Extraordinary acclaim for David Foster Wallace's
BRIEF INTERVIEWS WITH HIDEOUS MEN

"A brilliant book. . . . One of the most ambitious and talented writers of his generation. Wallace's work is bitingly funny and remarkably, even wildly, imaginative; at the same time he aims for very large psychological, emotional, and social issues, issues of how we live or fail to live, love and fail to love, survive or destroy ourselves. . . . Wallace has planted himself firmly as the American writer of his generation to watch, to match, and, most urgently, to read."   — Vince Passaro, *Salon*

"A strikingly original collection. . . . *Brief Interviews with Hideous Men* is meant to interrogate the reader, to elicit fresh responses to horrors that have lost their edge in the age of information overload. . . . It displays a range of intellect and talent that is unseemly for any one writer to have, let alone show off."   — R. Z. Sheppard, *Time*

"An astonishing collection. . . . A brutally magnificent book. . . . Not least among David Foster Wallace's many accomplishments is his almost single-handed rehabilitation of the footnote as a literary device."
—Will Blythe, *Spin*

"Often funny and very often hugely impressive. . . . Now we know Mr. Wallace can write short. Let's just hope he writes for a long, long time."
— Adam Begley, *New York Observer*

"Evocative and challenging. . . . A virtuoso performance of voice, imagination, footnotes, and black humor, showing once again that Wallace is the dark prince of contemporary American fiction."
— Rob Spillman, *Details*

"A demonstration of ironic virtuosity. . . . Savaging and redeeming this culture is what Wallace does, with the authority of a perfect master."
— Andrei Codrescu, *Chicago Tribune*

T0371949

"Wallace's command of various vernacular systems is deft, his creation of fantastical counter-worlds is sublime, and his skill at following the dialectical contortions of human thought through to their endless series of non-conclusions is unparalleled." — Jim Hanas, *Memphis Flyer*

"Wallace has a sensibility that is anarchistic and kaleidoscopic. . . . He makes you feel really smart without in any way flattering you. . . . He creates verbal ecosystems that, if you are patient with them for just long enough, pull you into their own self-contained universe and make you so happy to be there you're reluctant to leave."
— Thomas Beller, *BookForum*

"Darkly funny entertainment. Wallace has an astonishing repertoire of voices, an endless array of characters brilliantly rendered."
— Karen Sandstrom, *Cleveland Plain Dealer*

"Wallace is outrageously funny, ironically dissecting the psychological distortions that pass for normal turn-of-the-century mainstream America. . . . The humor and disturbance that dominate his prose are rendered so skillfully that anyone interested in cutting-edge American fiction should give this book a careful reading. . . . Wallace shows that he is a writer to be reckoned with."
— Stephen-Paul Martin, *San Diego Union-Trubune*

"Page by page he's more fun to read than anyone. . . . It's as if Wallace's mission is to combine the audacity of metafiction with the moral passions of classic fiction and to offer, as well, the entertainment value of the best of pop culture. His verbal brio, the glittering joy of his writing, brings Nabokov to mind." — Damaris Moore, *Express Books*

"Something at once marvelous and fearful: a writer of great power and intelligence grappling with the very act of his writing and your reading." — Duane Davis, *Denver Rocky Mountain News*

"A joy to read. . . . David Foster Wallace is one of the few contemporary authors who actually sounds like he's writing in the present. . . . *Brief Interviews with Hideous Men* is not only a state-of-the-art demonstration of the short-story form, but a rebuke to almost every other short-story writer to *move* on, to try something new."
— Steven Moore, *Rain Taxi* (Minneapolis)

"Wallace proves that he is still an expert ethnographer of contemporary America. . . . At times you are awed by his audacity. . . . Even when his post-modernist chemistry projects simply fizzle out, there is always at least a whiff of genius to make you savor the attempt."
— Adam Goodheart, *New York Times Book Review*

"The fun of the collection — and it is fun, and often very funny — is partly the thrill of watching Wallace do his stuff as an inventor of character, voice, and situation, and partly the weird pleasure of watching the moralist in him burn all this extravagance to ashes."
— Lorin Stein, *Newsday*

"All [of these stories] display an intelligence and a swagger that make them hard to put down." — Jeffrey A. Trachtenberg, *Wall Street Journal*

"Wallace is, for my money, the most exciting fiction writer out there at the moment, right on top of the Zeitgeist and more attuned to the formal possibilities of fiction than anyone else. What's more, he's naming the secrets of the generation that is now to inherit America's cultural legacy."
— Cornel Bonca, *OC Weekly*

"Wallace, the alarmingly talented author of the brilliant magnum opus of American novels in 1995, *Infinite Jest,* has set himself an admirable goal this time: a blistering series of satires on the intellectual vacuity and self-serving character of the contemporary culture of therapy."
— Greg Burkman, *Seattle Times*

"*Brief Interviews with Hideous Men* boosts Wallace's reputation as the finest young inventor in American fiction. . . . No other American writer seems as boldly impatient with the old or as daringly willing to fail so spectacularly trying to make it new."

— Eric Hanson, *Minneapolis Star-Tribune*

"Spellbinding. . . . At his best, Wallace rivals Vladimir Nabokov in his ability to observe and describe. His ear for contemporary double-talk and his eye for the telltale visual icons of our culture are unerring."

— George Gurley, *Kansas City Star*

"Damn funny stuff. . . . Wallace is America's best articulator of the comedy and tragedy of just about any living moment."

— Celia Farber, *Gear*

"A wild ride through a deranged, brilliant cortex (and 800 pages shorter than *Infinite Jest*)."

— *Entertainment Weekly*

"At his best . . . Wallace is thrilling to read. . . . You feel challenged and entertained and somewhat intellectually violated, but you know you like it, you know Wallace is brilliant, and you ask yourself days later what other writer makes you so frustrated in such a wonderfully weird way. . . . It is ripping good fun."

— Eric Celeste, *Ft. Worth Star-Telegram*

"Dazzling. . . . David Foster Wallace is a brilliant guy . . . funny, daring . . . ceaseless in his determination to subvert literary convention . . . capable of passages of inspired lyricism. . . . *Brief Interviews with Hideous Men* left me perversely hungry for more."

— Dan DeLuca, *Philadelphia Inquirer*

[BRIEF INTERVIEWS
WITH HIDEOUS MEN]

ALSO BY
DAVID FOSTER WALLACE

THE BROOM OF THE SYSTEM

GIRL WITH CURIOUS HAIR

INFINITE JEST

A SUPPOSEDLY FUN THING
I'LL NEVER DO AGAIN

EVERYTHING AND MORE

OBLIVION

CONSIDER THE LOBSTER

MCCAIN'S PROMISE

THIS IS WATER

[BRIEF INTERVIEWS
WITH HIDEOUS MEN]

DAVID FOSTER WALLACE

BACK BAY BOOKS

LITTLE, BROWN AND COMPANY

NEW YORK BOSTON LONDON

For Beth-Ellen Siciliano and Alice Dall, hideous ears *sine pari*

Back Bay Books / Little, Brown and Company
Hachette Book Group
1290 Avenue of the Americas, New York, NY 10104
littlebrown.com

Originally published in hardcover by Little, Brown and Company, 1999
First Back Bay paperback edition, 2000

Back Bay Books is an imprint of Little, Brown and Company.
The Back Bay Books name and logo are trademarks of Hachette Book Group, Inc.

The publisher is not responsible for websites (or their content) that are not owned
by the publisher.

Author herewith acknowledges the generous and broad-minded support of
The Lannan Foundation
The John D. and Catherine T. MacArthur Foundation
The Paris Review
The Staff and Management of Denny's 24-Hour Family Restaurant, Bloomington IL

Acknowledgment is made to the following publications in which various forms of this book's pieces first appeared: *Between C&D, Conjunctions, Esquire, Fiction International, Grand Street, Harper's,* Houghton Mifflin's *Best American Short Stories 1992, Mid-American Review, New York Times Magazine, Open City, The Paris Review, Ploughshares, Private Arts, Santa Monica Review, spelunker flophouse,* and *Tin House.*

LIBRARY OF CONGRESS CATALOGING-IN-PUBLICATION DATA

Wallace, David Foster.
  Brief interviews with hideous men / David Foster Wallace. — 1st ed.
    p.   cm.
  ISBN 978-0-316-92541-9 (hc) / 978-0-316-92519-8 (pb)
  I. Title.
PS3573.A425635B65   1999
813'.54 — dc21   98-50944

Printing 31, 2023

LSC-C

Book design by Melodie Wertelet

Printed in the United States of America

CONTENTS

BRIEF INTERVIEWS
WITH HIDEOUS MEN

A RADICALLY CONDENSED HISTORY
OF POSTINDUSTRIAL LIFE

When they were introduced, he made a witticism, hoping to be liked. She laughed extremely hard, hoping to be liked. Then each drove home alone, staring straight ahead, with the very same twist to their faces.

The man who'd introduced them didn't much like either of them, though he acted as if he did, anxious as he was to preserve good relations at all times. One never knew, after all, now did one now did one now did one.

DEATH IS NOT THE END

The fifty-six-year-old American poet, a Nobel Laureate, a poet known in American literary circles as 'the poet's poet' or sometimes simply 'the Poet,' lay outside on the deck, bare-chested, moderately overweight, in a partially reclined deck chair, in the sun, reading, half supine, moderately but not severely overweight, winner of two National Book Awards, a National Book Critics Circle Award, a Lamont Prize, two grants from the National Endowment for the Arts, a Prix de Rome, a Lannan Foundation Fellowship, a MacDowell Medal, and a Mildred and Harold Strauss Living Award from the American Academy and Institute of Arts and Letters, a president emeritus of PEN, a poet two separate American generations have hailed as the voice of their generation, now fifty-six, lying in an unwet XL Speedo-brand swimsuit in an incrementally reclinable canvas deck chair on the tile deck beside the home's pool, a poet who was among the first ten Americans to receive a 'Genius Grant' from the prestigious John D. and Catherine T. MacArthur Foundation, one of only three American recipients of the Nobel Prize for Literature now living, 5'8", 181 lbs., brown/brown, hairline unevenly recessed because of the inconsistent acceptance/rejection of various Hair Augmentation Systems–brand transplants, he sat, or lay — or perhaps most accurately just 'reclined' — in a black Speedo swimsuit by the home's kidney-shaped pool,[1] on the pool's

---

[1] Also the first American-born poet ever in the Nobel Prize for Literature's distinguished 94-year history to receive it, the coveted Nobel Prize for Literature.

tile deck, in a portable deck chair whose back was now reclined four
clicks to an angle of 35° w/r/t the deck's mosaic tile, at 10:20 A.M.
on 15 May 1995, the fourth most anthologized poet in the history
of American belles lettres, near an umbrella but not in the actual
shade of the umbrella, reading *Newsweek* magazine,[2] using the modest swell of his abdomen as an angled support for the magazine, also
wearing thongs, one hand behind his head, the other hand out to the
side and trailing on the dun-and-ochre filigree of the deck's expensive Spanish ceramic tile, occasionally wetting a finger to turn the
page, wearing prescription sunglasses whose lenses were chemically
treated to darken in fractional proportion to the luminous intensity
of the light to which they were exposed, wearing on the trailing
hand a wristwatch of middling quality and expense, simulated-
rubber thongs on his feet, legs crossed at the ankle and knees
slightly spread, the sky cloudless and brightening as the morning's
sun moved up and right, wetting a finger not with saliva or perspiration but with the condensation on the slender frosted glass of iced
tea that rested now just on the border of his body's shadow to the
chair's upper left and would have to be moved to remain in that cool
shadow, tracing a finger idly down the glass's side before bringing
the moist finger idly up to the page, occasionally turning the pages
of the 19 September 1994 edition of *Newsweek* magazine, reading
about American health-care reform and about USAir's tragic Flight
427, reading a summary and favorable review of the popular nonfic-
tion volumes *Hot Zone* and *The Coming Plague*, sometimes turning

---

[2] Never the recipient of a John Simon Guggenheim Foundation Fellowship, however: thrice rejected early in his career, he had reason to believe that something
personal and/or political was afoot with the Guggenheim Fellowship committee,
and had decided that he'd simply be damned, starve utterly, before he would ever
again hire a graduate assistant to fill out the tiresome triplicate Guggenheim
Foundation Fellowship application and go through the tiresome contemptible
farce of 'objective' consideration ever again.

several pages in succession, skimming certain articles and summaries, an eminent American poet now four months short of his fifty-seventh birthday, a poet whom *Newsweek* magazine's chief competitor, *Time*, had once rather absurdly called 'the closest thing to a genuine literary immortal now living,' his shins nearly hairless, the open umbrella's elliptic shadow tightening slightly, the thongs' simulated rubber pebbled on both sides of the sole, the poet's forehead dotted with perspiration, his tan deep and rich, the insides of his upper legs nearly hairless, his penis curled tightly on itself inside the tight swimsuit, his Vandyke neatly trimmed, an ashtray on the iron table, not drinking his iced tea, occasionally clearing his throat, at intervals shifting slightly in the pastel deck chair to scratch idly at the instep of one foot with the big toe of the other foot without removing his thongs or looking at either foot, seemingly intent on the magazine, the blue pool to his right and the home's thick glass sliding rear door to his oblique left, between himself and the pool a round table of white woven iron impaled at the center by a large beach umbrella whose shadow now no longer touches the pool, an indisputably accomplished poet, reading his magazine in his chair on his deck by his pool behind his home. The home's pool and deck area is surrounded on three sides by trees and shrubbery. The trees and shrubbery, installed years before, are densely interwoven and tangled and serve the same essential function as a redwood privacy fence or a wall of fine stone. It is the height of spring, and the trees and shrubbery are in full leaf and are intensely green and still, and are complexly shadowed, and the sky is wholly blue and still, so that the whole enclosed tableau of pool and deck and poet and chair and table and trees and home's rear façade is very still and composed and very nearly wholly silent, the soft gurgle of the pool's pump and drain and the occasional sound of the poet clearing his throat or turning the pages of *Newsweek* magazine the only sounds — not a bird, no distant lawn mowers or hedge trimmers or weed-eating devices, no jets overhead or distant muffled sounds from the pools of the homes on either side of the poet's home — nothing but the pool's respiration and poet's occasional cleared throat, wholly still and composed and enclosed, not even a hint of a breeze to stir the leaves of the trees and shrubbery, the silent living enclosing flora's motionless green vivid and inescapable and not like anything else in the world in either appearance or suggestion.[3]

---

[3] That is not wholly true.

FOREVER OVERHEAD

Happy Birthday. Your thirteenth is important. Maybe your first really public day. Your thirteenth is the chance for people to recognize that important things are happening to you.

Things have been happening to you for the past half year. You have seven hairs in your left armpit now. Twelve in your right. Hard dangerous spirals of brittle black hair. Crunchy, animal hair. There are now more of the hard curled hairs around your privates than you can count without losing track. Other things. Your voice is rich and scratchy and moves between octaves without any warning. Your face has begun to get shiny when you don't wash it. And two weeks of a deep and frightening ache this past spring left you with something dropped down from inside: your sack is now full and vulnerable, a commodity to be protected. Hefted and strapped in tight supporters that stripe your buttocks red. You have grown into a new fragility.

And dreams. For months there have been dreams like nothing before: moist and busy and distant, full of yielding curves, frantic pistons, warmth and a great falling; and you have awakened through fluttering lids to a rush and a gush and a toe-curling scalp-snapping jolt of feeling from an inside deeper than you knew you had, spasms of a deep sweet hurt, the streetlights through your window blinds cracking into sharp stars against the black bedroom ceiling, and on you a dense white jam that lisps between legs, trickles and sticks, cools on you, hardens and clears until there is nothing but gnarled knots of pale solid animal hair in the morning shower, and in the wet tangle a clean sweet smell you can't believe comes from anything you made inside you.

The smell is, more than anything, like this swimming pool: a bleached sweet salt, a flower with chemical petals. The pool has a strong clear blue smell, though you know the smell is never as strong when you are actually in the blue water, as you are now, all swum out, resting back along the shallow end, the hip-high water lapping at where it's all changed.

Around the deck of this old public pool on the western edge of Tucson is a Cyclone fence the color of pewter, decorated with a bright tangle of locked bicycles. Beyond this a hot black parking lot full of white lines and glittering cars. A dull field of dry grass and hard weeds, old dandelions' downy heads exploding and snowing up in a rising wind. And past all this, reddened by a round slow September sun, are mountains, jagged, their tops' sharp angles darkening into definition against a deep red tired light. Against the red their sharp connected tops form a spiked line, an EKG of the dying day.

The clouds are taking on color by the rim of the sky. The water is spangles off soft blue, five-o'clock warm, and the pool's smell, like the other smell, connects with a chemical haze inside you, an interior dimness that bends light to its own ends, softens the difference between what leaves off and what begins.

Your party is tonight. This afternoon, on your birthday, you have asked to come to the pool. You wanted to come alone, but a birthday is a family day, your family wants to be with you. This is nice, and you can't talk about why you wanted to come alone, and really truly maybe you didn't want to come alone, so they are here. Sunning. Both your parents sun. Their deck chairs have been marking time all afternoon, rotating, tracking the sun's curve across a desert sky heated to an eggy film. Your sister plays Marco Polo near you in the shallows with a group of thin girls from her grade. She is being blind now, her Marco's being Polo'd. She is shut-eyed and twirling to different cries, spinning at the hub of a wheel of shrill girls in bathing caps. Her cap has raised rubber flowers. There are limp old pink petals that shake as she lunges at blind sound.

There at the other end of the pool is the diving tank and the high board's tower. Back on the deck behind is the SN CK BAR, and on either side, bolted above the cement entrances to dark wet showers and lockers, are gray metal bullhorn speakers that send out the pool's radio music, the jangle flat and tinny thin.

Your family likes you. You are bright and quiet, respectful to elders — though you are not without spine. You are largely good. You look out for your little sister. You are her ally. You were six when she was zero and you had the mumps when they brought her home in a very soft yellow blanket; you kissed her hello on her feet out of concern that she not catch your mumps. Your parents say that this augured well. That it set the tone. They now feel they were right. In all things they are proud of you, satisfied, and they have retreated to the warm distance from which pride and satisfaction travel. You all get along well.

Happy Birthday. It is a big day, big as the roof of the whole southwest sky. You have thought it over. There is the high board. They will want to leave soon. Climb out and do the thing.

Shake off the blue clean. You're half-bleached, loose and soft, tenderized, pads of fingers wrinkled. The mist of the pool's too-clean smell is in your eyes; it breaks light into gentle color. Knock your head with the heel of your hand. One side has a flabby echo. Cock your head to the side and hop — sudden heat in your ear, delicious, and brain-warmed water turns cold on the nautilus of your ear's outside. You can hear harder tinnier music, closer shouts, much movement in much water.

The pool is crowded for this late. Here are thin children, hairy animal men. Disproportionate boys, all necks and legs and knobby joints, shallow-chested, vaguely birdlike. Like you. Here are old people moving tentatively through shallows on stick legs, feeling at the water with their hands, out of every element at once.

And girl-women, women, curved like instruments or fruit, skin burnished brown-bright, suit tops held by delicate knots of fragile colored string against the pull of mysterious weights, suit bottoms riding low over the gentle juts of hips totally unlike your own, immoderate swells and swivels that melt in light into a surrounding space that cups and accommodates the soft curves as things precious. You almost understand.

The pool is a system of movement. Here now there are: laps, splash fights, dives, corner tag, cannonballs, Sharks and Minnows, high fallings, Marco Polo (your sister still It, halfway to tears, too long to be It, the game teetering on the edge of cruelty, not your business to save or embarrass). Two clean little bright-white boys caped in cotton towels run along the poolside until the guard stops them dead with a shout through his bullhorn. The guard is brown as a tree, blond hair in a vertical line on his stomach, his head in a jungle explorer hat, his nose a white triangle of cream. A girl has an arm around a leg of his little tower. He's bored.

Get out now and go past your parents, who are sunning and reading, not looking up. Forget your towel. Stopping for the towel means talking and talking means thinking. You have decided being scared is caused mostly by thinking. Go right by, toward the tank at the deep end. Over the tank is a great iron tower of dirty white. A board protrudes from the top of the tower like a tongue. The pool's concrete deck is rough and hot against your bleached feet.

Each of your footprints is thinner and fainter. Each shrinks behind you on the hot stone and disappears.

Lines of plastic wieners bob around the tank, which is entirely its own thing, empty of the rest of the pool's convulsive ballet of heads and arms. The tank is blue as energy, small and deep and perfectly square, flanked by lap lanes and SN CK BAR and rough hot deck and the bent late shadow of the tower and board. The tank is quiet and still and healed smooth between fallings.

There is a rhythm to it. Like breathing. Like a machine. The line for the board curves back from the tower's ladder. The line moves in its curve, straightens as it nears the ladder. One by one, people reach the ladder and climb. One by one, spaced by the beat of hearts, they reach the tongue of the board at the top. And once on the board, they pause, each exactly the same tiny heartbeat pause. And their legs take them to the end, where they all give the same sort of stomping hop, arms curving out as if to describe something circular, total; they come down heavy on the edge of the board and make it throw them up and out.

It's a swooping machine, lines of stuttered movement in a sweet late bleach mist. You can watch from the deck as they hit the cold blue sheet of the tank. Each fall makes a white that plumes and falls into itself and spreads and fizzes. Then blue clean comes up in the middle of the white and spreads like pudding, making it all new. The tank heals itself. Three times as you go by.

You are in line. Look around. Look bored. Few talk in the line. Everyone seems by himself. Most look at the ladder, look bored. You almost all have crossed arms, chilled by a late dry rising wind on the constellations of blue-clean chlorine beads that cover your backs and shoulders. It seems impossible that everybody could really be this bored. Beside you is the edge of the tower's shadow, the tilted black tongue of the board's image. The system of shadow is huge, long, off to the side, joined to the tower's base at a sharp late angle.

Almost everyone in line for the board watches the ladder. Older boys watch older girls' bottoms as they go up. The bottoms are in soft thin cloth, tight nylon stretch. The good bottoms move up the ladder like pendulums in liquid, a gentle uncrackable code. The girls' legs make you think of deer. Look bored.

Look out past it. Look across. You can see so well. Your mother is in her deck chair, reading, squinting, her face tilted up to get light on her cheeks. She hasn't looked to see where you are. She sips something sweet out of a bright can. Your father is on his big stomach, back like the hint of a hump of a whale, shoulders curling with animal spirals, skin oiled and soaked red-brown with too much sun. Your towel is hanging off your chair and a corner of the cloth now moves — your mother hit it as she waved away a sweat bee that likes what she has in the can. The bee is back right away, seeming to hang motionless over the can in a sweet blur. Your towel is one big face of Yogi Bear.

At some point there has gotten to be more line behind you than in front of you. Now no one in front except three on the slender ladder. The woman right before you is on the low rungs, looking up, wearing a tight black nylon suit that is all one piece. She climbs. From above there is a rumble, then a great falling, then a plume and the tank reheals. Now two on the ladder. The pool rules say one on the ladder at a time, but the guard never shouts about it. The guard makes the real rules by shouting or not shouting.

This woman above you should not wear a suit as tight as the suit she is wearing. She is as old as your mother, and as big. She is too big and too white. Her suit is full of her. The backs of her thighs are squeezed by the suit and look like cheese. Her legs have abrupt little squiggles of cold blue shattered vein under the white skin, as if something were broken, hurt, in her legs. Her legs look like they hurt to be squeezed, full of curled Arabic lines of cold broken blue. Her legs make you feel like your own legs hurt.

The rungs are very thin. It's unexpected. Thin round iron rungs laced in slick wet Safe-T felt. You taste metal from the smell of wet iron in shadow. Each rung presses into the bottoms of your feet and dents them. The dents feel deep and they hurt. You feel heavy. How the big woman over you must feel. The handrails along the ladder's sides are also very thin. It's like you might not hold on. You've got to hope the woman holds on, too. And of course it looked like fewer rungs from far away. You are not stupid.

Get halfway up, up in the open, big woman placed above you, a solid bald muscular man on the ladder underneath your feet. The board is still high overhead, invisible from here. But it rumbles and makes a heavy flapping sound, and a boy you can see for a few contained feet through the thin rungs falls in a flash of a line, a knee held to his chest, doing a splasher. There is a huge exclamation point of foam up into your field of sight, then scattered claps into a great fizzing. Then the silent sound of the tank healing to new blue all over again.

More thin rungs. Hold on tight. The radio is loudest here, one speaker at ear-level over a concrete locker room entrance. A cool dank whiff of the locker room inside. Grab the iron bars tight and twist and look down behind you and you can see people buying snacks and refreshments below. You can see down into it: the clean white top of the vendor's cap, tubs of ice cream, steaming brass freezers, scuba tanks of soft drink syrup, snakes of soda hose, bulging boxes of salty popcorn kept hot in the sun. Now that you're overhead you can see the whole thing.

There's wind. It's windier the higher you get. The wind is thin; through the shadow it's cold on your wet skin. On the ladder in the shadow your skin looks very white. The wind makes a thin whistle in your ears. Four more rungs to the top of the tower. The rungs hurt your feet. They are thin and let you know just how much you weigh. You have real weight on the ladder. The ground wants you back.

Now you can see just over the top of the ladder. You can see the board. The woman is there. There are two ridges of red, hurt-looking callus on the backs of her ankles. She stands at the start of the board, your eyes on her ankles. Now you're up above the tower's shadow. The solid man under you is looking through the rungs into the contained space the woman's fall will pass through.

She pauses for just that beat of a pause. There's nothing slow about it at all. It makes you cold. In no time she's at the end of the board, up, down on it, it bends low like it doesn't want her. Then it nods and flaps and throws her violently up and out, her arms opening out to inscribe that circle, and gone. She disappears in a dark blink. And there's time before you hear the hit below.

Listen. It does not seem good, the way she disappears into a time that passes before she sounds. Like a stone down a well. But you think she did not think so. She was part of a rhythm that excludes thinking. And now you have made yourself part of it, too. The rhythm seems blind. Like ants. Like a machine.

You decide this needs to be thought about. It may, after all, be all right to do something scary without thinking, but not when the scariness is the not thinking itself. Not when not thinking turns out to be wrong. At some point the wrongnesses have piled up blind: pretend-boredom, weight, thin rungs, hurt feet, space cut into laddered parts that melt together only in a disappearance that takes time. The wind on the ladder not what anyone would have expected. The way the board protrudes from shadow into light and you can't see past the end. When it all turns out to be different you should get to think. It should be required.

The ladder is full beneath you. Stacked up, everyone a few rungs apart. The ladder is fed by a solid line that stretches back and curves into the dark of the tower's canted shadow. People's arms are crossed in the line. Those on the ladder's feet hurt and they are all looking up. It is a machine that moves only forward.

Climb up onto the tower's tongue. The board turns out to be long. As long as the time you stand there. Time slows. It thickens around you as your heart gets more and more beats out of every second, every movement in the system of the pool below.

The board is long. From where you stand it seems to stretch off into nothing. It's going to send you someplace which its own length keeps you from seeing, which seems wrong to submit to without even thinking.

Looked at another way, the same board is just a long thin flat thing covered with a rough white plastic stuff. The white surface is very rough and is freckled and lined with a pale watered red that is nevertheless still red and not yet pink — drops of old pool water that are catching the light of the late sun over sharp mountains. The rough white stuff of the board is wet. And cold. Your feet are hurt from the thin rungs and have a great ability to feel. They feel your weight. There are handrails running above the beginning of the board. They are not like the ladder's handrails just were. They are thick and set very low, so you almost have to bend over to hold on to them. They are just for show, no one holds them. Holding on takes time and alters the rhythm of the machine.

It is a long cold rough white plastic or fiberglass board, veined with the sad near-pink color of bad candy.

But at the end of the white board, the edge, where you'll come down with your weight to make it send you off, there are two areas of darkness. Two flat shadows in the broad light. Two vague black ovals. The end of the board has two dirty spots.

They are from all the people who've gone before you. Your feet as you stand here are tender and dented, hurt by the rough wet surface, and you see that the two dark spots are from people's skin. They are skin abraded from feet by the violence of the disappearance of people with real weight. More people than you could count without losing track. The weight and abrasion of their disappearance leaves little bits of soft tender feet behind, bits and shards and curls of skin that dirty and darken and tan as they lie tiny and smeared in the sun at the end of the board. They pile up and get smeared and mixed together. They darken in two circles.

No time is passing outside you at all. It is amazing. The late ballet below is slow motion, the overbroad movements of mimes in blue jelly. If you wanted you could really stay here forever, vibrating inside so fast you float motionless in time, like a bee over something sweet.

But they should clean the board. Anybody who thought about it for even a second would see that they should clean the end of the board of people's skin, of two black collections of what's left of before, spots that from back here look like eyes, like blind and cross-eyed eyes.

Where you are now is still and quiet. Wind radio shouting splashing not here. No time and no real sound but your blood squeaking in your head.

Overhead here means sight and smell. The smells are intimate, newly clear. The smell of bleach's special flower, but out of it other things rise to you like a weed's seeded snow. You smell deep yellow popcorn. Sweet tan oil like hot coconut. Either hot dogs or corn dogs. A thin cruel hint of very dark Pepsi in paper cups. And the special smell of tons of water coming off tons of skin, rising like steam off a new bath. Animal heat. From overhead it is more real than anything.

Look at it. You can see the whole complicated thing, blue and white and brown and white, soaked in a watery spangle of deepening red. Everybody. This is what people call a view. And you knew that from below you wouldn't look nearly so high overhead. You see now how high overhead you are. You knew from down there no one could tell.

He says it behind you, his eyes on your ankles, the solid bald man, Hey kid. They want to know. Do your plans up here involve the whole day or what exactly is the story. Hey kid are you okay.

There's been time this whole time. You can't kill time with your heart. Everything takes time. Bees have to move very fast to stay still.

Hey kid he says Hey kid are you okay.

Metal flowers bloom on your tongue. No more time for thinking. Now that there is time you don't have time.

Hey.

Slowly now, out across everything, there's a watching that spreads like hit water's rings. Watch it spread out from the ladder. Your sighted sister and her thin white pack, pointing. Your mother looks to the shallows where you used to be, then makes a visor of her hand. The whale stirs and jiggles. The guard looks up, the girl around his leg looks up, he reaches for his horn.

Forever below is rough deck, snacks, thin metal music, down where you once used to be; the line is solid and has no reverse gear; and the water, of course, is only soft when you're inside it. Look down. Now it moves in the sun, full of hard coins of light that shimmer red as they stretch away into a mist that is your own sweet salt. The coins crack into new moons, long shards of light from the hearts of sad stars. The square tank is a cold blue sheet. Cold is just a kind of hard. A kind of blind. You have been taken off guard. Happy Birthday. Did you think it over. Yes and no. Hey kid.

Two black spots, violence, and disappear into a well of time.

Height is not the problem. It all changes when you get back down. When you hit, with your weight.

So which is the lie? Hard or soft? Silence or time?

The lie is that it's one or the other. A still, floating bee is moving faster than it can think. From overhead the sweetness drives it crazy.

The board will nod and you will go, and eyes of skin can cross blind into a cloud-blotched sky, punctured light emptying behind sharp stone that is forever. That is forever. Step into the skin and disappear.

Hello.

BRIEF INTERVIEWS
WITH HIDEOUS MEN

B.I. #14 08-96
ST. DAVIDS PA

'It's cost me every sexual relationship I ever had. I don't know why I do it. I'm not a political person, I don't consider myself. I'm not one of these America First, read the newspaper, will Buchanan get the nod people. I'll be doing it with some girl, it doesn't matter who. It's when I start to come. That it happens. I'm not a Democrat. I don't even vote. I freaked out about it one time and called a radio show about it, a doctor on the radio, anonymously, and he diagnosed it as the uncontrolled yelling of involuntary words or phrases, frequently insulting or scatological, which is coprolalia is the official term. Except when I start to come and always start yelling it it's not insulting, it's not obscene, it's always the same thing, and it's always so weird but I don't think insulting. I think it's just weird. And uncontrolled. It's like it comes out the same way the spooge comes out, it feels like that. I don't know what it's about and I can't help it.'

Q.

'"Victory for the Forces of Democratic Freedom!" Only way louder. As in really shouting it. Uncontrollably. I'm not even thinking it until it comes out and I hear it. "Victory for the Forces of Democratic Freedom!" Only louder than that: "VICTORY —"'

Q.

'Well it totally freaks them out, what do you think? And I just about die of the embarrassment. I don't ever know what to say. What do you say if you just shouted "Victory for the Forces of Democratic Freedom!" right when you came?'

Q.

'It wouldn't be so embarrassing if it wasn't so totally fucking weird. If I had any clue about what it was about. You know?'

Q. . . .

'God, now I'm embarrassed as hell.'

Q.

'But all there *is* is the once. That's what I mean about it costing. I can tell how bad it freaks them out, and I get embarrassed and never call them again. Even if I try to explain. And it's the ones that'll act all understanding like they don't care and it's OK and they understand and it doesn't matter that embarrass me the worst, because it's so fucking weird to yell "Victory for the Forces of Democratic Freedom!" when you're shooting off that I can always tell they're totally freaked out and just condescending down to me and pretending they understand, and those are the ones where actually I actually end up almost getting pissed off and don't even feel embarrassed not calling them or totally avoiding them, the ones that say "I think I could love you anyway." '

B.I. #15 08-96

MCI-Bridgewater Observation & Assessment Facility
Bridgewater MA

'It is a proclivity, and provided there's minimal coercion and no real harm it's essentially benign, I think you'll have to agree. And that there are a surprisingly small number who require any coercion at all, be apprised.'

Q.

'From a psychological standpoint the origins appear obvious. Various therapists concur, I might add, here and elsewhere. So it's all quite tidy.'

Q.

'Well, my own father was, you might say, a man who was by natural proclivity not a good man but who nevertheless tried diligently to be a good man. Temper and so forth.'

Q.

'I mean, it's not as if I'm torturing them or burning them.'

Q.

'My father's proclivity for rage, especially [unintelligible or distorted] the Emergency Room for the umpteenth time, afraid of his own temper and proclivity for domestic violence, this built over a period of time, and eventually he resorted, after a period of time and periods of unsuccessful counseling, to the practice of handcuffing his own wrists behind his back whenever he lost his temper with any of us. In the house. Domestically. Small domestic incidents that try one's temper and so forth. This self-restraint eventually progressed over a period of time such that the more enraged he might become at any of us, the more coercively he began to restrain himself. Often the day would end with the poor man hogtied on the living room floor, screaming furiously at us to put his goddamn motherfucking gag in. Whatever possible interest that bit of history might hold for anyone not privileged to have been there. Trying to get the gag in without getting bitten. But of course so now we can explain my proclivities and trace their origins and have everything tied up all nice and tight and tidy for you, can't we.'

B.I. #11 06-96

Vienna VA

'All right, I am, okay, yes, but hang on a second, okay? I need you to try and understand this. Okay? Look. I know I'm moody. I know I'm kind of withdrawn sometimes. I know I'm hard to be in this with, okay? All right? But this every time I get moody or withdrawn you thinking I'm leaving or getting ready to ditch you — I can't take it. This thing of you being afraid all the time. It wears me out. It makes me feel like I have to, like, hide whatever mood I might be in because right away you're going to think it's about you and that I'm getting ready to ditch you and leave. You don't trust me. You don't. It's not like I'm saying given our history I deserved a whole lot of trust right off the bat. But you still don't at all. There's like zero security no matter what I do. Okay? I said I'd promise I wouldn't leave and you said you believed me that I was in this with you for the long haul this time, but you didn't. Okay? Just admit it, all right? You don't trust me. I'm on eggshells all the time. Do you see? I can't keep going around reassuring you all the time.'

Q.

'No, I'm not saying *this* is reassuring. What *this* is is just trying to get you to see — okay, look, things ebb and flow, okay? Sometimes people are just more into it than other times. This is just how it is. But you can't stand ebb. It feels like no ebb's allowed. And I know that's partly my fault, okay? I know the other times didn't exactly make you feel secure. But I can't change that, okay? But this is now. And now I feel like anytime I'd just rather not talk or get a little moody or withdrawn you think I'm plotting to ditch you. And that breaks my heart. Okay? It just breaks my heart. Maybe if I loved you a little less or cared about you less I could take it. But I can't. So yes, that's what the bags are, I'm leaving.'

Q.

'And I was — this is just how I was afraid you'd take it. I knew it, that you'd think this means you were right to be afraid all the time and never feel secure or trust me. I knew it'd be "See, you're leaving after all when you promised you wouldn't." I knew it but I'm trying to explain anyway, okay? And I know you probably won't understand this either, but — wait — just try to listen and maybe absorb this, okay? Ready? Me leaving is *not* the confirmation of all your fears about me. It is *not*. It's *because* of them. Okay? Can you see that? It's your fear I can't take. It's your distrust and fear I've been trying to fight. And I can't anymore. I'm out of gas on it. If I loved you even a little less maybe I could take it. But this is killing me, this constant feeling that I'm always scaring you and never making you feel secure. Can you see that?'

Q.

'It *is* ironic from your point of view, I can see that. Okay. And I can see you totally hate me now. And I've spent a long time getting myself to where I'm ready to face your totally hating me for this and this look of like total confirmation of all your fears and suspicions on your face if you could see it, okay? I swear if you could see your face right now anybody'd understand why I'm leaving.'

Q.

'I'm sorry. I don't mean to put it all on you. I'm sorry. It's not you, okay? I mean, it has to be something about me if you can't trust me after all these weeks or stand even just a little normal ebb and flow without always thinking I'm getting ready to leave. I don't know what, but there must be. Okay, and I know our history's not great, but I swear to you I meant everything I said, and I've tried a hundred-plus percent. I swear to God I did. I'm so sorry. I'd give anything in the world not to hurt you. I love you. I always will love you. I hope you believe that, but I'm giving up trying to get you to. Just please believe I tried. And don't think this is about something wrong with you. Don't do that to yourself. It's us, us is why I'm leaving, okay? Can you see that? That it's not what you've always been so afraid of? Okay? Can you see that? Can you maybe see you just *might* have been wrong, even *possibly*? Could you give me that much, do you think? Because this isn't exactly fun for me either, okay? Leaving like this, seeing your face like this as my last mental picture of you. Can you see I might be pretty torn up about it too? Can you? That you're not alone in this?'

B.I. #3 11-94

Trenton NJ [Overheard]

R———: 'So I'm last off again as usual and all that business like that there.'

A———: 'Yes just wait and relax in your seat be the last off why everybody right away all the time has to get up the minute it stops and cram into the aisle so you just stand there with your bags all crammed in pouring sweat in the aisle for five minutes just to be the —'

R———: 'Just wait and finally coming out of the jetway thing and out into the you know gate area greeting area as usual thinking I'll just get a cab out to —'

A———: 'Still but always depressing on these cold calls to come out into the gate greeting area and see everybody getting met and with the squeals and the hugs and limo guys holding up all the names on cardboard that aren't your name and the l—'

R———: 'Just shut it for one fucking second will you because listen to this because except it's mostly emptied out by the time I get out there.'

A———: 'The people by this juncture are mostly all dispersed you're saying.'

R———: 'Except for over by there's this one girl left over by the rope looking in peering gazing in down the jetway thing there as she sees it's me as I'm looking at her as I come out because it's emptied out except for her, our eyes meet and all that business like that there, and what does she she up and goes down on her knees drops crying and with the waterworks and all that business hitting slapping the carpet and scratching at gouging little tufts and fibers out of the cheapass product they buy where the low-polymer glue starts the backing separating almost right away and ends up tripling their twenty-quarter M and R costs as I sure don't have to tell you and all bent over slapping and gouging at the product with the nails, bent over so you can you know just about see her tits. Totally hysterical and with the waterworks and all like that there.'

A——: 'Another cheery welcome to Dayton for your fucking cold calls, we're pleased to wel—'

R——: 'No but the story it turns out the story when I you know go over to say are you OK is anything the matter and like that and get a better shot of I have to tell you some pretty fucking incredible tits under this like tight little top like leotard top thing under this coat she's all down and bent over in like bitchslapping herself in the head and still doing manual field stresses on this gate area product where she says this guy that she was in love with and all that business there that said he was in love with her too except he was already engaged from priorly when they meet and fall vehemiently in love so there's all this back and forth and storm and drag business like that and I'm lending the ear to her standing there but finally she says but finally the guy gets off the fence and finally says how he's surrendering to his love for this girl here with the tits and commits to her and says how he's going to go and tell this other girl in Tulsa where the guy lives that he's engaged to about this girl here and break it off in Tulsa and finally surrender and commit to this hysterical girl with the tits that loves him more than life herself and feels a merger of "souls" with him and all that violin business like that and felt like finally for chrissakes after all the onetrack shitheels she'd got the runaround from she finally she felt like here at last she's met a guy she could trust and love and merge "souls" with the sort of violins and hearts and fl—'

A——: 'And blah blah blah.'

R——: 'Blah and says off the guy goes flying back to Tulsa to finally break the engagement off with the prior girl like he committed he would and then fly right back to the arms of this girl standing with the Kleenex with the tits in Dayton here in the gate area with the waterworks crying out her eyes now to yours truly.'

A——: 'Oh like we can't see *this* coming.'

R——: 'Fuck you and that he puts his hand over his heart and all like that there and swears he's coming back to her and he'll be on that plane there with the flightnumber and time and she swears she'll be there with the tits to meet him, and how she tells all her friends she's finally in love with the real thing and how he's breaking it off and coming right back and she cleans up her place for him to stay there when he comes back and gets her hair done up all big with spray like they do and dribbles perfume on her you know zones and all that business like the usual story and puts on her best pink jeans did I mention she's got on these pink jeans and heels that say fuck me in like myriads of major world languages —'

A——: 'Heh *heh.*'

R——: 'By this juncture now we're in that little coffeeshop thing just in from the USAir gates that shitty one with no chairs that you have to with your shitty two-dollar coffee stand up at the tables with your sample case and bag and all your shit on the low-end tile not even thermoset of the floor they got that's already starting to curl at the grout and keep handing her Kleenexes and lend the ear and all that business there after she vacuums out the car and even replaces the little freshener thing hanging off the rearview and hauls ass to be on time to the airport to meet the flightnumber this so-called trustable guy swore on his fucking mother's life he'd be on.'

A———: 'Guy's a shitheel from the old school.'

R———: 'Shut up and that how she says how he even called her she gets the call right as she's smearing the last drib of perfume on her zone and gets her hair all sprayed out in directions like they do to haul ass to the airport it rings and it's this guy and there's all this hiss and static on the phone and she says he says how he's calling from the sky is how romantically he puts it calling her inflight on the flight on that little inflight phone you're supposed to slide your card through out of the back of the seat in front of you and saying how —'

A———: 'The markup on those things go six bucks a minute it's a racket and all the surcharges rated out of the region you're flying over right then with a double spread if the region they say adjoins at the grid's desig—'

R———: 'But that's not the point do you want to hear this how the point's this girl says she gets there early in the gate area greeting area and already with some of the waterworks already from love and violins of commitment finally and trust and stands she says all joy and trusting like a pathetic fool she says while it gets in finally the flight and we they all start herding all in their big rush out the jetway thing and he's not in the first wave out and he's not in the second wave how they come out in these little waves clumps like the thing's taking some kind of almost shit you know how —'

A———: 'Jesus I ought to the amount of fucking times I spend on jetw—'

R———: 'And says like a pathetic a total fool her faith never faldering she kept peering gazing over the octoweave rope maroon octoweave with that nice fauxvelvet finish the rope of the area over at the side during all the hugging and everybody meeting or going off to Baggage and every time expecting this guy in the next wave out, clump, and then the next and the next and like that, waiting.'

A———: 'Poor little muttski.'

R———: 'That then at the end there I come off the last off as usual and nobody else after except the crew pulling their little neat identical little bags those neat little bags that always bug me somehow and that's it I'm the last and she —'

A———: 'So you're explaining it wasn't you that she's screaming and hitting the floor it's just that you're the last of them off and you're not this shitheel guy. The bastard even must of faked that call, the static if you run your Remington it makes static that'll sound like a —'

R———: 'And I'm telling you you never saw anybody so the word heartbroken you think it's just words blah blah but then you see this girl with her hand knocking herself in the head for being such a fool crying so hard she can't mostly breathe and all that business like that, hugging herself and rocking and slapping the shit out of the table so bad you have to lift the coffee off to keep it from knocking over and how men are shits and don't trust them all her friends said and she finally she met one she thinks she can finally trust to really give in and surrender and commit to do the right thing and they're right, she's a fool, men are just shit.'

A———: 'Men mostly are shit, you're right, heh heh.'

R———: 'And I'm basically, I'm standing there holding coffee I don't even it's too late I don't want even decaf I'm lending the ear and my heart I got to say it my heart going out a little bit to this girl for this heartbreak. I swear kid but you have never seen anything like this heartbreak on this girl with the tits, and I start telling her how she's right the guy's a shit and don't even deserve and how it's true most guys are shit and how my heart's going out and all like that.'

A——: 'Heh heh. So then what happened?'

R——: 'Heh heh.'

A——: 'Heh heh *heh*.'

R——: 'You really got to ask?'

A——: 'You bastard. You shitheel.'

R——: 'Well you know how it is I mean what are you going to do.'

A——: 'You shitheel.'

R——: 'Well you know.'

B.I. #30 03-97

DRURY UT

'I have to admit it was a big reason for marrying her, thinking I wasn't likely going to do better than this because of the way she had a good body even after she'd had a kid. Trim and good and good legs — she'd had a kid but wasn't all blown out and veiny and sagged. It probably sounds shallow, but it's the truth. I'd always had this major dread of marrying some good-looking woman and then we have a kid and it blows her body out but I still have to have sex with her because this is who I've signed on to have sex with the whole rest of my life. This probably sounds awful, but in her case it was like she was pre-tested — the kid didn't blow her body out, so I knew she'd be a good bet to sign on and have kids with and still try to have sex. Does that sound shallow? Tell me what you think. Or does the real truth about this kind of thing always sound shallow, you know, everybody's real reasons? What do you think? How does it sound?'

B.I. #31 03-97

Roswell GA

'But you want to know how to really be great? How your Great Lover really pleases a lady? Now, all your basic smoothie-type fellows will always say they know, they're an authority and such. It's not a fag, darlin', you have to hold it in. Most of these fellows, they haven't got the first damn idea how to really please a lady. Not really. A lot of them don't even care, to tell you the truth. That's your first type, your Joe Sixpack cracker-type fellow there, your basic pig. This fellow's barely even semiconscious about life anyhow, and when it comes to lovemaking why he's just pure selfishness. He wants whatever he can get, and as long as he gets it that's all there is to it far as he's concerned. The type that rolls on and has at her and the minute he comes he rolls back off and commences to snoring. Go easy there. Why I suppose this is your old-fashioned stereotype male fellow, older, the fellow that's been married twenty years and don't even know if the wife even ever comes. Never thinks to even ask her. *He* comes, and that's all that counts far as he's concerned.'

Q.

'These aren't the fellows that I'm talking about. These are more like just animals, roll on and roll off and that's all she wrote. Hold it closer to the end there and don't inhale as much in as a regular fag. You want to hold it in and let it absorb. This is mine, I grow it, I got a room all lined with Mylar and lights, darlin' you would not believe what it goes for down here. Those fellows are just animals, they're not even in the type of game we're talking about here. No, because the ones we're talking about here are your basic secondary type of fellow, the fellow that thinks he's a Great Lover. And it's real important to these fellows that they think of themselves as Great. This preoccupies a major block of their time, thinking they're

Great and they know how to please her. These right here are your sensitive male smoothie type. Now, they're going to look like the complete opposite of your white-trash fellow that don't even give a shit. That's it but go easy. But now don't go thinking these fellows are really any better than your basic pigs are. Seeing themselves as a Great Lover doesn't mean they give any more of a shit about her than the pigs do, and deep down they aren't one little bit less selfish in bed. It's just with this type of fellow what they get off on in bed is their own idea of themselves as a Great Lover that can make the little lady just about lose her mind in bed. What they're into is a woman's pleasure and giving her pleasure. That's this type's whole trip.'

Q.

'Oh like oh say going down on her yingyang for hours on hours, holding off their own coming so they can keep at it for hours, knowing the G-spot and Ecstasy Posture and such. Running down to Barnes & Noble's for all your latest female sexuality–type books so they can keep up on their knowledge about what's going on. I'm guessing from looking you over out here now you've run up against a smoothie a time or two, with his pheromone aftershave and strawberry oil and hand massages and the holding and touching, that know about the earlobe and what kind of flush means what and the aureole and the backside of the knee and that new little ultrasensitive spot they say they found now just back of the G, this type of fellow knows them all, and you can be damn sure he's going to let *you* know he knows how to — here, give it here. I'll show you. Well and now darlin' you can just bet *this* type of fellow wants to know if she came, and how many times, and was it the best she ever — and like that. See there? When you blow out you don't want to even be able to see anything. That means you got 'er all. I thought you said you did this before. This is not your average cracker ditchweed. It's like a notch on this fellow's gun for each time he can make her come. That's how he thinks about it. It's too damn good to go blowing half back out, it's like you got a Porsche and you're only driving it to church. No, he's a Notcher, this fellow. That's a good way to compare them maybe. The two types. Your pig might put a notch for every one they nail, that's their notches, they don't care. But your so-called Great Lover–type fellow puts a notch for every time each one comes. But they're both of them just Notchers. They're both really the same-type fellow underneath. Their trip is different, but it's still only just their own trip they're on, in bed, and the little lady deep down's going to feel like she's just getting used just the same. That's if the lady's got any sense at all, which is another story. And now darlin' when it goes down a little more you take and don't grind it out with your boot there like you do a regular fag. You want to wet up your finger and gently pat the end of it and put it out and then save it, I got something to save them in. Me, I got something a little special but your more run-of-the-mill is one of them little film canisters from the developer, that's how come nobody ever throws those out. See if you ever see you a little film canister thing in the trash someplace.'

Q.

'No but here's your classic symptom to tell if it's one of these Great Lover fellows is they'll spend whole major blocks of time in bed going down on a lady's yingyang over and over and making her come seventeen straight times and such, but afterward just watch and see if there's any way on God's good green earth he's going to let *her* turn around and go down on *his* precious little pizzle for him. How he'll go Oh no baby no let me do you I want to see you come again baby oh baby you just lie there and let me work my love-magic and such like that right there. Or he'll know all his special Korean massage shit and give her deep-tissue backrubs or haul out the special black-cherry oil and massage her feet and hands — which darlin' I got to admit if you never had a quality hand massage you have not heretofore even really lived, trust me — but will he let the little lady reciplacate and give him just even one back-rub? Nosir he will not. Because this-type fellow's whole trip is *he's* got to be the one giving the pleasure here thank you ma'am. See, it's different, it's got a screw-lid with a airtight seal so it don't smell up your pocket, they're stinky little boogers, and then it goes right in this little flap thing here where why it could be anything at all. Because this is where your smoothie type is being stupid. This is what gives me my contempt for these fellows that go around thinking they're the Lord's own gift to the female species. Because at least your cracker type's halfway honest about it, they want to nail her and then roll off and that's all she wrote. Whereas but your basic smoothie thinks he's all sensitive and knows how to please a lady just because they know clitoral suction and shy-atsu, and watching them in bed's like watching one of these stupid-ass mechanics in white coats work on a Porsche all swelled up on their expertise and such. They think they're a Great Lover. They think they're generous in bed. No, but the catch is they're *selfish* about being generous. They're no better than the pig is, they're just sneakier about it. Now you're going to be thirsty, now you're going to want some Evian. This shit'll dry out your mouth something fierce. I carry these little portable Evians with me in here in this inside part, see? Custom-made. Go on and take one, you're going to want it. Go on.'

Q.

'Darlin' no problem, hang on to it, you're going to want some more in about half a minute. I could of sworn you said you did this before. I hope I'm not corrupting a Utah Mormon here am I? My-lar's better than foil, it reflects more of the light so it all goes right into the plant. They got special seeds now where the plant don't get any higher than this here, but it's lethal, it's death on a cracker.

Atlanta in particular seems full of these fellows. What they don't
understand is their type's an even worse drag for a lady with any
sense than your on-and-off pig ever was. Because how'd you like to
just lie there and get worked on like a Porsche and never get to feel
like *you're* generous and sexy and good in bed and a Great Lover too?
Hmm? Hmm? That's where your smoothie-type fellows always lose
the game. They want to be the only Great Lover in the bed. They
forget a lady's got feelings too. Who wants to lie there feeling all
ungenerous and greedy while some Yuppie with a Porsche shows off
his Tantric Clouds and Rain Half-Lotus on you and mentally notch-
ing off how many times you come? If you swish it around a little
your mouth'll stay wet longer, Evian's real good for that, who cares
if it's a dumb-ass Yuppie water if it's good, know what I mean? The
thing to watch for is if the fellow when he's going down on you if
he keeps one hand on the low part of your stomach there to really
make sure you're coming, why then you'll know. Wants to make
sure. This son of a bitch isn't a Lover, he's just putting on a show.
He doesn't give a shit about you. You want my opinion? You want
to know how to really be Great if you want to please her, that there's
not one fellow in a thousand that's figured out?'

   Q. . . .

   'Do you?'

   Q.

   'The secret is you got to both give the little lady pleasure and be
able to also take it, with equal technique to both and equal pleasure. Or at least you got to make *her* think so. Don't forget it's about
her. Go on and eat her yingyang till she begs, sure, go on, but also
let her at your pizzle, and even if she's no prize at it why you carry
on and make her think she is. And like if her notion of a backrub's
just some of those little pissant karate chops on your backbone, why
you go on and let her, and you carry on like you never knew a karate

chop could be like this. That's if a fellow wants to be a genuine Great Lover and go and think about *her* for one damn second.'

Q.

'Not on me darlin', no. I mean I usually do but I nibbled them up already I'm afraid. The real falldown of these wannabe-Great-type fellows is they think a lady is, when you come right down to it, dumb. Like all a lady wants to do is just lie there and come. The real secret is: assume she feels the same way. That she wants to see herself as a Great Lover that can blow the top of a man's head clean off in bed. Let her. Put your picture of yourself on the goddamn back burner for once in your life. The smoothies think if they blow the little lady's head off down there they got her. Bull*shit*.'

Q.

'But you're not going to just want one, though, darlin', trust me. There's a little Mart thing a couple blocks if we — whoa, watch your —'

Q.

'No, you go on and make her think she's blowing *your* damn head off. That's what they really want. Then you really and truly got her, if she thinks you'll never forget her. Never ever. You follow?'

B.I. #36 05-97

METROPOLITAN DOMESTIC VIOLENCE COMMUNITY OUTREACH,
COUNSELING, AND SERVICES CENTER ANNEX
AURORA IL

'So I decided to get help. I got in touch with the fact that the real problem had nothing to do with her. I saw that she would forever go on playing victim to my villain. I was powerless to change her. She was not the part of the problem I could, you know, address. So I made a decision. To get help for *me*. I now know it was the best thing I've ever done, and the hardest. It hasn't been easy, but my self-esteem is much higher now. I've halted the shame spiral. I've learned forgiveness. I *like* myself.'

    Q.

    'Who?'

YET ANOTHER EXAMPLE OF
THE POROUSNESS OF CERTAIN BORDERS (XI)

As in all those other dreams, I'm with somebody I know but don't know how I know them, and now this person suddenly points out to me that I'm blind. As in literally blind, unsighted, etc. Or else it's in the presence of this person that I suddenly realize I'm blind. What happens when I realize this is I get sad. It makes me incredibly sad that I'm blind. The person somehow knows how sad I am and warns me that crying will hurt my eyes somehow and make the blindness even worse, but I can't help it. I sit down and start crying really hard. I wake up crying in bed, and I'm crying so hard I can't really see anything or make anything out or anything. This makes me cry even harder. My girlfriend is concerned and wakes up and asks what's the matter, and it's a minute or more before I can even get it together enough to realize that I was dreaming and I'm awake and not really blind and that I'm crying for no reason, then to tell my girlfriend about the dream and get her input on it. Then all day at work then I'm incredibly conscious of my eyesight and my eyes and how good it is to be able to see colors and people's faces and to know exactly where I am, and of how fragile it all is, the human eye mechanism and the ability to see, how easily it could be lost, how I'm always seeing blind people around with their canes and strange-looking faces and am always just thinking of them as interesting to spend a couple seconds looking at and never thinking they had anything to do with me or my eyes, and how it's really just a lucky coincidence that I can see instead of being one of those blind people I see on the subway. And all day at work whenever this stuff strikes me I start tearing up again, getting ready to start crying, and only keeping myself from crying because of the cubicles' low partitions and how everybody can see me and would be concerned, and the whole day after the dream is like this, and it's tiring as hell, my girlfriend would say emotionally draining, and I sign out early and go home and I'm so tired and sleepy I can barely keep my eyes open, and when I get home I go right in and crawl in bed at like 4:00 in the afternoon and more or less pass out.

THE DEPRESSED PERSON

The depressed person was in terrible and unceasing emotional pain, and the impossibility of sharing or articulating this pain was itself a component of the pain and a contributing factor in its essential horror.

Despairing, then, of describing the emotional pain or expressing its utterness to those around her, the depressed person instead described circumstances, both past and ongoing, which were somehow related to the pain, to its etiology and cause, hoping at least to be able to express to others something of the pain's context, its — as it were — shape and texture. The depressed person's parents, for example, who had divorced when she was a child, had used her as a pawn in the sick games they played. The depressed person had, as a child, required orthodonture, and each parent had claimed — not without some cause, given the Medicean legal ambiguities of the divorce settlement, the depressed person always inserted when she described the painful struggle between her parents over the expense of her orthodonture — that the other should be required to pay for it. And the venomous rage of each parent over the other's petty, selfish refusal to pay was vented on their daughter, who had to hear over and over again from each parent how the other was unloving and selfish. Both parents were well off, and each had privately expressed to the depressed person that s/he was, of course, if push came to shove, willing to pay for all the orthodonture the depressed person needed and then some, that it was, at its heart, a matter not of money or dentition but of "principle." And the depressed person always took care, when as an adult she attempted to describe to a trusted friend the circumstances of the struggle over the cost of her orthodonture and that struggle's legacy of emotional pain for her, to concede that it may very well truly have appeared to each parent to have been, in fact, just that (i.e., a matter of "principle"), though unfortunately not a "principle" that took into account their daughter's needs or her feelings at receiving the emotional message that scoring petty points off each other was more important to her parents than her own maxillofacial health and thus constituted, if considered from a certain perspective, a form of parental neglect or abandonment or even outright abuse, an abuse clearly connected — here the depressed person nearly always inserted that her therapist concurred with this assessment — to the bottomless, chronic adult despair she suffered every day and felt hopelessly trapped in. This was just one example. The depressed person averaged four interpolated apologies each time she recounted for supportive friends this type of painful and damaging past circumstance on the telephone, as well as a sort of preamble in which she attempted to describe how painful and frightening it was not to feel able to articulate the chronic depression's excruciating pain itself but to have to resort to recounting examples that probably sounded, she always took care to acknowledge, dreary or self-pitying or like one of those people who are narcissistically obsessed with their "painful childhoods" and "painful lives" and wallow in their burdens and insist on recounting them at tiresome length to friends who are trying to be supportive and nurturing, and bore them and repel them.

The friends whom the depressed person reached out to for support and tried to open up to and share at least the contextual shape of her unceasing psychic agony and feelings of isolation with numbered around half a dozen and underwent a certain amount of rotation. The depressed person's therapist — who had earned both a terminal graduate degree and a medical degree, and who was the self-professed exponent of a school of therapy which stressed the cultivation and regular use of a supportive peer-community in any endogenously depressed adult's journey toward healing — referred to these female friends as the depressed person's Support System. The approximately half-dozen rotating members of this Support System tended to be either former acquaintances from the depressed person's childhood or else girls she had roomed with at various stages of her school career, nurturing and comparatively undamaged women who now lived in all manner of different cities and whom the depressed person often had not seen in person for years and years, and whom she often called late in the evening, long-distance, for sharing and support and just a few well-chosen words to help her get some realistic perspective on the day's despair and get centered and gather together the strength to fight through the emotional agony of the next day, and to whom, when she telephoned, the depressed person always began by saying that she apologized if she was dragging them down or coming off as boring or self-pitying or repellent or taking them away from their active, vibrant, largely pain-free long-distance lives.

The depressed person also made it a point, when reaching out to members of her Support System, never to cite circumstances like her parents' endless battle over her orthodonture as the *cause* of her unceasing adult depression. The "Blame Game" was too easy, she said; it was pathetic and contemptible; and besides, she'd had quite enough of the "Blame Game" just listening to her fucking parents all those years, the endless blame and recrimination the two had exchanged over her, through her, using the depressed person's (i.e., the depressed person as a child's) own feelings and needs as ammunition, as if her valid feelings and needs were nothing more than a battlefield or theater of conflict, weapons which the parents felt they could deploy against each other. They had displayed far more interest and passion and emotional availability in their hatred of each other than either had shown toward the depressed person herself, as a child, the depressed person confessed to feeling, sometimes, still.

The depressed person's therapist, whose school of therapy rejected the transference relation as a therapeutic resource and thus deliberately eschewed confrontation and "should"-statements and all normative, judging, "authority"-based theory in favor of a more value-neutral bioexperiential model and the creative use of analogy and narrative (including, but not necessarily mandating, the use of hand puppets, polystyrene props and toys, role-playing, human sculpture, mirroring, drama therapy, and, in appropriate cases, whole meticulously scripted and storyboarded Childhood Reconstructions), had deployed the following medications in an attempt to help the depressed person find some relief from her acute affective discomfort and progress in her (i.e., the depressed person's) journey toward enjoying some semblance of a normal adult life: Paxil, Zoloft, Prozac, Tofranil, Welbutrin, Elavil, Metrazol in combination with unilateral ECT (during a two-week voluntary in-patient course of treatment at a regional Mood Disorders clinic), Parnate both with and without lithium salts, Nardil both with and without Xanax. None had delivered any significant relief from the pain and feelings of emotional isolation that rendered the depressed person's every waking hour an indescribable hell on earth, and many of the medications themselves had had side effects which the depressed person had found intolerable. The depressed person was currently taking only very tiny daily doses of Prozac, for her A.D.D. symptoms, and of Ativan, a mild nonaddictive tranquilizer, for the panic attacks which made the hours at her toxically dysfunctional and unsupportive workplace such a living hell. Her therapist gently but repeatedly shared with the depressed person her (i.e., the therapist's) belief that the very best medicine for her (i.e., the depressed person's) endoge-

nous depression was the cultivation and regular use of a Support System the depressed person felt she could reach out to share with and
lean on for unconditional caring and support. The exact composition
of this Support System and its one or two most special, most trusted
"core" members underwent a certain amount of change and rotation
as time passed, which the therapist had encouraged the depressed
person to see as perfectly normal and OK, since it was only by taking the risks and exposing the vulnerabilities required to deepen
supportive relationships that an individual could discover which
friendships could meet her needs and to what degree.

The depressed person felt that she trusted the therapist and made
a concerted effort to be as completely open and honest with her as
she possibly could. She admitted to the therapist that she was always extremely careful to share with whomever she called long-
distance at night her (i.e., the depressed person's) belief that it
would be whiny and pathetic to blame her constant, indescribable
adult pain on her parents' traumatic divorce or their cynical use of
her while they hypocritically pretended that each cared for her more
than the other did. Her parents had, after all — as her therapist had
helped the depressed person to see — done the very best they could
with the emotional resources they'd had at the time. And she had,
after all, the depressed person always inserted, laughing weakly,
eventually gotten the orthodonture she'd needed. The former acquaintances and roommates who composed her Support System often told the depressed person that they wished she could be a little
less hard on herself, to which the depressed person often responded
by bursting involuntarily into tears and telling them that she knew
all too well that she was one of those dreaded types of people of
everyone's grim acquaintance who call at inconvenient times and
just go on and on about themselves and whom it often takes several
increasingly awkward attempts to get off the telephone with. The

depressed person said that she was all too horribly aware of what a joyless burden she was to her friends, and during the long-distance calls she always made it a point to express the enormous gratitude she felt at having a friend she could call and share with and get nurturing and support from, however briefly, before the demands of that friend's full, joyful, active life took understandable precedence and required her (i.e., the friend) to get off the telephone.

The excruciating feelings of shame and inadequacy which the depressed person experienced about calling supportive members of her Support System long-distance late at night and burdening them with her clumsy attempts to articulate at least the overall context of her emotional agony were an issue on which the depressed person and her therapist were currently doing a great deal of work in their time together. The depressed person confessed that when whatever empathetic friend she was sharing with finally confessed that she (i.e., the friend) was dreadfully sorry but there was no helping it she absolutely *had* to get off the telephone, and had finally detached the depressed person's needy fingers from her pantcuff and gotten off the telephone and back to her full, vibrant long-distance life, the depressed person almost always sat there listening to the empty apian drone of the dial tone and feeling even more isolated and inadequate and contemptible than she had before she'd called. These feelings of toxic shame at reaching out to others for community and support were issues which the therapist encouraged the depressed person to try to get in touch with and explore so that they could be processed in detail. The depressed person admitted to the therapist that whenever she (i.e., the depressed person) reached out long-distance to a member of her Support System she almost always visualized the friend's face, on the telephone, assuming a combined expression of boredom and pity and repulsion and abstract guilt, and almost always imagined she (i.e., the depressed person) could detect, in the friend's increasingly long silences and/or tedious repetitions of encouraging clichés, the boredom and frustration people always feel when someone is clinging to them and being a burden. She confessed that she could all too well imagine each friend now wincing when the telephone rang late at night, or during the conversation looking impatiently at the clock or directing silent gestures and facial expressions of helpless entrapment to all the other people in the room with her (i.e., the other people in the room with the "friend"), these inaudible gestures and expressions becoming more and more extreme and desperate as the depressed person just went on and on and on. The depressed person's therapist's most noticeable unconscious personal habit or tic consisted of placing the tips of all her fingers together in her lap as she listened attentively to the depressed person and manipulating the fingers idly so that her mated hands formed various enclosing shapes — e.g., cube, sphere, pyramid, right cylinder — and then appearing to study or contemplate them. The depressed person disliked this habit, though she would be the first to admit that this was chiefly because it drew her attention to the therapist's fingers and fingernails and caused her to compare them with her own.

The depressed person had shared with both the therapist and her Support System that she could recall, all too clearly, at her third boarding school, once watching her roommate talk to some unknown boy on their room's telephone as she (i.e., the roommate) made faces and gestures of repulsion and boredom with the call, this self-assured, popular and attractive roommate finally directing at the depressed person an exaggerated pantomime of someone knocking on a door, continuing the pantomime with a desperate expression until the depressed person understood that she was to open the room's door and step outside and knock loudly on the open door so as to give the roommate an excuse to get off the telephone. As a schoolgirl, the depressed person had never spoken of the incident of the boy's telephone call and the mendacious pantomime with that particular roommate — a roommate with whom the depressed person hadn't clicked or connected at all, and whom she had resented in a bitter, cringing way that had made the depressed person despise herself, and had not made any attempt to stay in touch with after that endless sophomore second semester was finished — but she (i.e., the depressed person) had shared her agonizing memory of the incident with many of the friends in her Support System, and had also shared how bottomlessly horrible and pathetic she had felt it would have been to have been that nameless, unknown boy at the other end of that telephone, a boy trying in good faith to take an emotional risk and to reach out and try to connect with the confident roommate, unaware that he was an unwelcome burden, pathetically unaware of the silent pantomimed boredom and contempt at the telephone's other end, and how the depressed person dreaded more than almost anything ever being in the position of being someone you had to appeal silently to someone else in the room to help you contrive an excuse to get off the telephone with. The depressed person would therefore always implore any friend she was on the telephone with to tell her the very *second* she (i.e., the friend) was getting bored or frustrated or repelled or felt she had other more urgent or interesting things to do, to please for God's sake be utterly up-front and frank and not spend one second longer on the phone with the depressed person than she (i.e., the friend) was absolutely glad to spend. The depressed person knew perfectly well, of course, she assured the therapist, how pathetic such a need for reassurance might come off to someone, how it could all too possibly be heard not as an open invitation to get off the telephone but actually as a needy, self-pitying, contemptibly manipulative plea for the friend *not* to get off the telephone, *never* to get off the telephone. The therapist[1] was diligent, whenever the depressed person shared her concern about how some statement or action might "seem" or "appear," in supporting the depressed person in exploring how these beliefs about how she "seemed" or "came off" to others made her feel.

It felt demeaning; the depressed person felt demeaned. She said it felt demeaning to call childhood friends long-distance late at night when they clearly had other things to do and lives to lead and vibrant, healthy, nurturing, intimate, caring partner-relationships to be in; it felt demeaning and pathetic to constantly apologize for boring someone or to feel that you had to thank them effusively just for being your friend. The depressed person's parents had eventually split the cost of her orthodonture; a professional arbitrator had finally been hired by their lawyers to structure the compromise. Arbitration had also been required to negotiate shared payment schedules for the depressed person's boarding schools and Healthy Eating Lifestyles summer camps and oboe lessons and car and collision insurance, as well as for the cosmetic surgery needed to correct a malformation of the anterior spine and alar cartilage of the depressed person's nose which had given her what felt like an excruciatingly pronounced and snoutish pug nose and had, coupled with the external orthodontic retainer she had to wear twenty-two hours a day, made looking at herself in the mirrors of her rooms at her boarding schools feel like more than any person could possibly

---

[1] The multiform shapes the therapist's mated fingers assumed nearly always resembled, for the depressed person, various forms of geometrically diverse cages, an association which the depressed person had not shared with the therapist because its symbolic significance seemed too overt and simple-minded to waste their time together on. The therapist's fingernails were long and shapely and well maintained, whereas the depressed person's fingernails were compulsively bitten so short and ragged that the quick sometimes protruded and began spontaneously to bleed.

stand. And yet also, in the year that the depressed person's father had remarried, he — in either a gesture of rare uncompromised caring or a *coup de grâce* which the depressed person's mother had said was designed to make her own feelings of humiliation and superfluousness complete — had paid in toto for the riding lessons, jodhpurs, and outrageously expensive boots the depressed person had needed in order to gain admission to her second-to-last boarding school's Riding Club, a few of whose members were the only girls at this particular boarding school whom the depressed person felt, she had confessed to her father on the telephone in tears late one truly horrible night, even remotely accepted her and had even minimal empathy or compassion in them at all and around whom the depressed person hadn't felt so totally snout-nosed and brace-faced and inadequate and rejected that it had felt like a daily act of enormous personal courage even to leave her room to go eat dinner in the dining hall.

The professional arbitrator her parents' lawyers had finally agreed on for help in structuring compromises on the costs of meeting the depressed person's childhood needs had been a highly respected Conflict-Resolution Specialist named Walter D. ("Walt") DeLasandro Jr. As a child, the depressed person had never met or even laid eyes on Walter D. ("Walt") DeLasandro Jr., though she had been shown his business card — complete with its parenthesized invitation to informality — and his name had been invoked in her hearing on countless childhood occasions, along with the fact that he billed for his services at a staggering $130 an hour plus expenses. Despite overwhelming feelings of reluctance on the part of the depressed person — who knew very well how much like the "Blame Game" it might sound — her therapist had strongly supported her in taking the risk of sharing with members of her Support System an important emotional breakthrough she (i.e., the depressed person) had achieved during an Inner-Child-Focused Experiential Therapy Retreat Weekend which the therapist had supported her in taking the risk of enrolling in and giving herself open-mindedly over to the experience of. In the I.-C.-F.E.T. Retreat Weekend's Small-Group Drama-Therapy Room, other members of her Small Group had role-played the depressed person's parents and the parents' significant others and attorneys and myriad other emotionally toxic figures from the depressed person's childhood and, at the crucial phase of the drama-therapy exercise, had slowly encircled the depressed person, moving in and pressing steadily in together on her so that she could not escape or avoid or minimize, and had (i.e., the small group had) dramatically recited specially prescripted lines designed to evoke and awaken blocked trauma, which had almost immediately provoked the depressed person into a surge of agonizing emotional memories and long-buried trauma and had resulted in the emergence of the depressed person's Inner Child and a cathartic tantrum in which the depressed person had struck repeatedly at a stack of velour cushions with a bat made of polystyrene foam and had shrieked obscenities and had reexperienced long-pent-up and festering emotional wounds, one of which[2] being a deep vestigial rage over the fact that Walter D. ("Walt") De-Lasandro Jr. had been able to bill her parents $130 an hour plus expenses for being put in the middle and playing the role of mediator and absorber of shit from both sides while she (i.e., the depressed person, as a child) had had to perform essentially the same coprophagous services on a more or less daily basis for *free,* for *nothing,* services which were not only grossly unfair and inappropriate for an emotionally sensitive child to be made to feel required to perform but about which her parents had then turned around and tried to make *her,* the depressed person *herself,* as a *child,* feel *guilty* about

---

[2] (i.e., one of which purulent wounds)

the staggering cost of Walter D. DeLasandro Jr. the Conflict-Resolution Specialist's services, as if the repeated hassle and expense of Walter D. DeLasandro Jr. were *her* fault and only undertaken on *her* spoiled little snout-nosed snaggletoothed behalf instead of simply because of her fucking parents' utterly fucking *sick* inability to communicate and share honestly and work through their own sick, dysfunctional issues with each other. This exercise and cathartic rage had enabled the depressed person to get in touch with some really core resentment-issues, the Small-Group Facilitator at the Inner-Child-Focused Experiential Therapy Retreat Weekend had said, and could have represented a real turning point in the depressed person's journey toward healing, had the rage and velour-cushion-pummeling not left the depressed person so emotionally shattered and drained and traumatized and embarrassed that she had felt she had no choice but to fly back home that night and miss the rest of the I.-C.-F.E.T.R. Weekend and the Small-Group Processing of all the exhumed feelings and issues.

The eventual compromise which the depressed person and her therapist worked out together as they processed the unburied resentments and the consequent guilt and shame at what could all too easily appear to be just more of the self-pitying "Blame Game" that attended the depressed person's experience at the Retreat Weekend was that the depressed person would take the emotional risk of reaching out and sharing the experience's feelings and realizations with her Support System, but only with the two or three elite, "core" members whom the depressed person currently felt were there for her in the very most empathetic and unjudgingly supportive way. The most important provision of the compromise was that the depressed person would be permitted to reveal to them her reluctance about sharing these resentments and realizations and to inform them that she was aware of how pathetic and blaming they (i.e., the resentments and realizations) might sound, and to reveal that she was sharing this potentially pathetic "breakthrough" with them only at her therapist's firm and explicit suggestion. In validating this provision, the therapist had objected only to the depressed person's proposed use of the word "pathetic" in her sharing with the Support System. The therapist said that she felt she could support the depressed person's use of the word "vulnerable" far more wholeheartedly than she could support the use of "pathetic," since her gut (i.e., the therapist's gut) was telling her that the depressed person's proposed use of "pathetic" felt not only self-hating but also needy and even somewhat manipulative. The word "pathetic," the therapist candidly shared, often felt to her like a defense-mechanism the depressed person used to protect herself against a listener's possible negative judgments by making it clear that the depressed person was already judging herself far more severely than any listener could possibly have the heart to. The therapist was careful to point out that she was not judging or critiquing or rejecting the depressed person's use of "pathetic" but was merely trying to openly and honestly share the feelings which its use brought up for her in the context of their relationship. The therapist, who by this time had less than a year to live, took a brief time-out at this point to share once again with the depressed person her (i.e., the therapist's) conviction that self-hatred, toxic guilt, narcissism, self-pity, neediness, manipulation, and many of the other shame-based behaviors with which endogenously depressed adults typically presented were best understood as psychological defenses erected by a vestigial wounded Inner Child against the possibility of trauma and abandonment. The behaviors, in other words, were primitive emotional prophylaxes whose real function was to preclude intimacy; they were psychic armor designed to keep others at a distance so that they (i.e., others) could not get emotionally close enough to the depressed person to inflict any wounds that might echo and mirror the deep vestigial wounds of the depressed person's childhood, wounds which the depressed person was unconsciously determined to keep repressed at all costs. The therapist — who during the year's cold months, when the abundant fenestration of her home office kept the room chilly, wore a pelisse of hand-tanned Native American buckskin that formed a somewhat ghastlily moist-looking flesh-colored background for the enclosing shapes her joined hands formed in her lap as she spoke — assured the depressed person that she was not trying to lecture her or impose on her (i.e., on the depressed person) the therapist's own particular model of depressive etiology. Rather, it simply felt appropriate on an intuitive "gut" level at this particular point in time for the therapist to share some of her own feelings. Indeed, as the therapist said that she felt comfortable about positing at this point in the therapeutic relationship between them, the depressed person's acute chronic mood disorder could actually itself be seen as constituting an emotional defense-mechanism: i.e., as long as the depressed person had the depression's acute affective discomfort to preoccupy her and take up her emotional attention, she could avoid feeling or getting in touch with the deep vestigial childhood wounds which she (i.e., the depressed person) was apparently still determined to keep repressed.[3]

---

[3] The depressed person's therapist was always extremely careful to avoid appearing to judge or blame the depressed person for clinging to her defenses, or to suggest that the depressed person had in any way consciously *chosen* or *chosen to cling to* a chronic depression whose agony made her (i.e., the depressed person's) every waking hour feel like more than any person could possibly endure. This renunciation of judgment or imposed value was held by the therapeutic school in which the therapist's philosophy of healing had evolved over almost fifteen years of clinical experience to be integral to the combination of unconditional support and complete honesty about feelings which composed the nurturing professionalism required for a productive therapeutic journey toward authenticity and intrapersonal wholeness. Defenses against intimacy, the depressed person's therapist's experiential theory held, were nearly always arrested or vestigial survival-mechanisms; i.e.,

Several months later, when the depressed person's therapist suddenly and unexpectedly died — as the result of what was determined by authorities to be an "accidentally" toxic combination of caffeine and homeopathic appetite suppressant but which, given the therapist's extensive medical background and knowledge of chemical interactions, only a person in very deep denial indeed could fail to see must have been, on some level, intentional — without leaving any sort of note or cassette or encouraging final words for any of the persons and/or clients in her life who had, despite all their debilitating fear and isolation and defense-mechanisms and vestigial wounds from past traumas, come to connect intimately with her and let her in emotionally even though it meant making themselves vulnerable to the possibility of loss- and abandonment-traumas, the depressed person found the trauma of this fresh loss and abandonment so shattering, its resultant agony and despair and hopelessness so unbearable, that she was, ironically, now forced to reach frantically and repeatedly out on a nightly basis to her Support System, sometimes calling three or even four long-distance friends in an evening, sometimes calling the same friends twice in one night, sometimes at a very late hour, sometimes even — the depressed person felt sicken-

they had, at one time, been environmentally appropriate and necessary and had very probably served to shield a defenseless childhood psyche against potentially unbearable trauma, but in nearly all cases they (i.e., the defense-mechanisms) had become inappropriately imprinted and arrested and were now, in adulthood, no longer environmentally appropriate and in fact now, paradoxically, actually caused a great deal more trauma and pain than they prevented. Nevertheless, the therapist had made it clear from the outset that she was in no way going to pressure, hector, cajole, argue, persuade, flummox, trick, harangue, shame, or manipulate the depressed person into letting go of her arrested or vestigial defenses before she (i.e., the depressed person) felt ready and able to risk taking the leap of faith in her own internal resources and self-esteem and personal growth and healing to do so (i.e., to leave the nest of her defenses and freely and joyfully fly).

ingly sure — waking them up or interrupting them in the midst of healthy, joyful sexual intimacy with their partner. In other words, sheer survival, in the turbulent wake of her feelings of shock and grief and loss and abandonment and bitter betrayal following the therapist's sudden death, now compelled the depressed person to put aside her innate feelings of shame and inadequacy and embarrassment at being a pathetic burden and to lean with all her might on the empathy and emotional nurture of her Support System, despite the fact that this, ironically, had been one of the two areas in which the depressed person had most vigorously resisted the therapist's counsel.

Even on top of the shattering abandonment-issues it brought up, the therapist's unexpected death also could not have occurred at a worse time from the perspective of the depressed person's journey toward inner healing, coming as it (i.e., the suspicious death) did just as the depressed person was beginning to work through and process some of her core shame- and resentment-issues concerning the therapeutic process itself and the intimate therapist-patient relationship's impact on her (i.e., on the depressed person's) unbearable isolation and pain. As part of her grieving process, the depressed person shared with supportive members of her Support System the fact that she felt she had, she had realized, experienced significant trauma and anguish and isolation-feelings even in the therapeutic relationship itself, a realization which she said she and the therapist had been working intensively together to explore and process. For just one example, the depressed person shared long-distance, she had discovered and struggled in therapy to work through her feeling that it was ironic and demeaning, given her parents' dysfunctional preoccupation with money and all that that preoccupation had cost her as a child, that she was now, as an adult, in the position of having to pay a therapist $90 an hour to listen patiently to her and respond honestly and empathetically; i.e., it felt demeaning and pathetic to feel forced to *buy* patience and empathy, the depressed person had confessed to her therapist, and was an agonizing echo of the exact same childhood pain which she (i.e., the depressed person) was so very anxious to put behind her. The therapist — after attending closely and unjudgingly to what the depressed person later admitted to her Support System could all too easily have been interpreted as mere niggardly whining about the expense of therapy, and after a long and considered pause during which both the therapist and the depressed person had gazed at the ovoid cage which the therapist's mated hands in her lap at that moment composed[4] — had responded that, while on a purely intellec-

---

[4] The therapist — who was substantially older than the depressed person but still younger than the depressed person's mother, and who, other than in the condition of her fingernails, resembled that mother in almost no physical or stylistic respects — sometimes annoyed the depressed person with her habit of making a digiform cage in her lap and changing the shapes of the cage and gazing down at the geometrically diverse cages during their work together. Over time, however, as the therapeutic relationship deepened in terms of intimacy and sharing and trust, the sight of the digiform cages irked the depressed person less and less, eventually becoming little more than a distraction. Far more problematic in terms of the depressed person's trust- and self-esteem-issues was the therapist's habit of from time to time glancing up very quickly at the large sunburst-design clock on the wall behind the suede easy chair in which the depressed person customarily sat during their time together, glancing (i.e., the therapist glancing) very quickly and almost furtively at the clock, such that what came to bother the depressed person more and more over time was not that the therapist was looking at the clock but that the therapist was apparently trying to *hide* or *disguise* the fact that she was looking at the clock. The depressed person — who was agonizingly sensitive, she admitted, to the possibility that anyone she was trying to reach out and share with was secretly bored or repelled or desperate to get away from her as quickly as possible, and was commensurately hypervigilant about any slight movements or gestures which might imply that a listener was conscious of the time or eager for time to pass, and never once failed to notice when the therapist glanced ever so quickly either up at the clock or down at the slender, elegant wristwatch whose timepiece rested hidden

tual or "head" level she might respectfully disagree with the substance or "propositional content" of what the depressed person was saying, she (i.e., the therapist) nevertheless wholeheartedly supported the depressed person in sharing whatever feelings the therapeutic relationship itself brought up in her (i.e., in the depressed

---

from the depressed person's view against the underside of the therapist's slim wrist — had finally, late in the first year of the therapeutic relationship, broken into sobs and shared that it made her feel totally demeaned and invalidated whenever the therapist appeared to try to hide the fact that she wished to know the exact time. Much of the depressed person's work with the therapist in the first year of her (i.e., the depressed person's) journey toward healing and intrapersonal wholeness had concerned her feelings of being uniquely and repulsively boring or convoluted or pathetically self-involved, and of not being able to trust that there was genuine interest and compassion and caring on the part of a person to whom she was reaching out for support; and in fact the therapeutic relationship's first significant breakthrough, the depressed person told members of her Support System in the agonizing period following the therapist's death, had come when the depressed person, late in the therapeutic relationship's second year, had gotten sufficiently in touch with her own inner worth and resources to be able to share assertively with the therapist that she (i.e., the respectful but assertive depressed person) would prefer it if the therapist would simply look openly up at the helioform clock or openly turn her wrist over to look at the underside's wristwatch instead of apparently believing — or at least engaging in behavior which made it appear, from the depressed person's admittedly hypersensitive perspective, as if the therapist believed — that the depressed person could be fooled by her dishonestly sneaking an observation of the time into some gesture that tried to look like a meaningless glance at the wall or an absent manipulation of the cagelike digiform shape in her lap.

Another important piece of therapeutic work the depressed person and her therapist had accomplished together — a piece of work which the therapist had said she personally felt constituted a seminal leap of growth and deepening of the trust and level of honest sharing between them — occurred in the therapeutic relationship's third year, when the depressed person had finally confessed that she also felt it was demeaning to be spoken to as the therapist sometimes spoke to her, i.e., that the depressed person felt patronized, condescended to, and/or treated like a child at those times during their work together when the therapist would start tiresomely lallating over and over and over again what her therapeutic philoso-

person[5]) so that they could work together on processing them and exploring safe and appropriate environments and contexts for their expression.

The depressed person's recollections of the therapist's patient, attentive, and unjudging responses to even her (i.e., the depressed

---

phies and goals and wishes for the depressed person were; plus not to mention, while they were on the whole subject, that she (i.e., the depressed person) also sometimes felt demeaned and resentful whenever the therapist would look up from her lap's hands' cage at the depressed person and her (i.e., the therapist's) face would once again assume its customary expression of calm and boundless patience, an expression which the depressed person admitted she knew (i.e., the depressed person knew) was intended to communicate unjudging attention and interest and support but which nevertheless sometimes from the depressed person's perspective looked to her more like emotional detachment, like clinical distance, like mere professional interest the depressed person was purchasing instead of the intensely *personal* interest and empathy and compassion she often felt she had spent her whole life starved for. It made her angry, the depressed person confessed; she often felt angry and resentful at being nothing but the object of the therapist's professional compassion or of the putative "friends" in her pathetic "Support System"'s charity and abstract guilt.

[5] Though the depressed person had, she later acknowledged to her Support System, been anxiously watching the therapist's face for evidence of a negative reaction as she (i.e., the depressed person) opened up and vomited out all these potentially repulsive feelings about the therapeutic relationship, she nevertheless was by this point in the session benefiting enough from a kind of momentum of emotional honesty to be able to open up even further and tearfully share with the therapist that it also felt demeaning and even somehow abusive to know that, for example, today (i.e., the day of the depressed person and her therapist's seminally honest and important piece of relationship-work together), at the moment the depressed person's time with the therapist was up and they had risen from their respective recliners and hugged stiffly goodbye until their next appointment together, that at that very moment all of the therapist's seemingly intensely personally focused attention and support and interest in the depressed person would be withdrawn and then effortlessly transferred onto the next pathetic contemptible whiny self-involved snaggletoothed pig-nosed fat-thighed *shiteater* who was waiting out there right outside reading a used magazine and waiting to lurch in and cling pathetically to the hem of the therapist's pelisse for an hour, so des-

person's) most spiteful and childishly arrested complaints felt as if they brought on further, even more unbearable feelings of loss and abandonment, as well as fresh waves of resentment and self-pity which the depressed person knew all too well were repellent in the extreme, she assured the friends who composed her Support System,

---

perate for a personally interested friend that they would pay almost as much per month for the pathetic temporary illusion of a friend as they paid in fucking *rent*. The depressed person knew all too perfectly well, she conceded — holding up a pica-gnawed hand to prevent the therapist from interrupting — that the therapist's professional detachment was in fact not at all incompatible with true caring, and that the therapist's careful maintenance of a professional, rather than a personal, level of caring and support and commitment meant that this support and caring could be counted on to always Be There for the depressed person and not fall prey to the normal vicissitudes of less professional and more personal interpersonal relationships' inevitable conflicts and misunderstandings or natural fluctuations in the therapist's own personal mood and emotional availability and capacity for empathy on any particular day; not to mention that her (i.e., the therapist's) professional detachment meant that at least within the confines of the therapist's chilly but attractive home office and of their appointed three hours together each week the depressed person could be totally honest and open about her own feelings without ever having to be afraid that the therapist would take those feelings personally and become angry or cold or judgmental or derisive or rejecting or would ever shame or deride or abandon the depressed person; in fact that, ironically, in many ways, as the depressed person said she was all too aware, the therapist was actually the depressed person's — or at any rate the isolated, agonized, needy, pathetic, selfish, spoiled, wounded-Inner-Child part of the depressed person's — absolutely *ideal* personal friend: i.e. here, after all, was a person (viz., the therapist) who would always Be There to listen and really care and empathize and be emotionally available and giving and to nurture and support the depressed person and yet would demand absolutely nothing back from the depressed person in terms of empathy or emotional support or in terms of the depressed person ever really caring about or even considering the therapist's own valid feelings and needs as a human being. The depressed person also knew perfectly well, she had acknowledged, that it was in fact the $90 an hour which made the therapeutic relationship's simulacrum of friendship so ideally one-sided: i.e. the only expectation or demand the therapist placed on the depressed person was for the contracted hourly $90; after that one demand was satisfied, everything in the relationship got to be for and

trusted friends whom the depressed person was by this time calling almost constantly, sometimes now even during the day, from her workplace, dialing her closest friends' long-distance work numbers and asking them to take time away from their own challenging, stimulating careers to listen supportively and share and dialogue

---

about the depressed person. On a rational, intellectual, "head" level, the depressed person was completely aware of all these realities and compensations, she told the therapist, and so of course felt that she (i.e., the depressed person) had no rational reason or excuse for feeling the vain, needy, childish feelings she had just taken the unprecedented emotional risk of sharing that she felt; and yet the depressed person confessed to the therapist that she nevertheless still felt, on a more basic, emotionally intuitive or "gut" level, that it truly was demeaning and insulting and pathetic that her chronic emotional pain and isolation and inability to reach out forced her to spend $1,080 a month to purchase what was in many respects a kind of fantasy-friend who could fulfill her childishly narcissistic fantasies of getting her own emotional needs met by another without having to reciprocally meet or empathize with or even consider the other's own emotional needs, an other-directed empathy and consideration which the depressed person tearfully confessed she sometimes despaired of ever having it in her to give. The depressed person here inserted that she often worried, despite the numerous traumas she had suffered at the hands of attempted relationships with men, that it was in fact her own inability to get outside her own toxic neediness and to Be There for another and truly emotionally *give* which had made those attempts at intimate, mutually nurturing partner-relationships with men such an agonizingly demeaning across-the-board failure.

The depressed person had further inserted in her seminal sharing with the therapist, she later told the select elite "core" members of her Support System after the therapist's death, that her (i.e., the depressed person's) resentments about the $1,080/month cost of the therapeutic relationship were in truth less about the actual expense — which she freely admitted she could afford — than about the demeaning *idea* of paying for artificially one-sided friendship and narcissistic-fantasy-fulfillment, then had laughed hollowly (i.e., the depressed person had laughed hollowly during the original insertion in her sharing with the therapist) to indicate that she heard and acknowledged the unwitting echo of her cold, niggardly, emotionally unavailable parents in the stipulation that what was objectionable was not the actual expense but the idea or "*principle*" of the expense. What it really felt like, the depressed person later admitted to supportive friends that she had

and help the depressed person find some way to process this grief and loss and find some way to survive. Her apologies for burdening these friends during daylight hours at their workplaces were elaborate, involved, vociferous, baroque, mercilessly self-critical, and very nearly constant, as were her expressions of gratitude to the

---

confessed to the compassionate therapist, was as if the $90 hourly therapeutic fee were almost a kind of ransom or "protection money," purchasing the depressed person an exemption from the scalding internal shame and mortification of telephoning distant former friends she hadn't even laid fucking *eyes* on in years and had no legitimate claim on the friendship of anymore and telephoning them uninvited at night and intruding on their functional and blissfully ignorantly joyful if perhaps somewhat shallow lives and leaning shamelessly on them and constantly reaching out and trying to articulate the essence of the depression's terrible and unceasing pain even when it was this very pain and despair and loneliness that rendered her, she knew, far too emotionally starved and needy and self-involved to be able ever to truly Be There in return for her long-distance friends to reach out to and share with and lean on in return, i.e. that hers (i.e., the depressed person's) was a contemptibly greedy and narcissistic omnineediness that only a complete idiot would not fully expect the members of her so-called "Support System" to detect all too easily in her, and to be totally repelled by, and to stay on the telephone with only out of the barest and most abstract human charity, all the while rolling their eyes and making faces and looking at the clock and wishing that the telephone call were over or that she (i.e., the pathetically needy depressed person on the phone) would call anyone else but her (i.e., the bored, repelled, eye-rolling putative "friend") or that she'd never historically been assigned to room with the depressed person or had never even gone to that particular boarding school or even that the depressed person had never been born and didn't even exist, such that the whole thing felt totally, unendurably pathetic and demeaning "*if the truth be told,*" if the therapist really wanted the "*totally honest and uncensored sharing*" she always kept "alleging [she] want[ed]," the depressed person later confessed to her Support System she had hissed derisively at the therapist, her face (i.e., the depressed person's face during the seminal but increasingly ugly and humiliating third-year therapy session) working in what she imagined must have been a grotesque admixture of rage and self-pity and complete humiliation. It had been the imaginative visualization of what her own enraged face must have looked like which had caused the depressed person to begin at this late juncture in the session to weep, pule, snuffle, and sob in real earnest, she shared later with trusted friends. For no,

Support System just for Being There for her, just for allowing her to begin again to be able to trust and take the risk of reaching out, even just a little, because the depressed person shared that she felt as if she had been discovering all over again, and with a shattering new clarity now in the wake of the therapist's abrupt and wordless abandonment, she shared over her workstation's headset telephone, just how agonizingly few and far between were the people whom she could ever hope to really communicate and share with and forge healthy, open, trusting, mutually nurturing relationships to lean on. For example, her work environment — as the depressed person readily acknowledged she'd whined about at tiresome length many times before — was totally dysfunctional and toxic, and the totally

---

if the therapist really wanted the truth, the actual "gut"-level truth underneath all her childishly defensive anger and shame, the depressed person had shared from a hunched and near-fetal position beneath the sunburst clock, sobbing but making a conscious choice not to bother wiping her eyes or even her nose, the depressed person *really* felt that what was *really* unfair was that she felt able — even here in therapy with the trusted and compassionate therapist — that she felt able to share only painful circumstances and historical insights about her depression and its etiology and texture and numerous symptoms instead of feeling truly able to communicate and articulate and express the depression's terrible unceasing agony *itself*, an agony that was the overriding and unendurable reality of her every black minute on earth — i.e., not being able to share the way it truly *felt*, what the depression made her *feel like* inside on a daily basis, she had wailed hysterically, striking repeatedly at her recliner's suede armrests — or to reach out and communicate and express it to someone who could not only listen and understand and care but could or would actually *feel it* with her (i.e., feel what the depressed person felt). The depressed person confessed to the therapist that what she felt *truly* starved for and really *truly* fantasized about was having the ability to somehow really truly literally "*share*" it (i.e., the chronic depression's ceaseless torment). She said that the depression felt as if it was so central and inescapable to her identity and who she was as a person that not being able to share the depression's inner feeling or even really describe what it felt like felt to her for example like feeling a desperate, life-or-death need to describe the sun in the sky and yet being able or permitted only to point to shadows on the ground. She was so very tired of point-

unsupportive emotional atmosphere there made the idea of trying to bond in any mutually nurturing way with coworkers a grotesque joke. And the depressed person's attempts to reach out in her emotional isolation and try to cultivate and develop caring friends and relationships in the community through church groups or nutrition and holistic stretching classes or community woodwind ensembles and the like had proved so excruciating, she shared, that she had all but begged the therapist to withdraw her gentle suggestion that the depressed person try her best to do so. And then as for the idea of girding herself once again and venturing out there into the emotionally Hobbesian meat market of the "dating scene" and trying once again to find and establish any healthy, caring, functional connections with men, whether in a physically intimate partner-

---

ing at shadows, she had sobbed. She (i.e., the depressed person) had then immediately broken off and laughed hollowly at herself and apologized to the therapist for employing such a floridly melodramatic and self-pitying analogy. The depressed person shared all this later with her Support System, in great detail and sometimes more than once a night, as part of her grieving process following the therapist's death from homeopathic caffeinism, including her (i.e., the depressed person's) reminiscence that the therapist's display of compassionate and unjudging attention to everything the depressed person had finally opened up and vented and hissed and spewed and whined and puled about during the traumatically seminal breakthrough session had been so formidable and uncompromising that she (i.e., the therapist) had blinked far less often than any nonprofessional listener the depressed person had ever shared with face-to-face had ever blinked. The two currently most trusted and supportive "core" members of the depressed person's Support System had responded, almost verbatim, that it sounded as though the depressed person's therapist had been very special, and that the depressed person clearly missed her very much; and the one particularly valuable and empathetic and elite, physically ill "core" friend whom the depressed person leaned on more heavily than on any other support during the grieving process suggested that the single most loving and appropriate way to honor both the therapist's memory and the depressed person's own grief over her loss might be for the depressed person to try to become as special and caring and unflaggingly nurturing a friend to herself as the late therapist had been.

relationship or even just as close and supportive friends — at this juncture in her sharing the depressed person laughed hollowly into the headset telephone she wore at the terminal inside her cubicle at her workplace and asked whether it was really even necessary, with a friend who knew her as well as whatever member of her Support System she was presently sharing with did, to go into why the depressed person's intractable depression and highly charged self-esteem- and trust-issues rendered that idea a pie-in-the-sky flight of Icarusian fancy and denial. To take just one example, the depressed person shared from her workstation, in the second semester of her junior year at college there had been a traumatic incident in which the depressed person had been sitting alone on the grass near a group of popular, self-assured male students at an intercollegiate lacrosse game and had distinctly overheard one of the men laughingly say, of a female student the depressed person knew slightly, that the only substantive difference between this woman and a restroom toilet was that the toilet did not keep pathetically following you around after you'd used it. Sharing with supportive friends, the depressed person was now suddenly and unexpectedly flooded with emotional memories of the early session during which she had first told the therapist of this incident: they had been doing basic feelings-work together during this awkward opening stage of the therapeutic process, and the therapist had challenged the depressed person to identify whether the overheard slur had made her (i.e., the depressed person) feel primarily more angry, lonely, frightened, or sad.[6, 6(A)]

---

[6] The depressed person, trying desperately to open up and allow her Support System to help her honor and process her feelings about the therapist's death, took the risk of sharing her realization that she herself had rarely if ever used the word "sad" in the therapeutic process's dialogues. She had usually used the words "despair" and "agony," and the therapist had, for the most part, acquiesced to this admittedly melodramatic choice of words, though the depressed person had long sus-

By this stage in the grieving process following the therapist's possible death by her own (i.e., by the therapist's own) hand, the depressed person's feelings of loss and abandonment had become so intense and overwhelming and had so completely overridden her vestigial defense-mechanisms that, for example, when whatever long-distance friend the depressed person had reached out to finally confessed that she (i.e., the "friend") was dreadfully sorry but there was no helping it she absolutely *had* to get off the telephone and back to the demands of her own full, vibrant, undepressed life, a primal instinct for what felt like nothing more than basic emotional survival now drove the depressed person to swallow every last pulverized remnant of pride and to beg shamelessly for two or even just one more minute of the friend's time and attention; and, if the "empathetic friend," after expressing her hope that the depressed person would find a way to be more gentle and compassionate with herself, held firm and gracefully terminated the conversation, the depressed person now spent hardly any time at all listening dully to the dial tone or gnawing the cuticle of her index finger or grinding the heel of her hand savagely into her forehead or feeling anything much at all beyond sheer primal desperation as she hurriedly dialed the next ten-digit number on her Support System Telephone List, a list which by this point in the grieving process had been photocopied several times and placed in the depressed person's address book, workstation terminal's PHONE.VIP file, billfold, zippered interior security compartment of her purse, minilocker at the Holistic Stretching and Nutrition Center, and in a special home-

---

pected that the therapist probably felt that her (i.e., the depressed person's) choice of "agony," "despair," "torment," and the like was at once melodramatic — hence needy and manipulative — on the one hand, and minimizing — hence shame-based and toxic — on the other. The depressed person also shared with long-distance friends during the shattering grieving process the painful realization that she had never once actually come right out and asked the therapist what she (i.e.,

made pocket inside the back cover of the leatherbound Feelings Journal which the depressed person — at her late therapist's suggestion — carried with her at all times.

The depressed person shared, with each available member of her Support System in turn, some portion of the flood of emotionally sensuous memories of the session during which she had first opened up and told the late therapist of the incident in which the laughing men had compared the female college student to a toilet, and shared that she had never been able to forget the incident, and that, even though she had not had much of a personal relationship or connection to the female student whom the men had compared to a toilet or even known her very well at all, the depressed person had, at the intercollegiate lacrosse game, been filled with horror and empathic despair at the pathos of the idea of that female student being the object of such derision and laughing intergender contempt without her (i.e., the female student, to whom the depressed person again admitted she had had very little connection) ever even knowing it. It seemed to the depressed person very likely that her (i.e., the depressed person's) whole later emotional development and ability to trust and reach out and connect had been deeply scarred by this incident; she chose to make herself open and vulnerable by sharing — albeit only with the one single most trusted and elite and special "core" member of her current Support System — that she had admitted to the therapist that she was, even today, as a

---

the therapist) was thinking or feeling at any given moment during their time together, nor had asked, even once, what she (i.e., the therapist) actually thought of her (i.e., of the depressed person) as a human being, i.e., whether the therapist personally liked her, didn't like her, thought she was a basically decent v. repellent person, etc. These were merely two examples.

6(A)As a natural part of the grieving process, sensuous details and emotional memories flooded the depressed person's agonized psyche at random moments and in ways impossible to predict, pressing in on her and clamoring for expression and

putative adult, often preoccupied with the idea that laughing groups of people were often derisive and demeaning of her (i.e., of the depressed person) without her knowledge. The late therapist, the depressed person shared with her very closest long-distance confidante, had pointed to the memory of the traumatic incident in college and the depressed person's reactive presumption of derision and ridicule as a classic example of the way an adult's arrested vestigial emotional defense-mechanisms could become toxic and dysfunctional and could keep the adult emotionally isolated and deprived of community and nurturing, even from herself, and could (i.e., the toxic vestigial defenses could) deny the depressed adult access to her own precious inner resources and tools for both reaching out for support and for being gentle and compassionate and affirming with herself, and that thus, paradoxically, arrested defense-mechanisms helped contribute to the very pain and sadness they had originally been erected to forestall.

It was while sharing this candid, vulnerable four-year-old reminiscence with the one particular "core" Support System–member whom the grieving depressed person felt she now most deeply trusted and leaned on and could really communicate over the headset telephone with that she (i.e., the depressed person) suddenly experienced what she would later describe as an emotional realization nearly as traumatic and valuable as the realization she had experienced nine months prior at the Inner-Child-Focused

---

processing. The therapist's buckskin pelisse, for example, though the therapist had seemed almost fetishistically attached to the Native American garment and had worn it, seemingly, on a near-daily basis, was always immaculately clean and always presented an immaculately raw- and moist-looking flesh-tone backdrop to the variform cagelike shapes the therapist's unconscious hands composed — and the depressed person shared with members of her Support System, after the therapist's death, that it had never been clear to her how or by what process the pelisse's buckskin was able to stay so clean. The depressed person confessed to sometimes imag-

Experiential Therapy Retreat Weekend before she had felt simply too cathartically drained and enervated to be able to continue and had had to fly home. I.e., the depressed person told her very most trusted and supportive long-distance friend that, paradoxically, she (i.e., the depressed person) appeared to have somehow found, in the extremity of her feelings of loss and abandonment in the wake of the therapist's overdose of natural stimulants, the resources and inner respect for her own emotional survival required for her finally to feel able to risk trying to follow the second of the late therapist's two most challenging and difficult suggestions and to begin openly asking certain demonstrably honest and supportive others to tell her straight out whether they ever secretly felt contempt, derision, judgment, or repulsion for her. And the depressed person shared that she now, finally, after four years of whiny and truculent resistance, proposed at last really to begin actually asking trusted others this seminally honest and possibly shattering question, and that because she was all too aware of her own essential weakness and defensive capacities for denial and avoidance she (i.e., the depressed person) was choosing to commence this unprecedentedly vulnerable interrogative process now, i.e., with the elite, incomparably honest and compassionate "core" Support System–member with whom she was sharing via her workstation's headset right this mo-

---

ining narcissistically that the therapist wore the immaculate flesh-colored garment only for their particular appointments together. The therapist's chilly home office also contained, on the wall opposite the bronze clock and behind the therapist's recliner, a stunning molybdenum desk-and-personal-computer-hutch ensemble, one shelf of which was lined, on either side of the deluxe Braun coffeemaker, with small framed photographs of the late therapist's husband and sisters and son; and the depressed person often broke into fresh sobs of loss and despair and self-excoriation on her cubicle's headset telephone as she confessed to her Support System that she had never once even asked the therapist's loved ones' names.

ment.[7] The depressed person here paused momentarily to insert the additional fact that she had firmly resolved to herself to ask this potentially deeply traumatizing question without the usual pathetic and irritating defense-mechanisms of preamble or apology or interpolated self-criticism. She wished to hear, with no holds barred, the depressed person averred, the one very most valuable and intimate friend in her current Support System's brutally honest opinion of her as a person, the potentially negative and judging and hurtful parts as well as the positive and affirming and supportive and nurturing parts. The depressed person stressed that she was serious about this: whether it sounded melodramatic or not, the brutally honest assessment of her by an objective but deeply caring other felt to her, at this point in time, like an almost literal matter of life and death.

For she was frightened, the depressed person confessed to the trusted and convalescing friend, profoundly, unprecedentedly frightened by what she was beginning to feel she was seeing and learning and getting in touch with about herself in the grieving process following the sudden death of a therapist who for nearly four years had been the depressed person's closest and most trusted confidante and source of support and affirmation and — with no offense in any way

---

[7] The singularly valuable and supportive long-distance friend to whom the depressed person had decided she was least mortified about posing a question this fraught with openness and vulnerability and emotional risk was an alumna of one of the depressed person's very first childhood boarding schools, a surpassingly generous and nurturing divorced mother of two in Bloomfield Hills, Michigan, who had recently undergone her second course of chemotherapy for a virulent neuroblastoma which had greatly reduced the number of responsibilities and activities in her full, functional, vibrantly other-directed adult life, and who thus was now not only almost always at home but also enjoyed nearly unlimited conflict-free availability and time to share on the telephone, for which the depressed person was always careful to enter a daily prayer of gratitude in her Feelings Journal.

intended to any members of her Support System — her very best friend in the world. Because what she had discovered, the depressed person confided long-distance, when she took her important daily Quiet Time[8] now, during the grieving process, and got quiet and centered and looked deep within, was that she could neither feel nor identify any real feelings within herself for the therapist, i.e. for the therapist as a person, a person who had died, a person who only somebody in truly stupefying denial could fail to see had probably taken her own life, and thus a person who, the depressed person posited, had possibly herself suffered levels of emotional agony and isolation and despair which were comparable to or perhaps — though it was only on a "head" or purely abstract intellectual level that she seemed to be able even to entertain this possibility, the depressed person confessed over the headset telephone — even exceeded the depressed person's own. The depressed person shared that the most frightening implication of this (i.e., of the fact that, even when she centered and looked deep within herself, she felt she could locate no real feelings for the therapist as an autonomously valid human being) appeared to be that all her agonized pain and despair since the therapist's suicide had in fact been all and only for *herself*, i.e. for *her* loss, *her* abandonment, *her* grief, *her* trauma and pain and primal affective survival. And, the depressed person shared that she was taking the additional risk of revealing, even more frightening, that this shatteringly terrifying set of realizations, instead now of awakening in her any feelings of compassion, empathy, and other-directed grief for the therapist as a person, had — and here the depressed person waited patiently for an episode of retch-

---

[8] (i.e., carefully arranging her morning schedule to permit the twenty minutes the therapist had long suggested for quiet centering and getting in touch with feelings and owning them and journaling about them, looking inside herself with a compassionate, unjudging, almost clinical detachment)

ing in the especially available trusted friend to pass so that she could take the risk of sharing this with her — that these shatteringly frightening realizations had seemed, terrifyingly, merely to have brought up and created still more and further feelings in the depressed person about *herself*. At this point in the sharing, the depressed person took a time-out to solemnly swear to her long-distance, gravely ill, frequently retching but still caring and intimate friend that there was no toxic or pathetically manipulative self-excoriation here in what she (i.e., the depressed person) was reaching out and opening up and confessing, only profound and unprecedented fear: the depressed person was frightened for herself, for as it were "[her]*self*" — i.e., for her own so-called "character" or "spirit" or as it were "soul," i.e., for her own capacity for basic human empathy and compassion and caring — she told the supportive friend with the neuroblastoma. She was asking sincerely, the depressed person said, honestly, desperately: what kind of person could seem to feel nothing — *"Nothing,"* she emphasized — for anyone but herself? Maybe not *ever?* The depressed person wept into the headset telephone and said that right here and now she was shamelessly begging her currently very best friend and confidante in the world to share her (i.e., the friend with the virulent malignancy in her adrenal medulla's) brutally candid assessment, to pull no punches, to say nothing reassuring or exculpatory or supportive which she did not honestly believe to be true. She trusted her, she assured her. For she had decided, she said, that her very life itself, however fraught with agony and despair and indescribable loneliness, depended, at this point in her journey toward true healing, on inviting — even if necessary laying aside all possible pride and defense and *begging for,* she interpolated — the judgment of certain trusted and very carefully selected members of her supportive community. So, the depressed person said, her voice breaking, she was begging her now single most trusted friend to share her very most private judgment of the depressed person's "character"'s or "spirit"'s capacity for human caring. She needed her feedback, the depressed person wept, even if that feedback was partly negative or hurtful or traumatic or had the potential to push her right over the emotional edge once and for all — even, she pleaded, if that feedback lay on nothing more than the coldly intellectual or "head" level of objective verbal description; she would settle even for that, she promised, hunched and trembling in a near-fetal position atop her workstation cubicle's ergonomic chair — and therefore now urged her terminally ill friend to go on, to not hold back, to let her have it: what words and terms might be applied to describe and assess such a solipsistic, self-consumed, endless emotional vacuum and sponge as she now appeared to herself to be? How was she to decide and describe — even to herself, looking inward and facing herself — what all she'd so painfully learned said about her?

THE DEVIL IS A BUSY MAN

Plus when he got something that was new or if he cleaned out the machine shed or the cellar oftentimes Daddy would find he had a item he didn't want anymore and had to get shed of and as it was a long haul to truck it to the dump or the Goodwill in town he'd just call up and put a notice in the *Trading Post* paper in town to give it away for nothing. Shit like a couch or a freezer or a old tiller. The notice would say Free Come And Get It. Yet even so it always took some time after it run before one soul even called up and the item would sit around in Daddy's drive pissing him off until one or two folks in town would finally come out to his place to look at it. And they'd be skittery about it too and their face all closed up like at cards and they'd walk around the thing and poke it with their toe and go Where'd you all get it at what's the matter with it how come you want shed of it so bad. They'd shake their head and talk to their Mrs. and dither around and about drive Daddy nuts because all he wanted was to give a old tiller away for nothing and get it out of the drive and here it was taking him all this time jickjacking around with these folks to get them to take it. Then so what he up and starts doing one time he wanted to get shed of something is he puts his notice in the *Trading Post* paper and he puts in some fool price he just makes up there on the phone with the *Trading Post* fellow. Some fool price next to nothing. Old Harrow With Some Teeth A Little Rusted $5, JCPenny Sleepersofa Green And Yellow $10 and like that. Then oftentimes folks called up the first day the *Trading*

Post run the notice and up and come out from town and even would haul in from further out in some little other towns that got the *Trading Post* and pull up spraying gravel and scarce even look at the item and press on Daddy to take the 5 or $10 right away before any other folks could take it and if it was something heavy like that one couch I'd help them load it up and they'd up and haul it off right then and there. Their faces was different and their wife's faces in the truck, fine and showing teeth and him with a arm around the Mrs. and a wave at Daddy as they back out. Tickled to death to get a old harrow for next to nothing. I asked Daddy about what lesson to draw here and he said he figured it's you don't try and teach a pig to sing and told me to go on and rake the drive's gravel back out of the ditch before it fucked up the drainage.

THINK

Her brassiere's snaps are in the front. His own forehead snaps clear. He thinks to kneel. But he knows what she might think if he kneels. What cleared his forehead's lines was a type of revelation. Her breasts have come free. He imagines his wife and son. Her breasts are unconfined now. The bed's comforter has a tulle hem, like a ballerina's little hem. This is the younger sister of his wife's college roommate. Everyone else has gone to the mall, some to shop, some to see a movie at the mall's multiplex. The sister with breasts by the bed has a level gaze and a slight smile, slight and smoky, media-taught. She sees his color heighten and forehead go smooth in a kind of revelation — why she'd begged off the mall, the meaning of certain comments, looks, distended moments over the weekend he'd thought were his vanity, imagination. We see these things a dozen times a day in entertainment but imagine we ourselves, our own imaginations, are mad. A different man might have said what he'd seen was her hand moved to her bra and *freed* her breasts. His legs might slightly tremble when she asks what he thinks. Her expression is from Page 18 of the Victoria's Secret catalogue. She is, he thinks, the sort of woman who'd keep her heels on if he asked her to. Even if she'd never kept heels on before she'd give him a knowing, smoky smile, Page 18. In quick profile as she turns to close the door her breast is a half-globe at the bottom, a ski-jump curve above. The languid half-turn and push of the door are tumid with some kind of significance; he realizes she's replaying a scene from some movie she loves. In his imagination's tableau his wife's hand is on his small son's shoulder in an almost fatherly way.

It's not even that he decides to kneel — he simply finds he feels weight against his knees. His position might make her think he wants her underwear off. His face is at the height of her underwear as she walks toward him. He can feel the weave of his slacks' fabric, the texture of the carpet below that, over that, against his knees. Her expression is a combination of seductive and aroused, with an overlay of slight amusement meant to convey sophistication, the loss of all illusions long ago. It's the sort of expression that looks devastating in a photograph but becomes awkward when it's maintained over real time. When he clasps his hands in front of his chest it's now clear he is kneeling to pray. There can now be no mistaking what he's doing. His color is very high. Her breasts stop their slight tremble and sway when she stops. She's now on the same side of the bed but not yet right up against him. His gaze at the room's ceiling is supplicatory. His lips are soundlessly moving. She stands confused. Her awareness of her own nudity becomes a different kind of awareness. She's not sure how to stand or look while he's gazing so intently upward. His eyes are not closed. Her sister and her husband and kids and the man's wife and tiny son have taken the man's Voyager minivan to the mall. She crosses her arms and looks briefly behind her: the door, her blouse and brassiere, the wife's antique dresser stippled with sunlight through the window's leaves. She could try, for just a moment, to imagine what is happening in his head. A bathroom scale barely peeking out from below the foot of the bed, beneath the gauzy hem of the comforter. Even for an instant, to try putting herself in his place.

The question she asks makes his forehead pucker as he winces. She has crossed her arms. It's a three-word question.

'It's not what you think,' he says. His eyes never leave the middle distance between the ceiling and themselves. She's now aware of

{*Think*}

just how she's standing, how silly it might look through a window.
It's not excitement that's hardened her nipples. Her forehead forms
a puzzled line.

He says, 'It's not what you think I'm afraid of.'

And what if she joined him on the floor, just like this, clasped in
supplication: just this way.

SIGNIFYING NOTHING

Here is a weird one for you. It was a couple of years ago, and I was 19, and getting ready to move out of my folks' house, and get out on my own, and one day as I was getting ready, I suddenly get this memory of my father waggling his dick in my face one time when I was a little kid. The memory comes up out of nowhere, but it is so detailed and solid-seeming, I know it is totally true. I suddenly know it really happened, and was not a dream, even though it had the same kind of bizarre weirdness to it dreams have. Here is the sudden memory. I was around 8 or 9, and I was down in the rec room by myself, after school, watching TV. My father came down and came into the rec room, and was standing in front of me, like between me and the TV, not saying anything, and I didn't say anything. And, without saying anything, he took his dick out, and started kind of waggling it in my face. I remember nobody else was home. I think it was winter, because I remember it was cold down in the rec room, and I had Mom's TV afghan wrapped around me. Part of the total weirdness of the incident of my father waggling his dick at me down there was that, the whole time, he did not say anything (I would have remembered it if he said anything), and there was nothing in the memory about what his face looked like, like what his expression looked like. I do not remember if he even looked at me. All I remember was the dick. The dick, like, claimed all of my attention. He was just sort of waggling it in my face, without saying anything or making any type of comment, shaking it kind of like you do in the can, like when you are shaking off, but, also, there was something threatening and a little bully-seeming about the way he did it, I remember, too, like the dick was a fist he was putting in my face and daring me to say anything, and I remember I was wrapped up in the afghan, and could not get up or move out of the way of the dick, and all I remembered doing was sort of moving my head all over the place, trying to get it out of my face (the dick). It was one of those totally bizarre incidents which are so weird, it seems like it is not happening even while it is happening. The only time I even had glimpsed my father's dick before was in locker rooms. I remember my head kind of moving around all over the place, on my neck, and the dick kind of following me all over the place, and having totally bizarre thoughts going through my head while he did it, like, 'I am moving my head just like a snake,' etc. He did not have a boner. I remember the dick was a little bit darker than the rest of him, and big, with a big ugly vein down one side of it. The little hole-thing at the end looked slitty and pissed off, and it opened and closed a little as my father waggled the dick, keeping the dick threateningly in my face no matter where I moved my head around to. That is the memory. After I had it (the memory), I went around my folks' house in a haze, in, like, a daze, totally freaked out, not telling anybody about it, and not asking anything. I know that was the only time my father ever did anything like that. This was when I was packing, and going around to stores getting old boxes to move with. Sometimes, I walked around my folks' house in shock, feeling totally weird. I kept thinking about the sudden memory. I went into my folks' room, and down to the rec room. The rec room had a new entertainment system, instead of the old TV, but my Mom's TV afghan was still there, spread over the back of the couch when not in use. It was still the same afghan as in the memory. I kept trying to think about why my father would do something like that, and what he could have been thinking of, like, what it could have meant, and trying to remember if there had been any kind of look or emotion, during it, on his face.

Now it gets even weirder, because I finally, the day my father took a half day off, and we went down and rented a van for me to pack and move out with, I, finally, in the van, on the way home from the rental place, brought it up, and asked him about the memory. I asked him about it straight up. It is not like there is a way to gradually lead up to something like that. My father had put the rental of the van on his card, and he was the one driving it home. I remember the radio in the van did not work. In the van, out of (from his perspective) nowhere, I suddenly tell my father I just had recently remembered the day he came down and waggled his dick in my face when I was a little kid, and I sort of briefly described what I had remembered, and asked him, 'What the fuck was up with *that?*' When he kept merely driving the van, and did not say or do anything to respond, I persisted, and brought the incident up again, and asked him the same question all over again. (I pretended like maybe he did not hear what I said the first time.) And then what my father does — we are in the van, on a brief straight away on the route home to my folks' house, so I can get ready to move out on my own — he, without moving his hands on the wheel or moving one muscle except for his neck, turns his head to look at me, and gives me this *look*. It is not a pissed off look, or a confused one like he believes he did not quite hear. And it is not like he says, 'What the hell is the matter with you,' or 'Get the fuck outta here,' or any of the usual things he says where you can tell he is pissed off. He does not say one thing, however this *look* he gives me says it all, like he can not believe he just heard this shit come out of my mouth, like he is in total disbelief, and total disgust, like not only did he never in his life waggle his dick at me for no reason when I was a little kid but just the fact that I could even fucking *imagine* that he

ever waggled his dick at me, and then, like, *believe* it, and then come
into his own presence in this rental van and, like, *accuse* him. Etc.,
etc. The look he reacted and gave me in the van while he drove, after I brought up the memory and asked him straight up about it —
this is what sent me totally over the edge, where my father was concerned. The look he turned and slowly gave me said he was embarrassed for me, and embarrassed for himself for even being related to
me. Imagine if you were at a large, fancy, and coat-and-tie dinner or
track banquet with your father, and if, like, you all of a sudden got
up on the banquet table and bent down and took a shit right there
on the table, in front of everybody at the dinner — this would be
the look your father would be giving you as you did it (took a shit).
Roughly, it was then, in the van, that I felt like I could have killed
him. For a second, I felt like I wished the van would open up and
swallow me whole, I was so embarrassed. But, just split seconds
later, what I felt was I was so totally pissed off I could have killed
him. It was weird — the memory in itself did not, at the time, get
me pissed off, but only freaked out, like in a shocked daze. But, in
the rented van that day, the way my father did not even say anything, but merely drove home to the house in silence, with both
hands on the wheel, and that look on his face about me asking about
it — now I was totally pissed off. I always thought that thing you
hear about seeing 'red' if you get mad enough was a figure of speech,
but it is real. After I packed up all my shit in the van, I moved away,
and did not get in contact with my folks for over a year. Not a word.
My apartment, in the same town, was maybe only two miles away,
but I did not even tell them my phone number. I pretended they
did not exist. I was so disgusted and pissed off. My Mom had no
clue why I was not in contact, but I sure was not going to mention
a word to her about any of it, and I knew, for fucking-'A' sure, my
father was not going to say anything to her about it. Everything I
saw stayed slightly red for months, after I moved out and broke off

contact, or at least a pink tinge. I did not think of the memory of my father waggling his dick at me as a little kid very often, but barely a day went by that I did not remember that look in the van he gave me when I brought it up again. I wanted to kill him. For months, I thought about going home when nobody was there and kicking his ass. My sisters had no clue why I was not in contact with my folks, and said I must have gone crazy, and was breaking my Mom's heart, and when I called them they gave me shit about breaking off contact without explanation constantly, but I was so pissed off, I knew I was going to go to my grave never saying another fucking word about it. It was not that I was chicken to say anything about it, but I was so fucking over the edge about it, it felt like, if I ever mentioned it again, and got any kind of look from somebody, something terrible would happen. Almost every day, I imagined that, as I went home and was kicking his ass, my father would keep asking me why I was doing it, and what it meant, but I would not say anything, nor would my face have any look or emotion on it as I beat the shit out of him.

Then, as time passed, I, little by little, got over the whole thing. I still knew that the memory of my father waggling his dick at me in the rec room was real, but, little by little, I started to realize, just because *I* remembered the incident, that did not mean, necessarily, my *father* did. I started to see that maybe he had forgotten the whole incident. It was possible that the whole incident was so weird and unexplained, that my father, psychologically, blocked it out of his memory, and that when I, out of (from his point of view) nowhere, brought it up to him in the van, he did not remember ever doing something as bizarre and unexplained as coming down and threateningly waggling his dick at a little kid, and thought I had lost my fucking mind, and gave me a look that said he was totally disgusted. It is not like I totally believed my father had no memory of it, but more like I was admitting, little by little, it was possible he blocked it out. Little by little, it seemed like the moral of a memory of any incident that weird is, anything is possible. After the year, I got to this position in my attitude where I figured that, if my father was willing to forget about the whole thing of me bringing up the memory of the incident in the van, and to never bring it up, then I was willing to forget the whole thing. I knew that I, for fucking-'A' god*damn* sure, would never bring any of it up again. When I arrived at this attitude about the whole thing, it was around early July, right before the 4th Of July, which is also my littlest sister's birthday, and so, out of (to them) nowhere, I call my folks' house, and ask if I can come along for my sister's birthday, and meet them at the special restaurant they traditionally take my sister to on her birthday, because she loves it so much (the restaurant). This restaurant, which is in our town's downtown, is Italian, kind of expensive, and has mostly dark, wooden decor, and has menus in Italian. (Our family is not Italian.) It was ironic that it was at this restaurant, on a birthday, that I would be getting back in contact with my folks, because, when I was a little kid, our family tradition was that this was 'my' special restaurant, where I always got to go for my birthday. I somewhere, as a kid, got the idea that it was run by the Mob, in which I had a total fascination, as a little kid, and always bugged my folks until they took me on at least my birthday — until, little by little, as I grew up, I outgrew it, and then, somehow, it passed into being my littlest sister's special restaurant, like she had inherited it. It has black and red checkered table cloths, and all the waiters look like enforcers for the Mob, and, on the restaurant's tables, there are always empty wine bottles with candles stuck in the hole, which have melted, and several colors of wax run and harden up all over the sides of the bottle in lines and varied patterns. As a little kid, I remembered having a weird fascination in the wine bottles with all the dried wax running all over them, and of having to be asked, over and over, by my father, not to keep picking the wax off. When I arrived at the restaurant, in a coat and tie, they were all already there, at a table. I remember my Mom looked totally enthusiastic and pleased just to see me, and I could tell she was willing to forget the whole year of me not contacting them, she was just so pleased to feel like a family again.

My father said, 'You're late.' His face had zero expression either way.

My Mom said, 'I'm afraid we already ordered, is that OK.'

My father said they had ordered for me already, being as I was a little late getting there.

I sat down, and smilingly asked what they ordered me.

My father said, 'A chicken presto dish thing your mother ordered for you.'

I said, 'But I hate chicken. I always hated it. How could you forget I hate chicken?'

We all looked at each other for a second, around the table, even my littlest sister, and her boyfriend with the hair. There was one long split second of all looking at each other. This was when the waiter was bringing everybody's chicken. Then my father smiled, and drew one of his fists back jokingly, and said, 'Get the fuck outta here.' Then my Mom put her hand up against her upper chest, like she does when she is afraid she's going to laugh too hard, and laughed. The waiter put my plate in front of me, and I pretended to look down and make a face, and we all laughed. It was good.

BRIEF INTERVIEWS
WITH HIDEOUS MEN

B.I. #40 06-97
BENTON RIDGE OH

'It's the arm. You wouldn't think of it as a asset like that would
you. But it's the arm. You want to see it? You won't get disgusted?
Well here it is. Here's the arm. This is why I go by the name Johnny
One-Arm. I made it up, not anybody being, like, hardhearted —
me. I see how you're trying to be polite and not look at it. Go ahead
and look though. It don't bother me. Inside my head I don't call it
the arm I call it the Asset. How all would you describe it? Go on.
You think it'll hurt my feelings? You want to hear me describe it?
It looks like a arm that changed its mind early on in the game when
it was in Mama's stomach with the rest of me. It's more like a itty
tiny little flipper, it's little and wet-looking and darker than the rest
of me is. It looks wet even when it's dry. It's not a pretty sight at all.
I usually keep it in the sleeve until it's time to haul it out and use it
for the Asset. Notice the shoulder's normal, it's just like the other
shoulder. It's just the arm. It'll only go down to like the titty-nipple
of my chest here, see? It's a little sucker. It ain't pretty. It moves
fine, I can move it around fine. If you look close here at the end
there's these little majiggers you can tell started out wanting to
be fingers but didn't form. When I was in her stomach. The other
arm — see? It's a normal arm, a little muscley on account of using it
all the time. It's normal and long and the right color, that's the arm

I show all the time, most times I keep the other sleeve pinned up so it don't look to be even anything like a arm in there at all. It's strong though. The arm is. It's hard on the eyes but it's strong, sometimes I'll try and get them to armwrestle it to see how strong it is. It's a strong little flippery sucker. If they think they can stand to touch it. I always say if they don't think they can stand touching it why that's OK, it don't hurt my feelings. You want to touch it?'

Q.

'That's all right. That is all right.'

Q.

'What it is is — well first there's always some girls around. You know what I mean? At the foundry there, at the Lanes. There's a tavern right down by the bus stop there. Jackpot — that's my best friend — Jackpot and Kenny Kirk — Kenny Kirk's his cousin, Jackpot's, that are both over me at the foundry cause I finished school and didn't get in the union till after — they're real good-looking and normal-looking and Good With The Ladies if you know what I mean, and there's always girls hanging back around. Like in a group, a bunch or group of all of us, we'll all just hang back, drink some beers. Jackpot and Kenny're always going with one of them or the other and then the ones they're going with got friends. You know. A whole, say, group of us there. You follow the picture here? And I'll start hanging back with this one or that one, and after a while the first stage is I'll start in to telling them how I got the name Johnny One-Arm and about the arm. That's a stage of the thing. Of getting some pussy using the Asset. I'll describe the arm while it's still up in the sleeve and make it sound like just about the ugliest thing you ever did see. They'll get this look on their face like Oh You Poor Little Fella You're Being Too Hard On Yourself You Shouldn't Be Shameful Of The Arm. So on. How I'm such a nice young fella and it breaks their heart to see me talk about my own part of me that way especially since it weren't any fault of mine to get born with the arm. At which time when they start with that stage of it the next stage is I ask them do they want to see it. I say how I'm shameful of the arm but somehow I trust them and they seem real nice and if they want I'll unpin the sleeve and let the arm out and let them look at the arm if they think they could stand it. I'll go on about the arm until they can't hardly stand to hear no more about it. Sometimes it's a ex of Jackpot's that's the one that starts hanging back with me down at Frame Eleven over to the Lanes and saying how I'm such a good listener and sensitive not like Jackpot or Kenny and she can't believe there's any way the arm's as bad as I'm making out and like that. Or we'll be hanging back at her place in the kitchenette or some such and I'll go It's So Hot I Feel Like Taking My Shirt Off But I Don't Want To On Account Of I'm Shameful Of The Arm. Like that. There's numerous, like, stages. I never out loud call it the Asset believe you me. Go on and touch it whenever you get a mind to. One of the stages is I know after some time I really am starting to come off creepy to the girl, I can tell, cause all I can talk about is the arm and how wet and flippery it is but how it's strong but how I'd just about up and die if a girl as nice and pretty and perfect as I think she is saw it and got disgusted, and I can tell all the talk starts creeping them up inside and they start to secretly think I'm kind of a loser but they can't back out on me cause after all here they been all this time saying all this nice shit about what a sensitive young fella I am and how I shouldn't be shameful and there's no way the arm can be that bad. In this stage it's like they're committed into a corner and if they quit hanging back with me now why they know I can go It Was Because Of The Arm.'

Q.

'Usually long about two weeks, like that. The next is your critical-type stage where I show them the arm. I wait till it's just her and me alone someplace and I haul the sucker out. I make it seem like they talked me into it and now I trust them and they're who I finally feel like I can let it out of the sleeve and show it. And I show it to her just like I just did you. There's some additional things too I can do with it that look even worse, make it look — see that? See this right here? It's cause there ain't even really a elbow bone, it's just a —'

Q.

'Or some of your ointments or Vaseline-type jelly on it to make it look even wetter and shinier. The arm's not a pretty sight at all when I up and haul it out on them I'm telling you right now. It just about makes them puke, the sight of it the way I get it. Oh and a couple run out, some skedoodle right out the door. But your majority? Your majority of them'll swallow hard a time or two and go Oh It's It's It's Not Too Bad At All but they're looking over all away and try and not look at my face which I've got this totally shy and scared and trusting face on at the time like this one thing I can do where I can make my lip even tremble a little. Ee? Ee anh? And ever time sooner or later within inside, like, five minutes of it they'll up and start crying. They're in way over their head, see. They're, like, committed into a corner of saying how it can't be that ugly and I shouldn't be shameful and then they see it and I see to it it is ugly, ugly ugly ugly and now what do they do? Pretend? Shit girl most of these girls around here think Elvis is alive someplace. These are not girl wonders of the brain. It breaks them down ever time. They get even worse if I ask them Oh Golly What's Wrong, how come they're crying, Is It The Arm and they have to say It Ain't The Arm, they have to, they have to try and pretend it ain't the arm that it's how they feel so sad for me being so shameful of something that ain't a big deal at all they have to say. Oftentimes with their face in their hands and crying. Your climatic stage then is then I up and come over to where she's at and sit down and now I'm the one that's comforting them. A, like, factor here I found out the hard way is when I go in to hold them and comfort them I hold them with the good side. I don't give them no more of the Asset. The Asset's wrapped back up safe out of sight in the sleeve now. They're broke down crying and I'm the one holding them with the good arm and go It's OK Don't Cry Don't Be Sad Being Able To Trust You Not To Get Disgusted By The Arm Means So Very Very Much To Me Don't You See You Have Set Me Free Of Being Shameful Of The Arm Thank You Thank You and so on while they put their face in my neck and just cry and cry. Sometimes they get me crying too. You following all this?'

Q. . . .

'More pussy than a toilet seat, man. I shit you not. Go on and ask Jackpot and Kenny if you want about it. Kenny Kirk's the one named it the Asset. You go on.'

B.I. #42 06-97

PEORIA HEIGHTS IL

'The soft plopping sounds. The slight gassy sounds. The little involuntary grunts. The special sigh of an older man at a urinal, the way he establishes himself there and sets his feet and aims and then lets out a timeless sigh you know he's not aware of.

'This was his environment. Six days a week he stood there. Saturdays a double shift. The needles-and-nails quality of urine into water. The unseen rustle of newspapers on bare laps. The odors.'

Q.

'Top-rated historic hotel in the state. The finest lobby, the single finest men's room between the two coasts, surely. Marble shipped from Italy. Stall doors of seasoned cherry. Since 1969 he's stood there. Rococo fixtures and scalloped basins. Opulent and echoing. A large opulent echoing room for men of business, substantial men, men with places to go and people to see. The odors. Don't ask about the odors. The difference in some men's odors, the sameness in all men's odors. All sounds amplified by tile and Florentine stone. The moans of the prostatic. The hiss of the sinks. The ripping extractions of deep-lying phlegm, the plosive and porcelain splat. The sound of fine shoes on dolomite flooring. The inguinal rumbles. The hellacious ripping explosions of gas and the sound of stuff hitting the water. Half-atomized by pressures brought to bear. Solid, liquid, gas. All the odors. Odor as environment. All day. Nine hours a day. Standing there in Good Humor white. All sounds magnified, reverberating slightly. Men coming in, men going out. Eight stalls, six urinals, sixteen sinks. Do the math. What were they thinking?'

Q. . . .

'It's what he stands in. In the sonic center. Where the shine stand used to be. In the crafted space between the end of the sinks and the start of the stalls. The space designed for him to stand. The vortex. Just outside the long mirror's frame, by the sinks — a continuous sink of Florentine marble, sixteen scalloped basins, leaves of gold foil around the fixtures, mirror of good Danish plate. In which men of substance drag material out of the corners of their eyes and squeeze their pores, blow their nose in the sinks and walk off without rinsing. He stood all day with his towels and small cases of personal-size toiletries. A trace of balsam in the three vents' whisper. The vents' threnody is inaudible unless the room is empty. He stands there when it's empty, too. This is his occupation, this is his career. Dressed all in white like a masseur. Plain white Hanes T and white pants and tennis shoes he had to throw out if so much as a spot. He takes their cases and topcoats, guards them, remembers without asking whose is whose. Speaking as little as possible in all those acoustics. Appearing at men's elbows to hand them towels. An impassivity that is effacement. This is my father's career.'

Q. . . .

'The stalls' fine doors end a foot from the floor — why is this? Why this tradition? Is it descended from animals' stalls? Is the word *stall* related to *stable?* Fine stalls that afford some visual privacy and nothing else. If anything they amplify the sounds inside, bullhorns on end. You hear it all. The balsam makes the odors worse by sweetening them. The toes of dress shoes defiled along the row of spaces beneath the doors. The stalls full after lunch. A long rectangular box of shoes. Some tapping. Some of them humming, speaking aloud to themselves, forgetting they are not alone. The flatus and tussis and meaty splats. Defecation, egestion, extrusion, dejection, purgation, voidance. The unmistakable rumble of the toilet paper dispensers. The occasional click of nail-clippers or depilatory scissors. Effluence. Emission. Orduration, micturition, transudation, emiction, feculence, catharsis — so many synonyms: why? what are we trying to say to ourselves in so many ways?'

Q. . . .

'The olfactory clash of different men's colognes, deodorants, hair tonic, mustache wax. The rich smell of the foreign and unbathed. Some of the stalls' shoes touching their mate hesitantly, tentatively, as if sniffing it. The damp lisp of buttocks shifting on padded seats. The tiny pulse of each bowl's pool. The little dottles that survive flushing. The urinals' ceaseless purl and trickle. The indole stink of putrefied food, the eccrine tang to the jackets, the uremic breeze that follows each flush. Men who flush toilets with their feet. Men who will touch fixtures only with tissue. Men who trail paper out of the stalls, their own comet's tail, the paper lodged in their anus. Anus. The word *anus*. The anuses of the well-to-do ranging above the bowls' water, flexing, puckering, distending. Soft faces squeezed tight in effort. Old men who require all kinds of ghastly help — lowering and arranging another man's shanks, wiping another man.

Silent, wordless, impassive. Whisking the shoulders of another man, shaking off another man, removing a pubic hair from the pleat of another man's slacks. For coins. The sign says it all. Men who tip, men who do not tip. The effacement cannot be too complete or they forget he is there when it comes time to tip. The trick of his demeanor is to appear only provisionally there, to exist all and only if needed. Aid without intrusion. Service without servant. No man wants to know another man can smell him. Millionaires who do not tip. Natty men who splatter the bowls and tip a nickel. Heirs who steal towels. Tycoons who pick their noses with their thumb. Philanthropists who throw cigar butts on the floor. Self-made men who spit in the sink. Wildly rich men who do not flush and without a thought leave it to someone else to flush because this is literally what they are used to — the old saw *Would you do this at home.*

'He bleached his work clothes himself, ironed them. Never a word of complaint. Impassive. The sort of man who stands in one place all day. Sometimes the very soles of the shoes visible under there, in the stalls, of vomiting men. The word *vomit*. The mere word. Men being ill in a room with acoustics. All the mortal sound he stood in every day. Try to imagine. The soft expletives of constipated men, men with colitis, ileus, irritable bowel, lientery, dyspepsia, diverticulitis, ulcers, bloody flux. Men with colostomies handing him the bag to dispose of. An equerry of the human. Hearing without hearing. Seeing only need. The slight nod that in men's rooms is acknowledgment and deferral at once. The ghastly metastasized odors of continental breakfasts and business dinners. A double shift when he could. Food on the table, a roof, children to educate. His arches would swell from the standing. His bare feet were blancmanges. He showered thrice daily and scrubbed himself raw but the job still followed him. Never a word.

'The door tells the whole story. *MEN.* I haven't seen him since 1978 and I know he's still there, all in white, standing. Averting his eyes to preserve their dignity. But his own? His own five senses? What are those three monkeys' names? His task is to stand there as if he were not there. Not really. There's a trick to it. A special nothing you look at.'

Q.

'I didn't learn it in a men's room, I can tell you that.'

Q. . . .

'Imagine not existing until a man needs you. Being there and yet not there. A willed translucence. Provisionally there, contingently there. The old saw *Lives to serve*. His career. Breadwinner. Every morning up at six, kiss us all goodbye, a piece of toast for the bus. He could eat for real on his break. A bellman would go to the deli. The pressure produced by pressure. The rich belches of expense-account lunches. The mirrors' remains of sebum and pus and sneezed detritus. Twenty-six-no-seven years at the same station. The grave nod he'd receive a tip with. The inaudible thank-you to the regulars. Sometimes a name. All those solids tumbling out of all those large soft warm fat moist white anuses, flexing. Imagine. To attend so much passage. To see men of substance at their most elemental. His career. A career man.'

Q.

'Because he brought his work home. The face he wore in the men's room. He couldn't take it off. His skull conformed to fit it. This expression or rather lack of expression. Attendant and no more. Alert but absent. His face. Beyond reserved. As if forever conserving himself for some ordeal to come.'

Q. . . .

'I wear nothing white. Not one white thing, I can tell you that much. I eliminate in silence or not at all. I tip. I never forget that someone is there.

'Yes and do I admire the fortitude of this humblest of working men? The stoicism? The Old World grit? To stand there all those

years, never one sick day, serving? Or do I despise him, you're wondering, feel disgust, contempt for any man who'd stand effaced in
that miasma and dispense towels for coins?'

Q.

'. . .'

Q.

'What were the two choices again?'

B.I. #2 10-94
CAPITOLA CA

'Sweetie, we need to talk. We've needed to for a while. I have I
mean, I feel like. Can you sit?'

Q.

'Well, I'd rather almost anything, but I care about you, and I'd
rather anything than you getting hurt. That concerns me a lot, believe me.'

Q.

'Because I care. Because I love you. Enough to really be honest.'

Q.

'That sometimes I worry you're going to get hurt. And that you
don't deserve it. To get hurt I mean.'

Q, Q.

'Because, to be honest, my record is not good. Almost every intimate relationship I get into with women seems to end up with
them getting hurt, somehow. To be honest, sometimes I worry I
might be one of those guys who uses people, women. I worry about
it somet— no, damn it, I'm going to be honest with you because I
care about you and you deserve it. Sweetie, my relationship record
indicates a guy who's bad news. And more and more now lately I've
been afraid that you're going to get hurt, that I might hurt you the
way I seem to have hurt others who —'

Q.

'That I have a history, a pattern so to speak, of, for instance, coming on very fast and hard in the beginning of a relationship and pursuing very hard and very intensely and wooing very intensely and being head over heels in love right from the very start, of saying I Love You very early on in the relationship, of starting to talk future-tense right from the outset, of having nothing be too much to say or do to show how much I care, which all of course has the effect, naturally, of seeming to make them truly believe I really am in love — which I am — which then, I think, seems to make them feel loved enough and so to speak safe enough to start letting them say I Love You back and acknowledging that they're in love with me, too. And it's not — let me stress this because it's the God's honest truth — it's not that I don't mean it when I say it.'

Q.

'Well, it's not as if how many of them I've said it to isn't an understandable question or concern but if it's all right it's just that it's not what I'm trying to talk to you about, so if it's all right I want to hold off on things like numbers or names and try to just be totally honest with you about what my concerns are, because I care. I care about you a lot, sweetie. A whole lot. I know it's insecure, but it's very important to me that you believe this and hang on to it all through our talk here, that what I'm saying or what I'm afraid I might do to in any way end up hurting you doesn't in any way lessen or mean that I don't care or that I have not meant it absolutely every time I've told you I love you. Every time. I hope you believe that. You deserve to. Plus it's true.'

Q. . . .

'But what it is is that it seems as if for a while everything I say and do has the effect of pulling them into thinking of it as a very — a very serious relationship and almost you could say somehow like *lulling* them into thinking in terms of the future.'

Q.

'Because then the as it were pattern seems to be that once I've *got* you, so to speak, and you're as much into the relationship as I've been, then it's as if I'm almost constitutionally unable somehow to push all the way through and follow through and make a . . . what's the right word —'

Q.

'Yes, all right, that's the word, even though I have to tell you the way you say it fills me with dread that you're already feeling hurt and not taking what I'm trying to say in the spirit which I'm trying to talk to you about this, which is that I honestly do care enough about you to share some honest concerns that have been troubling me about even the possibility of you getting hurt, which believe me is the absolute last thing I want.'

Q.

'That, from examining the record and trying to make some kind of sense of it, it seems as if something in me goes into a sort of over-drive in the early intense part and gets me right up to the point of yes of commitment, and then but then can't quite seem to push all the way through and actually make the commitment to do a truly serious, future-tense, committed thing with them. As Mr. Chitwin would put it I am just not a *closer*. Does any of this make any sense? I don't feel as though I'm saying it very well. Where the real hurt seems to come in is because this inability seems to kick in only af-ter doing and saying and behaving in all sorts of ways that on some level I surely must know are leading them to think that I want a truly committed future-tense thing as much as they do. So, to be honest, this is my record with this sort of thing, and as far as I can tell it seems to indicate a guy who's bad news for women, which concerns me. A lot. That I seem to maybe seem like a woman's com-pletely ideal guy up to a certain point in the relationship where now they've dropped all their resistance and defenses and are commit-

tedly in love, which of course seems to be what I had wanted right
from the beginning and had worked so hard and wooed them so intensely to get them to do and just as I know all too well I've done
with you, to get serious and think in terms of the future and the
word *commitment* and then — and sweetie trust me this is hard to
explain because I far from fully understand it myself — but then at
just this point, historically, as best as I can figure out it's as if something in me as it were kind of reverses thrust and now puts all its
overdrive into somehow pulling back.'

    Q.

'All I can really figure out is that I seem to sort of freak out and
feel I have to reverse thrust and get out of it, except usually I'm not
totally sure, I can't tell if I really want out of it or whether I'm simply freaking out somehow, and even though I'm freaking out and
want out I still don't want to lose them, it seems, so I tend to give
a lot of mixed signals and say and do a lot of things that seem to
confuse them and yank them around and cause them pain, which
believe me I always end up feeling horrible about, even while I'm
doing it. Which I'll tell you the truth is what I'm freaking out
about with you and me, because yanking you around or causing you
pain is the absolute last thing in —'

    Q, Q.

'The God's honest truth is I don't know. I do not know. I haven't
been able to figure it out. I think all I'm trying to do here in our sitting down and talking about it is really care about you and be honest about myself and my relationship record and do it in the middle
of something instead of the end. Because my record is that historically it seems to be only at the end of a relationship that I seem to
be willing to open up about some of my fears about myself and my
record of causing women who love me pain. Which, of course,
causes them pain, the sudden honesty does, and serves to get me out
of the relationship, which then afterward I worry might have been

my subconscious agenda all along in terms of bringing it up and finally getting honest with them, maybe. I'm not sure.'

Q. . . .

'So anyway the truth is I'm not sure about any of it. I'm just trying to look honestly at my record and honestly see what seems to be the pattern and what's the likelihood of my continuing this pattern with you, which believe me I'd rather anything than do. Please believe that inflicting any pain on you is the last thing I want, sweetie. This pulling-away thing and inability to push through and as Mr. Chitwin would say *close the deal* — this is what I want to try and be honest with you about.'

Q. . . .

'And the harder and faster I've come after them at the beginning, wooing and pursuing and feeling completely in love, the intensity of that drive seems to be directly proportional to the intensity and urgency with which it seems I then find ways to pull away, back away. The record indicates that this sort of sudden reversal of thrust happens right when I have the sense that I've *got* them. Whatever *got* means — to be honest I'm not sure. It seems to mean once I know for sure and feel that now they're as into the relationship and the future tense as I am. Have been. Was. It happens that fast. It's terrifying when it happens. Sometimes I don't even know what even happened until after it's over and I'm looking back on it and trying to understand how she could have gotten so hurt, was she crazy or unnaturally clingy and dependent or am I just bad news as far as relationships go. It happens incredibly fast. It feels both fast and slow, like a car crash, where it's almost more like you're watching it happen than that you're actually involved in it. Does any of this make any sense?'

Q.

'I seem to need to keep admitting I'm really terrified you're not going to understand. That I won't explain it well enough or you'll

somehow through no fault of your own misinterpret what I'm saying and turn it around somehow and be hurt. I'm feeling unbelievable terror here, I have to tell you.'

Q.

'All right. That's the bad part. Dozens of times. At least. Forty,
forty-five times, maybe. To be honest, possibly more. As in a lot
more, I'm afraid. I guess I'm not even sure anymore.'

Q. . . .

'On the surface, in terms of the specifics, a lot of them looked
pretty different, the relationships and what exactly ended up happening. Sweetie, but I've somehow started to see that underneath
the surface all of them were largely the same. The same basic pattern. In a way, sweetie, my seeing this gives me a certain amount of
hope, because maybe it means I'm becoming more able to understand myself and be honest with myself. I seem to be developing
more of a sort of conscience in this area. Which a part of me finds
terrifying, to be honest. The starting out so intense, in almost over-
drive, and feeling as if everything depends on getting them to drop
their defenses and plunge in and love me as totally as I love them,
then the freaking-out thing kicks in and reverses thrust. I admit
there's a kind of dread at the idea of having a conscience in this area,
as if it seems as if it's going to take away all room to maneuver,
somehow. Which is bizarre, I know, because at the beginning of the
pattern I don't *want* room to maneuver, the *last* thing I want is room
to maneuver, what I *want* is to plunge in and get them to plunge in
with me and believe in me and be together in it forever. I swear, I
really almost every time seem to have believed that's what I wanted.
Which is why it doesn't quite seem to me as if I was evil or anything, or as if I was actually lying to them or anything — even
though at the end, when I seem to have reversed thrust and suddenly pulled totally out of it, they almost always all feel as if I've
lied to them, as if if I meant what I said there's no way I could be

reversing thrust the way I'm doing now. Which I still, to be honest, don't quite think I've ever done: lied. Unless I'm just rationalizing. Unless I'm some kind of psychopath who can rationalize anything and can't even see the most obvious kinds of evil he's perpetrating, or who doesn't even care but wants to delude himself into believing he cares so that he can continue to see himself as a basically decent guy. The whole thing is incredibly confusing, and it's one reason I'm so hesitant to bring it up with you, out of fear that I won't be able to be clear about it and that you'll misunderstand and be hurt, but I decided that if I care about you I have to have the courage to really act as if I care about you, to put caring about you before my own petty worries and confusions.'

Q.

'Sweetie, you're welcome. I pray you're not being sarcastic. I'm so mixed up and terrified right now I probably couldn't even tell.'

Q.

'I know I should have told you some of all this about me sooner, and the pattern. Before you moved all the way out here, which believe me meant so — it made me really feel you really cared about this, us, being with me, and I want to be as caring and honest toward you as you've been with me. Especially because I know your moving out here was something I lobbied so hard for. School, your apartment, having to get rid of your cat — just please don't misunderstand — your doing all that just to be with me means a great deal to me, and it's a huge part of why I really do feel as if I love you and care so much about you, too much not to feel terrified about in any way yanking you around or hurting you somewhere down the road, which trust me given my record in this area is a possibility I'd have to be a total psychopath not to consider. That's what I want to be able to make clear enough so that you'll understand. Is it making at least a little sense?'

Q.

'It's not as simple as that. At least not the way I see it. And believe me my way of seeing it is not that I'm a totally decent guy who never does anything wrong. A better guy probably would have told you about this pattern and warned you before we even slept together, to be honest. Because I know I felt guilty after we did. Sleep together. Despite how unbelievably magical and ecstatic and *right* it was, you were. Probably I felt guilty because I'd been the one lobbying so hard for sleeping together so soon, and even though you were completely honest about being uncomfortable about sleeping together so soon and I already even then respected and cared for you a lot and wanted to respect your feelings but I was still so incredibly attracted to you, one of these almost irresistible thunderbolts of attraction, and felt so overwhelmed with it that even without necessarily meaning to I know I plunged in too fast and probably pressured you and rushed you to plunge into sleeping together, even though I think now on some level I probably knew how guilty and uncomfortable I was going to feel afterward.'

Q.

'I'm not explaining it well enough. I'm not getting through. All right, now I'm really freaking out that you're starting to feel hurt. Please believe me. The whole reason I'm having us talk about my record and what I get afraid might happen is that I don't *want* it to happen, see? that I don't *want* suddenly to reverse thrust and begin trying to extricate myself after you've given up so much and moved out here and now I've — now that we're so involved. I'm praying you'll be able to see that my telling you what always happens is a kind of proof that with you I don't *want* it to happen. That I don't *want* to get all testy or hypercritical or pull away and not be around for days at a time or be blatantly unfaithful in a way you're guaranteed to find out about or any of the shitty cowardly ways I've used before to get out of something I'd just spent months of intensive pursuit and effort trying to get the other person to plunge into with me. Does this make any sense? Can you believe that I'm honestly trying to *respect* you by warning you about me, in a way? That I'm trying to be honest instead of dishonest? That I've decided the best way to head off this pattern where you get hurt and feel abandoned and I feel like shit is to try to be honest for once? Even if I should have done it sooner? Even when I admit it's maybe possible that you might even interpret what I'm saying *now* as dishonest, as trying somehow to maybe freak you out enough so that you'll move back out and I can get out of this? Which I don't *think* is what I'm do-ing, but to be totally honest I can't be a hundred percent sure? To risk that with you? Do you understand? That I'm trying as hard as I can to love you? That I'm terrified I can't love? That I'm afraid maybe I'm just constitutionally incapable of doing anything other than pursuing and seducing and then running, plunging in and then reversing, never being honest with anybody? That I'll never be a closer? That I might be a psychopath? Can you imagine what it takes to tell you this? That I'm terrified that after I've told you all this I'm going to feel so guilty and ashamed that I won't be able even to look at you or stand to be around you, knowing that you know all this about me and now being constantly afraid of what you're thinking all the time? That it's even possible that my hon-estly here trying to head off the pattern of sending out mixed sig-nals and pulling away is just another type of way of pulling away? Or to get *you* to pull away, now that I've got you, and maybe deep down I'm such a cowardly shit that I don't even want to make the commitment of pulling away myself, that I want to somehow force you into doing it?'

Q. Q.

'Those are valid, totally understandable questions, sweetie, and I swear to you I'll do my absolute best to answer them as honestly as possible.'

Q. . . .

'There's just one more thing I feel like I have to tell you about first, though. So the slate's clean for once, and everything's out in the open. I'm terrified to tell you, but I'm going to. Then it'll be your turn. But listen: this thing is not good. I'm afraid it might hurt you. It's not going to sound good at all, I'm afraid. Can you do me a favor and sort of brace yourself and promise to try not to react for a couple seconds when I tell you? Can we talk about it before you react? Can you promise?'

B.I. #48 08-97
APPLETON WI

'It is on the third date that I will invite them back to the apartment. It is important to understand that, for there even to be a third date, there must exist some sort of palpable affinity between us, something by which I can sense that they will go along. Perhaps *go along* [flexion of upraised fingers to signify tone quotes] is not a fortuitous phrase for it. I mean, perhaps, [flexion of upraised fingers to signify tone quotes] *play*. Meaning to join me in the contract and subsequent activity.'

Q.

'Nor can I explain how I sense this mysterious affinity. This sense that a willingness to go along would not be out of the question. Someone once told me of an Australian profession known as [flexion of upraised fingers] *chicken-sexing*, in —'

Q.

'Bear with me a moment, now. Chicken sexing. Since hens have a far greater commercial value than males, cocks, roosters, it is apparently vital to determine the sex of a newly hatched chick. In order to know whether to expend capital on raising it or not, you see. A cock is nearly worthless, apparently, on the open market. The sex characteristics of newly hatched chicks, however, are entirely internal, and it is impossible with the naked eye to tell whether a given chick is a hen or a cock. This is what I have been told, at any rate. A professional chicken-sexer, however, can nevertheless tell. The sex. He can go through a brood of freshly hatched chicks, examining each one entirely by eye, and tell the poultry farmer which chicks to keep and which are cocks. The cocks are to be allowed to perish. "Hen, hen, cock, cock, hen," and so on and so forth. This is apparently in Australia. The profession. And they are nearly always right. Correct. The fowl determined to be hens do in fact grow up to be hens and return the poultry farmer's investment. What the chicken-sexer cannot do, however, is explain how he knows. The sex. It's apparently often a patrilineal profession, handed down from father to son. Australia, New Zealand. Have him hold up a new-hatched chick, a young cock shall we say, and ask him how he can tell that it is a cock, and the professional chicken-sexer will apparently shrug his shoulders and say "Looks like a cock to me." Doubtless adding "mate," much the way you or I would add "my friend" or "sir.'"

Q. . . .

'This is the aptest analogy I can adduce to explain it. Some mysterious sixth sense, perhaps. Not that I'm right one hundred percent of the time. But you would be surprised. We will be on the ottoman, having a drink, enjoying some music, light conversation. This is now on the third date together, late in the evening, after dinner and perhaps a film or a bit of dancing. I do very much like to dance. We are not seated close together on the ottoman. Usually I am at one end and she at the other. Though it is only a four-and-a-half-foot ottoman. It's not a terribly long piece of furniture. However, the point is that we are not in a posture of particular intimacy.

Very casual and so on. A great deal of complex body language is involved and has taken place over all the prior time spent in one another's company, which I will not bore you by attempting to go into. So then. When I sense the moment is right — on the ottoman, comfortable, with drinks, perhaps some Ligeti on the audio system — I will say, without any discernible context or lead-in that you could point to as such, "How would you feel about my tying you up?" Those nine words. Just so. Some rebuff me on the spot. But it is a small percentage. Very small. Perhaps shockingly small. I will know whether it's going to happen the moment I ask. I can nearly always tell. Again, I cannot fully explain how. There will always be a moment of complete silence, heavy. You are, of course, aware that social silences have varied textures, and these textures communicate a great deal. This silence will occur whether I'm to be rebuffed or not, whether I have been incorrect about the [flexion of upraised fingers to signify tone quotes] *hen* or not. Her silence, and the weight of it — a perfectly natural reaction to such a shift in the texture of a hitherto casual conversation. And it brings to a sudden head all the romantic tensions and cues and body language of the first three dates. Initial or early-stage dates are fantastically rich from a psychological standpoint. Doubtless you are aware of this. Any sort of courtship ritual, game of sizing one another up, gauging. There is, afterward, always that eight-beat silence. They must allow the question to [finger flexion] *sink in.* This was an expression of my mother's, by the way. To let such-and-such [finger flexion] *sink in,* and as it happens it is nearly perfect as a descriptor of what occurs.'

Q.

'Alive and kicking. She lives with my sister and her husband and their two small children. Very much alive. Nor do — rest assured that I do not delude myself that the low percentage of rebuffs is due to any overwhelming allure on my part. This is not how an activity like this works. In fact, it is one reason why I propose the possibility in such a bold and apparently graceless way. I withhold any attempt at charm or assuasion. Because I know, full well, that their response to the proposal depends on factors internal to them. Some will wish to play. A few will not. That is all there is to it. The only real [finger flexion] *talent* I profess is the ability to gauge them, screen them, so that by the — such that a preponderance of the third dates are, if you will, [finger flexion] *hens* rather than [finger flexion] *cocks*. I use these avian tropes as metaphors, not in any way to characterize the subjects but rather to emphasize my own unanalyzable ability to know, intuitively, as early as the first date, whether they are, if you will, [f.f.] *ripe* for the proposal. To tie them up. And that is just how I put it. I do not dress it up or attempt to make it seem any more [sustained f.f.] *romantic* or *exotic* than that. Now, as to the rebuffs. The rebuffs are very rarely hostile, very rarely, and then only if the subject in question really in fact does wish to play but is conflicted or emotionally inequipped to accept this wish and so must use hostility to the proposal as a means of assuring herself that no such wish or affinity exists. This is sometimes known as [f.f.] *aversion coding*. It is very easy to discern and decipher, and as such it is nearly impossible to take the hostility personally. The rare subjects about whom I've simply been incorrect, on the other hand, are often amused, or sometimes curious and thus interrogative, but in all events in the end they simply decline the proposal in clear and forthright terms. These are the cocks I have mistaken for hens. It happens. As of my last reckoning, I have been rebuffed just over fifteen percent of the time. On the third date. This figure is actually a bit high, because it includes the hostile, hysterical, or affronted rebuffs, which do not result — at least in my opinion — which do not result from my misjudging a [f.f.] *cock.*'

Q.

'Again, please note that I do not possess or pretend to possess specialized knowledge about poultry or professional brood-management. I use the metaphors only to convey the apparent ineffability of my intuition about prospective players in the [f.f.] *game* I propose. Nor, please also note, do I so much as touch them or in any way flirt with them before the third date. Nor, on that third date, do I launch myself at them or move toward them in any way as I hit them with the proposal. I propose it bluntly but unthreateningly from my end of a four-and-a-half-foot ottoman. I do not force myself on them in any way. I am not a Lothario. I know what the contract is about, and it is not about seduction, conquest, intercourse, or algolagnia. What it is about is my desire symbolically to work out certain internal complexes consequent to my rather irregular childhood relations with my mother and twin sister. It is not [f.f.] *S and M,* and I am not a [f.f.] *sadist,* and I am not interested in subjects who wish to be [f.f.] *hurt.* My sister and I are fraternal twins, by the way, and in adulthood look scarcely anything alike. What I am about, when I suddenly inquire, à propos nothing, whether I might take them into the other room and tie them up, is describable, at least in part, in the phrase of Marchesani and van Slyke's theory of masochistic symbolism, as *proposing a contractual scenario* [no f.f.]. The crucial factor here is that I am every bit as interested in the contract as in the scenario. Hence the blunt formality, the mix of aggression and decorum in my proposal. They took her in after she suffered a series of small but not life-threatening strokes, cerebral events, and simply could no longer get around well enough to live on her own. She refused even to consider institutional care. This was not even a possibility so far as she was concerned. My sister, of course, came immediately to the rescue. Mummy has her own room while my sister's two children must now share one. The room is on the first floor to prevent her having to negotiate the staircase, which is steep and uncarpeted. I have to tell you, I know precisely what the whole thing is about.'

Q.

'It is easy to know, there on the ottoman, that it is going to happen. That I have gauged the affinity correctly. Ligeti, whose work, you are doubtless aware, is abstract nearly to the point of atonality, provides the ideal atmosphere in which to propose the contractual scenario. Over eighty-five percent of the time the subject accepts. There is no [f.f.] *predatory thrill* at the subject's [f.f.] *acquiescence,* because it is not a matter of acquiescence at all. Not at all. I will ask how they feel about the idea of my tying them up. There will be a dense and heavily charged silence, a gathering voltage in the air above the ottoman. In that voltage the question dwells until it has, comme on dit, [f.f.] *sunk in.* They will, in most cases, abruptly change their position on the ottoman so as suddenly to straighten their posture, [f.f.] *sit up straight* and so on — this is an unconscious gesture designed to communicate strength and autonomy, to assert that they alone have the power to decide how to respond to the proposal. It stems from an insecure fear that something ostensibly weak or pliable in their character might have led me to view them as candidates for [sustained f.f.] *domination* or *bondage.* People's psychological dynamics are fascinating — that a subject's first, unconscious concern is what it might be about her that might prompt such a proposal, might lead a man to think such a thing might be possible. Reflexively concerned, in other words, about their self-presentation. You would almost have to be there in the room with us to appreciate the very, very complex and fascinating dynamics that accompany this charged silence. In point of fact, in its naked assertion of personal power, the sudden improvement in posture in fact communicates a clear desire to submit. To accept. To play. In other words, any assertion of [f.f.] *power* signifies, in this charged context, a hen. In the heavily stylized formalism of [f.f.] *masochistic play,* you see, the ritual is contracted and organized in such a way that the apparent inequality in power is, in fact, fully empowered and autonomous.'

Q.

'Thank you. This shows me you really are attending. That you are an acute and assertive auditor. Nor have I put it very gracefully. What would render you and I, for example, going to my apartment and entering into some contractual activity that included my tying you up true [f.f.] *play* is that it would be entirely different from my somehow luring you to my home and once there launching myself at you and overpowering you and tying you up. There would be no play in that. The play is in your freely and autonomously submitting to being tied up. The purpose of the contractual nature of masochistic or [f.f.] *bonded* play — I propose, she accepts, I propose something further, she accepts — is to formalize the power structure. Ritualize it. The [f.f.] *play* is the submission to bondage, the giving up of power to another, but the [f.f.] *contract* — the [f.f.] *rules,* as it were, of the game — the contract ensures that all abdications of power are freely chosen. In other words, an assertion that one is secure enough in one's concept of one's own personal power to ritualistically give up that power to another person — in this example, me — who will then proceed to take off your slacks and sweater and underthings and tie your wrists and ankles to my antique bedposts with satin thongs. I am, of course, for the purposes of this conversation, merely using you as an example. Do not think that I am actually proposing any contractual possibility with you. I scarcely know you. Not to mention the amount of context and explanation I am granting you here — this is not how I operate. [Laughter.] No, my dear, you have nothing to fear from me.'

Q.

'But of course you are. My own mother was, by all accounts, a magnificent individual, but of somewhat shall we say uneven temperament. Erratic and uneven in her domestic and day-to-day affairs. Erratic in her dealings with, of her two twin children, most specifically me. This has bequeathed me certain psychological complexes having to do with power and, perhaps, trust. The regularity of the acquiescence is nearly astounding. As the shoulders come up and her overall posture becomes more erect, the head is thrown back as well, such that she is now sitting up very straight and appears almost to be withdrawing from the conversational space, still on the ottoman but withdrawing as far as she possibly can within the strictures of that space. This apparent withdrawal, while intended to communicate shock and surprise and thus that she is most decidedly not the sort of person to whom the possibility ever of being invited to permit someone to tie her up would ever even occur, actually signifies a profound ambivalence. A [finger flexion] *conflict.* By which I mean that a possibility which had hitherto existed only internally, potentially, abstractly, as a part of the subject's unconscious fantasies or repressed wishes, has now suddenly been externalized and given conscious weight, made [f.f.] *real* as an actual possibility. Hence the fascinating irony that body language intended to convey shock does indeed convey shock but a very different sort of shock indeed. Namely the abreactive shock of repressed wishes bursting their strictures and penetrating consciousness, but from an external source, from a concrete other who is also male and a partner in the mating ritual and thus always ripe for transference. The phrase [no f.f.] *sink in* is thus far more appropriate than you might originally have imagined. Such penetration, of course, requires time only when there is [f.f.] *resistance.* Or for example doubtless you know the hoary cliché [f.f.] *I can't believe my ears.* Consider its import.'

Q. . . . .

'My own experience indicates that the cliché does not mean [sustained f.f.] *I can't believe that this possibility now exists in my consciousness* but rather something more along the lines of [sustained and increasingly annoying f.f.] *I cannot believe that this possibility is now originating from a point external to my consciousness.* It is the same sort of shock, the several-second delay in internalizing or processing, which accompanies sudden bad news or a sudden, inexplicable betrayal by a hitherto trusted authority figure and so on and so forth. This interval of shocked silence is one during which entire psychological maps are being redrawn, and during this interval any gesture or affect on the subject's part will reveal a great deal more about her than any amount of banal conversation or even clinical experimentation ever would. Reveal.'

Q.

'I meant woman or young woman, not [f.f.] *subject* per se.'

Q.

'The true cocks, the rare ones I have misjudged, will yield the briefest of these shocked pauses. They will smile politely, or even laugh, and then will decline the proposal in very direct and forthright terms. No harm, no foul. [Laughter.] No pun intended — [f.f.] *cock, foul.* These subjects' internal psychological maps have ample room for the possibility of being tied up, and they freely consider it, and freely reject it. They are simply not interested. I have no problem with this, with discovering I've mistaken a cock for a hen. Again, I am not interested in forcing or cajoling or persuading anyone against her will. I am certainly not going to beg her. That is not what this is about. I know what this is about. The — and force is not what this is about. The others — the long, weighted, high-voltage pause, the postural and affective shock — whether they acquiesce or become offended, outraged, these are the true hens, players, these are the ones whom I have not at all misjudged. As

their heads are thrown back — but their eyes are on me, fixed, looking at me, [f.f.] *gazing* and so on, with all the intensity one associ-
ates with someone trying to decide whether or not they can [f.f.]
trust you. With [f.f.] *trust* now connoting a great many different
possible things — whether you are having them on, whether you
are serious but are pretending to have them on in order to forestall
embarrassment should they be outraged or disgusted, or whether
you are in earnest but mean the proposal abstractly, as a hypotheti-
cal question such as [f.f.] *What would you do with a million dollars?*
meant to elicit information about their personality in possible deliberation as to a fourth date. And so on and so forth. Or rather
whether it is in fact a serious proposal. Even as — they are looking
at you because they are trying to read you. To size you up, as you
have apparently sized them up, as the proposal appears to imply.
This is why I always propose it in a blunt, undisguised way, abjur-
ing wit or segue or preparation or coloratura in the pronunciation of
the contractual possibility. I want to communicate to them as best
I can that the proposal is serious and concrete. That I am opening
my own consciousness up to them and to the possibility of rejection
or even disgust. This is why I answer their intense gaze with a
rather bland gaze of my own and say nothing to embellish or com-
plicate or color or interrupt the processing of their own internal
psychic reaction. I force them to acknowledge to themselves that
both I and the proposal are in deadly earnest.'

Q. . . .

'But again please note I am in no way aggressive or threatening
about it. This is what I meant by [f.f.] *bland gaze.* I do not propose
it in a creepy or lascivious way, and I do not appear in any way eager or hesitant or conflicted. Nor aggressive or threatening. This is
crucial. You're doubtless aware, from your own experience, that
one's natural unconscious reaction, when someone's body language
suggests a withdrawal or leaning-away from him, is automatically

to lean forward, or in, as a way to compensate and preserve the original spatial relation. I consciously avoid this reflex. This is extremely important. One does not nervously shift or lean or lick one's lips or straighten one's tie while a proposal like this is sinking in. I once, on a third date, found myself with one of those annoying isolated jumping muscles or twitches in my scalp which seized on and off throughout the evening and, on the ottoman, made it appear that I was raising and lowering one eyebrow in a rapid and lascivious way, which in the psychically charged aftermath of the sudden proposal simply torpedoed the whole thing. And this subject was by no stretch of the imagination a cock — this was a hen or I've never inspected a hen — yet one involuntary twitch in one eyebrow decapitated the whole possibility, such that the subject not only left in such a frenzy of conflicted disgust that she forgot her purse and not only never returned for the purse but refused even to return telephone messages in which I phoned several times and offered simply to return the purse to her at some neutral public location. The disappointment nevertheless drove home a valuable lesson as to just how delicate a period of internal processing and cartography this post-proposal moment can be. My mother's problem was that toward me — her eldest child, the elder of the twins, significantly — her nurturing instincts ran to rather erratic extremes of as it were [f.f.] *hot* and *cold*. She could at one moment be very, very, very warm and maternal, and then in the flash of an instant would become angry with me over some real or imagined trifle and would completely withdraw her affection. She became cold and rejecting, rebuffing any attempts as a small child on my part to receive reassurance and affection, sometimes sending me alone to my bedroom and refusing to let me out for some rigidly specified period while my twin sister continued to enjoy unconfined freedom of movement about the house and also continued to receive warmth and maternal affection. Then, after the rigid period of confinement was over — I mean to say the precise instant my [f.f.] *time-out* was completed — Mummy would open the door and embrace me warmly and blot my tears away with her sleeve and would claim that all was forgiven, all was well again. This flood of reassurance and nurture would once again seduce me into [f.f.] *trusting* her and revering her and ceding emotional power to her, rendering me vulnerable to devastation all over again whenever she might choose again to turn cold and look at me as if I were some sort of laboratory specimen she'd never inspected before. This cycle played itself out repeatedly throughout our childhood relation, I am afraid.'

Q.

'Yes, accentuated by the fact that she was by vocation a professional clinician, a psychiatric case-worker who administered tests and diagnostic exercises at a sanitarium in the neighboring town. A career she recommenced the moment my sister and I entered the school system as barely toddlers. My mother's imago all but rules my adult psychological life, I am aware, forcing me again and again to propose and negotiate contracted rituals where power is freely given and taken and submission ritualized and control ceded and then returned of my own free will. [Laughter.] Of the subject's, rather. Will. It is also my mother's legacy that I know precisely what my interest in carefully gauging a subject and on the third evening suddenly proposing that she allow me to immobilize her with satin restraints is, derives, comes from. Much of the annoying, pedantic jargon I use to describe the rituals also derives from my mother, who, far more than did our kindly but repressed and somewhat castrated father, modeled speech and behavior for us as children. My sister and I. My mother possessed a *Master's Degree in Clinical Social Work* [sustained f.f.], one of the first conferred upon a female diagnostician in the upper Midwest. My sister is a housewife and mother and aspires to be nothing more, at least not consciously. For example, [f.f.] *ottoman* was Mummy's term for both the sofa and the twin love seats in our living room. My own apartment's sofa has a back and arms and is, of course, technically a sofa or couch, but I seem unconsciously to insist on referring to it as an ottoman. This is an unconscious habit I seem unable to modify. In fact I have ceased trying. Some complexes are better accepted and simply yielded to rather than struggling against the imago by sheer force of will. Mummy — who was, of course, after all, you are aware, someone whose profession involved keeping persons confined and probing and testing them and breaking them and bending them to the will of what the state authorities deemed mental health — quite hopelessly broke my own will early on. I have accepted this and reached an accord with it and have erected complex structures in which to come symbolically to terms with it and redeem it. That is what this is about. Neither my sister's husband nor my father were ever involved in poultry in any way. My father, until his stroke, was a low-level executive in the insurance industry. Though of course the term [f.f.] *chicken* was often used in our subdivision — by the children with whom I played and acted out various primitive rituals of socialization — to describe a weak, cowardly individual, an individual whose will could easily be bent to the purposes of others. Unconsciously, I may perhaps employ poultry metaphors in describing the contractual rituals as a symbolic way of asserting my own power over those who, paradoxically, autonomously agree to submit. With little other fanfare we will proceed into the other room, to the bed. I am very excited. My manner has now changed, somewhat, to a more commanding, authoritative demeanor. But not creepy and not threatening. Some subjects have professed to see it as [f.f.] *menacing,* but I can assure you no menace is intended. What is being communicated now is a certain authoritative command based solely on contractual experience as I inform the subject that I am going to [no f.f.] *instruct* her. I radiate an expertise that may, I admit, to someone of a particular psychological makeup, appear menacing. All but the most hardened fowl begin asking me what it is I want them to do. I, on the other hand, very deliberately exclude the word [f.f.] *want* and its analogues from my instructions. I am not about expressing wishes or asking or pleading or persuading here, I inform them. That is not what this is about. We are now in my bedroom, which is small and dominated by a king-sized Edwardian-style four-poster bed. The bed itself, which appears enormous and deceptively sturdy, might communicate a certain menace, conceivably, in view of the contract we have entered into. I always phrase it as [no f.f.] *This is what you are to do, You are to do such-and-such,* and so on and so forth. I tell them how to stand and when to turn and how to look at me. Articles of clothing are to be removed in a certain very particular order.'

Q.

'Yes but the order is less important than that there *is* an order, and that they comply. Underthings are always last. I am intensely but unconventionally excited. My manner is brusque and commanding but not menacing. It is no-nonsense. Some appear nervous, some affect to appear nervous. A few roll their eyes or make small dry jokes to reassure themselves that they are merely [f.f.] *playing along.* They are to fold their clothes and place them at the foot of the bed and to recline and lie supine and to erase all vestige of affect or expression from their face as I remove my own clothing.'

Q.

'Sometimes, sometimes not. The excitement is intense but not specifically genital. My own undressing has been matter-of-fact. Neither ceremonial nor hurried. I radiate command. A few chicken out part of the way through, but very, very few. Those who wish to go, go. The confinement is very abstract. The thongs are black satin, mail-order. You would be surprised. As they comply with each request, command, I utter little phrases of positive reinforcement, such as, for instance, *Good* and *That's a good girl.* I tell them that the knots are *double-slips* and will tighten automatically if they struggle or resist. In fact they are not. In fact there is no such thing as a double-slip knot. The crucial moment occurs when they lie nude before me, bound tightly at wrists and ankles to the bed's four posts. Unknown to them, the bedposts are decorative and not at all sturdy and could no doubt be snapped by a determined effort to free themselves. I say, *You are now entirely in my power*. Recall that she is nude and bound to the bedposts, spread-eagled. I am standing un-clothed at the foot of the bed. I then consciously alter the expression on my face and ask, *Are you frightened?* Depending on their own de-meanor here, I sometimes alter this to, <u>*Aren't*</u> *you frightened?* This is the crucial moment. This is the moment of truth. The entire rit-ual — perhaps *ceremony* would be better, more evocative, because we — of course the whole thing from proposal onward is *about* cer-emony — and the climax is the subject's response to this prompt. To *Are you frightened?* What is required is a twin acknowledgment. She is to acknowledge that she is wholly in my power at this mo-ment. And she must also say she trusts me. She must acknowledge that she is not afraid I will betray or abuse the power I've been ceded. The excitement is at its absolute peak during this inter-change, reaching a sustained climax which persists for exactly as long as it takes me to extract these assurances from her.'

Q.

'Pardon me?'

Q.

'I've already told you. I weep. It is then that I weep. Have you been paying even the slightest attention, slouched over there? I lie down beside them and weep and explain to them the psychological origins of the game and the needs it serves in me. I open my inner-most psyche to them and beg compassion. Rare is the subject who is not deeply, deeply moved. They comfort me as best they can, re-stricted as they are by the bonds I've made.'

Q.

'Whether it ends in actual intercourse depends. It's unpredictable. There's simply no way to tell.'

Q. . . .

'Sometimes one just has to go with the mood.'

B.I. #51 11-97

FORT DODGE IA

'I always think, "What if I can't?" Then I always think, "Oh shit, don't think that." Because thinking about it can make it happen. Not like it's happened that often. But I get scared about it. We all do. Anybody tells you they don't they're full of it. They're always scared it might happen. Then I always think, "I wouldn't even be worried about it if she wasn't here." Then I get pissed off. It's like I think she's expecting something. That if she wasn't lying there expecting it and wondering and, like, evaluating, it wouldn't have even occurred to me. Then I get almost kind of pissed off. I'll get so pissed off, I'll stop even giving a shit about can I or not. It's like I want to show her up. It's like, "OK, bitch, you asked for it." Then everything goes fine.'

B.I. #19 10-96

NEWPORT OR

'Why? Why. Well, it's not just that you're beautiful. Even though you are. It's that you're so darn *smart*. There. That's why. Beautiful girls are a dime a dozen, but not — hey, let's face it, genuinely smart people are rare. Of either sex. You know that. I think for me, it's your smartness more than anything else.'

Q.

'Ha. That's possible, I suppose, from your point of view. I suppose it could be. Except think about it a minute: would that possibility have even *occurred* to a girl who wasn't so darn smart? Would a dumb girl have had the sense to suspect that?'

Q.

'So in a way you've proved my point. So you can believe I mean it and not dismiss it as just some kind of come-on. Right?'

Q. . . .

'So c'mere.'

B.I. #46   07-97
NUTLEY NJ

'Alls I'm — or think about the Holocaust. Was the Holocaust a good thing? No way. Does anybody think it was good it happened? No way. But did you ever read Victor Frankl? Victor Frankl's *Man's Search for Meaning?* It's a great, great book. Frankl was in a camp in the Holocaust and the book comes out of that experience, it's about his experience in the human Dark Side and preserving his human identity in the face of the camp's degradation and violence and suffering's total ripping away of his identity. It's a totally great book and now think about it, if there wasn't a Holocaust there wouldn't be a *Man's Search for Meaning*.'

Q.

'Alls I was trying to say is you have got to be careful of taking a knee-jerk attitude about violence and degradation in the case of women also. Having a knee-jerk attitude about *anything* is a total mistake, that's what I'm saying. But I'm saying especially in the case of women, where it adds up to this very limited condescending thing of saying they're fragile or breakable things and can be destroyed so easily. Like we have to wrap them in cotton and protect them more than everybody else. That it's knee-jerk and condescending. I'm talking about dignity and respect, not treating them like they're fragile little dolls or whatever. Everybody gets hurt and violated and broken sometimes, why are women so special?'

Q.

'Alls I'm saying is who are we to say getting incested or abused or violated or whatever or any of those things can't also have their positive aspects for a human being in the long run. Not that it necessarily does all the time, but who are we to say it *never* does, in a knee-jerk way? Not that anybody ever ought to get raped or abused, not that it's not totally terrible and negative and wrong while it's going on, no question. Nobody'd ever say that. But that's while it's going on. The rape or violation or incest or abuse, while it's going on. What about afterwards? What about down the line, what about the bigger picture then of the way her mind deals with what happened to her, adjusts to deal with it, the way what happened becomes part of who she is? Alls I'm saying, it's not impossible there are cases where it can enlarge you. Make you more than you were before. More of a complete human being. Like Victor Frankl. Or that saying about how whatever doesn't kill you makes you stronger. You think whoever it was that said that was *for* a woman getting raped? No way. He just wasn't being knee-jerk.'

Q. . . .

'I'm not saying there's no such thing as a victim. Alls I'm saying is we tend to sometimes be so narrow-minded about the myriads of different things that go into making somebody into who he is. I'm saying we get so knee-jerk and condescending about rights and perfect fairness and protecting people we don't stop and remember nobody's *just* a victim and nothing is *just* negative and *just* unfair — almost nothing is like that. Alls — how it's possible even the worst things that can happen to you can end up being positive factors in who you are. What you are, being a full human being instead of just a — think about getting gang-raped and degraded and beaten down to within an inch of your life for example. Nobody's going to say that's a good thing, I'm not saying that, nobody's going to say the sick bastards that did it shouldn't go to jail. Nobody's suggesting she was liking it while it was happening or that it should have happened. But let's put two things into the perspective here. One is, afterwards she knows something about herself she didn't know before.'

Q.

'What she knows is that the totally most terrible degrading thing that she ever could have even imagined happening to her has really happened to her now. And she survived. She's still here. I'm not saying she's thrilled, I'm not saying she's thrilled about it or she's in great shape or clicking her heels together out of joy it happened, but she's still here, and she knows it, and now she knows something. I mean really *knows*. Her idea of herself and what she can live through and survive is bigger now. Enlarged, larger, deeper. She's stronger than she ever deep-down thought, and now she knows it, she knows she's strong in a totally different way from knowing it just because your folks tell you or some speechmaker at a school assembly has you all repeat you're Somebody you're Strong over and over. Alls I'm saying is she's not the same and how some of the ways she's not the same — like, if she's still afraid at midnight walking to her car in a parking garage or whatever of getting jumped and gang-raped, now she's afraid in a different way. Not that she wants it to ever happen again, getting gang-raped, no way. But now she knows it won't kill her, she can survive it, it won't obliterate her or make her, like, subhuman.'

Q. . . .

'And plus now also she knows more about the human condition and suffering and terror and degradation. I mean, all of us will admit suffering and horror are part of being alive and existing, or at least we all pay lip service to knowing it, the human condition. But now she really *knows* it. I'm not saying she's thrilled about it. But think how much bigger now her view of the world is, how much more broad and deep the big picture is now in her mind. She can understand suffering in a totally different way. She's more than she was. That's what I'm saying. More of a human being. Now she knows something you don't.'

Q.

'That's the knee-jerk reaction, that's what I'm talking about, taking everything I say and taking and filtering it through your own narrow view of the world and saying what I'm saying is Oh so the guys that gang-raped her did her a *favor.* Because that's not what I'm saying. I'm not saying it was good or right or it should have happened or that she's not totally fucked up by it and shattered or it ever should have happened. For any one case of a woman getting gang-raped or violated or whatever, if I was there and I could have the power to either say Go ahead or Stop, I'd stop it. But I couldn't. Nobody could. Totally terrible things happen. Existence and life break people in all kinds of awful fucking ways all the time. Trust me I know, I've been there.'

Q.

'And I get the feeling this is the real difference. You and me here. Because this isn't really about politics or feminism or whatever. For you this is all ideas, you think we're talking about ideas. You haven't been there. I'm not saying nothing bad ever happened to you, you're not bad-looking and I bet there's been some degradation or whatever that came your way in your life. That's not what I'm saying. But we're talking Frankl's *Man's Search for Meaning*—Holocaust-type total violation and suffering and terror here. The real Dark Side. And baby I can tell just from just looking at you you never. You wouldn't even wear what you're wearing, trust me.'

Q.

'That you might admit you believe yeah OK the human condition is full of terrible awful human suffering and you can survive almost anything or whatever. Even if you really believe it. You believe it, but what if I said I don't just believe it I *know* it? Does that make a difference in what I'm saying? What if I told you my own wife got gang-raped? Not so sure of yourself now are you. What if I told you a little story about a sixteen-year-old girl that went to the wrong party with the wrong guy and his buddies and ended up get— having done to her just about everything four guys could do to you in terms of violation. Six weeks in the hospital. What if I told you she still has to go in for dialysis twice a week, that's how bad they did her?'

Q.

'What if I told you she'd never say she in any way asked for it or enjoyed it or liked it or likes only having half a kidney and if she could go back and have a way to stop it she would but if you asked her if she could go into her head and forget it or like erase the tape of it happening in her memory, what do you think she'd say? Are you so sure what she'd say? That she wishes she never had to, like, structure her mind to deal with it happening to her or to all of a sudden know the world can break you just like: *that*. To know that another human being, these guys, can look at you lying there and in the totally deepest way understand you as a thing, not a person a thing, a fuck-doll or punching-dog or a hole, as just a hole to shove a Jack Daniel's bottle in so far it blows out your kidneys — if she said after that, totally negative as what happened was, now at least she understood it was possible, people can.'

Q.

'See you as a thing, that they can see you as a thing. Do you know what that means? It's terrible, we know how terrible it is as an idea, and that it's wrong, and we think we know all these things about human rights and human dignity and how terrible it is to take away somebody's humanity that's what we call it somebody's humanity but to have it *happen* to you, see, and now you really *know*. Now it's not just an idea or cause to get all knee-jerk about. Have it happen and you get a real taste of the Dark Side. Not just the *idea* of darkness, the genuine Dark Side. And now you know the power of it. The total power. Because if you can really see somebody just as a thing you can do anything to him, all bets are off, humanity and dignity and rights and fairness — all bets are off. Alls — what if she said it's like a quick expensive little tour of a side of the human condition everybody talks about like they know but really they can't even imagine it, not really, not unless you been there. So if alls it is is her way of seeing the world was *broadened,* what if I said that? What would you say? And of herself, how she understood herself. That now she understood she could be understood as a thing. Can you see how much this would change — rip away, how much this would rip away? Of yourself, you, what you used to think of as you? It would rip all that away. Then what would be left? Can you even imagine do you think? It's like Victor Frankl in his book says that at the very worst of it in the camp in the Holocaust, when your freedom's taken away, and your privacy and dignity because you're naked in a crowded camp and you have to go to the bathroom in front of everybody else because there's no such thing as privacy anymore, and your wife's dead and your kids starved while you had to watch and you don't have any food or heat or blankets and they treat you like rats because to them really you really are rats you're not a human being, and they call you out and bring you in and torture you, like scientific torture so they can show you they can even take your body away, your body isn't even you anymore it's the enemy it's this thing they use to torture you because to them it's just a thing and they're running lab experiments on it, it's not even sadistic they're not being sadistic because to them it's not a human being they're torturing — that when everything that has any like connection to the you you think you are gets ripped away and now all that's left is only: what, what's left, is there anything left? You're

still alive so what's left is you? What's that? What does *you* mean
now? See now it's showtime, now's when you find out what you
even *are* to yourself. Which most people with dignity and humanity and rights and all that there don't ever get to know. What's possible. That nothing is automatically sacred. That's what Frankl's
talking about. That it's through suffering and terror and the Dark
Side that whatever's left gets to open up, and then after that you
know.'

Q.

'What if I told you she said it wasn't the violation or the terror or
the pain or any of that, that it — that the biggest part, afterwards,
of trying to like structure her mind around it, to fit what happened
into the world of her, that the worst part the hardest part of it was
now knowing she could think of *herself* that way too if she wanted?
As a thing. That it's totally possible to think of yourself not as you
or even a person but just a thing, just like it was for the four guys.
And how easy and powerful that was to do that, to think that, even
while the violation's going on, to just split yourself off and like float
up to the ceiling and there you are looking down at this thing getting worse and worse things done to it and the thing is you and it
doesn't mean anything, there's nothing that it just automatically
means, and it's a very intensive freedom and power in many ways,
that now all bets are off and everything's taken away and you can do
anything to anybody or even to yourself if you want because who
cares because what does it really matter because what are you anyway just this thing to shove a Jack Daniel's bottle into, and who
cares if it's a bottle what difference does it make if it's a dick or a fist
or a plumber's helper or this cane right here — what would it be
like to be able to be like this? You think you can imagine it? You
think you can but you can't. But what if I said now she could?
What if I told you she could because she's had this happen and she
totally knows it's possible to be just a thing but just like Victor

Frankl that every minute from then on minute by minute if you want you can *choose* to be more if you want, you can *choose* to be a human being and have it *mean* something? Then what would you say?'

Q.

'I'm calm, don't worry about me. It's like Frankl's thing of learning it's not automatic, how it's a matter of choice to be a human being with sacred rights instead of a thing or a rat and most people are so smug and knee-jerk and walking around asleep they don't even know it's something you have to actually choose for yourself that only has meaning when all the like props and stage-settings that let you just go around smugly assuming you're not a thing are ripped away and broken because all of a sudden now the world understands you as a thing, everybody else thinks you're a rat or a thing and now it's up to you, you're the only one that can decide if you're more. What if I said I wasn't even married? Then what? Then it's show-time, believe you me baby, which believe me everybody that's never had that kind of total attack and violation happen where everything they thought they were just automatically born with that smugly lets them walk around assuming they're automatically more than a thing gets skinned off and folded up and put in a Jack Daniel's bottle and shoved up your ass by four drunk guys who your suffering and violation was just their idea of fun, a way to kill a couple hours, no big deal, none of them probably even remember it, that nobody that hasn't had that kind of thing really happen to them ever gets to be this *broad* afterwards, to always deep-down know it's always a choice, that it's you that is making yourself up second by second every second from now on, that the only one that thinks you're even a person every second is you and you could stop anytime you wanted and whenever you want go back to just being a thing that eats fucks shits tries to sleep goes for dialysis and gets square bottles shoved so far up their ass it breaks by four guys that knee-jerked

you in the balls to make you bend over that you didn't even know
or ever saw before and never did anything to to make it make any
sense for them to want to knee you or rape you or ever ask for that
kind of total degradation. That don't even know your name, that do
this to you and don't even know your name, you don't even have a
name. You don't automatically have a name, it's not something you
just have, you know. To get to find out you even have to choose to
even have a name or to be more than just a machine programmed
with different reactions when they do different things to you when
they think of them to pass the time until they get bored and that
it's all up to you every second afterwards and what if I said it happened to me? Would that make a difference? You that are all full of
knee-jerk politics about your ideas about victims? Does it have to
be a woman? You think, maybe you think you can imagine it better if it was a woman because her external props look more like
yours so it's easier to see her as a human being that's being violated
so if it was somebody with a dick and no tits it wouldn't be as real
to you? Like if it wasn't Jewish people in the Holocaust if it was just
me in the Holocaust? Who do you think would care then? Do you
think anybody cared about Victor Frankl or admired his humanity
until he gave them *Man's Search for Meaning?* I'm not saying it happened to me or him or my wife or even if it happened but what if it
did? What if I did it to you? Right here? Raped you with a bottle?
Do you think it'd make any difference? Why? What are you? How
do you know? You don't know shit.'

DATUM CENTURIO

From *Leckie & Webster's Connotationally Gender-Specific Lexicon of Contemporary Usage,* a 600gb DVD₃ Product with 1.6gb of Hyperavailable Hot Text Keyed to 11.2gb of Contextual, Etymological, Historical, Usage, and Gender-Specific Connotational Notes, Available Also with Lavish Illustrative Support in All 5 Major Sense-Media*, ©2096 by R. Leckie DataFest Unltd. (NYPHDC/US/4Grid).

* *(compatible hardware required)*

date³ *(dāt) n.* [20C English, from Middle English, from Old French, from Medieval Latin *data,* feminine past participle of *dare,* to give.] **1.** *Informal.* (see also **soft date**) **a.** Consequent to the successful application for a License to Parent (KEY at PROCREATIVITY; at BREED/*(v.)*; at PARENT/*(v.)*; at OFFSPRING, SOFT), the process of voluntarily submitting one's nucleotide configurations and other Procreativity Designators to an agency empowered by law to identify an optimal female neurogenetic complement for the purposes of Procreative Genital Interface (KEY at PROCREATIVITY; at COMPLEMENTARITY, OPTIMAL NEUROGENETIC; at P.G.I.; at

---

ă pat / ā pay/ âr care / ä father / b bib / ch church / d deed / ĕ pet / ē be / f fife / g gag / h hat / hw which / ĭ pit / ī pie / îr pier / j judge / k kick / l lid / m mum / n no, sudden / ng thing / ŏ pot / ō toe / ô paw, for / oi noise / ou out / ŏŏ took / ōō boot / p pop / r roar / s sauce / sh ship, dish / t tight / th thin / *th* this, bath / ŭ cut / ûr urge / v valve / w with / y yes / z zebra, size / zh vision / ə about, item, edible, gallop, circus /
å *Fr.* ami / œ *Fr.* feu, *Ger.* schön / ü *Fr.* tu, *Ger.* über / KH *Ger.* ich, *Scot.* loch / N *Fr.* bon.

＊= Follows main vocabulary. †= Of obscure origin. ‡= Of idiomatic origin

For pentasensory illustrative support, affix neural plug and enter:
ROM\C.A.D.PAK\5MESH*.*.

NEUROGENETICS, STATISTICAL). **b.** A living female P.G.I.-complement identified via the procedures denoted by **date³1.a.**

---

date³1.a USAGE/CONTEXTUAL NOTE: "You are too old by far to be the type of man who checks his replicase levels before breakfast and has high-baud macros for places like Fruitful Union P.G.I. Coding or SoftSci Deoxyribonucleic Intercode Systems in his Mo.SyS deck, and yet here you are, parking the heads on your V.F.S.A. telediddler and checking your replicase levels and padding your gen-résumé like a randy freshman, preparing for what appears to all the world like an attempt at a soft date" (*McInerney et seq. {via OmniLit TRF Matrix}*, 2068).

---

2. *Vulgar.*‡ (see also **hard date**) **a.** The creation and/or use of a Virtual Female Sensory Array (KEY at V.F.S.A.; at Historical Note for REALITY, VIRTUAL; at TELEDIDDLER; at COITUS, DIGITAL; at POLIOEROTIC; at OBJECTIFICATION, LITERAL) for the purposes of Simulated Genital Interface (KEY at S.G.I.). **b.** A drive-captured and reusable V.F.S.A., to which proper names and various sexual and/or personality characteristics are sometimes applied by overwrought male users (KEY at MESH, DFX; at BABE, CYBER-; at FEMALE, HARD; at SYNDROME, V.F.S.A.-PERSONALIZATION).

---

date³2. USAGE/HISTORICAL NOTE: R. and F. Leckie, eds., *DFX Lattice of the Monochromosomatic Psyche,* and other authorities hold

---

ă pat / ā pay/ âr care / ä father / b bib / ch church / d deed / ĕ pet / ē be / f fife / g gag / h hat / hw which / ĭ pit / ī pie / îr pier / j judge / k kick / l lid / m mum / n no, sudden / ng thing / ŏ pot / ō toe / ô paw, for / oi noise / ou out / ŏŏ took / ōō boot / p pop / r roar / s sauce / sh ship, dish / t tight / th thin / *th* this, bath / ŭ cut / ûr urge / v valve / w with / y yes / z zebra, size / zh vision / ə about, item, edible, gallop, circus /

å *Fr.* ami / œ *Fr.* feu, *Ger.* schön / ü *Fr.* tu, *Ger.* über / KH *Ger.* ich, *Scot.* loch / N *Fr.* bon.

* =Follows main vocabulary. † =Of obscure origin. ‡ =Of idiomatic origin

For pentasensory illustrative support, affix neural plug and enter:
ROM\C.A.D.PAK\5MESH*.*.

standard definition **2** of **date**[3] to be connotationally descended from the *(n.)/(v.)* use of **date** by 20C prostitutes to solicit genital-financial interface without exposing themselves to statutory prosecution. The same authorities hold the euphemym **hard date** to be derived from the c. 2020 idiomatic/vulgar **hardware-dating** *(arch.)*, a compound gerund denoting (with the 20s' characteristic lack of subtlety) *"sex with a machine"/ "machine-assisted sex"* (*Webster's IX*, 2027, DVD/ROM/print). **Soft date** is held to have evolved as a natural antonym by at least 2030. Some authorities argue that **soft date**'s idiomatic longevity is also due to its apparently coincidental ability to connote the tender sentiments often associated with P.G.I. and soft offspring (see below; KEY at SENTIMENTS, TENDER).

=====

date[3] USAGE/HISTORICAL NOTE: Definitions **1** and **2** *supra* are both the connotational descendants of the univocal 20C definition of **date**[3]: *"(a) social engagement(s) with (a) member(s) of the opposite sex* (*Webster's V*, 1999, ROM/print). *Nash & Leckie's Condensed DVD$_2$ History of Male Sexuality* notes that for 20C males, **date** as intergender "social engagement" could connote either of two highly distinct endeavors: (A) the mutual exploration of possibilities for long-term neurogenetic compatibility (KEY at Historical Note (5) for RELATIONSHIP), leading to legally codified intergender union and P.G.I. and soft offspring; or (B) the unilateral pursuit of an immediate, vigorous, and uncodified episode of genital interface without regard to

---

ă pat / ā pay/ âr care / ä father / b bib / ch church / d deed / ĕ pet / ē be / f fife / g gag / h hat / hw which / ĭ pit / ī pie / îr pier / j judge / k kick / l lid / m mum / n no, sudden / ng thing / ŏ pot / ō toe / ô paw, for / oi noise / ou out / o͝o took / o͞o boot / p pop / r roar / s sauce / sh ship, dish / t tight / th thin / *th* this, bath / ŭ cut / ûr urge / v valve / w with / y yes / z zebra, size / zh vision / ə about, item, edible, gallop, circus / å *Fr.* ami / œ *Fr.* feu, *Ger.* schön / ü *Fr.* tu, *Ger.* über / KH *Ger.* ich, *Scot.* loch / N *Fr.* bon.

*= Follows main vocabulary. †= Of obscure origin. ‡= Of idiomatic origin

For pentasensory illustrative support, affix neural plug and enter:
ROM\C.A.D.PAK\5MESH*.*.

neurogenetic compatibility or soft offspring or even a telephone call the next day. Because — according to R. and F. Leckie, eds., *DFX Lattice of the Monochromosomatic Psyche* — the connotational range of **date**[3] as "social engagement" for 20C females was almost exclusively (A), whereas an implicit but often unspoken and just as often fraudulent interest in connotation (A) was often employed by 20C males for purposes related exclusively to connotation (B) (KEY at LOTHARIONISM; at SPORTFUCKING[‡]; at MISOGAMY; at LIZARDRY, LOUNGE-[‡]; at OEDIPAL, PRE-), the result of an estimated 86.5% of 20C **dates** was a state of severe emotional dissonance between the **date**'s participants, a dissonance attributed by most sources to basic psychosemantic miscodings (KEY at MISCODINGS, INTERGENDER; Secondary KEYS at Historical Notes for MISOGYNY, OSTENSIBLE PROJECTED FORMS OF; for VICTIMIZATION, CULTURE OF; for FEMINISM, MALEVOLENT SEPARATIST OF EARLY U.S. 21C; for SEXUAL REVOLUTION OF LATE 20C, PATHETIC DELUSIONS OF).

The A.D. 2006 patent and 2008 commercial introduction of Digitally Manipulable Video (KEY at D.M.V.[2]; at MICROSOFT-VCA D.M.V. VENTURES CORP.), in which video pornography could be home-edited to allow the simulated introduction of the viewer into filmed images of explicit genital interface, were upheld in U.S.S.C. Civil Action #181-9049, *Schumpkin et al. v. Microsoft-VCA D.M.V. Ventures Corp.* (2009), partly on the grounds that the availability to U.S. male consumers of wholly depersonalized simu-

---

ă pat / ā pay/ âr care / ä father / b bib / ch church / d deed / ĕ pet / ē be / f fife / g gag / h hat / hw which / ĭ pit / ī pie / îr pier / j judge / k kick / l lid / m mum / n no, sudden / ng thing / ŏ pot / ō toe / ô paw, for / oi noise / ou out / ŏŏ took / ōō boot / p pop / r roar / s sauce / sh ship, dish / t tight / th thin / *th* this, bath / ŭ cut / ûr urge / v valve / w with / y yes / z zebra, size / zh vision / ə about, item, edible, gallop, circus /

å Fr. ami / œ Fr. feu, Ger. schön / ü Fr. tu, Ger. über / KH Ger. ich, Scot. loch / N Fr. bon.

*–Follows main vocabulary. †=Of obscure origin. ‡=Of idiomatic origin

For pentasensory illustrative support, affix neural plug and enter:
ROM\C.A.D.PAK\5MESH*.*.

lacra of genital interface could reasonably be expected to palliate the 86.5% semioemotional conflict that attended genuine interpersonal **dating**; and this reasoning was subsequently (2012) extended to the legal introduction of Virtual Reality Sensory Arrays, whose costly full-body Joysuit with four extensions for human appendages rapidly gave way (2014) to the now familiar five-extension "Polioerotic Joysuit" and the first generation of three-dimensional Virtual Female DFX Meshes (KEY at JOYSUIT, POLIOEROTIC; at TELE-DIDDLER[†]; at MESH, DFX; at MODELING, NAUGHTY[‡]; Secondary KEY at Historical Notes for DESIGN, COMPUTER-ASSISTED; for FEMALE, VIRTUAL), home-entertainment innovations which, despite initial bugs and glitches (KEY at ELECTROCUTION, GENITAL), evolved rapidly into the current technology of V.F.S.A.'s and S.-R.J.A.'s (KEY at ARRAY, VIRTUAL FEMALE SENSORY; at APPENDAGE, SHOCK-RESISTANT JOYSUIT-), a technology which has all but forced today's modificatory split into the bivocal "hard" and "soft" denotations for **date**[3].

---

date[3] **GENDER-SPECIFIC CONNOTATIONAL NOTE:** Most contemporary-usage authorities observe a marked shift, for 21C males, in the "romantic" or "emotional" connotations of **date**[3] (KEY at SENTIMENTS, TENDER), affective connotations which, for most males, have now been removed altogether from "hard" or S.G.I.-**dating** (KEY at DYSPHORIA, HYPERORGASMIC; at N.G.O.S.; at SYNDROME, NARCISSISTIC GRATIFICATION OVERLOAD; at

---

ă pat / ā pay/ âr care / ä father / b bib / ch church / d deed / ĕ pet / ē be / f fife / g gag / h hat / hw which / ĭ pit / ī pie / îr pier / j judge / k kick / l lid / m mum / n no, sudden / ng thing / ŏ pot / ō toe / ô paw, for / oi noise / ou out / ŏŏ took / ōōboot / p pop / r roar / s sauce / sh ship, dish / t tight / th thin / *th* this, bath / ŭ cut / ûr urge / v valve / w with / y yes / z zebra, size / zh vision / ə about, item, edible, gallop, circus /

å *Fr.* ami / œ *Fr.* feu, *Ger.* schön / ü *Fr.* tu, *Ger.* über / KH *Ger.* ich, *Scot.* loch / N *Fr.* bon.

*= Follows main vocabulary. †= Of obscure origin. ‡= Of idiomatic origin

For pentasensory illustrative support, affix neural plug and enter:
ROM\C.A.D.PAK\5MESH*.*.

SOLIPSISM, TECHNOSEXUAL) and, in "soft" or P.G.I.-**dating**, have now been transferred almost entirely to the procreative function and the gratification associated with having one's Procreativity Designators affirmed by both culture and complement as neurogenetically desirable (KEY at PARADOXES, TECHNOSEXUAL; at DOGMA, PERVERSE VINDICATION OF CATHOLIC).

ă pat / ā pay/ âr care / ä father / b bib / ch church / d deed / ĕ pet / ē be / f fife / g gag / h hat / hw which / ĭ pit / ī pie / îr pier / j judge / k kick / l lid / m mum / n no, sudden / ng thing / ŏ pot / ō toe / ô paw, for / oi noise / ou out / ŏŏ took / ōō boot / p pop / r roar / s sauce / sh ship, dish / t tight / th thin / *th* this, bath / ŭ cut / ûr urge / v valve / w with / y yes / z zebra, size / zh vision / ə about, item, edible, gallop, circus /
â *Fr.* ami / œ *Fr.* feu, *Ger.* schön / ü *Fr.* tu, *Ger.* über / KH *Ger.* ich, *Scot.* loch / N *Fr.* bon.

* =Follows main vocabulary. †=Of obscure origin. ‡=Of idiomatic origin

For pentasensory illustrative support, affix neural plug and enter:
ROM\C.A.D.PAK\5MESH*.*.

OCTET

<u>POP QUIZ 4</u>

Two late-stage terminal drug addicts sat up against an alley's wall with nothing to inject and no means and nowhere to go or be. Only one had a coat. It was cold, and one of the terminal drug addicts' teeth chattered and he sweated and shook with fever. He seemed gravely ill. He smelled very bad. He sat up against the wall with his head on his knees. This took place in Cambridge MA in an alley behind the Commonwealth Aluminum Can Redemption Center on Massachusetts Avenue in the early hours of 12 January 1993. The terminal drug addict with the coat took off the coat and scooted over up close to the gravely ill terminal drug addict and took and spread the coat as far as it would go over the both of them and then scooted over some more and got himself pressed right up against him and put his arm around him and let him be sick on his arm, and they stayed like that up against the wall together all through the night.

Q: Which one lived.

<u>POP QUIZ 6</u>

Two men, X and Y, are close friends, but then Y does something to hurt, alienate, and/or infuriate X. They had been very close. In fact X's family had almost sort of adopted Y when Y arrived in town alone and had no family or friends yet and got a position in the same department of the same firm X worked for, and X and Y work side by side and become close *compadres,* and before long Y is usually over at X's house hanging out with the X family just about every night after work, and this goes on for quite some time. But then Y does X some kind of injury, like maybe writing an accurate but negative Peer Evaluation of X at their firm, or refusing to cover for X when X makes a serious error in judgment and gets himself in trouble and needs Y to lie to cover for him somehow. The point is that Y's done some honorable/upright thing that X sees as a disloyal and/or hurtful thing, and X is now totally furious at Y, and now when Y comes over to X's family's house every night to hang out as usual X is extremely frosty to him, or witheringly snide, or some-times even yells at Y in front of the X family's wife and kids. In re-sponse to all which, however, Y simply continues to come over to X's family's house and to hang around and take all the abuse X dishes out, nodding sort of studiously in response but not saying anything or in any other way responding to X's hostility. On one particular occasion X actually screams at Y to 'get the hell out of' his family's house and kind of half-hits-half-slaps Y, right in front of one of the family's kids, hard enough to make Y's glasses fall off, and all Y does by way of response is hold his cheek and nod sort of studiously at the floor while he picks his glasses up and repairs a bent arm-hinge as best he can by hand, and even after this he still continues to come around and hang out at X's house like an adopted member of the family, and to just stand there and take whatever X dishes out in retaliation for whatever it is Y apparently did to him. Just why Y does this (i.e., continues to come around and to hang out at the Xes') is unclear. Maybe Y is basically spineless and pa thetic and has noplace else to go and nobody else to hang out with. Or maybe Y's one of those quietly iron-spined people who are internally strong enough not to let any kind of abuse or humiliation get to them, and can see (Y can) through X's present pique to the generous and trusted friend he'd always been to Y before, and has decided (Y has, maybe) that he's just going to hang in there and stick it out and keep coming around and stoically allow X to vent whatever spleen he needs to vent, and that eventually X will probably get over being pissed off so long as Y doesn't respond or retaliate or do anything to aggravate the situation further. In other words, it's not clear whether Y is pathetic and spineless or incredibly strong and compassionate and wise. On only one specific further occasion, when X actually jumps up on an end table in front of the whole X family and screams at Y to 'take [his] ass and hat and get the fuck out of [his, i.e., X's] family's house and stay out,' does Y actually leave because of anything X says, but even after this further episode Y's still right back over there hanging out at the Xes' the very next night after work. Maybe Y just really likes X's wife and kids a lot, and that's what makes it worth it to him to keep coming around and enduring X's vitriole. Maybe Y is somehow both pathetic *and* strong . . . though it's hard to reconcile Y's being pathetic or weak with the obvious backbone it must have required to write a negatively truthful Peer Evaluation or to refuse to lie or whatever it was that X hasn't forgiven him for doing. Plus it's unclear how the whole thing plays out — i.e., whether Y's passive persistence pays off in the form of X finally getting over being furious and 'forgiving' Y and being his *compadre* again, or whether Y finally can't take the hostility anymore and eventually stops hanging around X's house . . . or whether the whole incredibly tense and unclear situation simply continues indefinitely. What made it a half-slap is that X had had a partly open hand when he hit Y that one time. There's also the factor of how X's overt unfriendliness to Y and Y's passive reaction to it affect certain intramural dynamics within the X family, like whether X's wife and kids are horrified by

X's treatment of Y or whether they agree with X that Y dicked him over somehow and so are basically sympathetic to X. This would affect how they feel about Y continuing to come around and hang out at their house every night even though X is making it crystal clear he's no longer welcome, like whether they admire Y's stoic fortitude or find it creepy and pathetic and wish he'd finally just get the message and quit acting like he's still an honorary part of the family, or what. In fact the whole *mise en scène* here seems too shot through with ambiguity to make a very good Pop Quiz, it turns out.

POP QUIZ 7

A lady marries a man from a very wealthy family and they have a baby together and they both love the baby a lot, although as time goes by they become less and less keen on each other, until eventually the lady files divorce papers on the man. The lady and the man both want primary custody of the baby, but the lady assumes she'll ultimately be the one to get primary custody because that's how things usually shake out in divorce law. But the man really wants primary custody a lot. Whether this is because he has a strong paternal urge and really wants to raise the baby or whether he just feels vindictive about getting served with divorce papers and wants to stick it to the lady by denying her primary custody is unclear. But that's not important, because what *is* clear is that the man's whole wealthy and powerful family all line up behind the man w/r/t this issue and think he should get primary custody (probably because they believe that since he's a scion of their family the man should get whatever he wants — it's that kind of family). But so the man's family comes around and tells the lady that if she fights their scion for primary custody of the baby they'll retaliate by taking away the lavish Trust Fund they'd established for the baby at birth, a Trust Fund sufficient to render the baby financially secure for life. No Primary Custody, No Trust Fund they say. So the lady (who'd signed a pre-nup, by the way, and has absolutely nothing in the way of remuneration or spousal support coming from the divorce settlement regardless of how the custody issue is resolved) walks away from the custody fight and lets the man and his hardass family have custody of the baby so that the baby will still have the Trust Fund.

Q: (A) Is she a good mother.[1]

POP QUIZ 6(A)

Try it again. Same guy X as in PQ6. X's wife's elderly father is diagnosed with inoperable brain cancer. X's wife's whole huge family is really close and intermeshed, and they all live right there in the same town as X and his wife and the father-in-law and his own wife, and since the diagnosis came down there's been a veritable Wagner opera of alarm and distress and grief going on in the family; and, closer to home as it were, X's wife and children are also terrifically distraught over the old man's inoperable brain cancer because X's wife has always been so close to her father and X's children love their Grampappy to distraction and are shamelessly spoiled and their affection purchased by him in return; and now X's wife's father is progressively enfeebled and suffering and dying of brain cancer, and X's whole family and family-in-law seem like they're getting a head start on grieving the old man's actual death and are all incredibly shattered and hysterical and sad all the time.

X himself is in a ticklish position w/r/t the whole father-in-law-

---

[1] (B)(*optional*) Explain whether and how receipt of the information that the lady had herself grown up in an environment of unbelievably desperate poverty would affect your response to (A).

with-inoperable-brain-cancer situation. He and his wife's father
have never had a very close or friendly relationship, and in fact the
old man had once actually urged X's wife to divorce X during a
rocky period some years prior when things in the marriage were
rocky and X had made some regrettable errors in judgment and had
committed some indiscretions which one of X's wife's pathologi-
cally nosy and garrulous sisters had told the father about and which
the old man had been typically judgmental and holier-than-thou
about and had loudly communicated to just about everyone in the
family that he considered X's behavior disgusting and wholly *infra-
dignitater* and had urged X's wife to leave him (i.e., X) over, none of
which X has forgotten over the years, not by a long shot, because
ever since that rocky period and the old man's h/t/t condemnations
X has felt somehow provisional and tangential and *non-grata* with
respect to his wife's whole teeming intermeshed close-knit family,
which family by this time includes his wife's six siblings' own
spouses and kids and various soricine great-aunts and -uncles and
ordinally disparate cousins, such that a local Conference Center has
to be rented every summer for his in-laws' family's traditional Family Get-Together (caps theirs), at which annual events X is always
somehow made to feel provisional and under continuing suspicion and judgment and pretty much like your classic outsider looking in.

X's sense of alienation from his wife's family has now intensified,
too, because the whole enormous roiling pack of them seem now to
be unable to think or talk about anything except the iron-eyed old
patriarch's brain cancer and grim treatment options and steady decline and apparently slim chances for lasting more than a few more
months at the very outside, and they seem to talk endlessly but only
with one another about all this, such that whenever X is there
alongside his wife during any of these lugubrious family councils he
always feels peripheral and otiose and subtly excluded, as if his

wife's close-knit family has woven in even tighter around itself in this time of crisis, forcing X even further out onto the periphery, he feels. And X's encounters with his father-in-law himself, whenever X now accompanies his wife on her ceaseless visits to the old man's sickroom in his (i.e., the old man's) and his wife's opulent neoromanesque home across town (and in what feels like a whole different economic galaxy) from the Xes' own rather modest house, are especially excruciating, for all the above reasons plus the fact that X's wife's father — who, even though by this time he's confined to a special top-of-the-line adjustable hospital bed the family has had brought in, and every time X is there he's lying stricken in this special high-tech bed being attended to by a Puerto Rican hospice technician, is nevertheless always still immaculately shaved and groomed and attired, with his club tie double-Windsored and his steel trifocals polished, as if ready at any moment to spring up and make the Puerto Rican fetch his Signor Pucci suit and juridical robes and return to 7th District Tax Court to hand down some more mercilessly well-reasoned decisions, a dress and demeanor which the distraught family all seem to regard as one more sign of the tough old bird's heartbreaking dignity and *dum spero joie de vivre* and strength of will — that the father-in-law always seems conspicuously chilly and aloof in his manner toward X during these dutiful visits, whereas X in turn, standing there awkwardly behind his wife as she is drawn tearfully in to incline over the sickbed like some spoon or metal rod drawn in and bent forward by the hideous force of a mentalist's will, usually feels overcome with first alienation and then distaste and resentment and then actual malevolence toward the iron-eyed old man who, if the truth be told, X has always secretly felt was a prick of the first rank, and now finds that even just the glint of the father-in-law's trifocals afflicts him, and can't help feeling that he hates him; and the father-in-law, in turn, seems to pick up on X's hidden involuntary hatred and gives back the clear impression of not feeling at all gladdened or bucked up or supported by X's presence and of wishing X weren't even there in the sickroom with Mrs. X and the glossy hospice technician, a wish X finds himself concurring bitterly with inside even as he exerts an even wider and more supportive and compassionate smile out into the space of the room, so that X always feels confused and disgusted and enraged in the old man's sickroom with his wife and always ends up wondering what he's even doing there in the first place.

X, however, of course, also always feels rather ashamed about feeling such dislike and resentment in the presence of a fellow human being and legal relative who's steadily and inoperably declining, and after each visit to the old man's luculent bedside, as he drives his distraught wife home in silence, X secretly castigates himself and wonders where his basic decency and compassion are. He locates an even deeper source of shame in the fact that ever since the father-in-law's terminal diagnosis came down, he (i.e., X) has spent so much time and energy thinking only of himself and of his own feelings of resentful exclusion from his wife's clannish family's *Drang* when, after all, his wife's father is suffering and dying right before their eyes and X's loving wife is nearly prostrate with agony and grief and the Xes' sensitive innocent children are also grieving terribly. X secretly worries that the obvious selfishness of his inner feelings during this time of family crisis when his wife and children so clearly deserve his compassion and support might constitute evidence of some horrific defect in his human makeup, some kind of hideous central ice where his heart's nodes of empathy and basic other-directedness ought to be, and is increasingly tormented by shame and self-doubt, and then is doubly ashamed and worried about the fact that the shame and self-doubt are themselves self-involving and thus further compromise his ability to be truly concerned and supportive toward his wife and kids; and he keeps all his secret feelings of alienation and distaste and resentment and of shame and self-urtication even about the shame itself completely to himself, and doesn't feel like he can possibly go to his distraught wife and burden/horrify her even further with his own self-involved *pons asinorum,* and in fact is so disgusted and ashamed about what he fears he might have discovered about his heart's makeup that he is unusually subdued and reserved and unforthcoming with everyone in his life for the first several months of his father-in-law's illness and says nothing to anyone of the storms raging centripetally inside him.

The father-in-law's agonizing inoperable degenerative neoplastic lingering goes on and on for so long, however — either because it's an unusually slow form of brain cancer or because the father-in-law is the sort of tough old nasty bird who clings grimly to life for just as long as possible, one of those cases X privately believes euthanasia was probably originally designed with in mind, viz. one where the patient keeps lingering and degenerating and suffering horribly but refuses to submit to the inevitable and give up the freaking ghost already and doesn't seem to give any thought to the coincident suffering that his ghastly degenerative lingering inflicts on those who, for whatever inscrutable reasons, love him, or both — and X's secret conflict and corrosive shame finally wear him down so utterly and make him so miserable at work and catatonic at home that he finally swallows all pride and goes hat in hand to his trusted friend and colleague Y and lays the whole situation *ab initio ad mala* out before him, confiding to Y the icy selfishness of his (X's) very deepest feelings during his family's crisis and detailing his indwelling shame over the antipathy he feels as he stands behind his wife's chair at the $6500 fully adjustable steel-alloy bedside of his now grotesquely wasted and incontinent father-in-law and the old man's tongue lolls and face contorts in gruesome clonic spasms and a yellowish froth collects steadily at the corners of his (the father-in-law's) writhing mouth in an attempt to speak and his[1] now obscenely oversized and asymmetrically bulging head rotates on the 300-thread-count Italian pillowcase and the old man's clouded but still cruelly ferrous eyes behind the steel trifocals travel up past the anguished face of Mrs. X and fall on the tight hearty expression of sympathy and support X always struggles in the car to form and wear for these excruciating visits and roll instantly away in opposite directions — the father-in-law's eyes do — accompanied always by a ragged exhalation of disgust, as if reading the mendacious hypocrisy of X's expression and discerning the antipathy and selfishness beneath it and questioning all over again his daughter's judgment in remaining bound to this marginal and reprobative CPA; and X confesses to Y the fact that he has begun, on these visits to the incontinent old h/t/t prick's sickbed, rooting silently for the tumor itself, mentally toasting its health and wishing it continued metastatic growth, and has begun secretly regarding these visits as rituals of sympathy and support for the malignancy in the old man's pons, X has, while allowing his poor wife to believe that X is there by her side out of shared commiserative concern for the old man himself . . . X now vomiting up every last dram of the prior months' internal conflict and alienation and self-castigation, and beseeching Y to please understand the difficulty for X of telling any living soul of his secret shame and to feel both honored and bound by X's confidence in him and to find in his heart the compassion to forgo any h/t/t judgments of X and to for God's sweet sake tell no one of the cryovelate and malignantly selfish heart X fears his innermost secret feelings during the whole hellish ordeal have maybe revealed.

Whether this cathartic interchange takes place before Y did

---

[1] (i.e., the father-in-law's)

whatever he did to make X so furious with him,[2] or whether the interchange took place afterward and thus signifies that Y's stoic passivity in bearing up under X's vituperations paid off and their friendship was restored — or whether even maybe this present interchange itself is what somehow engendered X's rage at Y's supposed 'betrayal,' i.e. whether X later got the idea that Y had maybe spilled some of the beans to Mrs. X w/r/t her husband's secret self-absorption during what was probably the single most emotionally cataclysmic period of her life so far — none of this is clear, but that is all right this time because it is not centrally important because what *is* centrally important is that X, out of a combination of pain and sheer fatigue, finally humbles himself and bares his necrotic heart to Y and asks Y what Y thinks he (X) ought maybe to do to resolve the inner conflict and extinguish the secret shame and sincerely be able to forgive his dying father-in-law for being such a titanic prick in life and to just put history aside and somehow ignore the smug old prick's self-righteous judgments and obvious dislike and X's own feelings of peripheral *non-grata*zation and just somehow hang in there and try to support the old man and feel empathy for the entire teeming hysterical mass of his wife's family and to truly be there and support and stand by Mrs. X and the little Xes in their time of crisis and truly think of *them* for a change instead of remaining all bent in on his own secret feelings of exclusion and resentment and *viva cancrosum* and self-loathing and -urtication and burning shame.

As was probably made clear in abortive PQ6, Y's nature is to be laconic and self-effacing to the point where you nearly have to get him in a half-nelson to get him to do anything as presumptuous as actually giving advice. But X, by finally resorting to having Y conduct a thought-experiment in which Y pretends to be X and rumi-

---

[2] See abortive PQ6 above.

nates aloud on what he (meaning Y, as X) might do if faced with this malignant and horripilative *pons asinorum,* gets Y finally to aver that the best he (i.e., Y as X, and thus by extension X himself) can probably do in the situation is simply to passively hang in there, i.e. just Show Up, continue to Be There — as in just physically, if nothing else — on the margins of the family councils and at Mrs. X's side in her father's sickroom. In other words, Y says, to make it his secret penance and gift to the old man to just hang in there and silently to suffer the feelings of loathing and hypocrisy and selfishness and discountenance, but not to stop accompanying his wife or going to visit the old man or lurking tangentially at the family councils, in other words for X simply to reduce himself to bare physical actions and processes, to get off his heart's back and stop worrying about his makeup and simply Show Up[3] . . . which, when X rejoins that for Christ's sweet sake this is what he's already been doing all along, Y tentatively pats his (i.e., X's) shoulder and ventures to say that X has always struck him (=Y) as a good deal stronger and wiser and more compassionate than he, X, is willing to give himself credit for.

All of which makes X feel somewhat better — either because Y's counsel is profound and uplifting or else just because X got some relief from finally vomiting up the malignant secrets he feels have been corroding him — and things continue pretty much as before with the odious father-in-law's slow decline and X's wife's grief and her family's endless histrionics and councils, and with X still, behind his tight hearty smile, feeling hateful and confused and self-urticative but now struggling to try to regard this whole septic emotional maelstrom as a heartfelt gift to his dear wife and —

---

[3] (The way Y says things like 'Show Up' and 'Be There' makes X somehow conceive the clichés as capitalized, not unlike the way he hears his wife's family talk about the insufferable annual 'Get-Togethers' at the Ramada C.C.)

wince — father-in-law, and with the only other significant developments over the next six months being that X's hollow-eyed wife and one of her sisters go on the antidepressant Paxil and that two of X's nephews-in-law are detained for the alleged molestation of a developmentally disabled girl in their junior high school's Special Education wing.

And things proceed this way — with X now periodically coming hat in hand to Y for a sympathetic ear and the occasional thought-experiment, and being such a passive but overwhelmingly constant presence at the patriarchal bedside and the involved family councils that the most waggish of X's wife's family's great-uncles begins making quips about having to dust him — until, finally, early one morning nearly a year after the initial diagnosis, the inoperably ravaged and agonized and illucid old father-in-law gives up the ghost at last, expiring with the mighty shudder of a clubbed tarpon,[4] and is embalmed and rouged and dressed (as per codicil) in his juridical robes and memorialized at a service throughout which a stilted bier holds the casket high above all those assembled, and at which service X's poor wife's eyes resemble two enormous raw cigar-burns in an acrylic blanket, and at which by her side X — to the first suspicious but eventually touched surprise of his massed and black-clad in-laws — weeps longer and louder than anyone there, his distress so extreme and sincere that, on the way out of the Episcopal vestry, it's the weedy mother-in-law herself who presses her own handkerchief into X's hand and consoles him with brief pressure on his left forearm as she's helped to her limo, and X is then later that afternoon invited by personal telephone call from the father-in-law's oldest and most iron-eyed son to attend, along with Mrs. X, a

---

[4] (This was according to one of X's brothers-in-law, a Big Six junior associate who hadn't cherished the old man any more than X had, and was right there bedside with his serotonin-flooded wife when it occurred.)

very private and exclusive inner-circle-of-the-bereaved-family post-interment Get-Together in the library of the deceased judge's opulent home, an inclusive gesture which moves Mrs. X to her first tears of joy since long before going on Paxil.

The exclusive Get-Together itself — which turns out, by X's on-site calculation, to include less than 38% of his in-laws' total family, and features pre-warmed snifters of Remy Martin and unabashedly virid Cuban cigars for the males — involves the arrangement of leather divans and antique ottomans and wing chairs and stout little Willis & Geiger three-step library stepladders into a large circle, around which circle X's in-laws' family's innermost and apparently now most intimate 37.5% are to sit and take turns declaiming briefly on their memories and feelings about the dead father-in-law and their own special and unique individual relationships with him during his long and extraordinarily distinguished life. And X — who is seated awkwardly on a small oaken stepladder next to his wife's wing chair, and from his position in the circle is to be the fourth-from-last to speak, and who is on his fifth snifter, and whose cigar for some mysterious reason keeps going out, and who is suffering moderate-to-severe prostatic twinges from the flitched texture of the ladder's top step — finds, as heartfelt and sometimes quite moving anecdotes and encomia circumscribe the inner circle, that he has less and less idea what he ought to say.

Q: (A) Self-evident.

(B) Throughout the year of her father's terminal illness, Mrs. X has given no indication that she knows anything of X's internal conflict and self-septic horror. X has thus succeeded in keeping his interior state a secret, which is what he has professed to want all year. X has, be apprised, kept secrets from Mrs. X on several prior occasions. Part of the interior confusion and flux of this whole premortem interval, however — as X confides to Y after the old bastard finally kicks — has been that, for the first time in their marriage, X's wife's not knowing something about X that X did not wish her to know has made X feel not relieved or secure or good but rather on the contrary sad and alienated and lonely and aggrieved. The crux: X now finds himself, behind his commiserative expression and solicitous gestures, secretly angry at his wife over an ignorance he has made every effort to cultivate in her, and sustain. Evaluate.

<u>Pop Quiz 9</u>

You are, unfortunately, a fiction writer. You are attempting a cycle of very short belletristic pieces, pieces which as it happens are not *contes philosophiques* and not vignettes or scenarios or allegories or fables, exactly, though neither are they really qualifiable as 'short stories' (not even as those upscale microbrewed Flash Fictions that have become so popular in recent years — even though these belletristic pieces are really short, they just don't work like Flash Fictions are supposed to). How exactly the cycle's short pieces are supposed to work is hard to describe. Maybe say they're supposed to compose a certain sort of '*interrogation*' of the person reading them, somehow — i.e. palpations, feelers into the interstices of her sense of something, etc. . . . though what that 'something' is remains maddeningly hard to pin down, even just for yourself as you're working on the pieces (pieces that are taking a truly grotesque amount of time, by the way, far more time than they ought to vis à vis their length and aesthetic 'weight,' etc. — after all, you're like everybody else and have only so much time at your disposal and have to allocate it judiciously, especially when it comes to career stuff (yes: things have come to such a pass that even belletristic fiction writers consider themselves to have 'careers')). You know for sure, though, that the narrative pieces really are just 'pieces' and nothing more, i.e. that it is the way they fit together into the larger cycle that comprises them that is crucial to whatever 'something' you want to 'interrogate' a human 'sense of,' and so on.

So you do an eight-part cycle of these little mortise-and-tenon pieces.[1] And it ends up a total fiasco. Five of the eight pieces don't work at all — meaning they don't interrogate or palpate what you want them to, plus are too contrived or too cartoonish or too annoying or all three — and you have to toss them out. The 6th piece works only after it's totally redone in a way that's forbiddingly long and digression-fraught and, you fear, maybe so dense and inbent that nobody'll even get to the interrogatory parts at the end; plus then in the dreaded Final Revision Phase you realize that the rewrite of the 6th piece depends so heavily on 6's first version that you have to stick that first version back into the octocycle too, even though it (i.e., the first version of the 6th piece) totally falls apart 75% of the way through. You decide to try to salvage the aesthetic disaster of having to stick in the first version of the 6th piece by having that first version be utterly up front about the fact that it falls apart and doesn't work as a 'Pop Quiz' and by having the rewrite of the 6th piece start out with some terse unapologetic acknowledgment that it's another 'try' at whatever you were trying to palpate into interrogability in the first version. These intranarrative acknowledgments have the additional advantage of slightly diluting the pretentiousness of structuring the little pieces as so-called 'Quizzes,' but it also has the disadvantage of flirting with metafictional self-reference — viz. the having 'This Pop Quiz isn't working' and 'Here's another stab at #6' within the text itself — which in the late 1990s, when even Wes Craven is cashing in on metafictional self-reference, might come off lame and tired and facile, and also runs the risk of compromising the queer *urgency* about whatever it is you feel you want the pieces to

---

[1] (Right from the start you'd imagined the series as an octet or octocycle, though best of British luck explaining to anyone why.)

interrogate in whoever's reading them. This is an urgency that you, the fiction writer, feel very . . . well, urgently, and want the reader to feel too — which is to say that by no means do you want a reader to come away thinking that the cycle is just a cute formal exercise in interrogative structure and S.O.P. metatext.[2]

---

[2] (Though it all gets a little complicated, because part of what you want these little Pop Quizzes to do is to break the textual fourth wall and kind of address (or 'interrogate') the reader directly, which desire is somehow related to the old 'meta'-device desire to puncture some sort of fourth wall of realist pretense, although it seems like the latter is less a puncturing of any sort of real wall and more a puncturing of the veil of impersonality or effacement around the writer himself, i.e. with the now-tired S.O.P. 'meta'-stuff it's more the dramatist himself coming onstage from the wings and reminding you that what's going on is artificial and that the artificer is him (the dramatist) and but that he's at least respectful enough of you as reader/audience to be honest about the fact that he's back there pulling the strings, an 'honesty' which personally you've always had the feeling is actually a highly rhetorical sham-honesty that's designed to get you to like him and approve of him (i.e., of the 'meta'-type writer) and feel flattered that he apparently thinks you're enough of a grownup to handle being reminded that what you're in the middle of is artificial (like you didn't know that already, like you needed to be reminded of it over and over again as if you were a myopic child who couldn't see what was right in front of you), which more than anything seems to resemble the type of real-world person who tries to manipulate you into liking him by making a big deal of how open and honest and unmanipulative he's being all the time, a type who's even more irritating than the sort of person who tries to manipulate you by just flat-out lying to you, since at least the latter isn't constantly congratulating himself for not doing precisely what the self-congratulation itself ends up doing, viz. not interrogating you or have any sort of interchange or even really *talking* to you but rather just *performing*[*] in some highly self-conscious and manipulative way.

None of that was very clearly put and might well ought to get cut. It may be that none of this real-narrative-honesty-v.-sham-narrative-honesty stuff can even be talked about up front.)

[*][Kundera here would say '*dancing*,' and actually he's a perfect example of a belletrist whose intermural honesty is both formally unimpeachable and wholly self-serving: a classic postmodern rhetorician.]

Which all sets up a serious (and seriously time-consuming) conundrum. Not only have you ended up with only half of the workable octet you'd originally conceived — and an admittedly makeshift and imperfect half at that[3] — but there's also the matter of the urgent and necessary way you'd envisioned the original eight

---

[3] Note — in the spirit of 100% candor — that it's not like it's any kind of Olympianly high aesthetic standards that have caused you to toss out 63% of the original octet. The five unworkable pieces just plain didn't work. One, e.g., had to do with this brilliant psychopharmacologist who'd patented an incredibly effective post-Prozac and -Zoloft type of antidepressant so efficacious that it completely wiped out every last trace of dysphoria/anhedonia/agoraphobia/OCD/existential despair in patients and replaced their affective maladjustments with an enormous sense of personal confidence and *joie de vivre*, a limitless capacity for vibrant interpersonal relations, and an almost mystical conviction of their elemental synecdochic union with the universe and everything therein, as well as an overwhelming and ebullient gratitude for all the above feelings; plus the new antidepressant had absolutely no side effects or contraindications or dangerous interactions with any other pharmaceuticals and practically flew through FDA approval hearings; plus the stuff was easy and inexpensive enough to synthesize and manufacture that the psychopharmacologist could make it himself in his little home laboratory in his basement and sell it at cost via direct mail to licensed psychiatric professionals, bypassing the rapacious markups of the large pharmaceutical companies; and the antidepressant meant a literal new lease on life for untold thousands of cyclothymic Americans, many of whom had been the most endogenous and obstinately miserable patients their psychiatrists had had, and now were positively bubbling over with *joie de vivre* and productive energy and a warm humble sense of their great good fortune for same, and had found out the brilliant psychopharmacologist's home address (i.e., some of the patients had, which turned out to be pretty easy, given that the psychopharmacologist direct-mailed the antidepressant and all anybody had to do was look at the return address on the cheap padded mailers he used to ship the stuff), and they began showing up at his house, first one at a time, then in small groups, and then after a while converging in greater and greater numbers on the psychopharmacologist's modest private home, wanting just to look the great man meaningfully in the eye and to shake his hand and to thank him from the bottom of their spiritually jump-started hearts; and the crowds of grateful patients outside the psychopharmacologist's home get steadily

belletristic pieces connecting to form a unified octoplicate whole, one that ended up subtly interrogating the reader w/r/t the protean but still unified single issue that all the overt, admittedly unsubtle 'Q''s at the end of each Pop Quiz would — if these queries were themselves fit together in the organic context of the larger whole —

---

bigger and bigger, and some of the more determinedly grateful people in the crowd have set up tents and mobile homes whose sewage hoses have to be fed down into the curb's storm drain, and the psychopharmacologist's doorbell and phone ring constantly, and his neighbor's yards get trampled and parked on, and untold dozens of municipal health ordinances are broken; and the psychopharmacologist inside the house eventually has to phone-order and install special extra-opaque shades across his front windows and to keep them drawn at all times because whenever the crowd outside catches any glance of any part of him moving around inside the house an enormous ebullient cheer of gratitude and praise rises from the massed thousands and there's an almost menacing-looking mass charge for the modest little house's porch and doorbell as the newly whole patients *en masse* are overwhelmed with a sincere desire just to shake the psychopharmacologist's hand with both of theirs and to tell him what a great and brilliant and self-less living saint he is and to say that if there's anything at all they can do to in any way even partly start to repay him for what he's done for them and their families and humanity as a whole, why, to just say the word, anything at all; so that of course the psychopharmacologist basically ends up a prisoner in his own home, with his special shades drawn and phone off the hook and doorbell unplugged and multiple expanding-foam earplugs crammed in his ears all the time to drown out the crowd-noise, unable to leave the house and already down to the last of the very most unappetizing canned food from the very back of his pantry and getting closer and closer to either slitting his radial arteries or else shimmying up the inside of the chimney to his roof with a megaphone and telling the maddeningly ebullient and grateful crowd of newly whole citizens to go fuck themselves and leave him the fuck alone for the love of fucking Christ he can't *take* it anymore . . . and then true to the cycle's Pop Quiz format there are some fairly predictable queries about whether and why the psychopharmacologist might deserve what's happened to him and whether it's true that any marked shift in the total joy/misery ratio in the world must always be compensated for by some equally radical shift on the other side of the relevant equation, etc. . . . and the whole thing just goes on too long and is at once too obvious and too obscure (e.g., the second part of the 'Q' part of

end up palpating. This weird univocal urgency may or may not make sense to anyone else, but it had made sense to you, and had seemed . . . well, again, urgent, and worth risking the initial appearance of shallow formal exercism or pseudometabelletristic gamesmanship in the pieces' unconventional Pop Quiz–type struc-

---

the Quiz spends five lines constructing a possible analogy between the world's joy/misery ratio and the seminal double-entry 'A = L + E' equation of modern accountancy, as if more than one person out of a thousand could possibly give a shit), plus the whole *mise en scène* is too cartoonish, such that it looks as if it's trying to be just grotesquely funny instead of both grotesquely funny and grotesquely serious at the same time, such that any real human urgency in the Quiz's scenario and palpations is obscured by what appears to be just more of the cynical, amusing-ourselves-to-death-type commercial comedy that's already sucked so much felt urgency out of contemporary life in the first place, a defect that in an ironic way is almost the opposite of what compels the deletion of another of the original eight little pieces, this one a PQ about a group of early-20th-century immigrants from an exotic part of E. Europe who land and get processed through Ellis Island and after passing their TB exam have the misfortune to draw this one certain Ellis Island Intake Processing Official who's psychotically jingoistic and sadistic and on their Intake documents transforms each immigrant's exotic native surname into whatever sort of disgusting ridiculous undignified English-language term it in any remote way resembles — Pavel Shitlick, Milorad Fucksalot, Djerdap Snott, doubtless you get the idea — which of course the immigrants' ignorance of their new country's tongue keeps them from objecting to or even noticing, but which of course soon becomes and remains over the balance of their U.S. lives a hellish source of ridicule and shame and discrimination and the source of a gnawing E.-European-*vendetta*-type resentment that lasts all the way into the nursing home in Brooklyn NY where a fair number of the nomologically afflicted immigrants end up in their old age; and then one day a ravaged but eerily familiar old face suddenly appears at the nursing home as the face's owner is processed and admitted and wheeled with his portable oxygen tank into the old immigrants' midst in the TV room, and first sharp-eyed old Ephrosin Mydickislittle and then gradually all the rest of them suddenly recognize the new guy as the enfeebled senescent husk of the malignant Ellis Island I.P.O., who's now paralyzed and mute and emphysematic and totally helpless; and the group of a dozen or so of the victimized immigrants who've borne ridicule and indignity and resentment almost every day for the last five

ture. You were betting that the queer emergent urgency of the organically unified whole of the octet's two-times-two-times-two pieces (which you'd envisioned as a Manichean duality raised to the triune power of a sort of Hegelian synthesis w/r/t issues which both characters and readers were required to 'decide') would attenuate the initial appearance of postclever metaformal hooey and end up (you hoped) actually interrogating the reader's initial inclination to dismiss the pieces as 'shallow formal exercises' simply on the basis of their shared formal features, forcing the reader to see that such a dismissal would be based on precisely the same sorts of shallow for-

---

decades have to decide whether they're going to exploit this now perfect chance at exacting their revenge, and thereupon there's a long debate about whether cutting the paralyzed old guy's O_2-cord or something is justified and whether it could be any accident that a just and merciful E.-European God caused this particular nursing home to be the one that the sadistic old former I.P.O. was wheeled into versus whether avenging their ridiculous names by torturing/killing an incapacitated old person would transform the immigrants into living embodiments of the very indignity and disgust their English names connoted, i.e. whether in avenging the insult of their names they would come, finally, to deserve those names . . . all of which is actually (in your opinion) kind of cool, and the scenario and debate do have traces of the odd sort of grotesque/redemptive urgency you'd wanted the octet to convey; but the problem is that the same spiritual/moral/human issues this piece's 'Quiz-questions' ((A), (B), and so on and so forth) would interrogate the reader on are already hashed out at enormous but narratively necessary length in the piece's climactic twelve-angry-immigrant-men-type debate, here rendering the post-scenario 'Q' little more than a Y/N referendum; plus it also turned out that this piece didn't fit with the octet's other, more 'workable' pieces to form the sort of plicated-yet-still-urgently-unified whole that'd make the cycle a real piece of belletristic art instead of just a trendy wink-nudge pseudo-avant-garde exercise; and so, as gravid with import and urgency as you find the story's issues of 'names' and of names 'fitting' instead of just denoting or connoting, you bite your lip and toss the piece out of the octet . . . which actually probably means that it turns out you *do* have standards, maybe not Olympian ones but standards and convictions just the same, which no matter how big a time-wasting fiasco the whole octet's become ought to be a source of at least some comfort.

malistic concerns she was (at least at first) inclined to accuse the octet of.

Except — and now here's the conundrum — even though you've tossed out and rewritten and reinserted the now-quartet's[4] pieces almost entirely out of a concern for organic unity and the communicative urgency thereof, you're now not at all sure that anybody else is going to have the remotest idea how the four[5] pieces the octet ended up with 'fit together' or 'have in common,' i.e. how they add up to a bona fide unified 'cycle' whose urgency transcends the sum-urgency of the discrete parts it comprises. Thus you're now in the unfortunate position of trying to read the semi-quartet 'objectively' and of trying to figure out whether the weird ambient urgency you yourself feel in and between the surviving pieces is going to be feelable or even discernible to somebody else, viz. to some total stranger who's probably sitting down at the end of a long hard day to try to unwind by reading this belletristic 'Octet' thing.[6] And you know that this is a very bad corner to have painted yourself into, as a fiction writer. There are right and fruitful ways to try to 'empathize' with the reader, but having to try to imagine yourself *as* the reader is not one of them; in fact it's perilously close to the dreaded trap of trying to anticipate whether the reader will '*like*' something you're working on, and both you and the very few other fiction writers you're friends with know that there is no quicker way to tie yourself in knots and kill any human urgency in the thing you're

---

[4] (or rather 'duo-plus-dual-attempts-at-the-third,' whatever the Latinate quantifier for this would be)

[5] (or whatever)

[6] You're still going to title the cycle 'Octet.' No matter if it makes any sense to anybody else or not. You're intransigent on this point. Whether this intransigence is a kind of integrity or just simply nuts is an issue you refuse to spend work-time stewing about. You've cast your lot with the title 'Octet,' and 'Octet' is what it's going to be.

working on than to try to calculate ahead of time whether that thing will be *'liked.'* It's just lethal. An analogy might be: Imagine you've gone to a party where you know very few of the people there, and then on your way home afterwards you suddenly realize that you just spent the whole party so concerned about whether the people there seemed to like you or not that you now have absolutely no idea whether you liked any of *them* or not. Anybody who's had that sort of experience knows what a totally lethal kind of attitude this is to bring to a party. (Plus of course it almost always turns out that the people at the party actually *didn't* like you, for the simple reason that you seemed so inbent and self-conscious the whole time that they got the creepy subliminal feeling that you were using the party merely as some sort of stage to perform on and that you barely even noticed them and that you'd probably left without any idea whether you even liked them or not, which hurts their feelings and causes them to dislike you (they are, after all, only human, and they have the same insecurities about being liked as you do).)

But after the requisite amount of time-intensive worry and fear and procrastination and Kleenex-fretting and knuckle-biting, it all of a sudden strikes you that it's just possible that the semi-octet's interrogative/'dialogic' formal structure — the same structure that at first seemed urgent because it was a way to flirt with the potential appearance of metatextual hooey for reasons that would (you had hoped) emerge as profound and far more urgent than the tired old 'Hey-look-at-me-looking-at-you-looking-at-me' agenda of tired old S.O.P. metafiction, but that then got you into the conundrum by requiring you to toss out the Pop Quizzes that didn't work or were ultimately S.O.P. and coy instead of urgently honest and to rewrite PQ6 in a way that seemed dangerously meta-ish and left you with an ablated and nakedly jerryrigged half-octet whose original ambient but univocal urgency you were now no longer at all sure would come through to anybody else after all the cuts and re-

tries and general futzing around, painting you into the lethal belletristic corner of trying to anticipate the workings of a reader's
mind and heart — that this same potentially disastrous-looking
avant-gardy heuristic form just might itself give you a way out of
the airless conundrum, a chance to salvage the potential fiasco of
you feeling that the 2+(2(1)) pieces add up to something urgent
and human and the reader not feeling that way at all. Because now
it occurs to you that you could simply ask her. The reader. That you
could poke your nose out the mural hole that '6 isn't working as a
Pop Quiz' and 'Here's another shot at it' etc. have already made and
address the reader directly and ask her straight out whether she's
feeling anything like what you feel.

The trick to this solution is that you'd have to be 100% honest.
Meaning not just sincere but almost naked. Worse than naked —
more like unarmed. Defenseless. 'This thing I feel, I can't name it
straight out but it seems important, do you feel it too?' — this sort
of direct question is not for the squeamish. For one thing, it's perilously close to '*Do you like me? Please like me,*' which you know quite
well that 99% of all the interhuman manipulation and bullshit
gamesmanship that goes on goes on precisely because the idea of
saying this sort of thing straight out is regarded as somehow obscene. In fact one of the very last few interpersonal taboos we have
is this kind of obscenely naked direct interrogation of somebody
else. It looks pathetic and desperate. That's how it'll look to the
reader. And it will have to. There's no way around it. If you step out
and ask her what and whether she's feeling, there can't be anything
coy or performative or sham-honest-so-she'll-like-you about it.
That'd kill it outright. Do you see? Anything less than completely
naked helpless pathetic sincerity and you're right back in the per-
nicious conundrum. You'll have to come to her 100% hat in hand.

In other words what you could do is you could now construct an
additional Pop Quiz — so the ninth overall, but in another sense

only the fifth or even fourth, and actually maybe none of these because this one'd be less a Quiz than (ulp) a kind of metaQuiz — in which you try your naked best to describe the conundrum and potential fiasco of the semi-octet and your own feeling that the surviving semiworkable pieces all seem to be trying to demonstrate[7] some sort of weird ambient *sameness* in different kinds of human relationships,[8] some nameless but inescapable '*price*' that all human beings are faced with having to pay at some point if they ever want truly 'to be with'[9] another person instead of just using that person somehow (like for example using the person as just an audience, or as an instrument of their own selfish ends, or as some piece of like moral

---

[7] That might not be the right word — too pedantic; you might want to use the word *transmit* or *evoke* or even *limn* (*palpate*'s been overused already, and it's possible that the weird psychospiritual probing you mean it to connote by medical analogy won't come across at all to anybody, which is probably marginally OK, because individual words the reader can sort of skip over and not get too bothered about, but there's no sense in pressing your luck and hammering on *palpate* over and over again). If *limn* doesn't end up seeming just off-the-charts pretentious I'd probably go with *limn*.

[8] Be warned that this has become a near-nauseous term in contemporary usage, *relationship*, treaclized by the same sorts of people who use *parent* as a verb and say *share* to mean talk, and for a late-1990s reader it's going to ooze all sorts of cloying PC- and New Age–associations; but if you decide to use the pseudometaQuiz tactic and the naked honesty it entails to try to salvage the fiasco you're probably going to have to come right out and use it, the dreaded 'R'-term, come what may.

[9] *Ibid.* on using the verb *to be* in this culturally envenomed way, too, as in 'I'll Be There For You,' which has become the sort of empty spun-sugar shibboleth that communicates nothing except a certain unreflective sappiness in the speaker. Let's not be naive about what this 100%-honest-naked-interrogation-of-reader tactic is going to cost you if you opt to try it. You're going to have to eat the big rat and go ahead and actually use terms like *be with* and *relationship*, and use them *sincerely* — i.e. without tone-quotes or ironic undercutting or any kind of winking or nudging — if you're going to be truly honest in the pseudometaQuiz instead of just ironically yanking the poor reader around (and she'll be able to tell which one you're doing; even if she can't articulate it she'll know if you're just trying to save your own belletristic ass by manipulating her — trust me on this).

gymnastics equipment on which they can demonstrate their virtu-
ous character (as in people who are generous to other people only because they want to be seen as generous, and so actually secretly like
it when people around them go broke or get into trouble, because it
means they can rush generously in and act all helpful — everybody's
seen people like this), or as a narcissistically cathected projection of
themselves, etc.),[10] a weird and nameless but apparently unavoid-
able 'price' that can actually sometimes equal death itself, or at least
usually equals your giving up something (either a thing or a person
or a precious long-held 'feeling'[11] or some certain idea of yourself
and your own virtue/worth/identity) whose loss will feel, in a true
and urgent way, like a kind of death, and to say that the fact that
there could be (you feel) such an overwhelming and elemental *sameness* to such totally different situations and *mise en scène*s and
conundra — that is, that these apparently different and formally
(admit it) kind of stilted and coy-looking 'Pop Quizzes' could all
reduce finally to the same question (whatever exactly that question
is) — seems to you urgent, truly urgent, something almost worth
shimmying up chimneys and shouting from roofs about.[12]

---

[10] You may or may not want to spend a line or two inviting the reader to consider
whether it's strange that there are literally a billion times more ways to 'use' somebody than there are to honestly just 'be with' them. It depends how long and/or
involved you want this PQ9 to be. My own inclination would be not to (probably
more out of worry about appearing potentially pious or obvious or longwinded
than out of any disinterested concerns about brevity and focus), but this'll be a
matter for you to sort of play by ear.

[11] *Ibid.* footnotes 8 and 9 on *feeling/feelings* too — look, nobody said this was going
to be painless, or free. It's a desperate last-ditch salvage operation. It's not unrisky.
Having to use words like *relationship* and *feeling* might simply make things worse.
There are no guarantees. All I can do is be honest and lay out some of the more
ghastly prices and risks for you and urge you to consider them very carefully before
you decide. I honestly don't see what else I can do.

[12] Yes: you are going to sound pious and melodramatic. Suck it up.

Which is all again to say that you — the unfortunate fiction writer — will have to puncture the fourth wall[13] and come onstage naked (except for your hand's hat) and say all this stuff right to a person who doesn't know you or particularly give a shit about you one way or the other and who probably wanted simply to come home and put her feet up at the end of a long day and unwind in one of the very few safe and innocuous ways of unwinding left anymore.[14] And then you'll have to ask the reader straight out whether she feels it, too, this queer nameless ambient urgent interhuman sameness. Meaning you'll have to ask whether she thinks the whole ragged jerryrigged heuristic semi-octet 'works' as an organically unified belletristic whole or not. Right there while she's reading it. Again: consider this carefully. You should *not* deploy this tactic until you've soberly considered what it might cost. What she might think of you. Because if you go ahead and do it (i.e., ask her straight out), this whole 'interrogation' thing won't be an innocuous formal belletristic device anymore. It'll be real. You'll be bothering her, the same way a solicitor who calls on the telephone just as you're sitting down to unwind over a good dinner is bothering you.[15] And consider the actual sort of question you'll be bothering her with. 'Does this work, do you like this,' etc. Consider what she might think of

---

[13] (among other things you'll have to puncture)

[14] Yes: things have come to such a pass that belletristic fiction is now considered *safe* and *innocuous* (the former predicate probably entailed or comprised by the latter predicate, if you think about it), but I'd opt to keep cultural politics out of it if I were you.

[15] (. . . Only *worse*, actually, because in this case it'd be more like if you'd just bought a fancy expensive take-out dinner from a restaurant and brought it home and were just sitting down to try to enjoy it when the phone rings and it's the chef or restaurateur or whoever you just bought the food from now calling and bothering you in the middle of trying to eat the dinner to ask how the dinner is and whether you're enjoying it and whether or not it 'works' as a dinner. Imagine how you'd feel about a restaurateur who did this to you.)

you just for asking something like this. It might very well make you (i.e. the *mise en scène*'s fiction writer) come off like the sort of person who not only goes to a party all obsessed about whether he'll be liked or not but actually goes around at the party and goes up to strangers and *asks* them whether they like him or not. What they think of him, what effect he's having on them, whether their view of him coincides at all with the complex throb of his own self-idea, etc. Coming up to innocent human beings who wanted only to come to a party and unwind a little and maybe meet some new people in a totally low-key and unthreatening setting and stepping directly into their visual field and breaking all kinds of basic unspoken rules of party- and first-encounter-between-strangers-etiquette and explicitly interrogating them about the very thing you're feeling inbent and self-conscious about.[16] Take a moment to

---

[16] . . . And of course it's very probably also the issue *they're* feeling self-conscious about — w/r/t themselves and whether other people at the party are liking *them* — and this is why it's an unspoken axiom of party-etiquette that you don't ask this sort of question outright or act in any way to plunge a party-interaction into this kind of maelstrom of interpersonal anxiety: because once even just one party-conversation reached this kind of urgent unmasked speak-your-innermost-thoughts level it would spread almost metastatically, and pretty soon everybody at the party would be talking about nothing but their own hopes and fears about what the other people at the party were thinking of them, which means that all distinguishing features of different people's surface personalities would be obliterated and everybody at the party would emerge as more or less exactly the same, and the party would reach this sort of entropic homeostasis of nakedly self-obsessed sameness, and it'd get incredibly boring,* plus the paradoxical fact that the distinctive colorful surface differences between people upon which other people base their like or dislike of those people would have vanished, and so the question 'Do you like me' would cease to admit of any meaningful response, and the whole party could very well undergo some sort of weird logical or metaphysical implosion, and none of the people at the party would ever again be able to function meaningfully in the outside world.**

*(It's maybe interesting to note that this corresponds closely to most atheists' idea of Heaven, which in turn helps explain the relative popularity of atheism.**)
**(I'd probably leave all this implicit, though, if I were you.)

imagine the faces of the people at a party where you did this. Imagine the faces' expression fully, in 3D and vibrant color, and then imagine the expression directed at you. Because this will be the risk run, the honesty-tactic's possible price — and keep in mind that it may be for nothing: it is not at all clear, if the precedent quartet of little mortise-and-tenon *quart d'heures* hasn't succeeded in 'interrogating' the reader or transmitting any felt 'sameness' or 'urgency,' that coming out hat in hand near the end and trying to interrogate her directly is going to induce any kind of revelation of urgent sameness that'll then somehow resonate back through the cycle's pieces and make her see them in a different light. It may well be that all it'll do is make you look like a self-consciously inbent schmuck, or like just another manipulative pseudopomo bullshit artist who's trying to salvage a fiasco by dropping back to a meta-dimension and commenting on the fiasco itself.[17] Even under the most charitable interpretation, it's going to look desperate. Possibly pathetic. At any rate it's *not* going to make you look wise or secure or accomplished or any of the things readers usually want to pretend they believe the literary artist who wrote what they're reading

---

[17] This tactic is sometimes, at belletristic-fiction conventions and whatnot, called 'Carsoning' or 'The Carson Maneuver' in honor of the fact that former *Tonight Show* host Johnny Carson used to salvage a lame joke by assuming a self-consciously mortified expression that sort of metacommented on the joke's lameness and showed the audience he knew very well it was lame, a strategy which year after year and decade after decade often produced an even bigger and more delighted laugh from the audience than a good original joke would have . . . and the fact that Carson was deploying this Maneuver in LCD commercial entertainment as far back as the late 1960s shows that it's not exactly a breathtakingly original device. You may want to consider including some of this information in PQ9 in order to show the reader that you're at least aware that metacommentary is now lame and old news and can't of itself salvage anything anymore — this may lend credibility to your claim that what you're trying to do is actually a good deal more urgent and real. Again, this will be for you to decide. Nobody's going to hold your hand.

is when they sit down to try to escape the insoluble flux of themselves and enter a world of prearranged meaning. Rather it's going to make you look fundamentally lost and confused and frightened and unsure about whether to trust even your most fundamental intuitions about urgency and sameness and whether other people deep inside experience things in anything like the same way you do . . . more like a reader, in other words, down here quivering in the mud of the trench with the rest of us, instead of a *Writer,* whom we imagine to be clean and dry and radiant of command presence and unwavering conviction as he coordinates the whole campaign from back at some gleaming abstract Olympian HQ.

So decide.

ADULT WORLD (I)

PART ONE. THE EVER-CHANGING STATUS OF THE YEN

For the first three years, the young wife worried that their love-making together was somehow hard on his thingie. The rawness and tenderness and spanked pink of the head of his thingie. The slight wince when he'd first enter her down there. The vague hot-penny taste of rawness when she took his thingie in her mouth — she seldom took him in her mouth, however; there was something about it that she felt he did not quite like.

For the first three to three-and-a-half years of their marriage together, this wife, being young (and full of herself (she realized only later)), believed it was something about her. The problem. She worried that there was something wrong with her. With her technique in making love. Or maybe that some unusual roughness or thickness or hitch down there was hard on his thingie, and hurt it. She was aware that she liked to press her pubic bone and the base of her button against him and grind when they made love together, sometimes. She ground against him as gently as she could force herself to remember to, but she was aware that she often did it as she was moving towards having her sexual climax and some-times forgot herself, and afterwards she was often worried that she had selfishly forgotten about his thingie and might have been too hard on it.

They were a young couple and had no children, though sometimes they talked about having children, and about all the irrevocable changes and responsibilities that this would commit them to.

The wife's method of contraception was a diaphragm until she began to worry that something about the design of its rim or the way she inserted or wore it might be wrong and hurt him, might add to whatever it was about their lovemaking together that seemed hard on him. She searched his face when he entered her; she remembered to keep her eyes open and watched for the slight wince that may or may not (she realized only later, when she had some mature perspective) have actually been pleasure, may have been the same kind of revelational pleasure of coming together as close as two married bodies could come and feeling the warmth and closeness that made it so hard to keep her eyes open and senses alert to whatever she might be doing wrong.

In those early years, the wife felt that she was totally happy with the reality of their sexlife together. The husband was a great lover, and his attentiveness and sweetness and skill drove her almost mad with pleasure, the wife felt. The only negative part was her irrational worry that something was wrong with her or that she was doing something wrong that kept him from enjoying their sexlife together as much as she did. She worried that the husband was too considerate and unselfish to risk hurting her feelings by talking about whatever was wrong. He had never complained about being sore or raw, or of slightly wincing when he first entered her, or said anything other than that he loved her and totally loved her down there more than he could even say. He said that she was indescribably soft and warm and sweet down there and that entering her was indescribably great. He said she drove him half insane with passion and love when she ground against him as she was getting ready to have her sexual climax. He said nothing but generous and reassuring things about their sexlife together. He always whispered compliments to her after they had made love, and held her, and considerately regathered the bedcovers around her legs as the wife's sexual heartrate slowed and she began to feel chilly. She loved to feel her legs still tremble slightly under the cocoon of bedcovers he gently regathered around her. They also developed the intimacy of him always getting her Virginia Slims and lighting one for her after they had made love together.

The young wife felt that the husband was a simply wonderful lovemaking partner, considerate and attentive and unselfish and virile and sweet, far better than she probably deserved; and as he slept, or if he arose in the middle of the night to check on foreign markets and turned on the light in the master bathroom adjoining their bedroom and inadvertently woke her (she slept lightly in those early years, she realized later), the wife's worries as she lay awake in their bed were all about herself. Sometimes she touched herself down there while she lay awake, but it wasn't in a pleasurable way. The husband slept on his right side, facing away. He had a hard time sleeping due to career stress, and could only fall asleep in one position. Sometimes she watched him sleep. Their master bedroom had a nightlight down near the baseboard. When he arose in the night she believed it was to check the status of the yen. Insomnia could cause him to drive all the way downtown to the firm in the middle of the night. There were the rupiah and the won and the baht to be monitored and checked, also. He was also in charge of the weekly chore of grocery shopping, which he habitually also performed late at night. Amazingly (she realized only later, after she had had an epiphany and rapidly matured), it had never occurred to her to check on anything.

She loved it when he gave oral sex but worried that he didn't like it as much when she reciprocated and took him in her mouth. He almost always stopped her after a short time, saying that it made him want to be inside her down there instead of in her mouth. She felt that there must be something wrong with her oral sex technique that made him not like it as much as she did, or hurt him. He had gone all the way to his sexual climax in her mouth only twice in their marriage together, and both the times had taken practically forever. Both the times took so long that her neck was stiff the next day, and she worried that he hadn't liked it even though he had said he couldn't even describe in words how much he liked it. She once gathered her nerve together and drove out to Adult World and bought a Dildo, but only to practice her oral sex technique on. She was inexperienced in this, she knew. The slight tension or distraction she thought she felt in him when she moved down the bed and took the husband's thingie in her mouth could have been nothing but her own selfish imagination; the whole problem could be just in her head, she worried. She had been tense and uncomfortable at Adult World. Except for the cashier, she had been the only female in the store, and the cashier had given her a look that she didn't think was very appropriate or professionally courteous at all, and the young wife had taken the dark plastic bag with the Dildo to her car and driven out of the crowded parking lot so fast that later she was afraid her tires might have squealed.

The husband never slept in the nude — he wore clean briefs and a T-shirt.

She sometimes had bad dreams in which they were driving someplace together and every single other vehicle on the road was an ambulance.

The husband never said anything about oral sex together except that he loved her and that she drove him mad with passion when she took him in her mouth. But when she took him in her mouth and flattened her tongue to suppress the well-known Gag Reflex and moved her head up and down as far as her ability allowed, making a ring of her thumb and first finger to stimulate the part of his shaft she could not fit in her mouth, giving him oral sex, the wife always sensed a tension in him; she always thought she could detect a slight rigidity in the muscles of his abdomen and legs and worried that he was tense or distracted. His thingie often tasted raw and/or sore, and she was concerned that her teeth or saliva might be stinging him and subtracting from his pleasure. She worried about her technique at it, and practiced in secret. Sometimes, during oral sex in their lovemaking together, she thought it felt as if he was trying to have his sexual climax quickly so as to have the oral sex be over A.S.A.P. and that that was why he couldn't for so long, usually. She tried making pleased, excited sounds with her mouth full of his thingie; then, lying awake later, she sometimes worried that the sounds she had made had perhaps sounded strangled or distressing and had only added to his tension.

This immature, inexperienced, emotionally labile young wife lay alone in their bed very late on the night of their third wedding anniversary. The husband, whose career was high-stress and caused insomnia and frequent awakenings, had arisen and gone into the master bathroom and then downstairs to his study, then later she had heard the sound of his car. The Dildo, which she kept hidden at the bottom of her sachet drawer, was so inhuman and impersonal and tasted so horrid that she had to all but force herself to practice with it. Sometimes he drove to his office in the middle of the night to check the overseas markets in more depth — trade never ceased somewhere in the world's many currencies. More and more often she lay awake in bed and worried. She had become woozy at their special anniversary dinner and had nearly spoiled their evening together. Sometimes, when she had him in her mouth, she became almost overwhelmed with fear that the husband wasn't enjoying it, and would have an overwhelming desire to bring him to his sexual climax A.S.A.P. in order to have some kind of selfish 'proof' that he enjoyed being in her mouth, and would sometimes forget herself and the techniques she had practiced and begin bobbing her head almost frantically and moving her fist frantically up and down his thingie, sometimes actually sucking at his thingie's little hole, exerting actual suction, and she worried that she chafed or bent or hurt him when she did this. She worried that the husband could unconsciously sense her anxiety about whether he enjoyed having his thingie in her mouth and that it actually was this that prevented him from enjoying oral sex together as much as she enjoyed it. Sometimes she berated herself for her insecurities — the husband was under enough stress already, due to his career. She felt that her fear was selfish, and worried that the husband could sense her fear and selfishness and that this drove a wedge into their intimacy together. There was also the riyal to be checked at night, the dirham, the Burmese kyat. Australia used the dollar but it was a different dollar and had to be monitored. Taiwan, Singapore, Zimbabwe, Liberia, New Zealand: all deployed dollars of fluctuant value. The determinants of the ever-changing status of the yen were very complex. The husband's promotion had resulted in the new career title Stochastic Currency Analyst; his business cards and stationery all included the title. There were complex equations. The husband's mastery of the computer's financial programs and currency software were already legendary at the firm, a colleague had told her during a party while the husband was using the bathroom again.

She worried that whatever the problem with her was, it felt impossible to sort out rationally in her mind to any true degree. There was no way to talk about it with him — there was no way the wife could think of to even start such a conversation. She would sometimes clear her throat in the special way that meant she had something on her mind, but then her mind froze. If she asked him whether there was anything wrong with her, he would believe she was asking for reassurance and instantly would reassure her — she knew him. His professional specialty was the yen, but other currencies impacted the yen and had to be continually analyzed. Hong Kong's dollar was also different and impacted the status of the yen. Sometimes at night she worried she might be crazy. She had ruined a previous intimate relationship with irrational feelings and fears, she knew. Almost in spite of herself, she later returned to the same Adult World store and bought an X-rated videotape, storing it in its retail box in the same hiding place as the Dildo, determined to study and compare the sex techniques of the women in the video. Sometimes, when he was asleep on his side at night, the wife would arise and walk around to the other side of the bed and kneel on the floor and watch the husband in the dim glow of their nightlight, study his sleeping face, as if hoping to discover there some unspoken thing that would help her stop worrying and feel more sure that their sexlife together pleased him as much as it pleased her. The X-rated videotape had explicit color photos of women giving their partners oral sex right there on the box. *Stochastic* meant random or conjectural or containing numerous variables that all had to be monitored closely; the husband joked sometimes that it really meant getting paid to drive yourself crazy.

Adult World, which had one side of marital aids and three sides of X-rated features, as well as a small dark hall leading to something else in the rear and a monitor playing an explicit X-rated scene right there above the cash register, smelled horrid in a way that reminded the wife of absolutely nothing else in her life experience. She later wrapped the Dildo in several plastic bags and put it out in the trash on the night before Trash Day. The only significant thing she felt she learned from studying the videotape was that the men often seemed to like to look down at the women when the women had them in their mouth and see their thingie going in and out of the woman's mouth. She believed that this might very well explain the husband's abdominal muscles tensing when she took him in her mouth — it could be him straining to raise up slightly to see it — and she began to debate with herself whether her hair might be too long to allow him to see his thingie go in and out of her mouth during oral sex, and began to debate whether or not to get her hair cut short. She was relieved that she had no worries about being less attractive or sexual than the actresses in the X-rated videotape: these women had gross measurements and obvious implants (as well as their own share of slight asymmetries, she noted), as well as dyed, bleached, and badly damaged hair that didn't look touchable or strokable at all. Most notably, the women's eyes were empty and hard — you could just tell they weren't experiencing any intimacy or pleasure and didn't care if their partners were pleased.

Sometimes the husband would arise at night and use the master bathroom and then go out to his workshop off the garage and try to unwind for an hour or two with his hobby of furniture refinishing.

Adult World was all the way out on the other side of town, in a tacky district of fast food and auto dealerships off the expressway; neither time she had hurried out of the parking lot did the young wife see any cars she ever recognized. The husband had explained before their wedding that he had slept in clean briefs and a T-shirt ever since he was a child — he was simply not comfortable sleeping in the nude. She had recurring bad dreams, and he would hold her and speak reassuringly until she was able to get back to sleep. The stakes of the Foreign Currency Game were high, and his study downstairs remained locked when not in use. She began to consider psychotherapy.

Insomnia actually referred not to difficulty falling asleep but to early and irrevocable awakening, he had explained.

Not once in the first three-and-a-half years of their marriage together did she ask the husband why his thingie was hurt or sore, or what she might do differently, or what the cause was. It simply felt impossible to do this. (The memory of this paralyzed feeling would astound her later in life, when she was a very different person.) Asleep, her husband sometimes looked to her like a child on its side sleeping, curled all tightly into itself, a fist to its face, the face flushed and its expression so concentrated it looked almost angry. She would kneel next to the bed at a slight angle to the husband so that the weak light of the baseboard's nightlight fell onto his face and watch his face and worry about why, irrationally, it felt impossible to simply ask him. She had no idea why he put up with her or what he saw in her. She loved him very much.

On the evening of their third wedding anniversary, the young wife had fainted in the special restaurant he had taken her to to celebrate. One minute she was trying to swallow her sorbet and looking at the husband over the candle and the next she was looking up at him as he knelt above her asking what was wrong, his face smooshy and distorted like the reflection of a face in a spoon. She was frightened and embarrassed. The bad dreams at night were brief and upsetting and seemed always to concern either the husband or his car in ways she could not pin down. Never once had she checked a Discover statement. It had never even occurred to her to inquire why the husband insisted on doing all the grocery shopping alone at night; she had only felt shame at the way his generosity highlighted her own irrational selfishness. When, later (long after the galvanic dream, the call, the discreet meeting, the question, the tears, and her epiphany at the window), she reflected on the towering self-absorption of her naiveté in those years, the wife always felt a mixture of contempt and compassion for the utter child she had been. She had never been what one would call a stupid person. Both times at Adult World, she had paid with cash. The credit cards were in the husband's name.

The way she finally concluded that something was wrong with her was: either something was really wrong with her, or something was wrong with her for irrationally worrying about whether something was wrong with her. The logic of this seemed airtight. She lay at night and held the conclusion in her mind and turned it this way and that and watched it make reflections of itself inside itself like a fine diamond.

The young wife had had only one other lover before meeting her husband. She was inexperienced and knew it. She suspected that her brief strange bad dreams might be her inexperienced Ego trying to shift the anxiety onto the husband, to protect itself from the knowledge that something was wrong with her and made her sexually hurtful or unpleasing. Things had ended badly with her first lover, she was well aware. The padlock on the door of his workshop off the garage was not unreasonable: power tools and refinished antiques were valuable assets. In one of the bad dreams, she and the husband lay together after lovemaking, snuggling contentedly, and the husband lit a Virginia Slims and then refused to give it to her, holding it away from her while it burned itself all the way down. In another, they again lay contentedly after making love together, and he asked her if it had been as good for him as it had for her. The door to his study was the only other door that stayed locked — the study contained a lot of sophisticated computer and telecommunications equipment, giving the husband up-to-the-minute information on foreign currency market activity.

In another of the bad dreams, the husband sneezed and then kept sneezing, over and over and over again, and nothing she did could help or make it stop. In another, she herself was the husband and was entering the wife sexually, ranging above the wife in the Missionary Position, thrusting, and he (that is, the wife, dreaming) felt the wife grind her pubis uncontrollably against him and start to have her sexual climax, and so then he began thrusting faster in a calculated way and making pleased male sounds in a calculating way and then feigned having his own sexual climax, calculatingly making the sounds and facial expressions of having his climax but withholding it, the climax, then afterwards going into the master bathroom and making horrid faces at himself while he climaxed into the toilet. The status of some currencies could fluctuate violently over the course of a single night, the husband had explained. Whenever she woke from a bad dream, he always woke up too, and held her and asked what was the matter, and lit a cigarette for her or stroked her side very attentively and reassured her that everything was all right. Then he would arise from bed, since he was now awake, and go downstairs to check the status of the yen. The wife liked to sleep in the nude after lovemaking together, but the husband almost always put his clean briefs back on before using the bathroom or turning away onto his side to sleep. The wife would lie awake and try not to spoil something so wonderful by driving herself crazy with worry. She worried that her tongue was rough and pulpy from smoking and might abrade his thingie, or that unbeknownst to her her teeth were scraping his thingie when she took the husband in her mouth for oral sex. She worried that her new haircut was too short and made her face look chubby. She worried about her breasts. She worried about the way her husband's face sometimes seemed to look when they made love together.

Another bad dream, which recurred more than once, involved the downtown street the husband's firm was on, a view of the empty street late at night, in a light rain, and the husband's car with its special license plate she'd surprised him with at Christmas driving very slowly up the street towards the firm and then passing the firm without stopping and proceeding off down the wet street to some other destination. The wife worried about the fact that this dream upset her so much — there was nothing in the scene of the dream to explain the crawly feeling it gave her — and about the way she could not seem to bring herself to talk openly to him about any of the dreams. She feared that she would feel somehow as if she were accusing him. She could not explain this feeling, and it gnawed at her. Nor could she think of any way to ask the husband about exploring the idea of psychotherapy — she knew he would agree at once, but he would be concerned, and the wife dreaded the feeling of being unable to explain in any rational way to ease his concern. She felt alone and trapped in her worry; she was lonely in it.

During their lovemaking together, the husband's face sometimes wore what sometimes seemed to her less an expression of pleasure than of intense concentration, as if he were about to sneeze and trying not to.

Early in the fourth year of their marriage, the wife felt herself becoming obsessed with the irrational suspicion that her husband was sexually climaxing into the master bathroom's toilet. She examined the toilet's rim and the bathroom trash basket closely almost every day, pretending to clean, feeling increasingly out of control. The old trouble with swallowing sometimes returned. She felt herself becoming obsessed with the suspicion that her husband maybe took no genuine pleasure in their lovemaking together but was concentrated only on making her feel pleasure, forcing her to feel pleasure and passion; lying awake at night, she feared that he took some kind of twisted pleasure in imposing pleasure on her. And yet, just experienced enough to be full of doubts (and of herself) at this innocent time, the young wife also believed that these irrational suspicions and obsessions could be merely her own youthful, self-centered Ego displacing its inadequacies and fears of true intimacy onto the innocent husband; and she was desperate not to spoil their relationship with insane displaced suspicions, like the way she had failed and wrecked the relationship with her previous lover because of irrational worries.

And so the wife fought with all her strength against her callow, inexperienced mind (she then believed), convinced that any real problem lay in her own selfish imagination and/or her inadequate sexual persona. She fought against the worry she felt about the way, nearly always, when she had moved down his body in the bed and taken him in her mouth, the husband would nearly always (it seemed then), after waiting with tense and rigid abdominal muscles for what felt somehow like the exact minimum considerate amount of time with his thingie in her mouth, would always reach gently down and pull her gently but firmly back up his body to kiss her passionately and enter her from below, gazing into her eyes with a very concentrated expression as she sat astride him, she sitting always slightly hunched out of embarrassment at the slight asymmetry of her breasts. The way he would exhale sharply in either passion or displeasure and reach down and pull the wife up and slide his thingie inside her in one smooth motion, the gasp sharp as if involuntary, as if trying to convince her that merely having his thingie in her mouth drove him mad with desire to be all the way up inside her down there, he said, and to have her, he said, 'right up close' against him instead of 'so far away' down his body. This nearly always made her feel somehow uneasy as she sat astride him, hunched and bobbing and with his hands on her hips and sometimes forgetting herself and grinding down with her pubic bone against his pubis, fearful that the grinding plus her weight on him could cause injury but often forgetting herself and involuntarily bearing down at a slight angle and grinding against him with less and less caution, sometimes even arching her back and thrusting out her breasts to be touched, until the moment he nearly always — nine times out of ten, on average — gave another gasp of either passion or impatience and rotated slightly onto his side with his hands on her hips, rolling her gently but firmly over with him until she was all the way beneath him and he ranged over her and either still had his thingie deep in her or else reentered her smoothly from above; he was very smooth and graceful in the movements and never hurt her when changing positions and rarely had to reenter, but it always caused the wife some worry, afterwards, that he almost never came to his sexual climax (if indeed he ever really did come to his climax) from beneath her, that as he felt his climax building inside himself he seemed to feel an obsessive need to rotate and be inside her from above, from the familiar Missionary Position of male dominance, which although it made his thingie feel even more deeply inside her down there, which the wife enjoyed very much, she worried that the husband's need to have her beneath him at the sexual climax indicated that something she did when sitting astride him and moving either hurt him or denied him the sort of intense pleasure that would lead to his sexual climax; and so the wife to her distress sometimes found herself preoccupied with worry even as they finished and she began to have another small aftershock of climax while grinding gently against him from below and searching his face for evidence of a truly genuine climax there and sometimes crying out in pleasure beneath him in a voice that sounded, she sometimes thought, less and less like her own.

The sexual relationship the wife had had prior to meeting her husband had occurred when she was a very young woman — hardly more than a child, she realized later. It had been a committed, monogamous relationship with a young man whom she had felt very close to and who was a wonderful lover, passionate and giving and very skilled (she had felt) in sexual technique, who was very vocal and affectionate during lovemaking, and attentive, and had loved to be in her mouth for oral sex, and had never seemed hurt or sore or distracted when she forgot herself and ground against him, and always closed both his eyes in passionate pleasure when he began to move uncontrollably into his sexual climax, and whom she had (at that young age) felt that she loved and loved being with and could easily imagine marrying and being in a committed relationship with forever — all until she had begun, late in the first year of their relationship together, to suffer from irrational suspicions that the lover was imagining making love with other women during their lovemaking together. The fact that the lover closed both his eyes when he experienced intense pleasure with her, which at first had made her feel sexually secure and pleased, began to worry her a great deal, and the suspicion that he was imagining being inside of other women when he was inside of her became more and more of a dreadful conviction, even though she also felt that it was groundless and irrational and only in her mind and would have hurt the lover's feelings just terribly if she had said anything to him about it, until finally it became an obsession, even though there was no tangible evidence for it and she had never said anything about it; and even though she believed the whole thing was almost surely just in her mind, the obsession became so terrible and overwhelming that she began to avoid making love with him, and began having sudden irrational bursts of emotion over trivial issues in their relationship, bursts of hysterical anger or tears that were in fact bursts of irrational worry that he was having fantasies about sexual encounters with other women. She had felt, towards the end of the relationship, as if she were totally inadequate and self-destructive and crazed, and she came away from the relationship with a terrible fear of her own mind's ability to torment her with irrational suspicions and to poison a committed relationship, and this added to the torment she felt about the obsessive worrying that she was now experiencing in her sexual relationship with her husband, a relationship that had also, at first, seemed to be more close and intimate and fulfilling than she could rationally believe she deserved, knowing about herself all (she believed) she did.

PART TWO. YEN4U

She once, as an adolescent, in an Interstate rest-stop women's room, on a wall, above and to the right of vending machines for tampons and feminine hygiene products, had seen, surrounded by the coarse declamations and crudely drawn genitalia and the simple and somehow plangent obscenities inscribed there in varied anonymous hands, standing out in both color and force, a single small red felt-tip block-capital rhyme,

> IN DAYS OF OLD
> WHEN MEN WERE BOLD
> AND WOMEN WEREN'T INVENTED
> THEY ALL DRILLED HOLES
> IN ROADSIDE POLES
> AND STOOD THERE QUITE
> CONTENTED[,]

tiny and precise and seeming somehow — via something about the tiny hand's precision against all that surrounding scrawl — less coarse or bitter than how simply sad, and had remembered it ever since, and sometimes thought of it, for no apparent reason, in the darkness of her marriage's immature years, although, to the best of her later recollection, the only real significance she had attached to the memory was that it was funny what stuck with you.

PART THREE. ADULT WORLD

Meanwhile, back in the present, the immature wife fell deeper and deeper inside herself and inside her worry and became more and more unhappy.

What changed everything and saved everything was that she had an epiphany. She had the epiphany three years and seven months into the marriage.

In secular psychodevelopmental terms, an epiphany is a sudden, life-changing realization, often one that catalyzes a person's emotional maturation. The person, in one blinding flash, 'grows up,' 'comes of age.' 'Put[s] away childish things.' Releases illusions gone moist and rank from a grip of years' duration. Becomes, for good or ill, a citizen of reality.

In reality, genuine epiphanies are extremely rare. In contemporary adult life, maturation and acquiescence to reality are gradual processes, incremental and often imperceptible, not unlike the formation of renal calculus. Modern usage usually deploys *epiphany* as a metaphor. It is usually only in dramatic representations, religious iconography, and the 'magical thinking' of children that achievement of insight is compressed to a sudden blinding flash.

What precipitated the young wife's sudden blinding epiphany was her abandonment of mentation in favor of concrete and frantic action.* She abruptly (within just hours of deciding) and frantically telephoned the ex-lover whom she'd formerly been in a committed relationship with, now by all accounts a successful associate manager at a local auto dealership, and implored him to agree to meet and talk with her. Placing this call was one of the most difficult, embarrassing things the wife (whose name was Jeni) had ever done. It appeared irrational and risked seeming totally inappropriate and disloyal: she was married, this was her former lover, they had not exchanged a word in almost five years, their relationship had ended badly. But she was in crisis — she feared, as she put it to the ex-lover over the telephone, for the soundness of her mind, and needed his help, and would, if necessary, beg for it. The former lover agreed to meet the wife for lunch at a fast food restaurant near the auto dealership the following day.

The crisis that had galvanized the wife, Jeni Roberts, into action was itself precipitated by nothing more than another of her bad dreams, albeit one that comprised a kind of compendium of many of the other bad dreams she'd suffered during the early years of her

---

* (In this, her epiphany accorded fully with the Western tradition, in which insight is the product of lived experience rather than mere thought.)

marriage. The dream was not itself the epiphany, but its effect was galvanic. The husband's car slowly passes his downtown firm and proceeds off down the street in a light rain, its YEN4U license plate receding, followed by Jeni Roberts' car. Then Jeni Roberts is driving on the heavy-flow expressway that circumscribes the city, trying desperately to catch up with the husband's car. Her wipers' beat matches that of her heart. She cannot see the car with its special personalized license plate anywhere up ahead but feels the particular special sort of anxious dream-certainty that it is there. In the dream, every other vehicle on the expressway is symbolically associated with emergency and crisis — all six lanes are filled with ambulances, police cars, paddywagons, fire engines, Highway Patrol cruisers, and emergency vehicles of every conceivable description, sirens all singing their heart-stopping arias and all their emergency lights activated and flashing in the rain so that Jeni Roberts feels as though her car is swimming in color. An ambulance directly in front of her will not let her by; it changes lanes whenever she does. The nameless anxiety of the dream is indescribably horrid — the wife, Jeni, feels she simply must (wiper) must (wiper) *must* catch the husband's car in order to avert some kind of crisis so horrible it has no name. A river of what looks to be sodden Kleenex flows windblown along the expressway's breakdown lane; Jeni's mouth feels full of raw hot sores; it is night and wet and the whole road swims with emergency colors — spanked pinks and slapped reds and the blue of critical asphyxia. It is when they are wet that you realize why they call Kleenex *tissue,* flowing by. The wipers match her urgent heart and the ambulance still, in the dream, will not let her pass; she slaps frantically at the steering wheel in desperation. And now in the window at the rear of the ambulance, as if in answer, appears a lone splayed hand at the glass, pressing and slapping at the glass, a hand reaching up from some sort of emergency stretcher or gurney and opening spiderishly out to stroke and slap and press whitely against the rear window's glass in full view of Jeni Roberts' Accord's retractable halogen headlights so that she sees the highly distinctive ring on the ring finger of the male hand splayed frantically against the emergency glass and screams (in the dream) in recognition and cuts hard left without signaling, cutting off various other emergency vehicles, to pull abreast of the ambulance and tell it to please stop because the stochastic husband she loves and must somehow catch up to is inside on a stretcher ceaselessly sneezing and slapping frantically at the window for someone he loves to catch up and help; but then (such is the dream's motive force that the wife actually *wets the bed,* she discovers on waking) and but then as she pulls abreast on the left of the ambulance and lowers her passenger window with the Accord's automatic feature in the rain and gesticulates for the ambulance driver to lower his own window so she can implore him to stop it's (in the dream) the *husband* driving the ambulance, it's his left profile at the wheel — which the wife has always somehow been able to tell he prefers to his right profile and customarily sleeps on his right side partly with this fact in mind, though they'd never spoken openly about the husband's possible insecurities about his right profile — and but then as the husband turns his face toward Jeni Roberts through the driver's window and lit-up rain as she gesticulates it seems to be both *him* and *not him,* her husband's familiar and much-loved face distorted and pulsed with red light and wearing a facial expression indescribable as anything other than: Obscene.

It was this look on the face that (slowly) turned left to look at her from the ambulance — a face that in the very most enuretic and disturbing way both *was* and *was not* the face of the husband she loved — that galvanized Jeni Roberts awake and prompted her to gather every bit of her nerve together and make the frantic humiliating call to the man she had once thought seriously of marrying, an associate sales manager and probationary Rotarian whose own facial asymmetry — he had suffered a serious childhood accident that subsequently caused the left half of his face to develop differently from the right side of his face; his left nostril was unusually large, and gaped, and his left eye, which appeared to be almost all iris, was surrounded by concentric rings and bags of slack flesh that constantly twitched and throbbed as irreversibly damaged nerves randomly fired — was what, Jeni had decided after their relationship foundered, had helped fuel her uncontrollable suspicion that he had a secret, impenetrable part to his character that fantasized about lovemaking with other women even while his healthy, perfectly symmetrical, and seemingly uninjurable thingie was inside her. The ex-lover's left eye also faced and scanned a markedly different direction than did his dextral, more normally developed eye, a feature that was somehow advantageous in his auto sales career, he tried to explain.

Galvanic crisis notwithstanding, Jeni Roberts felt awkward and very nearly mortified with embarrassment as she and the ex-lover met and selected their meal options and sat down together in a windowside booth of molded plastic and made radically incongruous small talk while she prepared to try to ask the question that would accidentally precipitate her epiphany and a whole new less innocent and self-deluded stage of her married life. She had decaf in a disposable cup and put in six prepackaged creamers as her former sexual partner sat with his entree's styrofoam box unopened and gazed both through the window and at her. He had a ring on his pinkiefinger and his sportcoat was unbuttoned, and the white shirt beneath the coat bore the distinctive furrows of an oxfordcloth dress shirt that had only recently been removed from its retail packaging. The sunlight through the big window was noon-colored and made the crowded franchise feel like a greenhouse; it was hard to breathe. The associate sales manager watched as she started the tops of the creamers with her teeth to safeguard her nails and removed them and placed them in the foil ashtray and dumped the thimblefuls of creamer into the disposable cup and stirred them in with a complimentary square-tipped stirrer one after another, the look in his developmentally appropriate eye the puddly look of nostalgia. She was still profligate with the creamer. She had both a wedding band and a diamond engagement ring, and the rock wasn't cheap by a long shot. The former lover's stomach hurt and eye-flesh ticced especially bad now because of how now they were in the dreaded last three bank days of the month and Mad Mike's Hyundai put unbelievable pressure on reps to move units in the last three days so they could go on that month's books and inflate the books for the clowns in the regional office. The young wife cleared her throat several times in her special way that the man solely responsible for the performance of all Mad Mike's reps remembered all too well, doing the dry nervous thing with her throat to communicate the fact that she recognized how inappropriate a question like this was going to appear now at this juncture, with them with their unhappy history and now no longer in any way even like marginally connected, and her happily married, and that she felt embarrassed but was also in some kind of she was saying genuine inner-crisis-type situation about something, and desperate — the way usually only serious credit problems made people look desperate and trapped like this — with her eyes with that drowning look in them of she was begging him not to take advantage of her desperate position in any way including judgment or ridicule at her expense. Plus and how she always drank her coffee with two hands around the cup even in a hot environs like this one here. Hyundai-U.S.'s volume, margins, and financing terms were among the countless economic conditions affected by fluctuations in the value of the yen and related Pacific currencies. The young wife had spent an hour at the mirror in order to choose the shapeless blouse and slacks she wore, actually taking her soft contacts back out in order to wear her glasses as well, and nothing on her face in the windowlight but a quick dab-and-blot of gloss. The expressway's heavy flow glittered through the window that lit up her right side with sun; and through the glass the Mad Mike's lot, with its plastic pennants and a man in a wheelchair with his wife or like nurse getting worked by fat Kidder in the hospital gown and arrow-through-head-prosthesis the reps all had to wear on the days Messerly was there to keep tabs, lay also within the divided purview of the booth's former lover — who still loved her, Jeni Ann Orzolek of Marketing 204, and not his current fiancée, he realized with the sickening wince of a mortal wound reopened — and just beyond it, shimmering in the heat, the Adult World lot, with its all makes and classes of vehicle day and night, moving them through like Mad Mike Messerly could only fantasize.

ADULT WORLD (II)

PART: 4
FORMAT: SCHEMA
TITLE: ONE FLESH

> 'As blindingly sudden and dramatic as any question about any
> man's sexual imagination is going to appear, it was not the ques-
> tion itself which caused Jeni Roberts' epiphany and rapid matura-
> tion, but what she found herself gazing at as she asked it.'
>
> — PT. 4 epigraph, in same stilted mode as 'Adult World
> (I)' [→ highlights format change from dramatic/stochastic
> to schematic/ordered]

1a. Question Jeni Roberts asks is whether Former Lover had indeed
in their past relationship ever fantasized about other women
during lovemaking w/ her.
> 1a(1) Inserted at beginning of question is participial phrase
> 'After apologizing for how irrational and inappropriate it
> might sound after all this time . . .'

1b. At some point during J.'s question, J. follows F.L.'s gaze out
fast-food window & sees husband's special vanity license plate
among vehicles in Adult World lot: → epiphany. Epiph un-
folds more or less independently as facially asymmetric F.L.
responds to J.'s question.

1c. Flat narr description of J.'s sudden pallor & inability to hold decaf steady as J. undergoes sddn blndng realization that hsbnd is

a Secret Compulsive Masturbator & that insomnia/yen is cover for secret trips to Adult World to purchase/view/masturbate self raw to XXX films & images & that suspicions of hsbnd's ambivalence about 'sexlife together' have in fact been prescient intuitions & that hsbnd has clearly been suffering from inner deficits/psychic pain of which J.'s own self-conscious anxieties have kept her from having any real idea [point of view (1c) all objective, exterior desc only].

2a. Meanwhile F.L. is answering J.'s orig question in vehement neg, tears appearing in eye: holy shit no, god, no, no, never, had loved her always, was never as fully *'there'* as when he & J. were making love [if in J.'s p.o.v., insert 'together' after 'love'].

  2a(1) At emotional height of dialogue, tears streaming down ½ face, F.L. confesses/declares that he still loves J., has all this time, 5 yrs, in fact sometimes still thinks of J. while making love to his current fiancée, which causes him to feel guilty (i.e. 'like I'm not really *there*') drng sex w/ fiancée. [Direct transcription of F.L.'s whole answer/confession → emotional focus of scene is off J. while J. undergoes trauma of sddnly realizing hsbnd is Secret Compulsive Masturbator → avoids nasty problem of trying to convey epiphany in narr expo.]

2b. Coincidence [N.B.: too heavy?]: F.L. confesses that he also still sometimes secretly masturbates to memories of former love-making w/ J., sometimes to point of making himself raw/sore. [→ F.L.'s 'confession' here both reinforcing J.'s epiph w/r/t male fantasy & providing her w/ much-needed injection of sexual esteem (i.e. it 'wasn't her fault'). [N.B. re Theme: implicit sadness of F.L. making soul-rending confession of love while J. is ½-distracted by trauma of (1b)/(1c)'s epiph; i.e. = further networks of misconnection, emotional asymmetry.]]

2b(1) Tone of F.L.'s confession trmndsly moving & high-affect, & J. (even tho traumatized w/r/t (1b)/(1c)'s shattering epiphany) never for one nanosec doubts the truth of what F.L. says; feels she 'really did know this man' & c.

    2b(1a) Narr {*not* J.} notes sudden appearance of red & demonic-looking gleam in hypertrophic iris of F.L.'s left ['bad'?] eye, which could be either trick of light or genuine demonic gleam [= p.o.v. shift/ narr intrusion].

2c. Mnwhile F.L., interpreting J.'s pallor & digital palsy as re-quital/positive response to his declarations of enduring love, begs her to leave hsbnd for him, or alternatively (*'at least'*) to proceed now to Holiday Inn just down the expressway & spend rest of afternoon making passionate love [→ w/ dmnc sinistral gleam & c.].

2d. J. (still gone 100% pale à la Dostoevsky's Nastasya F.) abruptly acquiesces w/r/t adulterous Holiday Inn interlude [tone flat = '"Mm, OK," she said.']. F.L. buses tray w/ uneaten entrée & empty cup & creamers & c., follows J. out into fast-food pkng lot. J. waits in Accord while F.L. attempts to sneak own Ford Probe [N.B.: too heavy?] out of M.M. Hyundai lot w/o Messerly or sales reps seeing him leave early on high-pressure end-of-month sales day.

    2d(1) J.'s precise mtvation for acquiescing to Holiday Inn in-terlude left opaque [→ entails that (2d) is in p.o.v. of F.L. only]. Comic dscrptn of F.L. crawling along row of vehicles on hands & knees in attempt to slip into Probe unseen from M.M. showroom has undercurrent of creepiness [→ congruence w/ subthemes of secrecy, creepy incongruity, opaque shame, 'crawliness'].

3a. J.'s Accord fllws F.L.'s Probe down xprswy toward Hday Inn. Sudden sun-shower forces J. to activate wipers.

3b. F.L. turns into Hday Inn lot, expects to see J.'s Accord turn in behind him. Accord does *not* turn in, continues down xprsway. [Abrupt p.o.v. change →] J., driving across town toward home, imagines F.L. leaping out of Probe & running dsprtly across Hday Inn lot in downpour to stand at roaring edge of xprsway & watch Accord recede, gradually disappearing in traffic. J. imagines F.L.'s wet/forlorn/asymm image dwndlng in rear-view mirror.

3c. Nearly home, J. finds herself weeping for F.L. & F.L.'s dwndlng image instead of for self. Weeps for hsbnd, '. . . how *lonely* his secrets must make him' [p.o.v.?]. Notes this & speculates on significance of 'weeping for' [= 'on behalf of'?] men. Bgning (3c), J.'s thoughts & spclations evince new sophistication/comprehension/maturity. Pulls into home's driveway feeling '[. . .] queerly exultant.'

3d. Narr intrusion, expo on Jeni Roberts [same flat & pedantic tone as ¶s 3, 4 of 'A.W.(I)' PT. 3]: While following F.L.'s teal/aqua Probe down xprsway, J. hadn't 'changed mind' about having secret adulterous sex w/ F.L., rather merely '. . . realized it was unnecessary.' Understands that she has had life-changing epiphany, has '. . . bec[o]me a woman as well as a wife' & c. & c.

 3d(1) J. hereafter referred to by narr as 'Ms. Jeni Orzolek Roberts'; hsbnd referred to as 'the Secret Compulsive Masturbator.'

4a(I) Epiloguous expo on J.O.R. → extension of narrative arc: 'Ms. Jeni Orzolek Roberts, from that day forward, kept the memory of her lover's desperate, ½-wet face faithfully shaped within her' & c. Realizes hsbnd has 'interior deficits' that '. . . ha[ve] nothing to do with her as a wife [/woman]' & c. Survives this aftershock of epiphany, + various other standard aftershocks.

[Possible mentn of psychotherapy, but now in upbeat terms: psychth now 'freely chosen' rather than 'straw dsprtly clutched at.'] J.O.R. establishes separate investment portfolio w/ substantial positions in gold futures & large-cap mining stock. Quits smoking w/ help of transdermal patches. Realizes/gradually accepts that hsbnd loves his secret loneliness & 'interior deficits' more than he loves [/is able to love] her; accepts her 'unalterable powerlessness' over hsbnd's secret cmplsions [possible mention of esoteric Support Group for spouses of S.C.M.'s — any such thing? 'MastAnon'? 'Co-Jack'? (N.B.: *avoid easy gags*)]. Realizes that true wellsprings of love, security, gratification must originate within self[*]; and w/ this realization, J.O.R. joins rest of adult hmn race, no longer 'full of herself'/'immature'/'irrational'/'young.'

4a(II) Marriage now enters new, more adult phase ['honeymoon over' an easy gag?]. Never once in sbsqnt yrs of marriage do J.O.R. & hsbnd discuss his S.C.M. or interior pain/loneliness/'deficits' [N.B.: hammer home fiduciary pun]. J.O.R. doesn't know whether hsbnd even suspects she knows about his S.C.M. or Discover charges at Adult World; she finds she does not care. J.O.R. reflects w/ amused irony on new 'significance' of persistent adlscnt memory of rest-stop graffito. Hsbnd [/'the S.C.M.'] continues to arise & leave master bdrm in wee hrs; sometimes J.O.R. hears his car start as she '. . . stirs only slightly and returns at once to sleep' & c. Ceases worrying w/r/t whether hsbnd enjoys 'sexlife' w/ her; continues to love [' '?] hsbnd even tho she no longer believes he's 'wonderful' [/'atten-

---

[*] [N.B.: narr tone here mxmly flat/affectless/distant/dry → no discernible endorsement of cliché.]

tive'?}] lvmking partner. Sex between them finds its own level; by 5th yr it's appr every 2 weeks. Their sex now characterized as 'nice' — less intense but also less scary [/'lonely']. J.O.R. ceases to search hsbnd's face drng sex [→ metaphor: Theme → eyes closed = 'eyes open'].

4a(II(1)) Taking 'authentic responsibility for self,' J.O.R. '. . . gradually begins exploring masturbation as a wellspring of personal pleasure' & c. Revisits Adult Wld svrl times; becomes almost a rglr. Purchases 2nd dildo [N.B.: 'dildo' now not captlzd], then 'Penetrator!!®' dildo w/ vibrator, later 'Pink Pistollero® Pistol-Grip Massager,' finally 'Scarlet Garden MX-1000® Vibrator with Clitoral Suction and Fully Electrified 12 Inch Cervical Stimulator' ['$179.99 retail']. Narr inserts that J.O.R.'s new dresser/vanity ensemble contains no sachet drawer. [Ironies: J.O.R.'s new hi-tech mastrbtory appliances are (a) manufactured in Asia & (b) displayed on Adult Wld wall labeled MARITAL AIDS (2 hvy/obvious?).] By marriage's 6th yr, hsbnd frqntly away on 'emergency trips to the Pacific Rim'; J.O.R. mastrbting almost daily.

4a(II(1a)) Narr intr, expo: J.O.R.'s most frequent/ pleasurable mastrbtion fantasy in 6th yr of marriage = a faceless, hypertrophic male figure who loves but cannot have J.O.R. spurns all other living women & chooses instead to mastrbte daily to fantasies of lvmking w/ J.O.R.

4a(III) Concl ¶: 7th, 8th yr: Hsbnd mastrbtes secretly, J.O.R. openly. Their now-bimonthly sex is '. . . both a submission to and celebration of certain freely embraced realities.' Neither appears to mind. Narr: binding them now is that deep & unspoken complicity that in adult marriage is covenant/love → 'They were now truly married, cleaved,** one flesh, [a union that] afforded Jeni O. Roberts a cool, steady joy. . . .'

4b. Concl [embed]: '. . . were ready thus to begin, in a calm and mutually respectful way, to discuss having children [together].'

** [/'cloven'? (*avoid ez gag*)]

THE DEVIL IS A BUSY MAN

Three weeks ago, I did a nice thing for someone. I can not say more than this, or it will empty what I did of any of its true, ultimate value. I can only say: a nice thing. In a general context, it involved money. It was not a matter of out and out "giving money" to someone. But it was close. It was more classifiable as "diverting" money to someone in "need." For me, this is as specific as I can be.

It was two weeks, six days, ago that the nice thing I did occurred. I can also mention that I was out of town — meaning, in other words, I was not where I live. Explaining why I was out of town, or where I was, or what the overall situation that was going on was, however, unfortunately, would endanger the value of what I did further. Thus, I was explicit with the lady that the person who would receive the money was to in no way know who had diverted it to them. Steps were explicitly taken so that my namelessness was structured into the arrangement which led to the diversion of the money. (Although the money was, technically, not mine, the secretive arrangement by which I diverted it was properly legal. This may lead one to wonder in what way the money was not "mine," but, unfortunately, I am unable to explain in detail. It is, however, true.) This is the reason. A lack of namelessness on my part would destroy the ultimate value of the nice act. Meaning, it would infect the "motivation" for my nice gesture — meaning, in other words, that part of my motivation for it would be, not generosity, but desiring gratitude, affection, and approval towards me to result.

Despairingly, this selfish motive would empty the nice gesture of any ultimate value, and cause me to once again fail in my efforts to be classifiable as a nice or "good" person.

Thus, I was very intransigent about the secrecy of my own name in the arrangement, and the lady, who was the only other person with any knowing part in the arrangement (she, because of her job, could be classified as "the instrument" of the diversion of the money) whatsoever, acquiesced, to the best of my knowledge, in full to this.

Two weeks, five days, later, one of the people I had done the nice thing for (the generous diversion of funds was to two people — more specifically, a common law married couple — but only one of them called) called, and said, "hello," and that did I, by any possible chance, know anything about who was responsible for _____ _____, because he just wanted to tell that person, "thank you!," and what a God-send this _____ dollars that came, seemingly, out of nowhere from the _____, was, etc.

Instantly, having cautiously rehearsed for such a possibility at great lengths, already, I said, coolly, and without emotion, "no," and that they were barking completely up the wrong tree for any knowledge on my part. Internally, however, I was almost dying with temptation. As everyone is well aware, it is so difficult to do something nice for someone and not want them, desperately, to know that the identity of the individual who did it for them was you, and to feel grateful and approving towards you, and to tell myriads of other people what you "did" for them, so that you can be widely acknowledged as a "good" person. Like the forces of darkness, evil, and hopelessness in the world at large itself, the temptation of this frequently can overwhelm resistance.

Therefore, impulsively, during the grateful, but inquisitive, call, unprescient of any danger, I said, after saying, very coolly, "no," and "the wrong tree," that, although I had no knowledge, I could well imagine that whoever, in fact, *was*, mysteriously responsible for _____ would be enthusiastic to know how the needed money, which they had received, was going to be utilized — meaning, for example, would they now plan to finally acquire health insurance for their new-born baby, or service the consumer debt in which they were deeply mired, or etc.?

My uttering this, however, was, in a fatal instant, interpreted by the person as an indirect hint from me that I was, despite my prior denials, indeed, the individual responsible for the generous, nice act, and he, throughout the remainder of the call, became lavish in his details on how the money would be applied to their specific needs, underlining what a God-send it was, with the tone of his voice's emotion transmitting both gratitude, approval, and something else (more specifically, something almost hostile, or embarrassed, or both, yet I can not describe the specific tone which brought this emotion to my attention adequately). This flood of emotion, on his part, caused me, sickeningly, too late, to realize, that what I had just done, during the call, was to not only let him know that I was the individual who was responsible for the generous gesture, but to make me do so in a subtle, sly manner that appeared to be, insinuationally, euphemistic, meaning, employing the euphemism: "whoever was responsible for _____," which, combined together with the interest I revealed in the money's "uses" by them, could fool no one about its implying of me as ultimately responsible, and had the effect, insidiously, of insinuating that, not only was I the one who had done such a generous, nice thing, but also, that I was so "nice" — meaning, in other words, "modest," "unselfish," or, "untempted by a desire for their gratitude" — a person, that I did not even want them to know that I was who was responsible. And I had, despairingly, in addition, given off these insinuations so "slyly," that not even I, until afterward — meaning, after the call was over —, knew what I had done. Thus, I showed an unconscious and, seemingly, natural, automatic ability to both deceive myself and other people, which, on the "motivational level," not only completely emptied the generous thing I tried to do of any true value, and caused me to fail, again, in my attempts to sincerely be what someone would classify as truly a "nice" or "good" person, but, despairingly, cast me in a light to myself which could only be classified as "dark," "evil," or "beyond hope of ever sincerely becoming good."

CHURCH NOT MADE WITH HANDS

(for E. Shofstahl, 1977–1987)

ART

Drawn lids one screen of skin, dreampaintings move across Day's colored dark. Tonight, in a lapse unfluttered by time, he travels what seems to be back. Shrinking, smoother, loses his belly and faint acne scars. Bird-boned gangle; bowl haircut and cup-handle ears; skin sucks hair, nose recedes into face; he swaddles in his pants and then curls, pink and mute and smaller until he feels himself split into something that wriggles and something that spins. Nothing stretches tight across everything else. A black point rotates. The point breaks open, jagged. His soul sails toward one color.

Birds, gray light. Day opens one eye. He is lying half off the bed Sarah breathes in. He sees the windows parallelograms, from the angle.

Day stands at a square window with a cup of something hot. A dead Cezanne does this August sunrise in any-angled smears of clouded red, a blue that darkles. A Berkshire's shadow retreats toward one blunt nipple: fire.

Sarah comes awake at the slightest touch. They lie open-eyed and silent, brightening under a sheet. Doves work the morning, sound from the belly. The sheet's printed pattern fades from Sarah's skin.

Sarah pins her hair for morning mass. Day packs another case for Esther. Dresses himself. He fails to find a shoe. On the big bed's edge, one shoe on, he watches cotton dust rotate through the butter-yellow columns of a morning that gets later.

BLACK ART

That day he buys them a janitor's broom. He sweeps rainwater off the tarp over Sarah's pool.

That night Sarah stays with Esther. Touches metal all night. Day sleeps alone.

Day stands at a black window in Sarah's bedroom. Over Massachusetts the sky is smeared with stars. The stars move slowly across the glass.

That day he goes to Esther with Sarah. Esther's bed's steel gleams in the bright room. Esther smiles dully as Day reads about giants.

"I am a giant," he reads:

"I am a giant, a mountain, a planet. Everything else is far off below. My footprints are counties, my shadow a time zone. I watch from high windows. I wash in high clouds."

"I am a giant," Esther tries to say.

Sarah, allergic, sneezes.

Day: "Yes."

BLACK AND WHITE

'All true art is music' (a different teacher). 'The visual arts are but one corner of true music's allcomprising room' (ibid.)

Music discloses itself as a relation between one key and two notes locked by the key in dance. Rhythm. And in Day's blown pre-dreams, too, music consumes all law: what is most solid discloses itself here as rhythms, nothing but. Rhythms are relations between what you believe and what you believed before.

The cleric appears tonight in monochrome and collar.

Bless me

Do you take this woman Sarah

To be my

How long

For I have

since your last confession to a body with the power to absolve.

Confession need

As I those who have swimmed against me

not entail absolution, lay bare, confession in the absence of awareness of sin,

Bless me father for there can be no awareness of sin without awareness of transgression without awareness of limit

Full of Grace

no such animal. Pray together for a revelation of limit

Red clouds in Warhol's coffee

arrange in yourself an awareness of.

ONE COLOR

That day he is back at work's first week. Sunlight reverses HEALTH pink through the windshield's sticker. Day drives the county car past a factory.

"Habla Espanol?" Eric Yang asks from the passenger's side.

Smoke from a smokestack hangs jagged as Day nods his head.

"You wanted to be shown ropes," Yang says. His eyes are closed as he rotates. "I'll show you a rope. Habla?"

"Yes," Day says. "Hablo."

They drive past homes.

Eric Yang's special talent is the mental rotation of three-dimensional objects.

"This case speaks only Spanish," Yang says. "Lady's son got him-self killed last month. In their apartment. Nasty. Sixteen. Gang thing, drug thing. Big area of the kid's blood on her kitchen floor."

They drive past hard hats and jackhammers.

"She says it's all she's got left of him!" Yang shouts. "She won't let us clean it up. She says it's him," he says.

Mental rotation is Yang's hobby. He is a certified counselor and caseworker.

"Your job today," Yang twirls an imaginary rope, lassoes some-thing mental on the dashboard, "is to get her to draw him. Even just the blood. Ndiawar said he didn't care which. Just so she has a picture he said. So we can maybe clean up the blood."

In the rearview, past himself, Day can see his case of supplies on the back seat. It's not supposed to be in the sun.

"Make her draw him," Yang says, releasing a rope Day can't see. Yang closes his eyes again. "I'm going to try to rotate this month's phone bill."

Day passes a white van. Its windows are tinted. Saucers of rust on the side.

"Today we see the poor lady who loves blood and the rich man who begs for time."

"Old teacher of mine. I told Ndiawar." Day checks his left. "Art teacher in a former life."

"The nuisance in the public, Ndiawar calls him," Yang says. He furrows, concentrating. "I'm rotating the duty log. We're going to go right by him. He's right on the way. But he's not first on the log."

"He was a teacher of mine," Day says again. "I had him in school."

"We go by the log."

"He influenced me. My work."

They pass a dry lot.

ART

Tonight, at the window, under stars that refuse to move, Day nearly makes it and dreampaints awake.

He paints it so that he's standing on the pool's baggy tarpaulin when he rises into the lunchtime sky. He ascends without weight, neither pulled from above nor pushed from below, one perfect line to a point in the sky overhead. Mountains sit blunt, humidity curls in the valleys like gauze. Holyoke and then Springfield and Chicopee and Longmeadow and Hadley are dull misshapen coins.

Day rises into the sky. The air gets more and more blue. Something in the sky blinks, and he's gone.

"Colors," he says to the screen's black lattice.

The screen breathes mint.

"She complains I turn colors in my sleep," Day says.

"Something understands," breathes the screen, "surely."

Knees sore, Day jangles pockets with his hands. So many coins.

TWO COLORS

Blue-eyed behind his County Mental Health Director's desk, Dr. Ndiawár is a darkly bald man of vague alien status. He likes to make a steeple with his hands and to look at it while he speaks.

"You paint," he says. "As a student, there was sculpture. You took psychology." He looks up. "In large amounts? You speak languages?"

Day's slow nod produces a dot of reflected office light on Ndiawar's scalp. Day births the dot and kills it. The Director's desk is large and strangely clean. Day's c.v. looks tiny against its expanse.

"There are doubts," Ndiawar says, "which I have in my mind." He broadens the hands' angle slightly. "There is not money in it."

Day gives the dot two brief lives.

"However you state there are independent means, through marriage, for you."

"And shows," Day says quietly. "Sales." A scarlet lie.

"You sell art you make in the past, you have stated," Ndiawar says.

Eric Yang is tall, late twenties, with long hair and muddy eyes that close and open instead of blink.

Day shakes Yang's hand. "How do you do."

"Surprisingly well."

Ndiawar is bent to an open drawer. "Your new art therapy person," he says to Yang.

Yang looks Day in the eye. "Look, man," he says. "I rotate three-dimension objects. Mentally."

"You and you, part-time, become a field team who travel cross-ward throughout the county and environs," Ndiawar reads to Day from something prepared. Both hands hold the page. "Yang is senior as, together, you visit the shut-ins. The very badly off. The no room for them here."

"It's a talent I have," Yang says, combing his bangs with four fingers. "I close my eyes and form a perfect detailed image of any object. From any angle. Then I rotate it."

"You visit the prepared log's schedule of shut-ins," Ndiawar reads. "Yang, who is senior, counsels these badly off people, while you encourage them, through skill, to express disordered feelings through artistic acts."

"I can see textures and imperfections and the play of light and shadow on the objects I rotate, too," Yang says. He is making small hand gestures that do not seem to signify anything in particular. "It's a very private talent." He looks to Ndiawar. "I just want to be up front with the guy."

Dr. Ndiawar ignores Yang. "Influencing them to direct aberrant or dysfunctioning affect onto things which they artistically make," he reads in a monotone. "On objects which cannot be harmed. This is a field-model of intervention. Such as clay, which as an object is good."

"I'm practically an MD," Yang says, tamping a cigarette on his knuckle.

The steeple reappears as Ndiawar leans back. "Yang is a case-worker who consumes medication. However he is cheap, and has in that chest of his a good heart . . ."

Yang stares at the Director. "What medication?"

". . . which goes out toward others."

Day stands. "I need to know when I start."

Ndiawar extends both hands. "Buy clay."

Sarah walks Day to the pool on the night before Esther gets hurt. She asks Day to touch water that's lit from below by lamps in the tile. He can see the center drain and what it does to the water around it. The water is so blue it even feels blue, he says.

She asks him to immerse himself in the shallow end.

Day and Sarah have sex in the shallow end of Sarah's childhood home's blue pool. Sarah around him is warm water in cold water. Day has his orgasm inside her. The drain outlet slaps and gurgles. Sarah begins to have her orgasm, her lids flutter, Day tries with wet fingers to hold her lids open, she hanging on to him, back ramming against the tiled side with a rhythmic lisping sound, whispering, "Oh."

FOUR COLORS

"I don't know who Soutine is," Yang says as they drive away from the home of the lady who speaks only Spanish. "You thought it looked like Soutine?"

The car's color is a noncolor, neither brown nor green. Day's seen nothing like it. He wipes sweat from his face. "It did." His supply case is in the back under a steel bucket. A mophandle rattles against the bucket. Sarah paid for the case and supplies.

Yang hits the dashboard's top. The air conditioner grinds out a smell of must. The car's heat is intense.

"Do the phone bill," Day says, falling in behind a city bus hairy with spraypaint. The bus's fumes are sweet.

Yang rolls down his window and lights a cigarette. The sunlight makes his exhalation pale.

"Ndiawar told me about your wife's little girl. I'm sorry about that crack about a vacation your first week here. I'm sorry I didn't know."

Day can see Yang's profile out of the corner. "I've always liked the blue of a phone bill."

The air conditioner begins to work against its own smell.

Yang has very black hair and a thin wool tie and eyes the color of trout. He closes them. "Now I've got the phone bill folded into a triangle. But one side doesn't quite come down and meet the base. But it's still a triangle. An order-in-chaos type of thing."

Day sees something yellow by the road.

"Eric?"

"The bill's got a tiny rip in the right leg of the triangle," Yang says, "and it's for sixty dollars. The rip is tiny and white and sort of hairy. That must be the paper's fibers or something."

Day guns to pass a pickup full of chickens. A spray of corn and feathers.

"I'm rotating the rip out of sight," Yang whispers. The side of his face breaks into crescents. "Now there's nothing but phone-bill blue."

There's a horn and the tug of a swerve.

Yang opens his eyes. "Whoa."

"Sorry."

They drive past some dark buildings with no glass in the windows. A dirty boy throws a tennis ball at a wall.

"I hope they," Yang is saying.

"What?"

"Catch the drunk driver."

Day looks over at Yang.

Yang looks at him. "The one who hit your little girl."

"What driver?"

"I just hope they catch the bastard."

Day looks at the windshield. "Esther had an accident in the pool."

"You guys have a pool?"

"My wife does. There was an accident. Esther got hurt."

"Ndiawar told me she got hit."

"The drain outlet got blocked. The drain's suction sucked her under."

"Jesus Christ."

"She was under a long time."

"Am I sorry."

"I can't swim."

"Jesus."

"I could see her very clearly. The pool's very clear."

"Ndiawar said you said the driver was drunk."

"She's still in the hospital. There's going to be brain damage."

Yang is looking at him. "Should you even be here today?"

Day cranes to see street signs. They're stopped at a light. "Which way."

Yang looks at the log book attached to the visor. Its rubber band was once green. Points.

VERY HIGH

The brushstrokes of the best-dreamt work, too, are visible as rhythms. This day's painting discloses its rhythms against a terrain in which light is susceptible to the influences of the wind. This is a wind that blows hard and inconstant across the school's campus, whistles against the De Chirico belltower from which it has scoured all shadow. This is a terrain in which there are alternating lulls and gusts of light. In which open spaces flash like diseased nerves and bent trees hang with a viscous aura that settles to set the grass on willemite fire, in which windrows of light pile up against fence-bottoms, walls, and undulate and glow. The belltower's sharp edges shiver gusts into spectra. Tall boys in blazers move knifelike through a parting shine with sketchbooks held eye-level; their shadows flee before them. The scintillant winds lull and gather, seem to coil, then brawl and whistle and strobe and strike to break faint pink through the Hall of Art's rose window. Day's sketched notes light up. On the machinelit screens at the front, two slides of the same thing project the frail and palmate shadow of the art professor at the podium, a dry old Jesuit hissing his s's into the illwired mike, reading a lecture to a hall half full of boys. His shadow is insectile against Vermeer's colored Delft as he feels at his eyes.

The withered priest reads his lecture about Vermeer and limpidity and luminosity and about light as attachment/vestment to objects' contour. Died 1675. Obscure in his time you see for painted very few. But now we know do we not, ahm. Blue-yellow hues predominate as against ahm shall we say de Hooch. The students wear blue blazers. Unparalleled representation light serves subtly to glorify God. Ahm, though some might say blaspheme. You see. Do you not see it. A notoriously dull lecturer. An immortality conferred upon implicit in the viewer. Do you ahm see it. 'The beautiful terrible stillness of Delft' in the seminal phrase of. The hall is dark behind Day's glowing row. The boys are permitted some personal expression in choice of necktie. The irreal evenness of focus which transforms the painting into what glass in glass's fondest dreams might wish to be. 'Windows onto interiors in which all conflicts have been resolved' in the much-referenced words of. All lit and rendered razor-clear you see and ahm. It meets TuTh after lunch and mail call. Resolving conflict, both organic and divine. Flesh and spirit. Day hears an envelope ripped open. The viewer sees as God sees, in other ahm. Lit up throughout time you see. Past time. Someone snaps gum. Whispered laughter somewhere up in a rear row. The hall is dimly lit. A boy off to Day's left groans and thrashes in a deep sleep. The teacher is, it is true, wholly dry, out of it, unalive. The boy next to Day is taking a deep interest in that part of his wrist which surrounds his watch.

The art professor is a sixty-year-old virgin in black and white who reads in a monotone about how one Dutchman's particular brushstrokes kill death and time in Delft. Well-barbered heads turn obliquely to see the angle of the clock's flashing hands. The notorious eternity of the Jesuit's lectures. The clock is against the back wall, between windows with theater shades that bump the glass with each gust.

Thin blotchy Day can see how it's the angle of the bright breeze against the screen that makes the wet face atop the priest's lit shadow glow. Big jelly tears shine above the old man's typed lecture. Day watches a teardrop move into another teardrop on the art teacher's cheek. The professor reads on about the use of four-colored hue in the river's sun's reflection in Delft, Holland. The two drops merge, pick up speed along the jaw, head for the text.

FOUR WINDOWS

And now in the starlit painting's third istoria the priest is truly old. Teacher in a former life. He kneels in the brittle field at the limit of an industrial park. His palms are together in an attitude of antique piety: a patron's pose. Day, who's failed twice, is somewhat outside the three-sided figure the field's other figures form. Cicadas scream in the dry weeds. The weeds a dead yellow and their shadows' lengths and angles make no sense; the August sun has a mind of its own.

"One faces . . . ," Ndiawar of the blinding head reads from a prepared memo in the sun. Yang shields his cigarette from a breeze.

". . . confinement as a natural consequence of behaving in manners which, toward others, are aberrant," Ndiawar reads.

The small white planet on a stalk Day sees is a dandelion gone to seed.

Yang sits tangent to the knelt shadow with his legs crossed, smoking. His T-shirt says ASK ME ABOUT MY INVISIBLE ENE-MIES. He combs at himself with a hand. "It's a question of venue, Sir," he says. "Out here like this, it becomes a public question. Am I right Dr. Ndiawar."

"Inform him a community of other persons is no vacuum."

"You're not in a vacuum here, Sir," Yang says.

"Rights exist in a state of tension. Rights necessarily tense." Ndiawar is skimming.

Yang buries a butt. "Here's the thing, Sir, Father if I may. You want to pray to a picture of yourself praying, that is okay. That is fine. That is your right. Except just not where other people have to watch you do it. Other people with their own rights to not have to see it against their will, which disturbs them. Isn't that pretty reasonable?"

Day is watching the exchange over his lollipop of snow. The canvas stands nailed to a weighted easel in the field. Its quadrate shadow distorted. The former Jesuit teacher of art kneels, in the painting.

"One faces" — Ndiawar — "additional confinement as a consequence of standing publicly on streets' corners to ask passersby for the gift of minutes from their day."

"Just one."

"There exists no right to accost, disturb, or solicit the innocent."

Yang has no shadow.

"One minute," says the art professor in the weighted painting. "Surely you can spare one minute."

"The venue plus the solicitation is going to equal confinement, Sir," Yang says.

"To accost and force to look at — these passersby are the innocents, tell him."

"I'll take any time you can spare. Name your time."

"To be a shut-in once more. Ask him if he liked it. Remind him of the term conditional release."

"A vacuum is one thing," Yang says, looking briefly over his shoulder in signal to Day. "Just not on the streets." Even though Day is not behind him.

The Director is replacing the memo in a cardboard portfolio. A hint of the steeple as he surveys the field. The Jesuit's eyes never leave his easel's square. Because the canvas is the viewer's point of access to the dreampainting, the as it were window onto the scene, his eyes are thus on Day's, a tiny dead seeded globe between them. The perspective makes no sense. Ndiawar's headless shadow is now over Day, over the white seeded ball, he sees. "Skills are required," Ndiawar says, "badly."

A mind of its own.

Day's own breath breaks the ball apart.

LIMIT

Esther's head is wrapped in gauze. Day's head is inclined over a page. Sarah's head is in the pastor's lap in the room's bright corner. The room is white. The cleric's head is thrown back, eyes on the ceiling.

"I'm sorry," Sarah's head says to the black lap. "The phone. The outlet. The drain. The suction. She turns white and he turns colors. I apologize."

"Though giants," Day is reading aloud. "Though giants come in just one size, they come in many forms. There are the Greek Cyclops and the French Pantagruel and the American Bunyan. There are wide and multicultural cycles that have giants as columns of flame, as clouds with legs, as mountains that walk inverted while the whole world sleeps."

"No, *I* apologize," says the pastor's head. A white hand strokes Sarah's pinned hair.

"There are red-hot giants, warm giants," Day reads. "There are also cold giants. These are forms. One form of cold giant is described in cycles as a mile-high skeleton made all of colored glass. The glass giant lives in a forest that is pure white with frost."

"Cold giants."

"After you," Sarah whispers, opening the door to Esther's room.

"It is this forest's master."

The head above black and white smiles. "After *you*."

"The glass giant's stride is a mile across. All day every day it strides. It never stops. It cannot rest. For it lives in fear of its frozen forest ever melting. This fear keeps it striding every minute."

"Won't sleep," Esther says.

"Yes never sleeping, the glass giant strides through the white forest, its stride a mile across, day and night, and the heat of its stride melts the forest behind it."

Esther tries to smile at the closing door. Her gauze is spotless. "The rainbow."

"Yes." Day shows the picture. "The melted forest rains, and the glass giant is the rainbow. This is the cycle."

"Melted are rain."

Sarah sneezes, muffled, out in the hall. Day waits for the cleric to say it.

CLOSE THEM

"Time your breathing," the desiccant and truly old former Jesuit instructs him. Yang and Ndiawar stand in the foam at the edge of the field's blue sea.

"Breathe air," the art professor says, pantomiming the stroke. "Spit water. A rhythm. In. Out."

Day imitates the stroke.

Eric Yang closes his eyes. "The rip in the bill is back."

The dreampainting of the teacher in ceaseless prayer stands nailed to the weighted display. The wind rises; dandelions snow up around them. Bees work the field's yellow against a growing blue.

"Breathe in from above. Breathe out from below," the old man instructs. "The crawl."

The dry field is an island. The blue water all around is peppered white with dry islands. Esther lies on a thin clean steel bed on the next island. Water moves in the channel between them.

Day imitates the stroke. His pronated hands bat down white seed. A plant has sprouted in no time. Its spire already reaches Day's knees.

Yang speaks to Ndiawar about the texture of the mental bill. Ndiawar complains to Yang that his one best church leaves no hand free to open the door. The symbolism of the interchange is unmistakable.

The art teacher has backstroked away from the fluttered growth of the black plant. Day flails in the pollen, trying to establish a rhythm.

Sarah floats supine in the channel before Esther's island. Then the plant's shadow shuts down the light. The shadow is the biggest thing Day has ever seen. Its facade heaves out of sight, summons the prefix bronto-. The ground booms under the weight of a buttress. The buttress curves upward out of sight toward the facade. A rose window glints at the sky's upper limit. The easel falls over. The doors of the thing have come out of nowhere, writhing like lips. It rushes at them.

"Help!" Esther calls, very faint, before the picture's church takes them inside. Day hears the distant groan of continued growth. The unconstructed church is dim, lit only through colored glass. Its doors have rushed on behind them, out of sight.

The rose window continues to rise. It is round and red. Refracting spikes radiate. Inside the window a sad woman tries to smile her way out of the glass.

Day still pantomimes the crawl, the only stroke he knows.

The window lets light through and nothing else, colors it.

"Close the eyes which are in your head," comes Ndiawar's wooden echo.

Yang faces the nave. "Close them."

Barrel vaults darkle above the rose. The window reverses all normal disclosure — everything solid is here black, all that is light is brilliant color. Day, on the inbreath, can see its shape. The color tapers up from the window, narrows to a refracting spike, its tip a dark point. Something in white revolves around it.

Day crawlstrokes for the pointed tip, ascending without weight.

The defrocked professor of art puts Day's waterproof watch on the altar. Kneels to it, blaspheming.

Esther floats gauzed in the dark point atop the sharpshaped color of the red rose window. Day sees the point through the wet starred curtain his arms have drawn. The air's blue looks black, he swims through the curtain, stars rain upward from his arms' strokes. He pantomimes the crawlstroke through the stars. He can see her clearly, revolving.

"Don't look!"

And again it is when he looks below him that he fails. Wanting only to see whence he'd risen. The merest second — less — it takes for it all to come down. It starts at the apsis. East rushes west and the west's facade can't take it, crumbling. The walls seem to shrug as they come down on themselves. The black point on the red spike cracks open. Esther spins wriggling between its jagged halves, falling toward the rose window even as the window tilts. It's all photo-clear. Yang says Whoa. The buttress bows outward and shears. Her fall takes time. Her body rotates slowly through the air, trails a gauze comet. The rose rushes up at her. A mile-high man could catch and cup her among the falling stars; the gauze would follow. It is Day's failed breath that turns him blue. The blood-colored pane holds the mother inside, awaiting the child to set her free.

There is the sound of impact at a great glass height: terrible, multihued.

ROTATE

The sky is an eye.

The dusk and the dawn are the blood that feeds the eye.

The night is the eye's drawn lid.

Each day the lid again comes open, disclosing blood, and the blue iris of a prone giant.

YET ANOTHER EXAMPLE OF
THE POROUSNESS OF CERTAIN BORDERS (VI)

RECONSTRUCTED TRANSCRIPT OF
MR. WALTER D. ("WALT") DELASANDRO JR.'S
PARENTS' MARRIAGE'S END, MAY 1956

"Don't love you no more."

"Right back at you."

"Divorce your ass."

"Suits me."

"Except now what about the doublewide."

"I get the truck is all I know."

"You're saying I get the doublewide you get the truck."

"All I'm saying is that truck out there's mine."

"Then what about the boy."

"For the truck you mean?"

"You mean you'd want him?"

"You mean otherwise?"

"I'm asking are you saying you'd want him."

"You're saying you'd want him then."

"Look I get the doublewide you get the truck we flip for the boy."

"That's what you're saying?"

"Right here and now we flip for him."

"Let's see it."

"For Christ's sake it's just a quarter."

"Just let's see it."

"Jesus here then."

"All right then."

"I flip you call?"

"Hows about you flip I call?"

"Quit screwing around."

BRIEF INTERVIEWS
WITH HIDEOUS MEN

B.I. #59 04-98

HAROLD R. AND PHYLLIS N. ENGMAN INSTITUTE

FOR CONTINUING CARE

EASTCHESTER NY

'As a child, I watched a great deal of American television. No matter of where my father was being posted, it seemed always that American television was available, with its glorious and powerful women performers. Perhaps this was one more advantage of the importance of my father's work to the defenses of the state, for we had privileges and lived comfortably. The television program I most preferred then was to watch *Bewitched,* featuring the American performer Elizabeth Montgomery. It was as a child, while watching this television program, that I experienced my first erotic sensations. It was not for several years, until late in my adolescence, that I was able, however, to trace my sensations and fantasies backward to these episodes of *Bewitched* and my experiences as the viewer when the protagonist, Elizabeth Montgomery, would perform a circular motion with her hand, accompanied by the sound of a zither or harp, and produce a supernatural effect in which all motion ceased and all the television program's other characters suddenly were frozen in mid-gesture and were oblivious and rigid, lacking all animation. In these instances time itself appeared to cease, leaving Elizabeth Montgomery free alone to maneuver at her will. Elizabeth

Montgomery employed this circular gesture within the program only as a desperate resort to help save her industrialist husband, Darion, from the political disasters which would come if she were exposed as a sorcerer, a frequent threat in the episodes. The program of *Bewitched* was poorly dubbed, and many details of the narratives I, at my age, did not understand. Yet my fascinations were attached to this great power to freeze the time of the program in its tracks, and to render all the other witnesses frozen and oblivious while she went about her rescue tactics among living statues whom she could again reanimate with the circular gesture when the circumstances called for this. Years later, I began, like many adolescent boys, to masturbate, creating erotic fantasies of my own construction in my imagination as I did so. I was a weak, unathletic, and somewhat sickly adolescent, a scholarly and dreamy youth more like my father, of nervous constitution and little confidence or social outgoingness in those years. It is little wonder that I sought compensation for these weaknesses in erotic fantasies in which I possessed supernatural powers over the women of my choosing in these fantasies. Linked heavily to this childhood program of *Bewitched,* these masturbation fantasies' connection to this television program were unknown to me. I had forgotten this. Yet, I learned too well the insupportable responsibilities which come along with power, responsibilities whose awesomeness I have since learned to decline in my adult life since arriving here, which is a story for another time. These masturbation fantasies took their setting from the settings of our actual existences during these times, which were located at the many different military posts to which my father, a great mathematician, brought us, his family, along. My brother and I, separated in age by less than one year, were nevertheless dissimilar in most things. Often, my masturbation fantasies took their settings from the State Exercise Facilities which my mother, a former competitive athlete in youth, religiously attended, exercising enthusiastically each afternoon no matter of where my father's duties brought us to live for that time. Willingly accompanying her to these facilities on most afternoons of our lives was my brother, an athletic and vigorous person, and often myself as well, at first with reluctance and direct force, and then, as my erotic reveries set there evolved and became more complex and powerful, with a willingness born of reasons of my own. By custom, I was permitted to bring my science books, and sat reading quietly upon a padded bench in a corner of the State Exercise Facility while my brother and mother performed their exercises. For purposes of envisioning, you may imagine these State Exercise Facilities as your nation's health spa of today, although the equipment used there was less varied and maintained, and an air of heightened security and seriousness was due to the military posts to which the facilities were attached for the uses of personnel. And the athletic clothing of women at the State Exercise Facilities was very different from today, constituting full suits of canvas with belts and straps of leather not unlike this, which was far less revealing than today's exercise clothing and leaving more to the mind's eye. Now I will describe the fantasy which evolved at these facilities as a youth and became my masturbation fantasy of those years. You are not offended by this word, *masturbate?*'

Q.

'And this is an adequate pronunciation of it?'

Q.

'In the fantasy which I am describing, I would envision myself on such an afternoon at the State Exercise Facilities, and, as I masturbated, I envision myself gazing out across the floor of vigorous exercises to let my gaze fall upon an attractive, sensual, but vigorous and athletic and so highly concentrated on her exercises as to appear unfriendly woman, often resembling many of the attractive, vigorous, humorless young women of the military or civilian atomic engineering services who possessed access to these facilities and exercised with the same forbidding seriousness and intensity as my mother and my brother, who spent long periods of their time often hurling a heavy leather medicine ball between them with extreme force. But in my masturbation fantasy, the supernatural power of my gaze would rattle the chosen woman's attention, and she would look up from her piece of exercise equipment, gazing around the facility for the source of the irresistible erotic power which had penetrated her consciousness, finally her gaze locating me in my corner across the activity-filled room, such that the object of my gaze and I locked both eyes in a gaze of strong erotic attraction to which the remainder of the vigorously exercising personnel in the room were oblivious. For you see, in the masturbation fantasy I possess a supernatural power, a power of the mind, of which the origin and mechanics are never elaborated, remaining mysterious even to I who possess this secret power and can employ it at my will, a power through which a certain expressive, highly concentrated gaze on my part, directed at the woman who was the object of it, renders her irresistibly attracted toward me. The sexual component of the fantasy, as I masturbate, proceeds to depict this chosen woman and myself copulating in variations of sexual frenzy upon an exercise mat in the room's center. There is little more to these components of this fantasy, which are sexual and adolescent and, in retrospect, somewhat average, I now realize. I have not yet explained the origins of the American program of *Bewitched* of my early youth for these fantasies of seduction. Nor of the great secondary power which I also possess in the masturbation fantasy, the supernatural power to halt time and magically to freeze all other of the room's exercisers in their tracks with a covert circular motion of my hand, to cause all motion and activity in the State Exercise Facility to cease. You must envision these: heavily muscled missile officers held motionless beneath the barbell of a lift, wrestling navigators frozen complexly together, computer technicians' whirling jump ropes frozen into parabolas of all angle, and the medicine ball hanging frozen between the outstretched arms of my brother and my mother. They and all other witnesses in the exercise room are rendered with but one gesture of my will petrified and insensate, such that the attractive, bewitched, overpowered woman of my choice and myself only remain animated and aware in this dim wooden room with its odors of liniment and unwashed sweating in which now all time has ceased — the seduction occurs outside of the time and movement of the most very basic physics — and as I beckon her to me with a powerful gaze and perhaps as well a slight circular motion of just one finger, and she, overpowered with erotic attraction, comes toward me, I also in turn arise from my bench in the corner and come also toward her as well, until, as in a formal minuet, the woman of the fantasy and I both meet together upon the exercise mat at the room's exact center, she removing the straps of her heavy clothing with a frenzy of sexual mania while my schoolboy's uniform is removed with a more controlled and amused deliberation, forcing her to wait in an agony of erotic need. To compress the matters, then there is copulation in varied indistinct positions and ways among the many other petrified, unseeing figures for whom I have stopped time with my hand's great power. Of course, it is here you may observe this linkage with the program of *Bewitched* of my childhood sensations. For this additional power, within the fantasy, to freeze living bodies and halt time in the State Exercise Facility, which began merely as a logistical contrivance, became swiftly I think the primary fuel source of the entire masturbation fantasy, a masturbation fantasy which was, as any onlooker can easily be able to tell, a fantasy much more of power than merely of copulation. By this I am saying that envisioning my own great powers — over citizens' wills and motion, over the flowing of time, the frozen obliviousness of witnesses, over whether my brother and my mother even may move the robust bodies of which they were so justly proud and vain — soon these formed the true nucleus of the fantasy's power, and it was, unknown to me, to fantasies of this power that I was more truly masturbating. I understand this now. In my youth I did not. I knew, as an adolescent, only that the sustaining of this fantasy of overpowering seduction and copulation required some strict logical plausibility. I am saying in order to masturbate successfully, the scene required a rational logic by which copulation with this exercising woman is plausible in the public of the State Exercise Facility. I was responsible to this logic.'

Q.

'This may appear so outlandish, of course, from the perspective of how little logic is in envisioning a sickly youth causing sexual desire with only a hand's motion. I have really no answer for this. The hand's supernatural power was perhaps the fantasy's First Premise or *aksioma,* itself unquestioned, from which all else then must rationally derive and cohere. Here, you must say I think *First Premise.* And all must cohere from this, for I was the son of a great figure of state science, thus if once a logical inconsistency in the fantasy's setting occurred to me, it demanded a resolution consistent with the enframing logic of the hand's powers, and I was responsible for this. If not, I found myself distracted by nagging thoughts of the inconsistency, and was unable to masturbate. This is following for you? By this I am saying, what began only as a childish fantasy of unlimited power became a series of problems, complications, inconsistencies, and the responsibilities to erect working, internally consistent solutions to these. It was these responsibilities which swiftly expanded to become too insupportable even within fantasy to permit me ever to exercise again true power of any type, hence placing me in the circumstances which you see all too plainly here.'

Q.

'The true problem begins for me in soon recognizing that the State Exercise Facility is in truth public, open to all those of the post's personnel with proper documentation desiring to exercise; therefore, some person at any time could with ease stride into the facility in the midst of the hand's seduction, witnessing this copulation amidst a surreal scene of frozen, insensate athletics. To me this was not acceptable.'

Q.

'Not because of so much anxiety at being caught or exposed, which had been the concerns of Elizabeth Montgomery in the program, but for myself more because this represented a loose thread in the tapestry of power which the masturbation fantasy, of course, represented. It seemed ridiculous that I, whose circular hand's gesture's power over the facility's physics and sexuality was so total, should suffer interruption at the hands of any random military person who wanders in from outside wishing to perform calisthenics. This was the first-stage indication that the metaphysical powers of my hand were, though supernatural, nevertheless too limited. A yet more serious inconsistency occurred to me soon in the fantasy, as well. For the immobile, oblivious personnel of the exercise room — when the woman of my choice under my power and myself had now satiated one another, and dressed, and returned to our two positions across the wide facility from one another, with she, her, recalling now of the interval now only a vague but powerful erotic attraction toward the pale boy reading across the room, which would permit the sexual relation to occur again at whatever future time I would choose, and I then performed the reversed second hand gesture which permitted time and conscious motion in the facility to again begin — the now resumed personnel in the midst of their exercises would, I realized, merely by glancing at their wristwatches, then they would be made aware that an inexplicable amount of time had passed. They would, therefore, be, in truth, not truly oblivious that something unusual had occurred. For instance, both my brother and our mother wore Pobyeda wristwatches. All witnesses were not truly *oblivious*. This inconsistency was unacceptable in the fantasy's logic of total power, and soon made successful masturbation to envisioning it impossible. Here you must say *distraction*. But it was more, yes?'

Q.

'Expanding the hand's imagined powers to stop all clocks, time-pieces, and wristwatches in this room was the initial solution, until the nagging realization occurred that, just at the moment the room's personnel, afterward, left the State Exercise Facility and reentered the external flow of the military post outside, any first glance at some other clock — or, for example, the remonstrance of an appointment with a superior for which they were too late — this nevertheless would once again bring them to realize that *something* strange and inexplicable had taken place, which once again compromised the premise that all are *oblivious*. This, I naggingly concluded, was the fantasy's more serious inconsistency. Despite my circular gesture and the brief harp which accompanied its power, I had not, as I had naively at the outset believed, caused time's flow to cease and taken myself and the bewitched, athletic women out of time's physics. Trying to masturbate, I was agitated that my fantasy's power had in reality succeeded only in halting the superficial *appearance* of time, and then only within the limited arena of the fantasy's State Exercise Facility. It was at this time that the imaginative labor of this fantasy of power became exponentially more difficult. For, within the enframing logic of the fantasy's power, I now required this circular hand's gesture to halt all time and freeze all personnel upon the entire military post of which the exercise facility was a part. The logic of this need was clear. But also it was incomplete.'

Q.

'Excellent, yes. You see where this is now heading for, this logical problem whose circumference will continue expanding as each solution discloses further inconsistencies and further needs for the exercise of my fantasy's powers. For, yes, because the posts to which my father's duties to the computers brought us along were in strategic communication with the entire defense apparatus of the state, thus I soon was required to fantasize that only my one single hand's gesture — taking place in only one bleak Siberian defense outpost, and for the sake of entrancing the will of merely one female programmer or clerical aide — nevertheless now must accomplish the instantaneous freezing of the entire state, to suspend in time and consciousness almost two hundred million citizens in the midst of whatever of their actions might happen to intrude upon my imaginations, actions as diverse as peeling an apple, traversing an intersection, mending a boot, interring a child's casket, plotting a trajectory, copulating, removing new-milled steel from an industrial forge, and so forth, unending and numberless sep—'

Q.

'Yes yes and because the state itself existed in close ideological and defensive alliance with many neighboring satellite states, and, of course, also was in communication and trade with countless other of the world's nations, I all too quickly, as an adolescent, trying merely to masturbate in private, found out that my single fantasy of unknown seduction outside time required that the very world's entire population itself must be frozen by the single hand's gesture, all of the entire world's timepieces and activities, from the activities of yam farming in Nigeria to those of affluent Westerners purchasing blue jeans and Rock and Roll, on, on . . . and you see of course yes not merely all human motion and time-measurings but of course the very movements of the earth's clouds, oceans, and prevailing winds, for it is hardly consistent to reanimate the earth's population to awareness at a resumed time of two o'clock with the tides and weathers, whose cycles have been scientifically catalogued to an exacting specificity, now in conditions corresponding to three o'clock or four. This is what I was meaning in referring to the *responsibilities* which come with such powers, responsibilities which the American program of *Bewitched* had wholly suppressed and neglected during my childish viewing. For this labor of freezing and holding suspended of each element of the natural world of earth which intruded to occur to me as I only am attempting to envision the attractive, athletic, uncontrollable cries of passion beneath me on the worn mat — these labors of imagination were exhausting to me. Episodes of masturbation fantasy which used to take up only fifteen brief minutes were now requiring many hours and enormous mental labors. My health, never good, declined in a dramatic fashion in this period, so much so so that I was often bedridden and absent from my schools and from the State Exercise Facilities which my brother attended with my mother after school period. Also, my brother began at this time to become a competitive power weight-lifter in the light divisions of his age and weight, competitions of lifting which our mother often attended, traveling along with him, while my father remained on duty with the targeting programs and I in bed in our empty quarters alone for whole days in a row. Most of my times alone in the bed in our room in their absence were increasingly devoted, not to masturbating, but in the labor of imagination of constructing a sufficiently motionless and atemporal planet earth to allow my fantasy merely to take place at all. I do not, in fact, remember now whether the American program's implicit doctrine required the circular hand motion of Elizabeth Montgomery to deanimate the whole of humanity and the natural world outside the suburban home she shared with Darion. But I vividly do remember that a new, different television performer assumed the role of Darion late in my childhood, near the end of the American program's availability from transmitters in the Aleutian, and my discomfiture, even as a child, at the inconsistency that Elizabeth Montgomery would fail to recognize that her industrialist mate and sexual partner was now altogether a different man. He did not look similar at all and she remained oblivious! This had caused me some great distress. Of course, also there was the sun.'

Q.

'Our sun up above, overhead, whose seeming movement across the southern horizon was, of course, time's first measure among man. This too must be suspended in its apparent movement, as well, by the logic of the fantasy, which, in reality, this entailed halting the very earth's own spin. Very well I recall the moment this further inconsistency occurred to me, in the bed, and the labors and responsibility it implied within the fantasy. Well, too, do I remember this envy I felt of my brutish, unimaginative brother, upon whom the excellent scientific instruction of so many of the posts' schools was sheerly wasted, and he would not be in the least overwhelmed by the consequences of realizing this further: that the earth's rotation was but one part of its temporal movements, and that in order not to betray the fantasy's First Premise through causing incongruities in the scientifically catalogued measurements of the Solar Day and the Synodic Period, the earth's elliptical orbit around the sun must itself be halted by my supernatural hand's gesture, an orbit whose plane, I had to my misfortune learned in childhood, included a 23.53-degrees angle to the axis of the earth's own spin, having as well variant equivalents in the measurement of the Synodic Period and Sidereal Period, which required then the rotational and orbital stopping of all other planets and their satellite bodies in the Solar System, each of which forced me to interrupt the masturbation fantasy to perform research and calculations based upon the varying planets' different spins and angles with respect to the planes of their own orbits around the sun. This was laborious in that era of only very simple hand-held calculators . . . and beyond, for you see where this nightmare is heading for, since, yes, the sun itself is in many complex orbits relative to such nearby stars as Sirius and Arcturus, stars which must now be brought under the hegemony of the hand's circular gesture's power, as did the Milky Way Galaxy, upon whose edge the neighboring cluster of stars which includes our own sun both com-

plexly spins and orbits the many other such clusters . . . and onward
and onward, an ever-expanding nightmare of responsibilities and labor, because yes the Milky Way Galaxy of itself also orbits the Local
Group of galaxies in counterpoint to the Andromeda Galaxy more
than some 200 million light-years distant, an orbit whose halting
entails also a halt in the Red Shift and thus the proven and measured
flight of the now-known galaxies from one another in an expanding
bloom of expansion of the Known Universe, with innumerable complications and factors to include in the nightly calculations which
kept me from the sleep my exhaustion cried increasingly out for,
such as, for example, the fact that such distant galaxies as 3C295 re-
ceded at rapid rates exceeding one-third the speed of light while far
closer-in galaxies, including the troublesome NGC253 Galaxy at
merely thirteen million light-years, appeared mathematically to actually be *approaching* our Milky Way Galaxy through its own mo-
mentums more rapidly than the larger expansions of the Red Shift
could impel it to recede from us, so that now the bed is so awash
with the piles of science volumes and journals and sheafs of my calculations that there would be no space for me to masturbate even if
I had been able to do so. And it was when it then dawned upon me,
amidst an agitated half-sleep in the littered bed, that all these many
months' datas and calculations had, so stupidly, been based upon
published astronomic observations from an earth whose spin, orbits,
and sidereal positions were in the naturally unfrozen, ever-changing
mode of reality, and that all of it therefore must be recalculated from
my fantasy's gesture's theoretical haltings of the earth and neighboring satellites if the seduction and copulation amidst the timeless
obliviousness of all citizens were to avoid hopeless inconsistency —
it was then I broke down from it. The fantasy's single gesture of one
adolescent hand had proven to entail an infinitely complex responsibility more befitting of a God than a mere boy. These broke me. It
was at this moment I renounced, resigned, became again merely a

sickly and unconfident youth. I abdicated at seventeen years and four months and 8.40344 days, reaching up high with now both of my hands to make the reversing gesture of linked circles which set all of it free once again in a bloom of renunciation that commenced at our bed and opened swiftly out to include all known bodies in motion. I think you have no idea what this cost for me. Delirium, confinement, my father's disappointments — but these were as nothing compared to the price and rewards of what I underwent in this time. This American program of *Bewitched* was merely the spark behind this infinite explosion and contraction of creative energy. Deluded, broken or not broken — but how many other men have felt the power to become a God, then renounced it all? This is the theme of my power you say you wished to hear of: *renunciation.* How many know the true meaning of it? None of these persons here, I can assure you. Going through their oblivious motions outside of here, crossing streets and peeling apples and copulating thoughtlessly with women they believe they love. What do they know of love? I, who am by my choosing a celibate of all eternity, have alone seen love in all its horror and unbounded power. I alone have any rights to speak of it. All the rest is merely noise, radiations of a background which is even now retreating always further. It cannot be stopped.'

B.I. #72 08-98

NORTH MIAMI BEACH FL

'I love women. I really do. I love them. Everything about them. I can't even describe it. Short ones, tall ones, fat ones, thin. From drop-dead to plain. To me, hey: all women are beautiful. Can't get enough of them. Some of my best friends are women. I love to watch them move. I love how different they all are. I love how you can never understand them. I love love love them. I love to hear them giggle, the different little sounds. The way you just can't keep them from shopping no matter what you do. I love it when they bat their eyes or pout or give you that little look. The way they look in heels. Their voice, their smell. Those teeny red bumps from shaving their legs. Their little dainty unmentionables and special little womanly products at the store. Everything about them drives me wild. When it comes to women I'm helpless. All they have to do is come into a room and I'm a goner. What would the world be without women? It'd — oh no not again behind you *look out!*'

B.I. #28 02-97

Ypsilanti MI [Simultaneous]

K———: 'What does today's woman want. That's the big one.'

E———: 'I agree. It's the big one all right. It's the what-do-you-call. . . .'

K———: 'Or put another way, what do today's women *think* they want versus what do they really deep down *want*.'

E———: 'Or what do they think they're *supposed* to want.'

Q.

K———: 'From a male.'

E———: 'From a guy.'

K———: 'Sexually.'

E———: 'In terms of the old mating dance.'

K———: 'Whether it sounds Neanderthal or not, I'm still going to argue it's the big one. Because the whole question's become such a mess.'

E———: 'You can say that again.'

K———: 'Because now the modern woman has an unprecedented amount of contradictory stuff laid on her about what it is she's supposed to want and how she's expected to conduct herself sexually.'

E———: 'The modern woman's a mess of contradictions that they lay on themselves that drives them nuts.'

K——: 'It's what makes it so difficult to know what they want. Difficult but not impossible.'

E——: 'Like take your classic Madonna-versus-whore contradiction. Good girl versus slut. The girl you respect and take home to meet Mom versus the girl you just fuck.'

K——: 'Yet let's not forget that overlayed atop this is the new feminist-slash-postfeminist expectation that women are sexual agents, too, just as men are. That it's OK to be sexual, that it's OK to whistle at a man's ass and be aggressive and go after what you want. That it's OK to fuck around. That for today's woman it's almost *mandatory* to fuck around.'

E——: 'With still, underneath, the old respectable-girl-versus-slut thing. It's OK to fuck around if you're a feminist but it's also not OK to fuck around because most guys aren't feminists and won't respect you and won't call you again if you fuck around.'

K——: 'Do but don't. A double bind.'

E——: 'A paradox. Damned either way. The media perpetuates it.'

K——: 'You can imagine the load of internal stress all this dumps on their psyches.'

E——: 'Come a long way baby my ass.'

K——: 'That's why so many of them are nuts.'

E——: 'Out of their minds with internal stress.'

K——: 'It's not even really their fault.'

E——: 'Who wouldn't be nuts with that kind of mess of contradictions laid on them all the time in today's media culture?'

K——: 'The point being that this is what makes it so difficult, when for example you're sexually interested in one, to figure out what she really wants from a male.'

E——: 'It's a total mess. You can go nuts trying to figure out what tack to take. She might go for it, she might not. Today's woman's a total crap-shoot. It's like trying to figure out a Zen koan.

Where what they want's concerned, you pretty much have to just shut your eyes and leap.'

K——: 'I disagree.'

E——: 'I meant metaphorically.'

K——: 'I disagree that it's impossible to determine what it is they really want.'

E——: 'I don't think I said *impossible*.'

K——: 'Though I do agree that in today's postfeminist era it's unprecedentedly difficult and takes some serious deductive fire-power and imagination.'

E——: 'I mean if it were really literally *impossible* then where would we be as a species?'

K——: 'And I do agree that you can't necessarily go just by what they *say* they want.'

E——: 'Because are they only saying it because they think they're supposed to?'

K——: 'My position is that actually most of the time you *can* figure out what they want, I mean almost logically deduce it, if you're willing to make the effort to understand them and to understand the impossible situation they're in.'

E——: 'But you can't just go by what they say, is the big thing.'

K——: 'There I'd have to agree. What modern feminists-slash-postfeminists will *say* they want is mutuality and respect of their individual autonomy. If sex is going to happen, they'll say, it has to be by mutual consensus and desire between two autonomous equals who are each equally responsible for their own sexuality and its expression.'

E——: 'That's almost word for word what I've heard them say.'

K——: 'And it's total horseshit.'

E——: 'They all sure have the empowerment-lingo down pat, that's for sure.'

K——: 'You can easily see what horseshit it is as long as you remember to start by recognizing the impossible double bind we already discussed.'

E——: 'It's not all that hard to see.'

Q.

K——: 'That she's expected to be both sexually liberated and autonomous and assertive, and yet at the same time she's still conscious of the old respectable-girl-versus-slut dichotomy, and knows that some girls still let themselves be used sexually out of a basic lack of self-respect, and she still recoils at the idea of ever being seen as this kind of pathetic roundheel sort of woman.'

E——: 'Plus remember the postfeminist girl now knows that the male sexual paradigm and the female's are fundamentally different —'

K——: '*Mars and Venus.*'

E——: 'Right, exactly, and she knows that as a woman she's naturally programmed to be more high-minded and long-term about sex and to be thinking more in relationship terms than just fucking terms, so if she just immediately breaks down and fucks you she's on some level still getting taken advantage of, she thinks.'

K——: 'This, of course, is because today's postfeminist era is also today's postmodern era, in which supposedly everybody now knows everything about what's really going on underneath all the semiotic codes and cultural conventions, and everybody supposedly knows what paradigms everybody is operating out of, and so we're all as individuals held to be far more responsible for our sexuality, since everything we do is now unprecedentedly conscious and informed.'

E——: 'While at the same time she's still under this incredible sheer biological pressure to find a mate and settle down and nest and breed, for instance go read this thing *The Rules* and try to explain its popularity any other way.'

K——: 'The point being that women today are now expected to be responsible both to modernity and to history.'

E——: 'Not to mention sheer biology.'

K——: 'Biology's already included in the range of what I mean by *history*.'

E——: 'So you're using *history* more in a Foucaultvian sense.'

K——: 'I'm talking about history being a set of conscious intentional human responses to a whole range of forces of which biology and evolution are a part.'

E——: 'The point is it's an intolerable burden on women.'

K——: 'The real point is that in fact they're just logically incompatible, these two responsibilities.'

E——: 'Even if modernity *itself* is a historical phenomenon, Foucault would say.'

K——: 'I'm just pointing out that nobody can honor two logically incompatible sets of perceived responsibilities. This has nothing to do with history, this is pure logic.'

E——: 'Personally, I blame the media.'

K——: 'So what's the solution.'

E——: 'Schizophrenic media discourse exemplified by like for example *Cosmo* — on one hand be liberated, on the other make sure you get a husband.'

K——: 'The solution is to realize that today's women are in an impossible situation in terms of what their perceived sexual responsibilities are.'

E——: 'I can bring home the bacon mm *mm* mm *mm* fry it up in a pan mm *mm* mm *mm*.'

K——: 'And that, as such, they're naturally going to want what any human being faced with two irresolvably conflicting sets of responsibilities is going to want. Meaning that what they're really going to want is some way *out* of these responsibilities.'

E——: 'An escape hatch.'

K——: 'Psychologically speaking.'

E——: 'A back door.'

K——: 'Hence the timeless importance of: *passion.*'

E——: 'They want to be both responsible and passionate.'

K——: 'No, what they want is to experience a passion so huge, overwhelming, powerful and irresistible that it obliterates any guilt or tension or culpability they might feel about betraying their perceived responsibilities.'

E——: 'In other words what they want from a guy is *passion.*'

K——: 'They want to be swept off their feet. Blown away. Carried off on the wings of. The logical conflict between their responsibilities can't be resolved, but their postmodern *awareness* of this conflict can be.'

E——: 'Escaped. Denied.'

K——: 'Meaning that, deep down, they want a man who's going to be so overwhelmingly passionate and powerful that they'll feel they have no choice, that this thing is bigger than both of them, that they can forget there's even such a *thing* as postfeminist responsibilities.'

E——: 'Deep down, they want to be irresponsible.'

K——: 'I suppose in a way I agree, though I don't think they can really be faulted for it, because I don't think it's conscious.'

E——: 'It dwells as a Lacanian cry in the infantile unconscious, the lingo would say.'

K——: 'I mean it's understandable, isn't it? The more these logically incompatible responsibilities are forced on today's females, the stronger their unconscious desire for an overwhelmingly powerful, passionate male who can render the whole double bind irrelevant by so totally overwhelming them with passion that they can allow themselves to believe they couldn't help it, that the sex wasn't a matter of conscious choice that they can be held responsible for, that ultimately if *anyone* was responsible it was the *male.*'

E——: 'Which explains why the bigger the so-called feminist, the more she'll hang on you and follow you around after you sleep with her.'

K——: 'I'm not sure I'd go along with that.'

E——: 'But it follows that the bigger the feminist, the more grateful and dependent she's going to be after you've ridden in on your white charger and relieved her of responsibility.'

K——: 'What I disagree with is the *so-called*. I don't believe that today's feminists are being consciously insincere in all their talk about autonomy. Just as I don't believe they're strictly to blame for the terrible bind they've found themselves in. Though deep down I suppose I do have to agree that women are historically ill-equipped for taking genuine responsibility for themselves.'

Q.

E——: 'I don't suppose either of you saw where the Little Wranglers' room was in this place.'

K——: 'I don't mean that in any kind of just-another-Neanderthal-male-grad-student-putting-down-women-because-he's-too-insecure-to-countenance-their-sexual-subjectivity way. And I'd go to the wall to defend them against scorn or culpability for a situation that is clearly not their fault.'

E——: 'Because it's getting to be time to answer nature's page if you know what I mean.'

K——: 'I mean, even simply looking at the evolutionary aspect, you have to agree that a certain lack of autonomy-slash-responsibility was an obvious genetic advantage as far as primitive human females went, since a weak sense of autonomy would drive a primitive female toward a primitive male to provide food and protection.'

E——: 'While your more autonomous, butch-type female would be out hunting on her own, actually competing with the males for food.'

K——: 'But the point is that it was the less self-sufficient, less autonomous females who found mates and bred.'

E——: 'And raised offspring.'

K——: 'And thus perpetuated the species.'

E——: 'Natural selection favored the ones who found mates instead of going out hunting. I mean, how many cave-paintings of *female* hunters do you ever see?'

K——: 'Historically, we should probably note that once the quote-unquote *weak* female has mated and bred, she shows an often spectacular sense of responsibility where her offspring are concerned. It's not that females have no capacity for responsibility. That's not what I'm talking about.'

E——: 'They do make great moms.'

K——: 'What we're talking about here is single adult preprimipara females, their genetic-slash-historical capacity for autonomy, for as it were *self*-responsibility, in their dealings with males.'

E——: 'Evolution has bred it out of them. Look at the magazines. Look at romance novels.'

K——: 'What today's woman wants, in short, is a male with both the passionate sensitivity and the deductive firepower to discern that all her pronouncements about autonomy are actually desperate cries in the wilderness of the double bind.'

E——: 'They all want it. They just can't *say* it.'

K——: 'Putting you, today's interested male, in the paradoxical role of almost their therapist or priest.'

E——: 'They want absolution.'

K——: 'When they say "*I am my own person,*" "*I do not need a man,*" "*I am responsible for my own sexuality,*" they are actually telling you just what they want you to make them forget.'

E——: 'They want to be rescued.'

K——: 'They want you on one level to wholeheartedly agree and respect what they're saying and on another, deeper level to recognize that it's total horseshit and to gallop in on your white charger and overwhelm them with passion, just as males have been doing since time immemorial.'

E——: 'That's why you can't take what they say at face value or it'll drive you nuts.'

K——: 'Basically it's all still an elaborate semiotic code, with the new postmodern semions of autonomy and responsibility replacing the old premodern semions of chivalry and courtship.'

E——: 'I really do have to see a man about a prancing pony.'

K——: 'The only way not to get lost in the code is to approach the whole issue logically. What is she really saying?'

E——: '*No* doesn't mean yes, but it doesn't mean no, either.'

K——: 'I mean, the capacity for logic is what distinguished us from animals to begin with.'

E——: 'Which, no offense, but logic's not exactly a woman's strong suit.'

K——: 'Although if the whole sexual *situation* is illogical, it hardly makes sense to blame today's woman for being weak on logic or for giving off a constant barrage of paradoxical signals.'

E——: 'In other words, they're not responsible for not being responsible, K——'s saying.'

K——: 'I'm saying it's tricky and difficult but that if you use your head it's not impossible.'

E——: 'Because think about it: if it was really *impossible* where would the whole species be?'

K——: 'Life always finds a way.'

TRI-STAN: I SOLD SISSEE NAR TO ECKO

The fuzzy Hensonian epiclete Ovid the Obtuse, syndicated chronicler of trans-human entertainment exchange in low-cost organs across the land, mythologizes the origins of the ghostly double that always shadows human figures on UHF broadcast bands thus:

There moved & shook, Before Cable, a wise & clever programming executive named Agon M. Nar. This Agon M. Nar was revered throughout medieval California's fluorescent basin for the clever wisdom & cojones with which he presided over Recombinant Programming for the Telephemus Studios division of Tri-Stan Entertainment Unltd. Agon M. Nar's programming *archē* was the metastasis of originality. He could shuffle & recombine proven entertainment formulae that allowed the muse of Familiarity to appear cross-dressed as Innovation. Agon M. Nar was also a devoted family man. & so it came to pass that, as his *Brady Bunch* & *All in the Family* flourished & begat *Family Ties* & *Diff'rent Strokes* & *Gimme a Break* & *Who's the Boss?,* from whose brows, hydra-like, sprang *Webster* & *Mr. Belvedere* & *Growing Pains* & *Married . . . With Children* & *Life Goes On* & the mythic *Cosby*, all with ads infinitum, Agon M. Nar in private family life did beget three semi-independent vehicles, daughters, maidens, Leigh & Coleptic & Sissee, who did then grow & thrive like kudzu among the fluorescent basin's palms & malls & beaches & temples.

So favored was Agon M. Nar, industry legend had it, by com-

pany CEOs Stanley, Stanley & Stanley, as well as by Stasis, God of
Passive Reception himself, & too so blest with savvy, that by the
time his three lovely maidens — whom he now saw & adored every
third weekend — had undergone their first Surgical Enhancements,
Agon M. Nar had actually vanquished the esurient, heavy-hitting
& high-profile Reggie Ecko of Venice as Recombinant Head of all
Tri-Stan, R. Ecko of V. falling then gently back to the basin's pastel
earth, deposed & just royally pissed, under a parachute's aegis of
golden silk.

& Agon M. Nar administered Tri-Stan Entertainment's affairs
wisely & cleverly indeed; &, as is recorded, recombinations of de-
rivations of rip-offs of spin-offs of pale imitations came to dominate
& soothe the formerly chaotic MHz, Before Cable.

& while recombination as *ēthos* metastasized, soothed, & remu-
nerated across the pink-orange landscape of medieval CA, Agon M.
Nar's unattested daughters blossomed into nymphetitude. Ever far-
sighted, Agon M. Nar wisely provided for monthly tribute to the
fluorescent basin's God of Surgical Enhancement, the spherically
crispate & sartorially retrograde but plasticly facile Herm ('Afro')
Deight MD, he of the plaid bellbottoms & lavender smock; &
H.('A.')D.MD, G. of S.E., well pleased at such tribute, fashioned
Agon M. Nar's daughters into nymphets far, far lovelier than the
stony vicissitudes of Nature would have provided solo. Nature was
a bit honked off over this, but she had more than enough on her
plate in medieval CA already. Anyway, Leigh & Coleptic Nar eventually blossomed into USC cheerleaders, post-vestal attendants at
the Saturday temple of the padded gods Ra & Sisboomba; on their
subsequent careers Ovid the Obtuse is mute.

But it was Agon M. Nar's youngest daughter, his Baby, his Love-
Dumpling, his Little Princess — viz. Sissee, the Nar family's lone
aspiring thespian, haunter of casting calls for commercials & day-

time serials — who did become Herm ('Afro') Deight the Enhancement *technē*cian's favorite & Personal Project; & after much non-HMO tribute, plus rituals & procedures so grisly as to compel lyric restraint, the eventually nearly 100%-Enhanced Sissee Nar so like totally surpassed her acrobatic sisters & all the fluorescent basin's other maidens that she seemed, according to *Varietae*, '. . . a very goddess consorting with mortals.'

& she consorted a *lot*. For as word of her trans-human charms spread throughout the basins & ranges & interior wastes of medieval CA, bronzed men with cleft chins & rigid hair from as far away as the Land of Huge Red Pines journeyed in loud & extraordinarily phallic chariots to gaze upon Sissee Nar's spandextral form with wonder & glandular excitement, & to consort. The tragic historian Dirk of Fresno records that so vertiginously protrusive was Sissee Nar's bust that she needed aid to recline, so juttingly sepulchral her cheekbones that she cast predatory shadows & had to do doorways in profile, & so perfectly otherworldly her teeth & tan that the BC demiurges Carie & Erythema, mortally affronted & blasphemed, entered an appeal for aesthetic justice (specific appeal: for a nasty attack of comedones & gingivitic recession) to Stasis — i.e. yes *the* Stasis, Overlord of San Fernandus, Board-Chair *ex off* of Tri-Stan's parent, the Sturm & Drang Family of Exceptionally Fine Companies; Stasis as in *summum solo,* Olympic Overseer, God of Passive Reception & all-around Big Mythopoeic Cheese. Carie & Erythema's case never even made it onto the Olympian docket, though; for Stasis, G. of P.R., had himself personally gazed down upon & admired Ms. Sissee Nar, & from his home-entertainment module kept distant video tabs on the riveting maiden at all times via the state-of-the-art hand-held *technai* of his foam-winged factota, Nike & Fila (who split shifts).

It's right around here that Ovid the O. tone-shifts to Lament. For alas, the God Stasis's immortal S.O., the basin's Queen Goddess,

Codependae, was seriously ill pleased that Stasis spent more quality time admiring Sissee Nar's camcorded image from the vantage of his module's exercycle than he spent even bothering to deny his infatuation with the much-Enhanced maiden to Codep. over the Olympian couple's oat-intensive breakfast. Stasis's denial was Codependae's ambrosia, & she found its absence inappropriate & irksome in the extremus. & plus then when she came out of the sauna & found the Reception-God on his cellular pricing swan-costume rentals — well, this was understandably impossible to detach from; & Codependae vowed retaliation against this mortal & undulant strumpet before her entire Support Group. The horn-mad Queen began teleconferencing with the affronted demiurges Carie & Erythema, plus had her administrative assistant contact Nature's administrative assistant & set up a brunch meeting; & Codep. basically got all these transmortals, their self-esteem compromised by Sissee Nar's Enhanced & Passively Received charms, to declare a covert action against Sissee & her much-favored father, Agon M. Nar of Tri-Stan Unltd. Having three divinities plus Nature all honked off at you at once is just not good karma at all, but mortally naive Sissee & workaholic Agon M. ignored sudden sharp increases in their insurance premia & went about their business of moving & shaking & recombining & undergoing Enhancement & auditioning & consorting & avoiding anything in the way of autoreflection more or less as usual. I.e. they were blithe.

It soon came to pass that Codependae & Co., after much interface, settled on a vengeance vehicle. This was the Telephemically dethroned, parachuted, & highly vengeance-oriented Reggie Ecko of Venice, who'd suffered a massive self-esteem-displacement & had sold his house & tank of pedigreed carp & moved into a freebase fleabag in an infamous Venetian residency hotel known along the boardwalk as The Temple of Very Short Prayers, & was now spending all his time & contract settlement hitting the alkaloid pipe &

drinking Crown Royal right out of the velvet bag & throwing darts at 8 × 10s of Agon M. Nar & watching incredibly massive amounts of late-night syndicated television, gnashing his increasingly discolored teeth &, like, totally embittered. A covertly active strategy went into effect. While the demiurge Erythema began to appear to Reggie Ecko in the mortal guise of Robert Vaughan hosting *Hair Loss Update* every night from 4 to 5 A.M. on Channel 13, & to work on him, Codependae herself began work on the heart, mind, & cojones of Agon M. Nar, insinuating herself into his 4–5 A.M. REM-stage as the Cerberian image of Tri-Stan's three CEO Stanleys, ancient entertainment-kabalists who never left their video center & shared but a single large-screen CCTV monitor & remote between them. Under Codependae's direction their images began to kibbitz at Nar's psyche, & to Foretell. There are at this point long, long Ovidian lyrics about the vengeful Goddess's CEO-mediated siren-songs to the oneirically impressionable A.M.N. . . . so long in fact that Ovid's copied at a certain glossy organ ended up deleting major portions of the epiclete's SIREN.SNG file. The thrust of what's stetted, however, is that Cod.'s covert plan begins, alas, to unfold with all the dark logic of a genuine entertainment-market inspiration.

This inspiration — the thesis Nar thought was his own, mortally, on awakening — appeared as inevitable as his Enhanced Love-Dumpling daughter's own part in it. Now, Telephemus Studios & Tri-Stan Entertainment, consulting the cassocked vestals at the Oracle of Nielsen, God of Life Itself, were much vexed by the nascent spread of Cable Television & the geometric expansion of grainy syndication's eternal return. Turner & ESP's Network & Chicago's Super 9 were then in utero. The industry was abuzz. It was said that Stasis Himself had personally placed shiny TelSat appliances in the star-chocked sky, with a per-use fee structure. It's now 4–5 A.M. O verily must Tri-Stan get its foot in the door of Cable's ground floor while there is still time, sings the three-headed siren; & Agon M. Nar, asleep & nystagmic, can feel the epiphanicity of what the three S.'s Foretell, the best of both possible worlds: no Sermonette, no Indian crying at litter, no anthem or flags or sign-off at the Close of the Broadcast Day, *no Close of the Broadcast Day at all:* instead, a 24-hr low-overhead loop of something so very archaic as to appear forward-looking, & not on any 'cable' but on & in the very air. The siren sings to Nar of oracular foresight, making the pitch with charts & pointer: Cable offers nothing new or improved & dies on the vine as hyperborean MHz TV expands to even the weeest of wee hours via black-and-white recycling. & not just recycled *Hazel* or *I Married Joan,* no, the callid & thrice-disguised C. did sing of the Ultimate Rerun, 100% echo: *myth,* classic & Classical *myth:* rich, ambiguous, archetypal, cosmological, polyvalent, susceptible of neverending renewal, ever fresh. The high-alto dreamsong was complex & mostly C#. Covert seeds were thus sowed by A.M.N.'s nightshade: a moebioid ticker-like loop that became its own REM mantra: ENDYMION PYRAMUS PHAETON MARPESSA EU-RYDICE LINUS THOR ESHU POLLUX THISBE BAAL EUROPA NIEBELUNGEN PSYCHE DEMETER ASMODEUS ENDYMION WALKÜRE PYRAMUS ETCETERA.

Awakening thus in fugues & paroxysms, Agon M. Nar did there-upon consult mediated Oracles, offer leveraged tribute to images of Nielsen & Stasis, & sacrifice two whole humidors of Davidoff 9" Deluxes upon the offering-pyre of Emmē, Winged Goddess of Vic-tory. There was much market research. Finally, journeying person-ally to the uniscreened video center of Stan 1–3 & (aided by charts & pointer) pitching his epiphany to the big boys, Agon M. Nar found Tri-Stan & S.&D.'s Executive ICOP well pleased. Codepen-dae kept intercepting emergency calls to Stasis's pager.

& so it came to pass that, on the same week Sissee Nar's nose was Enhanced into eternal aquilinity, Nar & Tri-Stan's much-ballyhooed *Satyr-Nymph Network* was born & licensed for analog broadcast. In brief, S-NN comprised an ingeniously simple 24-hr low-overhead loop of mythopoeia mined at 10¢/$1 from the loded stockrooms of the BBC's toga'd & grape-leafy mythophilic period 1961–7. Here the prefeminist epiclete Ovid the O. usurps & dithyrambicizes — without credit or tribute — the historian Dirk of Fresno's account of S-NN's philosophy, Codependae's invidious dreamsong, Agon M. Nar's oneirically inspired bid to launch the greatest kabal network of all BC time — the Satyr-Nymph Network: '. . . basically an ingeniously simple 24-hr interspliced loop of mythopoeia harvested from the gravid stockrooms of the BBC's antically antique '60s & targeted at that uneasily neoclassical demographic class that already consumed reruns without even chewing. This lonely & insomniac audience found the invariant sameness of S-NN's circuit of British b/w mythic skits — serial legends of e.g. Endymion & Pyramus & Phaeton & Baal & Marpessa & surreally cockney Niebelungs — good: reliable, familiar, hypnotic, & delicious as the taste of their own mouths. For Agon M. Nar, this appetite for repetitive echo spelled divine inspiration — in the words of statistical microecon, *autogenerative Demand*. For not only did S-NN feed at the syndicated trough of viewers' hunger for familiarity, but the familiarity fed the mythopoeia that fed the market: double-blind polls revealed that in a nation whose great informing myth is that it has no great informing myth, familiarity equaled timelessness, omniscience, immortality, a spark of the vicarious Divine.

'. . . that A.M.N., when deep asleep, heeding the song of a jaundiced Goddess with three gray heads & one Curtis Mathes remote, began actually to believe he could explain the very nation on whose left shoulder he moved & shook. There existed today, the three sham-Stans sang, an untapped national market for myth. History was dead. Linearity was a cul de sac. Novelty was old news. The national *I* was now about flux & eternal return. Difference in sameness. "Creativity" — see for instance Nar's recombinant own — now lay in the manipulation of received themes. & soon, the C# siren Foretold, this would itself be acknowledged, this apotheosis of static flux, & be itself put to the cynical use of just what it acknowledged, like a funnel that falls through itself. "*Soon, myths about myths*" was the sirens' prophecy & long-range proposal. TV shows about TV shows. Polls about the reliability of surveys. Soon, perhaps, respected & glossy high-art organs might even start inviting smartass little ironists to contemporize & miscegenate BC mythos; & all this pop irony would put a happy-face mask on a nation's terrible shamefaced hunger & need: translation, genuine *information*, would be allowed to lie, hidden & nourishing, inside the wooden belly of parodic camp.

'I.e., the Medium would handle the Message's P.R.

'& for the wise & clever Agon M. Nar, it had already begun. This process. For of course Codependae was doing to Agon M. Nar what Agon M. Nar's S-NN would do to the fluorescent BC market, viz. convincing him that those most bivalent of *pharmaka,* double-edged gifts so terribly precious & so heavy on the heart that a thousand sleepless weeping years couldn't even start to make good their price . . . persuading A.M.N. & USA that the unearnable gifts of inspiration were naught but the products of his own mortal genius, through recombination. Agon M. Nar was invited, in unseen short, to imitate a God. To re-present history. To let's say for instance combine the fall of Lucifer & the ascension of Aepytus into a *Dynasty*-type parable about the patricide of Cronos. Oprah as Isis, Sigurd as JFK. & *all in fun,* is the thing. Keep it light, self-mocking, Codependae sings in Nar's tri-Stanley'd dreamvoice. Let the heroes tell their "own story," & their confabulation of myth with fact & Classical with post-Enlightened will reveal meaning & compel marketshare. & there can be young upscale ads infinitum, hip paeans to Bacchus & Helen & ultrabuff Thor. & the revenues from the campy old BBC loops can then be plowed back into deliberately cheap & stagy S-NN/Telephemic myth-reproductions, which "original" remakes can then themselves be run over & over, really late at night, say from 4 to 5 A.M., laser-aimed at those sleepless pre-Cable repetiphiles who can't but get stoned just watching.

"That is to say," the covert Codependae spells it out behind A.M. Nar's multichart pitch to the three ancient Stanleys whose guise she'd used to dybbuk Nar in the first place, composing thus her own insidious loop, unseen, "that S-NN will purvey myth & compel -share by purveying myth about the transmogrification of 'timeless' myth into contemporary camp-image. A whole new kind of ritual narrative, neither Old Comic nor New Tragic — the sit-trag. Pure Legend: about itself, legend, theft, repetition, eternal return, self-regeneration as loss as self-regeneration. A kind of cosmic outtake, Gods flubbing lines, cracking up, mugging at cameras." Etcetera.'

All this according to Dirk of Fresno.

& the Satyr-Nymph Network came to be, is the rub. Three palsied liver-spotted thumbs were raised before resuming the eternal struggle for the Stans' one remote. S-NN was run up the E-M flagpole. & lo. *Sine* production costs or satellitic overhead but very much *cum* an Olympian advertising budget, S-NN kicked much 24-hr ass. The BBC's resuscitated situation-tragedies were instant syndication classics on the order of *Rascals* & Caesar/Coca. Obscure BBC contract players from the R.S.C.'s minor leagues, now well into their thespian senescence, enjoyed cult followings & sudden endorsement cachet. A muffler company put a toothless cockney Midas under lifetime contract & so did prosper; a bald & trifocal'd Samson did health-club spots; etc. Everyone was winning. Tri-Stan became an even more proud member of the Sturm & Drang Family of E.F.C.'s; Agon M. Nar received an honorary Emmē & was wisely & cleverly humble about it; Sissee Nar continued to Enhance, tan, aerobicize, flourish, & consort; Reggie Ecko of Venice bounced in &

out of detox facilities, returning ever to his high-N pipe & velvet Crown & Temple of Very Short Prayers & Trinitron to await, via the hirsutely groomed Robert Vaughan, the transformation of his benthic ire into narrative meaning.

At about this point Codependae & Carie & Erythema sat back to watch Nature, incited further by the brunch-rhetoric of Codep., take her place at the retributive helm.

Alas, we no longer get to say 'alas' with a straight face, but 'alas' used, according to legend, to be what you said in great stoic sorrow over tragedies ineluctable, over the blackly implacable *telos* of Nature's flawed unfolding. So *alas:* for given Sissee Nar's Deighted pulchritude & her modest, mirror-denying grace under technical beauty's great pressure, & given her own prescient father's position & prestige & marketing vision, plus his devotion to his Little Princess (not to mention his twin investments in both the Satyr-Nymph Network & the aesthetic *technē* of Herm ('A.') D. MD), it was both naturally & tragically ineluctable that one Sissee Nar, aspiring thespian, would, before two Nielsenial Sweeps had marked the seasons' circuit, audition & screen-test & survive two call-backs for & yes finally land a starring role in the very first ever original S-NN/Tri-Stan mythic reproduction. This was a recombinant update of *Endymion,* one of the most popular of the stagy old BBC sandal-fests. The reproduction, *Beach Blanket Endymion,* not only came in under its shoestring budget, but its prime-time debut nearly threatened the slot-supremacy of NBC's *roughly eighty,* a *thirtysomething* knockoff about flappers & hepcats struggling to find both themselves & sustained continence in a modern nursing-care context.

& both Focus Groups & mail confirmed it: Ms. Sissee Nar, in the S-NN original repro, was a phenom. It was, yes, nonpositive that she could not act, & that her unEnhanceable voice was like nails on a slate. But these flaws were not fatal. For Sissee Nar's title role, opposite the contemporary logos-legend Vanna of the White Hands as the lunar Selene in this somewhat Sapphic redux of a well-known minimyth, called only for catatonia. Sissee turned out to be a natural. Forever asleep on Mt. Latmus's rather incongruous beach, she had only to lie there, cross-dressed, Enhanced, & immortally desirable; her antinatural beauty was enough. She was poetry in stasis. Despite a slight tendency toward palpebral twitching, her closed eyes had a magic. Long-jaded viewers were rapt, Vanna's show stolen, critics indulgent, & sponsors all but manic. Stasis even taped the thing, up at home. Sissee Nar got a *Guide* cover & a *Varietae* profile. She became, as *B.B.E.* ran like clockwork every 23 hrs, a high-RF light in the small-screen firmament, albeit somewhat typecast: for Tri-Stan's F.G.-respondents did attest with one voice that they loved Sissee *for,* not despite, her eerie enactment of the vegetative state. Her morphean passivity touched a chivalric nerve, apparently. A market for large-r Romance. Classic-minded viewers yearned for a maiden comatose, gloriously unconscious — for who is yet more remote & unattainable & thus desirable than the oblivious? Dirk of Fresno's own editorial here is that there seems to be something death-tending at the very heart of all Romance ('. . . that every love story is also [a] ghost story . . .') & that Sissee Nar's voluptuous recumbency spoke to this black thanaticism in the contemporary erotic *Geist.* Whatever the source of Sissee's unconscious allure, the industry found it good, & thus recombinable. An 'original' S-NN reshuffling of the Norse myth of Siegfried, with Sissee as a narcoleptic Brynhild, was rushed into reproduction. Dyspeptic men in worsted blends journeyed far by air to feel both Nars out re merchandising tie-ins, for the Official Sissee Nar Doll — gloriously devoid of all function — seemed a Natural.

Safe to say that even the wise, clever, worldly & level-headed Agon M. Nar was extremely well pleased.

Alas, too well pleased. For prominent among the rapt red-eyed faithful who tuned in to watch Sissee as Endymion lie there desirably couchant as Selene ministered Sapphically to h/her over & over & over in the weeest of broadcast hours was the vexed & malevolent Reggie Ecko of Venice, late of Tri-Stan & Recombinant eparchy, more recently of obscurity & the B. Ford Clinic, & even more recently of the Erythemic Robert Vaughan's sibylant & Iagian late-night campaign. Erythema's visitations had gotten progressively more effective: after many liters & quarter-ounces & very short prayers over glass pipe & flame, diplomatic relations between R. Ecko & reality had pretty much broken down. & it so happened to be on the early morning of his pharmacological sanity's tether's frayed & final end, alas, that Ecko first laid eyes on Sissee Nar's androsupine performance in S-NN's *Beach Blanket Endymion,* the selfsame hour of which saw also Nature & Codependae, cross-dressed & adhesively whiskered, now insinuate themselves into his cloacal room as respectively a Domino's deliveryman & an assertive associate of a certain chemical creditor known only as 'Javier J.' . . . & as the littoral *Endymion* so gloriously failed to unfold they began to work on his psyche in earnest — as too, oblivious, did Sissee Nar, there on the Trinitron's screen.

Both Ovid the Obtuse & his usually reliable Hollinshed D. of F. leave obscure the dramatic question whether Ecko of Venice fell addled head over snakeskin heels in Romantic love with the comatose 2-D image of Sissee Nar because of the parthenopic blandishments of N. & C., or because of the Dionysian febrility associated with chronic ingestion of $C_{17}H_{21}NO_4$, or because he was just plain addled & at tether's end, or whether it was because the formerly high-profile Reggie Ecko had fallen into corporate invisibility & saw in Sissee Nar the apotheosis of commercial image; or whether on the other hand it was just one of those large-r Romantic love-at-initial-reception things, the stuff of chivalric myth, the Tristian/Lancelotian fuck-it-all plunge, the Sicilian thunderbolt, the Wagnerian *Liebestod*. It does not much matter. What matters, alas, is what this eros wrought.

Malignly serenaded by Vaughan, Domino's, & Latin creditor, plus of course no stranger to obsession since his corporate displacement & Lucifer-like fall into what had started as mere recreation, R. Ecko of Venice was ripe for metamorphosis into that most dread of the fluorescent basin's BC monsters: the lunatic stalker-type fan. What little psyche did remain to him was in a twinkling consumed & possessed by the image of what he saw lying there passive on Latmus before him. He began to live all & only for the reappearance of *Beach Blanket Endymion* every morning at 4–5 PT, at the same time that he began to see the cathode screen itself as the dimensional barrier that prevented his 3-D union with Sissee Nar's much-Enhanced 2-D image. He kept breaking his Sony in rages & then running out to buy another. Your standard lunatic love-hate thing. He wrote creepy unpunctuated letters to S-NN & Tri-Stan (red crayon), made supplicating/belligerent calls. The creepy letters he even more creepily signed 'Your Actæon The Huntsman.' He used his alkaloid plenty to lure & debrief those young Adoni with whom S. Nar'd consorted on her path to recombinant stardom. Plus he began keeping the rambling clinical diary expected of your classic stalker-type fan. In it he represents himself as an Errant Knight displaced from his proper place & time & embarked on your basic daemonic love-quest of chivalric Yore, yet also tormented by his post-Romantic awareness of the quest's chimericity: he knew full well his transdimensional love to be daemonic, unreal, puerile, compensatory, Wertherian — i.e. 'about FICTION not FRICTION' in his vulgate phrase — but he was helpless, driven, possessed, as if impotioned, & for this bewitchment he did blame both Nars, *pater et filia duae:* they had created, for him, in the Sissee of *B.B.E.,* the Ultimate

Erotic Object of the contemporary industry: ideally proportioned, aesthetically flawless, sartorially hermaphroditic, rapturously passive, &, most bewitching yet, in every way 2-D, dimensionally unattainable, ergo a blank screen for the agelessly projected fantasies of every man with a red car & shades & a 'tude behind which bulged a heart just starving to be allowed to buy w/o reservation into what it was far too late anymore to truly believe in. Reggie wrote that he'd hear, watching, Sissee sing, hear a waxproof $C^{\#}$ threnody as her buxom shepherd lay moon-caressed in the fulgence of a cathode pulse. More bedazzlement — he *knew* her part to be silent but *felt* her unmoving ventriloquent lips to be moving in song, for R.E. of the Temple of V.S.P. alone; & only because he wanted it so. (Ovid takes a rhetorical moment to ponder: was this musical interface Erythemically inspired? Codependaent? Unreal? No matter?) Reggie Ecko records singing phogistic duets with the comatose TV image, &, with that flaccid figure, reaching the sorts of unimaginable passion-heights one reaches only with dolls & dreams — dreams of the unattainably-dead-in-life. Malignant divinities or no, Ecko's was a flameout of the most classically Romantic sort: the agony of Sissee Nar's unattainability was in him a fisher that netted all other pains & frustrations & vexations & terrors in his wine-dark psyche & presented the haul in one unendurable anamnetic load, capsizing him. & so Ecko freebased heart-bursting amounts of product & composed creepy Crayola poems & communed with C. & Co. & through their assuasions bought wholly into this whole trite & trendy medieval CA codependent-inner-child-dysfunctionality deal, this men-who-love-too-much-not-wisely-type thanaphiliacal thing where he believed not only that the passive 2-D Sissee Nar was the timeless & ideal object of his deepest longings but that this love was by nature unconsummatable in the merciless daylight of 3-D reality. (LA-area Alanon, by the by, would diagnose this a lethal combination of Grandiosity & the Pity Pot.)

. . . Ovid's point finally being that Ecko of Venice & the T.V.S.P. decides that he can 'attain' Sissee Nar only in the unionized melt that is death's good night. Both Robert Vaughan & the high-alto sirens affirm this decision as meet & good (Codependae calling him 'esse').

Codependae then elects to afflict Agon M. Nar with the following dream. A.M.N.'s Pac 10 daughters Leigh & Coleptic are being held hostage by some extremely serious militant CA Hispanics who threaten to hang them by their own lustrous locks if Nar doesn't complete the single telemarketing labor they demand: he is to find a hypnotic avatar of the ancient-Greek Narcissus & air him, i.e. broadcast his irresistible image over & over, in order to entrance the Anglos of medieval CA into the glazed narcosis that will make them easy pickings for lean hungry barbarians from the Latin south. Their voices on Nar's cellular are high-alto. Agon M. goes as usual to seek counsel at Tri-Stan's videonic HQ, but the three antique Stans can't concentrate on his trouble: they have only one of everything among them, & when two or more of them have to visit the exec washroom at the same time there's always a hell of a row about time & trade, & A. Nar, in that aphasiac frustration so common to nightmares, can't make himself heard through the Empedoclean squabble over porcelain & part. Finally a mysterious pockmarked Hispanic custodian does that *psst* thing from the doorway — without context or explanation, he informs Nar that he has consulted the Oracle of Stasis & that the ortolan-entrails have Foretold that Agon M. Nar will never be able in time to find a qualified male Narcissus II (no modern man, even in the much-Enhanced fluorescent basin, being divine-looking enough to hold the rapt gaze of demographic millions), but that a bona fide *female* Narcissus-grade object will, ironically, be found by Nar no farther away than his own neocolonial home's bassinet or the cover of last week's *Guide:* yes his Love-Dumpling, *esse,* his Leettle Preenciss, who will, however, the custodian says the $88.95 entrails Foretell in no uncertain terms, herself prove to be the cause of Nar's own personal doom — vanishing then with an eerie & not all that Hispanic or even masculine laugh. Nevertheless, properly freaked by the prophecy, the still-dreaming Nar (yes this is all still in the dream, on which Codependae has spared no effort or expense) the still-dreaming A.M.N. remands Sissee's new Norse reproduction to the purgatory of a permanent 4–5 A.M. slot, when even 24-hr-loop demographics are grim. Yet fatalistically alas, for this weeest-hour slot is also the slot when all the really seriously insomniac drug freaks & neurasthenics & flameouts & lunatic stalker-type S-NN fans tune faithfully in; & no fewer than about 400 different lunatic stalker-type fans start stalking his narcoBrynhildic baby, sometimes actually bumping into one another in mid-stalk outside Sissee's S-NN dressing room; & but eventually in the dream one of the stalkers finally accomplishes his mission, & she dies in a hail of laser-scoped semiautomatic gas-tipped bullets; & even though in the dream's remainder Agon M. Nar himself doesn't get killed off (so the carbuncular custodian's prophecy isn't fulfilled within the dream itself) A.M.N. feels so horrible & benighted by REM-cycle's end that he's pretty sure when he wakes up at 5 A.M. that if the dream's epilogue hadn't been preempted by his Hispanic houseboy's gentle prod Nar would also have bought it just from sheer Laiusian grief & guilt.

The point being that Agon M. Nar is colossally frightened & upset by the dream (BC programming executives tending to place great importance on oneiromancy), & he immediately suspends pre-reproduction on the Siegfried thing & pages Sissee Nar & beseeches her to return to & secret herself in her Venice beach house & keep a very low & window-avoiding profile for a while . . . which Sissee immediately does, because she's pretty much passivity in motion & does whatever A.M.N. tells her, & also because she has an extremely small ego from never once having seen herself in a mirror. Except alas, it's child's play for the natively Venetian Reggie Ecko — who's now pawned his Trinitron & bought an AK-47 from an auto-weapon stand right on Dockweiler Beach in Playa del Rey — to find out exactly where the unlisted Sissee lives: her sleeping face is burned into CA's consciousness, & he has only to flash a glossy 4 × 5 around Venice's various health clubs & silicon wholesalers to have babes & dudes alike immediately recognize the image as of the un-listed S-NN girl who's living low-profile just over a certain set of dunes.

& so Reggie Ecko, adorned in finest Alfani & light-denying glasses, & suffering mightily from coke-bugs & general desiderative frenzy, journeys forthwith to Sissee's off-violet beach house &, after checking all the windows' drawn shades & repeatedly shaking the sand out of his loafers & ringing the Cyndi Lauper doorchime, booms the door & bursts the pathetically naive safety-chain, & Sis-see's in there innocently passing the time with Walkman & a Buns of Steel aerobics tape; &, as best forensic authorities could later de-termine, Ecko — crashing in & seeing Sissee Nar not only upright & awake but in what looked for all the world like vigorous purpo-sive motion — for a brief too-human moment hesitated to open up & actually fire, & Sissee had a moment's chance to run for her life & escape the fatal stalker-type tribute, except apparently she'd hap-pened to catch a doubled glimpse of herself in the mirrored sun-glasses Ecko wore to protect his rheumy Romantic retinae from the horrific light of the 3-D day, & Sissee was apparently just, like, to-tally transfixed by her own human image, literally frozen by what's got to have been the revelation of her Enhanced & trans-human charms in the first mirror of any sort she had ever gazed into, & apparently she was standing there so utterly static & passive & affectless w/ shock that Ecko's heart retumesced with doomed un-endurable ur-Romantic C#-aria-type love once more, flooding his ravaged CNS so utterly that he suddenly came to/departed from himself again & ventilated Sissee Nar, liberally, then somehow shot himself not once but three times in the head.

. . . w/ the tragicomic irony here being that Ecko's wacko & retrograde Romantic dream of union with Sissee in death turned out to *come true*. For S. Nar & Ecko were recombinantly joined in just precisely the 2-D world he'd Foreseen as their only possible union. For the syndicated vehicles *Donahue!* & *Entertainment Tonight* & its many avatars like *Oprah* & *Geraldo!* & *A Current Affair* & *Inside Edition* & *Unsolved Mysteries* & *Sally Jessy!* & *Solved But Still Really Interesting Mysteries* paid lavish & repetitive tribute to the now-tragic epic of Sissee Nar's cometic rise & Reggie Ecko's fall at the hands of Sissee's father & the father's epiphanic & Laiusian dreams & Sissee's paralysis in the mirror of Ecko's lenses & high-caliber ventilation & gruesome death with her Walkman still on & urging the first police on the scene to Flex That Fundament & Ecko's mysterious triballistic suicide & subsequently discovered Crayola diary. & the very most famous *Varietae* photo of an unconscious Endymionic Sissee & a photo of Reggie Ecko jet-skiing with Ricardo Montalban back when he'd moved & shaken at Tri-Stan's apex — these two images kept getting juxtaposed on-screen & placed side by side behind the commentators' variform heads; & the *Enquirer* even did the job right & spliced the negatives together & claimed they'd been lovers all along, Ecko & Sissee, with a fetish for cross-dressing & watersports . . . & so fan/lover & star/object really were, in a sort of cynically campy but still contemporarily deep & mythic way, united, melded in death, in 2-D, in tales & on screens.

& then when Ovid the Obtuse's gregarious Rolfer happened to be discussing his own obsession with the celebrated case one day during a spinogravitational alignment, & saying (the Rolfer was) how it seemed a terribly insensitive & grisly thing to say but that

Ecko & Sissee Nar looked, in 2-D juxtaposition, like just the sort of perfectly doomed couple that all good BC Americans of whatever erotic persuasion hear & read & fantasize Romantically about from the age of say Grimms' Tales on . . . at this point Ovid the O. got the idea to turn the entire affair into this sort of ironically contemporary & self-conscious but still mythically resonant & highly lyrical entertainment-property. The fact that Agon M. Nar — now so peripetially devastated that he has in public cursed the Gods via Prepared Statement & has ceased all moving/shaking/recombining & has allowed S-NN to be surpassed in the Sweeps by a rank cable imitator, Ted of Atlanta's Hit or Myth Network — that Nar had had his attorneys tell Ovid the Obtuse that any unauthorized Sissee-lyric would constitute grounds for legal action deterred O. the O. not one iota. Seeking, as his lapidary soliciting abstract put it, to '. . . renew our abiding puzzlement at such suffering,' Ovid proposed to reconstitute & present the story as a '. . . high-concept miscegenation-of-Romantic-archetypes-type metamyth,' a kind of hottub-swingers' incest among Tristan & Narcissus & Echo & Isolde; & in the abstract he not only confirmed but did in fact plagiarize Dirk of Fresno's theory that such were Stasis the P. Reception God's grief at the demise of his mortal Flavor-of-the-Month & wrath at the lovesick ex-exec who'd 86'd her that he denied Reggie Ecko's thrice-shot soul the peace of any sort of Underworld visa, that instead Stasis condemned Ecko's ghost to haunt forever those most ultra- of broadcast television's UHF bandwidths, to abide there annoyingly & imperfectly juxtaposed with all figures & imbricately to overlap & mimic their on-screen movements as an irksome visual echo to help remind impressionable mortals that what we're transfixed by is artificial & mediated by imperfect *technē*. (Like we didn't already know. (Plus reception was nearly perfect on Cable by this time anyway.))

& but one final & epexegetic 'alas.' For such proved to be the descantant Ovid's love for reflecting on his own periphrastic theories about what made Agon M. Nar & Stasis & Codependae & the Satyr-Nymph Network & the popularization of timeless lies resonate aesthetically that he neglected to make any substantive mention of the fact that Sissee Nar had in fact been Skinnerianly raised to fear & avoid & religiously eschew all mirrors, any surface with reflective burnish, her wise & clever but somewhat Behaviorist father fearing that her image's ever-Enhancing beauty would, seen, render her unattractively narcissistic, stoned on self-love; & Ovid neglected to reveal how the whole reason A.M.N. had chosen a comatose role for Sissee's debut was so that her eyes could remain demurely shut during shooting & she could be spared any involutant glimpses of herself on monitors or tape, etc.; that if A.M.N.'d maybe let his Enhanced Love-Dumpling have one or two quick mithridatitic glimpses of herself in mirrors — thus letting her glean even some slim bit of an idea what Herm Deight MD's aesthetic Enhancements had wrought — before at last Ecko of Venice's reflective shades hove into her unprepared view, she'd not have been so transfixed & shocked by an image which actually she alone in all the fluorescent basin saw in truth as *imperfect* nay *flawed* & inadequately Enhanced & like totally gnarlyly *mortal,* & she might have been able to keep it psychically together enough to run like hell & escape the semiautomatic Wagnerian intentions of the lunatic UHF-ghost-to-be. So Ovid ended up having to stick all this narratively important background in right at the end, pretentiously referring to it as an 'epexegesis,' & the Acquiring Editor of the respected glossy organ he'd solicited was ill pleased, & the organ didn't buy the thing after all, although Ted of Atlanta's cable H.o.M.N. bought the rights to Ovid's overall concept for one of those 'Remembering Sissee'–type tribute-specials that lets you use a whole lot of public-domain footage over & over again under the rubric of Encomium; & even though 'Remembering Sissee' didn't actually ever make it onto the wire (Hit or Myth was by then processing 660 myth-recombination concepts per diem), its Option Payment to Ovid was far from dishonoring, & between that & the respected glossy organ's Kill Fee Ovid the Obtuse ended up making out okay on the whole thing; don't you worry about Ovid.

ON HIS DEATHBED, HOLDING YOUR HAND, THE ACCLAIMED NEW YOUNG OFF-BROADWAY PLAYWRIGHT'S FATHER BEGS A BOON

THE FATHER: Listen: I did despise him. Do.
> [PAUSE for episode of ophthalmorrhagia; technician's
> swab/flush of dextrocular orbit; change of bandage]

THE FATHER: Why does no one tell you? Why do all regard it as a blessed event? There seems to be almost a conspiracy to keep you in the dark. Why does no one take you aside and tell you what is coming? Why not tell you the truth? That your life is to be forfeit? That you are expected now to give up everything and not only to receive no thanks but to expect none? Not one. To suspend the essential give-and-take you'd spent years learning was life and now want nothing? I tell you, worse than nothing: that you will have no more life that is *yours?* That all you wished for yourself you are now expected to wish for him instead? Whence this expectation? Does it sound reasonable to expect? Of a human being? To have nothing and wish nothing for *you?* That your entire human nature should somehow change, alter, as if magically, at the moment it emerges from her after causing her such pain and deforming her body so profoundly that ne— that she will herself somehow alter herself this way automatically, as if by magic, the instant he emerges, as if by some glandular bewitchment, but that you, who have not carried him or been joined by tubes, will remain, inside, as you have always been, yet be expected to change as well, drop everything, freely? Why does no one speak of it, this madness? That your failure to cast yourself away and change everything and be delirious with joy at —

that this will be judged. Not just as a quote unquote parent but as a man. Your human worth. The prim smug look of those who would judge parents, judge them for not magically changing, not instantly ceding everything you'd wished for heretofore and — *securus judicat orbis terrarum,* Father. But Father are we really to believe it is so obvious and natural that no one feels even any *need* to tell you? Instinctive as blinking? Never think to warn you? It did not seem obvious to me, I can assure you. Have you ever actually seen an afterbirth? watch drop-jawed as it emerged and hit the floor, and what they do with it? No one told me I assure you. That one's own wife might judge you deficient simply for remaining the man she married. Was I the only one not told? Why such silence when —

[PAUSE for episode of dyspnea]

THE FATHER: I despised him from the first. I do not exaggerate. From the first moment they finally saw fit to let me in and I looked down and saw him already attached to her, already sucking away. Sucking at her, draining her, and her upturned face — she who had made her views on the sucking of body parts very plain, I can — her face, she had changed, become an abstraction, The Mother, her natal face enraptured, radiant, as if nothing invasive or grotesque were taking place. She had screamed on the table, *screamed,* and now where was that girl? I had never seen her look so — the current term is 'out of it,' no? Has anyone considered this phrase? what it really implies? In that instant I knew I despised him. There is no other word. Despicable. The whole affair from then on. The truth: I found it neither natural nor fulfilling nor beautiful nor fair. Think of me what you will. It is the truth. It was all disgusting. Ceaseless. The sensory assault. You cannot know. The incontinence. The vomit. The sheer smell. The noise. The theft of sleep. The selfishness, the appalling selfishness of the newborn, you have no idea. No one prepared us for any of it, for the sheer *unpleasantness* of it. The insane expense of pastel plastic things. The

cloacal reek of the nursery. The endless laundry. The odors and constant noise. The disruption of any possible schedule. The slobber
and terror and piercing shrieks. Like a needle those shrieks. Perhaps
if someone had prepared, forewarned us. The endless reconfigura-
tion of all schedules around him. Around his desires. He ruled from
that crib, ruled from the first. Ruled her, reduced and remade her.
Even as an infant the power he wielded! I learned the bottomless
greed of him. Of my son. Of arrogance past imagining. The regal
greed and thoughtless disorder and mindless cruelty — the literal
thoughtlessness of him. Has anyone considered this phrase's real import? Of the *thoughtlessness* with which he treated the world? The
way he threw things aside and clutched at things, the way he broke
things and just walked away. As a toddler. Terrible Twos indeed. I
watched other children; I studied other children his age — something in him was different, missing. Psychotic, sociopathic. The
grotesque lack of care for what we gave him. Believe me. You were
of course forbidden to say 'I paid for that! Treat that with care!
Show some minim of respect for something outside yourself!' No
never that. Never that. You'd be a monster. What sort of parent
asks for a moment's thought to whence things came? Never. Not a
thought. I spent years drop-jawed with amazement, too appalled
even to know what — noplace to speak of it. No one else even appeared to see it. Him. An essential disorder of character. An absence
of whatever we mean by 'human.' A psychosis no one dares diagnose. No one says it — that you are to live for and serve a psychotic.
No one mentions the abuse of power. No one mentions that there
will be psychotic tantrums during which you will wish — even just
his face, I did, I detested his face. A small soft moist face, not human. A circle of cheese with features like hasty pinches in some
ghastly dough. Am — was I the only one? That an infant's face is
not in any way recognizable, not a human face — it's true — then
why do all clasp their hands and call it beauty? Why not simply ad-

mit to an ugliness that may well be outgrown? Why such — but
the way from the beginning his eye — my son's right eye — it protruded, subtly yes, slightly more than the left, and blinked in a
palsied and overrapid way, like the sputter of a defective circuit.
That fluttery blink. The subtle but once noticed never thenceforth
ignorable bulge of that same eye. Its subtle but aggressive forward
thrust. All was to be his, that eye betrayed the — a triumph in it, a
glazed exultation. Pediatric term was 'exophthalmic,' supposedly
harmless, correctable over time. I never told her what I knew: not
correctable, not an accidental sign. That was the eye to look at, into
it, if you wished to see what no one else wished to see or acknowledge. The mask's only gap. Hear this. I loathed my child. I loathed
the eye, the mouth, the lip, the pinched snout, the wet hanging lip.
His very skin was an affliction. 'Impetigo' the term, chronic. The
pediatricians could find no reason. The insurance a nightmare. I
spent half my days on the phone with these people. Wearing a mask
of concern to match hers. Never a word. A sickly child, weak and
cheese-white, chronically congested. The suppurating sores of his
chronic impetigo, the crust. The ruptured infections. 'Suppura-
tion': the term means ooze. My son oozed, exuded, flaked, suppurated, dribbled from every quadrant. To whom does one speak of
this? That he taught me to despise the body, what it is to have a
body — to be disgusted, repulsed. Often I had to look away, duck
outside, dart around corners. The absent thoughtless picking and
scratching and probing and toying, bottomless narcissistic fascination with his own body. As if his extremities were the very world's
four corners. A slave to himself. An engine of mindless will. A reign
of terror, trust me. The insane tantrums when his will was
thwarted. When some gratification was denied or delayed. It was
Kafkan — you were punished for protecting him from himself.
'No, no, child, my son, I cannot allow you to thrust your hand into
the vaporizer's hot water, the blades of the window fan, do not drink

that household solvent' — a tantrum. The insanity of it. You could not explain or reason. You could only walk away appalled. Will yourself not simply to let him the next time, not to smile and let him, 'Have at that solvent, my son,' learn the hard way. The whining and wheedling and tugging and towering rages. Not really psychotic, I came to see. Crazy like a fox. An agenda behind every outburst. 'Too much excitement, overtired, cranky, feverish, needs a lie-down, just frustrated, just a long day' — the litany of her excuses for him. His endless emotional manipulation of her. The ceaselessness of it and her inhuman reaction: even when she recognized what he was up to she excused him, she was charmed by the nakedness of his insecurity, his what she called 'need' for her, what she called my son's 'need for reassurance.' Need for reassurance? What reassurance? He never doubted. He knew it all belonged to him. He never doubted. As if it were due him. As if he deserved it. Insanity. Solipsism. He wanted it all. All I had, had had, never would. It never ended. Blind, reasonless appetite. I will say it: evil. There. I can imagine your face. But he was evil. And I alone seemed to know it. He afflicted me in a thousand ways and I could say nothing. My face fairly ached at day's end from the control I was forced to exert over — even the slight note of complaint you could hear in his breathing. The bruised circles of restless appetite beneath his eyes. Exhalation a whimper. The two different eyes, the one terrible eye. The redness and flaccidity of his mouth and the way the lip was always wet no matter how much one wiped at it for him. An inherently moist child, always clammy, the scent of him vaguely fungal. The vacancy of his face when he became absorbed in some pleasure. The utter shamelessness of his greed. The sense of utter entitlement. How long it took us to teach him even a perfunctory thank-you. And he never meant it, and she did not mind. She would — never minded. She was his servant. Slave mentality. This was not the girl I asked to marry me. She was his slave and believed she knew only joy. He played with her as a cat does a toy mouse and she felt joy. Madness? Where was my wife? What was this creature she stroked as he sucked at her? Most of his childhood — memory of it — most renders down to seeing myself standing there some meters away, watching them in appalled amazement. Behind my dutiful smile. Too weak ever to speak out, to ask it. This was my life. This is the truth I've hidden. You are good to listen. More important than you know. To speak it. *Te ju*— judge me as you wish. No, do. I am dying — no, I know — bedridden, near blind, gutted, catarrh, dying, alone and in pain. Look at all these bloody tubes. A life of such silence. And this is my confession. Good of you. Not what you — it is not your forgiveness I — just to hear the truth. About him. That I despised him. There is no other word. Often I was forced to avert my eyes from him, look away. Hide. I discovered why fathers hold the evening paper as they do.

[PAUSE for FATHER's attempted pantomime
of holding object spread before face]

THE FATHER: I am recalling now just one in un— something, a tantrum over something or other after dinner one evening. I did not want him eating in our living room. Not unreasonable I think. The dining room was for eating; I had explained to him the etymology and sense of '*dining* room.' The living room, where I reserved for myself but half an hour with the newspaper after dinner — and there he was, suddenly there before me, on the new carpet, eating his candy in the living room. Was I unreasonable? He had received the candy as his reward for eating the healthy dinner I had worked to buy for him and she had worked to prepare for him — feel it? the judgment, disgust? that one is never to say such a thing, to mention that one paid, that one's limited resources had been devoted to — that would be selfish, no? a bad parent, no? niggardly? *selfish?* And yet I had, had paid for the little colored chocolate candies, candies which here he stood upending the little bag to be able to get all of the candy into that mouth at once, never one by one, always all the sweets all at once, as much as fast as possible regardless of spillage, hence my gritted smile and carefully gentle reminder of the etymology of '*dining* room' and far less a command than — mindful of her reaction, always — *request* that, please, no candy in the — and with his mouth crammed with candy and chewing at it even as the tantrum began, puling and stamping his feet and shrieking now at the top of his lungs in the living room even as his mouth was filled with chocolate, that open red mouth filled with mashed candy which mixed with his spittle and as he howled overran his lip as he howled and stamped up and down and running down his chin and shirt, and peering timidly over the top of the paper held like a shield as I sat willing myself to remain in the chair and say nothing and watching now his mother down on one knee trying to wipe the chocolate drool off his chin as he screamed at her and batted the napkin away. Who could look on this and not be appalled? Who could — where was it determined that this sort of thing is acceptable, that such a creature must be not only tolerated no but *soothed*, actually *placated* as she was on her knees doing, tenderly, in gross contradiction to the unacceptability of what was going on. What sort of madness is this? That I can hear the soft little singsong tones she used to try to soothe him — for *what?* — as she patiently brings the napkin back again and again as he bats it away and screams that he hates her. I do not exaggerate; he said this: hates her. *Hates* her? *Her?* Down on one knee, pretending she hears nothing, that it's nothing, cranky, long day, that — what bewitchment lay behind this patience? What human being could remain on her knees wiping drool caused by *his, his* violation of a simple and reasonable prohibition against just this very sort of disgusting mess in the room in which we sought only to *live?* What chasm of insanity lay between us? What was this creature? Why did we go on like this? How could I be in any way culpable for lifting the evening paper to try to obscure this scene? It was either look away or kill him where he stood. How does doing what must be done to control my — how is this equal to my being remote or ungiving unquote or heaven forfend 'cruel'? Cruel to *that?* Why is 'cruel' applied only to those who pay for the little chocolates he spews onto the shirt-front you paid for to dribble onto the carpet you paid for and grinds under the shoes you paid for as he stamps up and down in fury at your mild request that he take reasonable steps to avert precisely the sort of mess he is causing? Am I the only one to whom this makes no sense? Is revolted, appalled? Why is even to speak of such revulsion not allowed? Who made this rule? Why was it I who must be seen and not heard? Whence this inversion of my own upbringing? What unthinkable discipline would my own father have —

[PAUSE for episode of dyspnea, blennorrhagia]

THE FATHER: Did. Sometimes I did, no, literally could not bear the sight of him. Impetigo is a skin disorder. His scalp's sores suppurated and formed a crust. The crust then turned yellow. A childhood skin disease. Condition of children. When he coughed it rained yellow crust. His bad eye wept constantly, a viscous stuff that has no name. His eyelashes at the breakfast his mother made would be clotted with a pale crust which someone would have to clean off with a swab while he writhed in complaint at being cleaned of repellent crust. About him hung a scent of spoilage, mildew. And she would nuzzle just to smell him. Nose running without cease or reason and caused small red raised sores on his nostrils and upper lip which then yielded more crust. Chronic ear infections meant not only a spike in the incidence of tantrums but an actual smell, a discharge whose odor I will spare you describing. Antibiotics. He was a veritable petri dish of infection and discharge and eruption and runoff, white as a root, blotched, moist, like something in a cellar. And yet all who saw him clasped their hands together and exclaimed. Beautiful child. Angel. Soulful. Delicate. Break such

hearts. The word 'beautiful' was used. I would simply stand there —
what could I say? My carefully pleased expression. But could they
have seen that inhuman little puke-white face during an infection,
an attack, a tantrum, the piggy malevolence of it, the truculent entitlement, the rapacity. The ugliness. 'Barked about most lazar-like
with vile' — the ugly truth. Mucus, pus, vomit, feces, diarrhea,
urine, wax, sputum, varicolored crusts. These were his dowry to —
the gifts he bore us. Thrashing in sleep or fever, clutching at the
very air as if to pull it to him. And always there bedside she was,
his, in thrall, bewitched, wiping and swabbing and stroking and
tending, never a word of acknowledgment of the sheer horror of
what he produced and expected her to wipe away. The endless
thankless expectation. Never acknowledged. The girl I married
would have reacted very, very differently to this creature, believe
me. Treating her breasts as if they were his. Property. Her nipples
the color of a skinned knee. Grasping, clutching. Making greedy
sounds. Manhandling her. Snorting, wheezing. Absorbed wholly in
his own sensations. Reflectionless. At home in his body as only one
whose body is not *his* job can be at home. Filled with himself, right
to the edges like a swollen pond. He *was* his body. I often could not
look. Even the speed of his growth that first year — statistically
unusual, the doctors remarked it — a rate that was weedy, aggressive, a willed imposition of self on space. That right eye's sputtering forward thrust. Sometimes she would grimace at the weight of
him, holding him, lifting, until she caught the brief grimace and
wiped it away — I was sure I saw it — replaced at once with that
expression of narcotic patience, abstract thrall, I several meters off,
extrorse, trying not —

[PAUSE for episode of dyspnea; technician's application
of tracheobronchial suction catheter]

THE FATHER: Never learned to breathe is why. Awful of me to
say, yes? And of course yes ironic, given — and she'd have died on

the spot to hear me say it. But it is the truth. Some chronic asthma and a tendency to bronchitis, yes, but that is not what I — I mean nasal. Nothing structurally wrong with his nose. Paid several times to have it examined, probed, they all concurred, nose normal, most of the occlusion from simple disuse. Chronic disuse. The truth: he never bothered to learn. Through it. Why bother? Breathed through his mouth, which is of course easier in the short term, requires less effort, maximizes intake, get it all in at once. And does, my son, breathes to this very day through his slack and much-loved adult mouth, which consequently is always partly open, this mouth, slack and wet, and white bits of rancid froth collect at the corners and are of course too much trouble ever to check in a lavatory mirror and attend to discreetly in private and spare others the sight of the pellets of paste at the corners of his mouth, forcing everyone to say nothing and pretend they do not see. The equivalent of long, unclean, or long nails on men, which I tirelessly tried to explain were in his own best interest to keep trimmed and clean. When I picture him it is always with his mouth partly open and lower lip wet and hanging and projecting outward far further than a lower lip ought, one eye dull with greed and the other's palsied bulge. This sounds ugly? It was ugly. Blame the messenger. Do. Silence me. Say the word. Verily, Father, but whose ugliness? For is she — that he was a sickly child as a child who — always in bed with asthma or ears, constant bronchitis and upper flu, slight chronic asthma yes true but bed for days at a time when some sun and fresh air could not poss— ring for, hurts — he had a little silver bell by the rocket's snout he'd ring, to summon her. Not a normal regular child's bed but a catalogue bed, battleship gray they called Authentic Silvery Finish plus postage and handling with aerodynamic booster fins and snout, assembly required and the instructions practically Cyrillic and yes and whom do you suppose was expec— the little silver tinkle of the bell and she'd fly, fly to him, bending uncomfortably over the booster fins of the bed, cold iron fins, minist— it rang and rang.

[PAUSE for episode of ophthalmorrhagia; technician's
swab/flush of dextrocular orbit; change of facial bandage]

THE FATHER: Bells of course employed throughout history to summon servants, domestics, an observation I kept to myself when she got him the bell. The official version was that the bell was to be used if he could not breathe, in lieu of calling out. It was to be an emergency bell. But he abused it. Whenever he was ill he continually rang the bell. Sometimes just to force her to come sit next to the bed. Her presence was demanded and off she went. Even in sleep, if the bell rang, however softly, slyly, sounding more like a wish than a ring, but she would hear it and be out of bed and off down the hall without even putting on her robe. The hall often cold. House poorly insulated and ferociously dear to heat. I, when I awoke, would take her her robe, slippers; she never thought of them. To see her arise still asleep at that maddening tinkle was to see mind-control at its most elemental. This was his genius: to *need*. The sleep he robbed her of, at will, daily, for years. Watching her face and body fall. Her body never had the chance to recover. Sometimes she looked like an old woman. Ghastly circles under her eyes. Legs swollen. He took years from her. And she'd have sworn she gave them freely. Sworn it. I'm not speaking now of *my* sleep, *my* life. He never thought of her except in reference to himself. This is the truth. I know him. If you had seen him at the funeral. As a child he — she'd hear the bell and without even coming fully awake pad off to the lavatory and turn on every faucet and fill the place with steam and sit for hours holding him on the commode in the steam while he slept — that he made her trade her own rest for his, night after — and that not only was all the hot water for all of us for the entire next morning exhausted but the constant steam then would infiltrate upstairs and everything was constantly sodden with his steam and in warm weathers came a rank odor of mold which she would have been appalled had I openly credited to him as its real source, his rocket and tinkle, all wood everywhere warping, wallpaper peeling off in sheets. The gifts he bestowed. That Christmas film — their joke was that he was giving angels wings each time. It was not that he was not sometimes truly ill, it would not be true to accuse him of — but he *used* it. The bell was only one of the more obvious — and she believed it was all her idea. To orbit him. To alter, cede herself. Vanish as a person. To become an abstraction: The Mother, Down On One Knee. This was life after he came — she orbits him, I chart her movements. That she could call him a blessing, the sun in her sky. She was no more the girl I'd married. And she never knew how I missed that girl, mourned her, how my heart went out to what she'd become. I was weak not to tell her the truth. Despised him. Couldn't. This was the insidious part, the part I truly despised, that he ruled *me*, as well, despite my seeing through him. I could not help it. After he came some chasm lay between us. My voice could not carry across it. How often on so many late nights I would lean weakly in the doorway of the lavatory wiping steam from my spectacles with the belt of the robe and was so desperate to say it, to utter it: 'What about *us?* Where had *our* lives gone? Why did this choking sucking thankless thing mean more than we? Who had decided that this should be so?' Beg her to come out of it, snap out. In despair, weak, not utter— she would not have heard me. That is why not. Afraid that what she would hear would — hear only a bad father, deficient man, uncaring, *selfish,* and then the last of the freely chosen bonds between us would be severed. That she would choose. Weak. Oh I was doomed, knew it. My self-respect was a plaything in those clammy little hands as well. The *genius* of his weakness. Nietzsche had no *idea*. Ballocks all reason for — and this, this was my thank-you — free tickets? A

black joke. *Free* he calls them? And airfare to come and applaud
and shape my face's grin to pretend with the rest of — *this* is my
thank-you? Oh the endless sense of entitlement. Endless. That you
understand eternal doom in all the late-night sickly hours forced
in a one-buttock hunch on the booster's bolted fin of the ridiculous
rocket-shaped bed he cajoled her — more plaything than bed,
impossible instructions on my knees with the wrong tool as he
stood in my light — ironized fin no broader than a ham but I'm
damned if I'll kneel by that ill-assembled bed. My job to maintain
the vaporizer and administer wet cloths and monitor the breathing
and fever as he lay holding the bell while again she was off un-
rested out in the cold to the all-night druggist to hunch there on
the booster-stage fin awash in the odor of mentholate gel and
yawning and checking my watch and looking down at him resting
with wet mouth agape and watching the chest make its diffident
minimal effort of rising and falling while he through the flutter
of that right lid staring without expression or making one
acknowledgment of — rising then up out of an almost oneiric
reverie to realize that I had been wishing it to cease, that chest, to
still its sluggish movement under the Gemini comforter he demanded to have upon him at — dreaming of it falling still, stilled,
the bell to cease its patrician tinkle, the last rattle of that weak and
omnipotent chest, and yes I would then strike my own breast,
crosswise thus —

[FATHER's weak pantomime of striking own chest]

— in punishment of my wish, ashamed, such was my own thrall to
him. He merely staring up slackly at my self-abuse with that red wet
lip hanging wetly, rancid froth, lazar-like crust, chin's spittle, chest's
unguent's menthol reek, a creamy little gout of snot protruding, that
blank eye sputtering like a bad bulb — put it out! put it out!

[PAUSE for technician's removal, cleaning,
reinsertion of O$_2$ feed into FATHER's nostril]

THE FATHER: That cramped on that fin and dabbing tender at his forehead and wiping away some of the chin's sputum and sitting gazing at it on the handkerchief, trying to — and — yes at the pillow, looking at the pillow, gazing at and thought of it, how quickly it — how few movements required not just to wish but to will it, to impose my own will as he so blithely always did, lying there pretending to be too feverish to see my — but it was, it was pathetic, not even — I was thinking of my weight on the pillow as a man in arrears thinks of sudden fortune, sweepstakes, inheritance. Wishful thinking. I believed then that I was struggling with my will, but it was mere fantasy. Not will. Aquinas's velleity. I lacked whatever it seems to take to be able to — or perhaps I failed to lack what must be lacking, yes? I could not have. Wishing it but not — both decency *and* weakness perhaps. *Te judice,* Father, yes? I know I was weak. But listen: I did wish it. That is no confession but just the truth. I did wish it. I did despise him. I did miss her and mourn. I did resent — I failed to see why his weakness should permit him to win. It was insane, made no sense — on the basis of what merit or capacity should *he* win? And she never knew. This was the worst, his *lèse majesté,* unforgivable: the chasm he opened between her and I. My unending pretense. My fear that she'd think me a monster, deficient. I pretended to love him as she did. This I confess. I subjected her to a — the last twenty-nine years of our life together were a lie. My lie. She never knew. I could pretend with the best of them. No adulterer was more careful a dissembler than I. I would help her off with her wrap and take the small sack from the druggist's and whisper my earnest little report on the state of his breathing and temperature throughout her absence, she listening but looking past me, at him, not noting how perfectly my expression's concern matched her own. I modeled my face on hers; she taught me to pretend. It never even occurred to her. Can you understand what this did to me? That she never for a moment doubted I felt the same, that I ceded myself as — that I too was under the sucking thing's spell?

> [PAUSE for episode of severe dyspnea; R.N.'s application
> of tracheobronchial suction catheter]

THE FATHER: That she never thenceforth knew me? That my wife had ceased to know me? That I let her go and pretended to join her? Might I hope that anyone could imagine the —

> [PAUSE for episode of ocular bobbing; technician's flush/evacuation
> of ophthalmorrhagic residue; change of ocular bandage]

THE FATHER: That we would make love and afterward lie curled together in our special position preparing to sleep and she'd not be still, whispering on and on about him, every conceivable ephemera about him, worries and wishes, a mother's prattle — and took my silence for agreement. The chasm's essence was that she believed there was no chasm. Our bed's width grew day by day and she never — not once occurred to her. That I saw through and loathed him. That I not merely failed to share her bewitchment but was appalled by it. It was my fault, not hers. I tell you this: he was the only secret I had from her. She was the very sun in my sky. The loneliness of the secret was an agony past — oh I loved her so. My feelings for her never wavered. I loved her from the first. We were meant to be together. Joined, united. I knew it the moment — saw her there on the arm of that Bowdoin twit in his fur collar. Holding her pennant as one would a parasol. That I loved her on the spot. I had a bit of an accent then; she twitted me for it. She would impersonate me when I was cross — only your life's one love could do this — the anger would vanish. The way she affected me. She followed American football and had a son who could not play and then later when he mysteriously ceased being sickly and grew sleek and vigorous would not play. She went instead to watch him swim. The nauseous diminutives, Wuggums, Tigerbear. He swam in public school. The stink of cheap bleach in the venues, barely breathe. Did she miss even one event? When did she stop following it, the football on the misaligned Zenith we would watch together — hold it still, the — making love and lying curled like twins in the womb, saying everything. I could tell her anything. When did that all go then. Just when did he take it from us. Why can't I remember. I remember the day we met as if it were yesterday but I'm bollixed if I can remember yesterday. Pathetic, disgusting. They do not care but if they knew what it — felt to hurt to bloody breathe. Enwebbed in tubes. Bastards, bleeding out every — yes I saw her and she me, the demurely held pennant I was new over and could not parse — our eyes met, all the clichés came instantly true — I knew she was the one to have all of me. A spotlight followed her across the lawn. I simply knew. Father, this was the acme of my life. Watching — that 'she was the girl for all of me/my unworthy life for thee' [melody unfamiliar, discordant]. To stand before Church and man and pledge it. To unwrap one another like gifts from God. Conversation's lifetime. If you could have seen her on our wedding — no of course not, that look as she — for me alone. To love at such depth. No better feeling in all creation. She would cock her head just so when amused. So much used to amuse her. We laughed at everything. We were our secret. She chose me. One another. I told her things I had not told my own brother. We belonged to one another. I felt chosen. Who chose *him,* pray? Who gave informed consent to everything hitherto's loss? I despised him for forcing me to hide the fact that I despised him. The common run is one thing, with their judgments, the demand to see you dandle and coo and toss the ball. But her? That I must wear this mask for her? Sounds monstrous but it's true: his fault. I simply couldn't. Tell her. That I — that he was in truth loathsome. That I so bitterly regretted letting her conceive. That she did not truly *see* him. To trust me, that she was under a spell, lost to herself. That she must come back. That I missed her so. None. And not for my sake, believe — she could not have borne it. It would have destroyed her. She'd have been destroyed, and on his account. He did this. Twisted everything his own way. Bewitched her. Fear that she'd — 'Poor dear defenseless Wuggums your father has a monstrous uncaring inhuman side to him I never saw but we see it now don't we but we don't need him do we no now let me make it up to you until I drop from bloody trying.' Missing something. 'Don't need him do we now there there.' Orbited him. Thought first and last. She had ceased to be the girl I'd — she was now The Mother, playing a part, a fairy story, emptying everything out to —. No, not true that it would have destroyed her, there was nothing left in her which would even have understood it, could so much as have *heard* the — she'd have cocked just so and looked at me without any comprehension whatever. It would have amounted to telling her the sun did not rise each day. He had made himself her world. *His* was the real lie. She believed *his* lie. She believed it: the sun rose and fell only —

[PAUSE for episode of dyspnea, visual evidence of erythruria;
R.N.'s location and clearing of pyuric obstruction
in urinary catheter; genital disinfection; technician's
reattachment of urinary catheter and gauge]

THE FATHER: The crux. The rub. Omit all else. This is why. The great black enormous lie that I for some reason I alone seemed able to see through — through, as if in a nightmare.

[PAUSE for episode of severe dyspnea; R.N.'s application
of tracheobronchial suction catheter, pulmonary
wedge pressure; technician (1)'s application of forcipital
swabs; location and attempted removal of mucoidal
obstruction in FATHER's trachea; technician (2)'s
administration of nebulized adrenaline; pertussive
expulsion of mucoidal mass; technician (2)'s removal
of mass in authorized Medical Waste Receptacle;
technician (1)'s reinsertion of O$_2$ feed into FATHER's nostril]

THE FATHER: Thrall. Listen. My son is evil. I know too well how this might sound, Father. *Te judice.* I am well beyond your judgment as you see. The word is '*evil.*' I do not exaggerate. He sucked something from her. Some discriminatory function. She lost her sense of humor, that was a clear sign I clung to. He cast some uncanny haze. Maddening to see through it and be unable — and not just her, Father, either. Everyone. Subtle at first but by oh shall we say middle school it was manifest: the wider world's bewitchment. No one seemed able to *see* him. Began then in blank shock at her side to endure the surreal enraptured soliloquies of instructors and headmasters, coaches and committees and deacons and even clergy which sent her into maternal raptures as I stood chewing my tongue in disbelief. It was as if they had all become his mother. She and they would enter into this complicity of bliss about my son as I beside her nodding with the careful, dutifully pleased expression I'd fashioned through years of practice, out of it as they went on. Then when we'd off to home and I would contrive some excuse and go sit alone in the den with my head in my hands. He seemed able to do it at will. Everyone around us. The great lie. He's taken in the bloody world. I do not exaggerate. You were not there to listen, drop-jawed: oh so brilliant, so sensitive, such discernment, precocity without vaunt, such a joy to know, so full of promise, such limitless gifts. On and on. Such an unqualified *asset,* such a *joy* to have on our roll, our team, our list, our staff, our dramaturgid panel, our minds. Such *limitless gifts* unquote. You cannot imagine the sensation of hearing that: '*gifts.*' As if freely given, as if not — had I even once had the backbone to seize one of them by the knot of his cravat and pull him to me and howl the truth in his face. Those glazed smiles. Thrall. If only I myself could have been taken in. My son. Oh and I did, prayed for it, pondered and sought, examined and studied him and prayed and sought without cease, praying to be taken in and bewitched and allow their scales to cover mine as well. I examined him from every angle. I sought diligently for what they all believed they saw, *natus ad glo*— headmaster pulling us aside at that function to take us aside and breathe gin that this was the single finest and most promising student he'd seen in his tenure at middle school, behind him a tweedy defile of instructors bearing down and leaning in to — such a joy, every so often the job worthwhile with one such as — limitless gifts. The sustained wince I'd molded into what appeared a grin while she with her hands clasped before her thanking them, thank— understand, I'd *read* with the boy. At length. I'd probed him. I'd sat trying to teach him sums. As he picked at his impetigo and stared vacantly at the page. I had circumspectly watched as he labored to read things and afterward searched him out thoroughly. I'd engaged him, examined, subtly and thoroughly and without prejudice. Please believe me. There was not one spark of brilliance in my son. I swear it. This was a child whose intellectual acme was a reasonable competence at sums acquired through endless grinding efforts at grasping the most elementary operations. Whose printed S's remained reversed until age eight despite — who pronounced 'epitome' as dactylic. A youth whose social persona was a blank affability and in whom a ready wit or appreciation for the nuances of accomplished English prose was wholly absent. No sin in that of course, a mediocre boy, ordinary — mediocrity is no sin. Nay but whence all this high estimate? What *gifts?* I went over his themes, every one, without fail, before they were passed in. I made it a policy to give my time. To this study of him. Willed myself to withhold prejudice. I lurked in doorways and watched. Even at university this was a boy for whom Sophocles' *Oresteia* was weeks of slack-jawed labor. I crept into doorways, alcoves, stacks. Observed him when no one's about. The *Oresteia* is not a difficult or inaccessible work. I searched without cease, in secret, for what they all seemed to see. And a *translation*. Weeks of grinding effort and not even Sophocles' Greek, some pablumesque adaptation, standing there unseen and appalled. Yet managed — he fooled them all. All of them, one great audience. Pulitzer indeed. Oh and all too well I know how this sounds; *te jude,* Father. But know the truth: I knew him, inside and out, and this was his one only true gift: this: a capacity for somehow *seeming* brilliant, *seeming* exceptional, precocious, gifted, promising. Yes to be *promising,* they all of them said it eventually, 'limitless *promise*,' for this was his gift, and do you see the dark art here, the genius for manipulating his audience? His gift was for somehow arousing admiration and raising everyone's estimate of him and everyone's expectations of him and so forcing you to pray for him to triumph and live up to and justify those expectations in order to spare not just her but everyone who had been duped into believing in his limitless promise the crushing disappointment of seeing the truth of his essential mediocrity. Do you see the perverse genius of this? The exquisite torment? Of forcing me to pray for his triumph? To desire the maintenance of his lie? And not for his sake but others'? Hers? This is brilliance of a certain very particular and perverse and despicable sort, yes? The Attics called one's particular gift or genius his *techno.* Was it *techno?* Odd for 'gift.' Do you decline it in the genitive? That he draws all into his web this way, *limitless gifts,* expectations of brilliant success. They come thus not only to believe the lie but to depend upon it. Whole rows of them in evening dress rising, applauding the lie. My dutifully proud — wear a mask and your face grows to fit it. Avoid all mirrors as though — and no, worst, the black irony: now his wife and girls are bewitched this way now as well you see. As his mother — the art he perfected upon her. I see it in their faces, the heartbreaking way they look at him, holding him whole in their eyes. Their perfect trusting innocent children's eyes, adoring. And he then in receipt, casually, passively, never — as if he actually *deserved* this sort of — as if it were the most natural thing in the world. Oh how I have longed to shout the truth and expose and break this spell he's cast over all who — this spell he's not even *aware* of, not even conscious of what he's about, what he so effortlessly casts over his — as if this sort of love were *due* him, itself of nature, inevitable as the sunrise, never a thought, never a moment's doubt that he deserves it all and more. The very thought of it chokes me. How many years he took from us. Our gift. Genitive, ablative, nominative — the accidence of 'gift.' He wept at her deathbed. Wept. Can you imagine? That *he* had the right to weep at her loss. That *he* had that right. I stood in abject shock beside him. The arrogance. And she in that bed suffering so. Her last conscious word — to him. *His* weeping. This was the closest I ever came. *Pervigilium.* To speaking it. The truth. Weeping, that soft slack face red and eyes squeezed tight like a child whose sweets are all gone, gobbled up, like some obscene pink — mouth open and lip wet and a snot-string hanging untended and his wife — *his* wife — lovely arm around, to comfort him, comforting *him, his* loss — imagine. That now even my loss, my shameless tears, the loss of the only — that even my grief must be usurped, without one thought, not once acknowledged, as if it were his right to weep. To weep for her. Who told him he had that right? Why was I alone undeluded? What had — what sins in my sad small life merited this curse, to see the truth and be impotent to speak it? What was I guilty of that this should visit upon me? Why did no one ever ask? What acuity were they absent and I cursed with, to ask why was he born? oh why was he born? The truth would have killed her. To realize her own life had been given for — ceded to a lie. It would have killed her where she stood. I tried. Came close once or twice, once at his wed— not in me to do it. I searched within and it was not there. That certain sliver of steel one requires to do what must be done come what may. And she did die happy, believing thc lic.

> [PAUSE for technician's change of ileostomy pouch and
> skin barrier; examination of stoma; partial sponge bath]

THE FATHER: Oh but *he* knew. He knew. That behind my face I despised him. My son alone knew. He alone saw me. From those I loved I hid it — at what cost, what life and love sacrificed for the need to spare them all, hide the truth — but he alone saw through. I could not hide it from him whom I despised. That fluttered thrusting eye would fall upon me and read my hatred of the living lie I'd wrought and borne. That ghastly extrusive right eye divined the secret repulsion its own repulsiveness caused in me. Father, you see this irony. She herself was blind to me, lost. He alone saw that I alone saw him for what he was. Ours was a black intimacy forged around that secret knowledge, for I knew that he knew I knew, and he that I knew he knew I knew. The profundity of our shared knowledge and complicity in that knowledge flew between us — *'I know you'*; *'Yes and I you'* — a terrible voltage charged the air when — if we two were alone, out of her sight, which was rare; she rarely left us alone together. Sometimes — rarely — once — it was at his first girl's birth, as my wife was leaning over the bed embracing his and I behind her facing him and he made as if to hold the infant out to me, his eyes on me, holding my eyes whole with his and the truth arcing back and forth between us over the lolling head of that beautiful child as he held it out as if his to give, and I could not then refrain from letting escape the briefest flicker of acknowledgment of the truth with the twist of my mouth's right side, a dark little half-smile, *'I know what you are,'* which he met with that baggy half-smile of his own, what doubtless all in the room perceived as filial thanks for my smile and the blessing it appeared to imply and — do you now see why I loathed him? The ultimate insult? That he alone knew my heart, knew the truth, which from those I loved I died inside from hiding? A terrible charge, my hatred of him and his blithe delight at my secret pain oscillating between us and de-forming the very air of any shared space commencing around shall we say just after his Confirmation, adolescence, when he stopped coughing and grew sleek. Though it's become ever worse as he's aged and consolidated his powers and more and more of the world has fallen under the — taken in.

[PAUSE]

THE FATHER: Rare that she left us alone in a room together, though. His mother. A reluctance. I'm convinced she did not know why. Some instinctive unease, intuition. She believed he and I loved one another in the strained stilted way of fathers and sons and that this was why we had so little to say to one another. She believed the love was unspoken and so intense that it made us awkward. Used gently to chide me in bed about what she called my 'awkwardness' with the boy. She rarely left a room, believed she had somehow to mediate between us, the strained circuit. Even when I taught him — taught him sums she contrived ways to sit at the table, to — she felt she had to protect us both. It broke — oh — broke my — oh oh bloody Christ please ring it the —

> [PAUSE for technician's removal of ileostomy pouch and
> skin barrier; FATHER's evacuation of digestive gases;
> catheter suction of edemic particulates; moderate dyspnea;
> R.N. remarks re fatigue and recommends truncation of visit;
> FATHER's outburst at R.N., technician, Charge Nurse]

THE FATHER: That she died without knowing my heart. Without the entirety of union we had promised one another before God and Church and her parents and my mother and brother standing with me. Out of love. It was, Father. Our marriage a lie and she did not know, never knew I was so alone. That I slunk through our life in silence and alone. My decision, to spare her. Out of love. God how I loved her. Such silence. I was weak. Bloody awful, pathetic, tragic that weakn— for the truth might have brought her to me; I might somehow have shown him to her. His true gift, what he was really about. Slight chance, granted. Long odds. Never able. I was too weak to risk causing her pain, a pain which would have been on his behalf. She orbited him, I her. My hatred of him made me weak. I came to know myself: I am weak. Deficient. Disgusted now by my own deficiency. Pathetic specimen. No backbone. Nor has he a backbone either, none, but requires none, a new species, needn't stand: others support him. Ingenious weakness. World owes him love. His gift that the world somehow believes it as well. Why? Why does *he* pay no price for his weakness? Under what possible scheme is this just? Who gave him my life? By what fiat? Because and he will, he will come to me today, here, later. Pay his respects, press my hand, play his solicitous part. Fresh flowers, girls' construction-paper cards. Genius of him. Has not missed a day I've been here. Lying here. Only he and I know why. Bring them here to see me. Loving son the staff all say, lovely family, how lucky, so very much to be grateful. Blessings. Brings his girls, holds them up for me to see whole. Above the rails. Stem to stern. Ship to shore. He calls them his apples. He may be in transit this very — even as we speak. Fit diminutive. 'Apples.' He devours people. Drains. Thank you for hearing this. Devoured my life and left me to my. I am loathsome, lying here. Good of you to listen. Charitable. Sister, I require a favor. I wish to try to — to find the strength. I am dying, I know it. One can feel it coming you know, know it's on its way. Oddly familiar the feeling. An old old friend come to pay his. I require a favor from you. I'll not say an indulgence. A boon. Listen. Soon he will come, and with him he will bring the delightful girl who married him and adores him and cocks her head when he delights her and adores him and weeps shamelessly at the sight of me here lying here in these webs of tubes, and the two girls he makes such a faultless show of loving — '*Apple of my eye*' — and who adore him. Adore him. You see the lie lives on. If I am weak it will outlive me. We shall see whether I have the backbone to cause the girl pain, who believes she does love him. To be judged a bad man.

When I do. Bitter spiteful old man. I am weak enough to hope in part it's taken for delirium. This is how weak a man I am. That her loving me and choosing and marrying me and having her child by me might well have been her mistake. I am dying, he impending, I have one more chance — the truth, to speak it aloud, to expose him, sunder the thrall, shift the scales, warn the innocents he's taken in. To sacrifice their opinion of me to the truth, out of love for those blameless children. If you saw the way he looked at them, his little apples, with that eye, the smug triumph, the weak lid peeled back to expose the — never doubting he deserves this joy. Taking joy as his due no matter the. They will be here soon standing here. Holding my hand as you are. What time is it? What time do you have? He is in transit even now, I feel it. He will look down again at me today on this bed, between these rails, entubed, incontinent, foul, wracked, struggling even to breathe, and his face's intrinsic vacancy will again disguise to all eyes but mine the exultation in his eyes, both the eyes, seeing me like this. And he will not even know he exults, he is that blind to himself, he himself believes the lie. This is the real affront. This is his *coup de théâtre*. That he too is taken in, that he too believes he loves me, believes he loves. For him, too, I would do it. Say it. Break the spell he's cast over even himself. That is true evil, not even to *know* one is evil, no? Save his soul you could say. Perhaps. Had I the spine. Velleity. Could find the steel. Shall set one free, no? Is that not promised Father? For say unto you verily. Yes? Forgive me, for I. Sister, I wish to make my peace. To close the circuit. To deliver it into the room's air: that I know what he is. That he disgusts me and desp— repels me and that I despise him and that his birth was a blot, unbearable. Perhaps yes even yes to raise both arms as I — the black joke my now suffocating here as he must know he should have so long ago in that rocket I paid for without —

[PAUSE]

THE FATHER: God, Aeschylus. The *Oresteia*: Aeschylus. His doorway, picking at himself in translation. Aeschylus, not Sophocles. Pathetic.

[PAUSE]

THE FATHER: Long nails on men are repellent. Keep them short and keep them clean. That is my motto.

[PAUSE for episode of ophthalmorrhagia; technician's swab/flush of dextrocular orbit; change of facial bandage]

THE FATHER: Now and now I have made it. My confession. To you merciful Sisters of Mercy. Not, not that I despised him. For if you knew him. If you saw what I saw you'd have smothered him with the pillow long ago believe me. My confession is that damnable weakness and misguided love send me to heaven without having spoken the truth. The forbidden truth. No one even says aloud that you are not to say it. *Te judice.* If only I could. Oh how I despise the loss of my strength! If you knew this hurt — how it — but do not weep. Weep not. Do not weep. Not for me. I do not deserve — why are you crying? Don't you dare pity me. What I need from — pity is not what I need from you. Not why. Far from — do stop it, don't want to see it. *Stop.*

YOU [cruelly]: But Father it's me. Your own son. All of us, standing here, loving you so.

THE FATHER: Father good and because I do I do do need something from you. Father, listen. It must not win. This evil. You are — you've heard the truth now. Good of you. Do this: hate him for me after I die. I beg you. Dying request. Pastoral service. Mercy. As you love truth, as God the — for I confess: I will say nothing. I know myself and it is too late. Not in me. Mere fantasy to think. For even now he is in transit, bearing gifts. His apples to hold out to me whole. Wishful thinking, to raise myself up Lazarus-like with vile and loathsome truth for all to — where is my bell? That they will gather about the bed and his weak eye will fall upon me in the midst of his wife's uxorious prattle. He will have a child in his arms. His eye will meet mine and his wet red wet labial lip curl invisibly in secret acknowledgment between he and I and I will try and try and fail to raise my arms and break the spell with my last breath, to depose — expose him, rebuke the evil he long ago used her to make me help him erect. Father *judicat orbis*. Never have I ever begged before. Down on one knee now for — do not forsake me. I beg you. Despise him for me. On my account. Promise you'll carry it. It must outlive all this. Of myself I am weak bear my burden save your servant *te judice* for thine is — not —

> [PAUSE for severe dyspnea; sterilization and partial
> anesthesis of dextral orbit; Code for attending MD]

THE FATHER: Not consign me. Be my bell. Unworthy life for all thee. Beg. Not to die in this appalling silence. This charged and pregnant vacuum all around. This wet and open sucking hole beneath that eye. That terrible eye impending. Such silence.

SUICIDE AS A SORT OF PRESENT

There was once a mother who had a very hard time indeed, emotionally, inside.

As she remembered it, she had always had a hard time, even as a child. She remembered few of her childhood's specifics, but what she could remember were feelings of self-loathing, terror, and despair that seemed to have been with her always.

From an objective perspective, it would not be inaccurate to say that this mother-to-be had had some very heavy psychic shit laid on her as a little girl, and that some of this shit qualified as parental abuse. Her childhood had not been as bad as some, but it had been no picnic. All this, while accurate, would not be to the point.

The point is that, from as early an age as she could recall, this mother-to-be loathed herself. She viewed everything in life with apprehension, as if every occasion or opportunity were some sort of dreadfully important exam for which she had been too lazy or stupid to prepare properly. It felt as if a perfect score on each such exam was necessary in order to avert some shattering punishment.[1] She was terrified of everything, and terrified to show it.

The mother-to-be knew perfectly well, from an early age, that this constant horrible pressure she felt was an internal pressure. That it was not anyone else's fault. Thus she loathed herself even

---

[1] Her parents, by the way, did not beat her or ever even really discipline her, nor did they pressure her.

more. Her expectations of herself were of utter perfection, and each time she fell short of perfection she was filled with an unbearable plunging despair that threatened to shatter her like a cheap mirror.[2] These very high expectations applied to every department of the future mother's life, particularly those departments which involved others' approval or disapproval. She was thus, in childhood and adolescence, viewed as bright, attractive, popular, impressive; she was commended and approved. Peers appeared to envy her energy, drive, appearance, intelligence, disposition, and unfailing consideration for the needs and feelings of others[3]; she had few close friends. Throughout her adolescence, authorities such as teachers, employers, troop leaders, pastors, and F.S.A. Faculty Advisers commented that the young mother-in-waiting 'seem[ed] to have very, very high expectations of [her]self,' and while these comments were often delivered in a spirit of gentle concern or reproof, there was no failing to discern in them that slight unmistakable note of approval — of an authority's detached, objective judgment and decision to approve — and at any rate the future mother felt (for the moment) approved. And felt seen: her standards *were* high. She took a sort of abject pride in her mercilessness toward herself.[4]

By the time she was grown up, it would be accurate to say that the mother-to-be was having a very hard interior time of it indeed.

When she became a mother, things became even harder. The mother's expectations of her small child were also, it turned out,

---

[2] Her parents had been low-income, physically imperfect, and not very bright — features which the child disliked herself for noting.

[3] The phrases *lighten up* and *chill out* had not at this time come into currency (nor, in fact, had *psychic shit;* nor had *parental abuse* or even *objective perspective*).

[4] In fact, one explanation the soon-to-be mother's own parents gave for their disciplining her so little was that their daughter had seemed so mercilessly to upbraid herself for any shortcoming or transgression that disciplining her would have felt 'a little bit like kicking a dog.'

impossibly high. And every time the child fell short, her natural inclination was to loathe it. In other words, every time it (the child)
threatened to compromise the high standards that were all the
mother felt she really had, inside, the mother's instinctive self-
loathing tended to project itself outward and downward onto the
child itself. This tendency was compounded by the fact that there
existed only a very tiny and indistinct separation in the mother's
mind between her own identity and that of her small child. The
child appeared in a sense to be the mother's own reflection in a di-
minishing and deeply flawed mirror. Thus every time the child was
rude, greedy, foul, dense, selfish, cruel, disobedient, lazy, foolish,
willful, or childish, the mother's deepest and most natural inclination was to loathe it.

But she could not loathe it. No good mother can loathe her child
or judge it or abuse it or wish it harm in any way. The mother knew
this. And her standards for herself as a mother were, as one would
expect, extremely high. It was thus that whenever she 'slipped,'
'snapped,' 'lost her patience' and expressed (or even felt) loathing
(however brief) for the child, the mother was instantly plunged into
such a chasm of self-recrimination and despair that she felt it just
could not be borne. Hence the mother was at war. Her expectations
were in fundamental conflict. It was a conflict in which she felt her
very life was at stake: to fail to overcome her instinctive dissatisfac-
tion with her child would result in a terrible, shattering punishment which she knew she herself would administer, inside. She was
determined — desperate — to succeed, to satisfy her expectations
of herself as a mother, no matter what it cost.

From an objective perspective, the mother was wildly successful
in her efforts at self-control. In her outward conduct toward the
child, the mother was indefatigably loving, compassionate, empathetic, patient, warm, effusive, unconditional, and devoid of any apparent capacity to judge or disapprove or withhold love in any

form. The more loathsome the child was, the more loving the mother required herself to be. Her conduct was, by any standard of what an outstanding mother might be expected to be, impeccable.

In return, the small child, as it grew, loved the mother more than all other things in the world put together. If it had had the capacity to speak of itself truly somehow, the child would have said that it felt itself to be a very wicked, loathsome child who through some undeserved stroke of good fortune got to have the very best, most loving and patient and beautiful mother in the whole world.

Inside, as the child grew, the mother was filled with self-loathing and despair. Surely, she felt, the fact that the child lied and cheated and terrorized neighborhood pets was her fault; surely the child was simply expressing for all the world to see her own grotesque and pathetic deficiencies as a mother. Thus, when the child stole his class's UNICEF money or swung a cat by its tail and struck it repeatedly against the sharp corner of a brick home next door, she took the child's grotesque deficiencies upon herself, rewarding the child's tears and self-recriminations with an unconditionally loving forgiveness that made her seem to the child to be his lone refuge in a world of impossible expectations and merciless judgment and unending psychic shit. As he (the child) grew, the mother took all that was imperfect in him deep into herself and bore it all and thus absolved him, redeemed and renewed him, even as she added to her own inner fund of loathing.

So it went, throughout his childhood and adolescence, such that, by the time the child was old enough to apply for various licenses and permits, the mother was almost entirely filled, deep inside, with loathing: loathing for herself, for the delinquent and unhappy child, for a world of impossible expectations and merciless judgment. She could not, of course, express any of this. And so the son — desperate, as are all children, to repay the perfect love we may expect only of mothers — expressed it all for her.

BRIEF INTERVIEWS
WITH HIDEOUS MEN

B.I. #20 12-96
New Haven CT

'And yet I did not fall in love with her until she had related the story of the unbelievably horrifying incident in which she was brutally accosted and held captive and very nearly killed.'

Q.

'Let me explain. I'm aware of how it might sound, believe me. I can explain. In bed together, in response to some sort of prompt or association, she related an anecdote about hitchhiking and once being picked up by what turned out to be a psychotic serial sex offender who then drove her to a secluded area and raped her and would almost surely have murdered her had she not been able to think effectively on her feet under enormous fear and stress. Irregardless of whatever I might have thought of the quality and substance of the thinking that enabled her to induce him to let her live.'

Q.

'Neither would I. Who would now, in an era when every — when psychotic serial killers have their own trading cards? I'm concerned in today's climate to steer clear of any suggestion of anyone quote asking for it, let's not even go there, but rest assured that it gives one pause about the capacities of judgment involved, or at the very least the naiveté —'

Q.

'Only that it was perhaps marginally less unbelievable in the context of her type, in that this was what one might call a quote Granola Cruncher, or post-Hippie, New Ager, what have you, in college where one is often first exposed to social taxonomies we called them Granola Crunchers or simply Crunchers, terms comprising the prototypical sandals, unrefined fibers, daffy arcana, emotional incontinence, flamboyantly long hair, extreme liberality on social issues, financial support from parents they revile, bare feet, obscure import religions, indifferent hygiene, a gooey and somewhat canned vocabulary, the whole predictable peace-and-love post-Hippie diction that im—'

Q.

'A large outdoor concert-dash-performance-art community festival thing in a park downtown where — it was a pickup, plain and simple. I will not try to represent it as anything nicer than that, or more fated. And I'm going to admit at the risk of appearing mercenary that her prototypical Cruncher morphology was evident right at first sight, from clear on the other side of the bandstand, and dictated the terms of the approach and the tactics of the pickup itself and made the whole thing almost criminally easy. Half the women — it is a less uncommon typology among educated girls out here than one might think. You don't want to know what kind of festival or why the three of us were there, trust me. I'll just bite the political bullet and confess that I classified her as a strictly one-night objective, and that my interest in her was almost entirely due to the fact that she was pretty. Sexually attractive, sexy. She had a phenomenal body, even under the poncho. It was her body that attracted me. Her face was a bit strange. Not homely but eccentric. Tad's assessment was that she looked like a really sexy duck. Nevertheless *nolo* to the charge that I spotted her on the blanket at the concert and sauntered carnivorously over with an overtly one-night objective. And, having had some prior dealings with the Cruncher genus prior to this, that the one-night proviso was due mostly to the grim unimaginability of having to *talk* with a New Age brigadier for more than one night. Whether or not you approve I think we can assume you understand.'

Q.

'That essential at-center-life-is-just-a-cute-pet-bunny *fluffiness* about them that makes it so exceedingly hard to take them seriously or not to end up feeling as if you're exploiting them in some way.'

Q.

'Fluffiness or daffiness or intellectual flaccidity or a somehow smug-seeming naiveté. Choose whichever offends you least. And yes and don't worry I'm aware of how all this sounds and can well imagine the judgments you're forming from the way I'm character- izing what drew me to her but if I'm really to explain this to you as requested then I have no choice but to be brutally candid rather than observing the pseudosensitive niceties of euphemism about the way a reasonably experienced, educated man is going to view an extraordinarily good-looking girl whose life philosophy is fluffy and unconsidered and when one comes right down to it kind of con- temptible. I'm going to pay you the compliment of not pretending to worry whether you understand what I'm referring to about the difficulty of not feeling impatience and even contempt — the hypocrisy, the blatant self-contradiction, the way you know from the outset that there will be the requisite enthusiasms for the rain forest and spotted owl, creative meditation, feel-good psychology, macrobiosis, rabid distrust of what they consider authority without evidently once stopping to consider the rigid authoritarianism im- plicit in the rigid uniformity of their own quote unquote noncon- formist uniform, vocabulary, attitudes. As someone who worked himself through both college and two years now of postgraduate school I have to confess to an almost blanket — these rich kids in torn jeans whose way of protesting apartheid was to boycott South African pot. Silverglade called them the Inward Bound. The smug naiveté, the condescension in the quote compassion they feel for those quote unquote trapped or imprisoned in orthodox American lifestyle choices. So on and so forth. The fact that the Inward Bound never consider that it's the probity and thrift of the re— to occur to them that they themselves have themselves become the distillate of everything about the culture they deride and define themselves as opposing, the narcissism, the materialism and complacency and unexamined conformity — nor the irony that the blithe teleology of this quote impending New Age is exactly the same cultural permission-slip that Manifest Destiny was, or the Reich or the dialectic of the proletariat or the Cultural Revolution — all the same. And it never even occurs to them their certainty that they are different is what makes them the same.'

Q.

'You would be surprised.'

Q.

'All right and the near-contempt here specifically in the way you can saunter casually over and bend down next to her blanket to initiate conversation and idly play with the blanket's fringe and easily create the sense of affinity and connection that will allow you to pick her up and somehow almost resent that it's so goddamn easy to make the conversation flow toward a sense of connection, how exploitative you feel when it is so easy to get this type to regard you as a kindred soul — you almost know what's going to be said next without her having even to open her pretty mouth. Tad said she was like some kind of smooth blank perfect piece of pseudo-art you want to buy so you can take it home and sm—'

Q.

'No, not at all, because I am trying to explain that the typology here dictated a tactic of what appeared to be a blend of embarrassed confession and brutal candor. The moment enough of a mood of conversational intimacy had been established to make a quote confession seem even remotely plausible I deployed a sensitive-slash-pained expression and quote confessed that I'd in fact not just been passing her blanket and had even though we didn't know one another felt a mysterious but overwhelming urge just to lean down and say Hi but no something about her that made it somehow impossible to deploy anything less than total honesty now forced me to confess that I had in fact deliberately approached her blanket and initiated conversation because I had seen her from across the bandstand and had felt some mysterious but overwhelmingly sensual energy seeming to emanate from her very being and had been helplessly drawn to it and had leaned down and introduced myself and started a conversation with her because I wanted to connect and make mutually nurturing and exquisite love with her, and had been ashamed of admitting this natural desire and so had fibbed at first in explaining my approach of her, though now some mysterious gentleness and generosity of soul I could intuit about her was now allowing me to feel serene enough to confess that I had, formerly, fibbed. Note the rhetorically specific blend of childish diction like *Hi* and *fib* with flaccid abstractions like *nurture* and *energy* and *serene*. This is the lingua franca of the Inward Bound. I actually truly did like her, I found, as an individual — she had an amused expression during the whole conversation that made it hard not to smile in return, and an involuntary need to smile is one of the best feelings available, no? A refill? It's refill time, yes?'

Q. . . .

'Yes and that prior experience has taught that the female Granola Cruncher tends to define herself in opposition to what she sees as the unconsidered and hypocrisy-bound attitudes of quote bourgeois women and is thus essentially unoffendable, rejects the whole concept of propriety and offense, views so-called honesty of even the most brutal or repellent sort as evidence of sincerity and respect, getting quote real, the impression that you respect her personhood too much to ply her with implausible fictions and leave very basic natural energies and desires uncommunicated. Not to mention — to render your own indignation and distaste complete, I'm sure — that extremely, off-the-charts pretty women of almost every type have, from my experience, tend all to have a uniform obsession with this idea of *respect,* and will do almost anything anywhere for any fellow who affords her a sufficient sense of being deeply and profoundly respected. I doubt I need to point out that this is nothing but a particular female variant of the psychological need to believe that others take you as seriously as you take yourself. There is nothing particularly wrong with this, as psychological needs go, but yet of course we should remember that a deep need for anything from other people makes us easy pickings. I can tell by your expression what *you* think of brutal candor. The fact is that she had a body that my body found sexually attractive and wanted to have intercourse with and it was not really any more noble or complicated than that. And she did indeed turn out to be straight out of Central Granola-Cruncher Casting, I should insert. She had some kind of monomaniacal hatred for the American timber industry, and professed membership in one of those apostrophe-heavy near-Eastern religions that I would defy anyone to pronounce correctly, and believed strongly in the superior value of vitamins and minerals in colloidal suspension rather than tablet form, et cetera, and then, when one thing had been led stolidly by me to another and there she was in my apartment and we had done what I had wanted to do with her and had exchanged the standard horizontal compliments and assurances, she was going on about her obscure Levantine denomination's views vis-à-vis energy fields and souls and connections between souls via what she kept calling quote focus, and using the,

well, the quote L-word itself several times without irony or even
any evident awareness that the word has through tactical over-
deployment become trite and requires invisible quotes around it now
at the very least, and I suppose I should tell you that I was planning
right from the outset to give her the special false number when we
exchanged numbers in the morning, which all but a very small and
cynical minority always want to. Exchange numbers. A fellow in
Tad's torts study group's great-uncle or grandparents or something
have a vacation home just outside Milford and are never there, with
a phone but no machine or service, so when someone you've given
the special number calls the special number it simply rings and
rings, so for a few days it's usually not evident to the girl that what
you've given her isn't your true number and for a few days allows
her to imagine that perhaps you've just been extremely busy and
scarce and that this is also perhaps why you haven't called her either. Which obviates the chance of hurt feelings and is therefore, I
submit, good, though I can well im—'

Q.

'The sort of glorious girl whose kiss tastes of liquor when she's
had no liquor to drink. Cassis, berries, gumdrops, all steamy and
soft. Quote unquote.'

Q. . . .

'Yes and so in the anecdote there she is, blithely hitchhiking
along the interstate, and on this particular day the fellow in the car
that stops almost the moment she puts her thumb out happens
to — she said she knew she'd made a mistake the moment she got
in. The car. Just from what she called the energy field inside the car,
she said, and that fear gripped her soul the moment she got in. And
sure enough, the fellow in the car soon exits the highway and exits
off into some kind of secluded area, which seems to be what psychotic sex criminals always do, you're always reading *secluded area* in
all the accounts of quote *brutal sex slayings* and *grisly discoveries* of

unidentified remains by a scout troop or amateur botanist, et cetera, common knowledge which you can be sure she was reviewing, horror-stricken, as the fellow began acting more and more creepy and psychotic even on the interstate and then soon exited into the first available secluded area.'

Q.

'Her explanation was that she did not in fact feel the psychotic energy field until she had shut the car's door and they were moving, at which time it was too late. She was not melodramatic about it but described herself as literally paralyzed with terror. Though you might be wondering as I did when one hears about cases like this as to why the victim doesn't simply bail out of the car the minute the fellow begins grinning maniacally or acting erratic or casually discussing how much he loathes his mother and dreams of raping her with her LPGA-endorsed sand wedge and then stabbing her 106 times, et cetera. But here she did point out that the prospect of bailing out of a rapidly moving car and hitting the macadam at sixty miles an — at the very least you break a leg or something, and then as you're trying to drag yourself off the road into the underbrush of course what's to keep the fellow from turning around to come back for you, which in addition let's keep in mind that he's now going to be additionally aggrieved about the rejection implicit in your preferring to hit the macadam at 60 m.p.h. rather than remain in his company, given that psychotic sex offenders have a notoriously low tolerance for rejection, and so forth.'

Q.

'Something about his aspect, eyes, the quote energy field in the car — she said she instantly knew in the depths of her soul that the fellow's intention was to brutally rape, torture, and kill her, she said. And I believed her here, that one can intuitively pick up on the epiphenomena of danger, sense psychosis in someone's aspect — you needn't buy into energy fields or ESP to accept mortal intuition. Nor would I even begin to try to describe what she looks like as she's telling the story, reliving it, she's naked, hair spilling all down her back, sitting meditatively cross-legged amid the wrecked bedding and smoking ultralight Merits from which she keeps removing the filters because she claims they're full of additives and unsafe — unsafe as she's sitting there *chain-smoking,* which was so patently irrational that I couldn't even bring — yes and some kind of blister on her Achilles tendon, from the sandals, leaning with her upper body to follow the oscillation of the fan so she's moving in and out of a wash of moon from the window whose angle of incidence itself alters as the moon moves up and across the window — all I can tell you is she was lovely. The bottoms of her feet dirty, almost black. The moon so full it looks engorged. And long hair spilling all over, more than — beautiful lustrous hair that makes you understand why women use conditioner. Tad's boon companion Silverglade telling me she looks like her hair grew her head instead of the other way around and asking how long estrus lasts in her species and droll ho ho. My memory is more verbal than visual, I'm afraid. It's on the sixth floor and my bedroom gets stuffy, she treated the fan like cold water and closed her eyes when it hit her. And by the time the psychotic fellow in question exits into the secluded area and finally comes straight out and indicates what his true intentions are — apparently detailing certain specific plans and procedures and implements — she's not the least bit surprised, she said she'd known the kind of hideously twisted soul-energy she'd gotten into the car into, the kind of pitiless and unappeasable psychotic he was and what sort of interaction they were headed for in this secluded area, and concluding that she was going to become just another grisly discovery for some amateur botanist a few days hence unless she could focus her way into the sort of profound soul-connection that would make it difficult for the fellow to murder her. These were her words, this was the sort of pseudo-abstract terminology she — and yet at the same time I was now captivated enough by the anecdote to simply accept the terminology as a kind of foreign language without trying to judge it or press for clarification, I just decided to presume that *focus* was her obscure denomination's euphemism for prayer, and that in a desperate situation like this who really was in any position to judge what would be a sound response to the sort of shock and terror she must be feeling, who could say with any certainty whether prayer wouldn't be appropriate. Foxholes and atheists and so on. What I remember best is that by this time it was, for the first time, taking much less effort to listen to her — she had an unexpected ability to recount it in such a way as to deflect attention from herself and displace maximum attention onto the anecdote itself. I have to confess that it was the first time I did not find her one bit dull. Care for another?'

Q.

'That she was not melodramatic about it, the anecdote, telling me, nor affecting an unnatural calm the way some people affect an unnatural nonchalance about narrating an incident that is meant to heighten their story's drama and/or make them appear nonchalant and sophisticated, one or the other of which is often the most annoying part of listening to certain types of beautiful women structure a story or anecdote — that they are used to high levels of people's attention, and need to feel that they control it, always trying to control the precise type and degree of your attention instead of simply trusting that you are paying the appropriate degree of attention. I'm sure you yourself have noticed this in very attractive women, that paying attention to them makes them immediately begin to pose, even if their pose is the affected nonchalance they affect to portray themselves as unposed. It becomes dull very quickly. But she was, or seemed, oddly unposed for someone this attractive and with this dramatic a story to tell. It struck me, listening. She seemed truly poseless in relating it, open to attention but not solicitous — nor contemptuous of the attention, or affecting disdain or contempt, which I hate. Some beautiful women, something wrong with their voice, some squeakiness or lack of inflection or a laugh like a machine gun and you flee in horror. Her speaking voice is a neutral alto without squeak or that long drawled *O* or vague air of nasal complaint that — also mercifully light on the *likes* and *you knows* that can make you chew the inside of your cheek with this type. Nor did she giggle. Her laugh was fully adult, full, good to hear. And that this was my first hint of sadness or melancholy, as I listened with increasing attention to the anecdote, that the qualities I found myself admiring in her narration of the anecdote were some of the same qualities about her I'd been contemptuous of when I'd first picked her up in the park.'

Q.

'Chief among them — and I mean this without irony — that she seemed, quote, *sincere* in a way that may in fact have been smug naiveté but was nevertheless attractive and very powerful in the context of listening to her encounter with the psychopath, in that I found it helped me focus almost entirely on the anecdote itself and thus helped me imagine in an almost terrifyingly vividly realistic way just what it must have *felt* like for her, for anyone, finding yourself through nothing but coincidence heading into a secluded woody area in the company of a dark man in a dungaree vest who says he is your own death incarnate and who is alternately smiling with psychotic cheer and ranting and apparently gets his first wave of jollies by singing creepily about the various sharp implements he has in the Cutlass's trunk and detailing what he's used them to do to others and now plans in exquisite detail to do to you. It was tribute to the — her odd affectless sincerity that I found myself hearing expressions like *fear gripping her soul,* unquote, as less as televisual clichés or melodrama but as sincere if not particularly artful attempts simply to describe what it must have felt like, the feelings of shock and unreality alternating with waves of pure terror, the sheer emotional *violence* of this magnitude of fear, the temptation to retreat into catatonia or shock or the delusion — yield to the seduction of the idea, riding deeper into the secluded area, that there must be some sort of mistake, that something as simple and random as getting into a 1987 maroon Cutlass with a bad muffler that just happened to be the first car to pull over to the side of a random interstate could not possibly result in the death not of some abstract other person but your own personal death, and at the hands of someone whose reasons have absolutely nothing to do with you or the content of your character, as if everything you'd ever been told about the relationship between character and intention and outcome had been a rank fiction from start to —'

Q.

'— to finish, that you'd feel the alternating pulls of hysteria and dissociation and bargaining for your life in the way of foxholes or simply to blank catatonically out and retreat into the roar in your mind of the ramifying idea that your whole seemingly random and somewhat flaccid and self-indulgent but nevertheless comparatively blameless life had somehow been connected all along in a terminal chain that has somehow justified or somehow connected, causally, to lead you inevitably to this terminal unreal point, your life's quote unquote *point,* its as it were sharp point or tip, and that canned clichés such as *fear seized me* or *this is something that only happens to other people* or even *moment of truth* now take on a horrendous neural resonance and vitality when —'

Q.

'Not of — just being left narratively alone in the self-sufficiency of her narrative aspect to contemplate just how little-kid-level *scared* you'd be, how much you'd resent and despise this sick twisted shit beside you ranting whom you'd kill without hesitation if you could while but at the same time feeling involuntarily the very highest respect, almost a deference — the sheer agential *power* of one who could make you feel this frightened, that he could bring you to this point simply by wishing it and now can, if he wished, take you past it, past yourself, turn you into a *grisly discovery, brutal sex slaying,* and the feeling that you'd do absolutely anything or say or trade anything to persuade him simply to settle for rape and then let you go, or even torture, even willing to bring to the bargaining table a bit of nonlethal torture if only he'd settle for hurting you and choose then for whatever reason to drive off and leave you hurt and breathing in the weeds and sobbing at the sky and traumatized beyond all recovery instead of as *nothing,* yes it's a cliché but this is to be *all*? this was to be *the end*? and at the hands of someone who probably didn't even finish Manual Arts High School and had nothing like a recognizable soul or capacity for empathy with anyone else, a blind ugly force like gravity or a rabid dog, and yet it was he who wished it to happen and who possessed the power and certainly the tools to make it happen, tools he names in a maddening singsong about knives and wives and scythes and dolls and awls, adzes and mattocks and other implements whose names she did not recognize but even so they even *sounded* like just what —'

Q.

'Yes and a good deal of the anecdote's medial part's rising action detailed this interior struggle between giving in to hysterical fear and maintaining the level-headedness to focus her concentration on the situation and to figure out something ingenious and persuasive to say to the sexual psychotic as he's driving deeper into the secluded area and looking ominously around for a propitious site and becoming more and more openly raveled and psychotic and alternately grinning and ranting and invoking God and the memory of his brutally slain mother and gripping the Cutlass's steering wheel so tightly that his knuckles are gray.'

Q.

'That's right, the psychopath is also a mulatto, although with aquiline and almost femininely delicate features, a fact that she has omitted or held back for a good portion of the anecdote. She said it hadn't struck her as important. In today's climate one wouldn't want to critique too harshly the idea of someone with a body like that getting into a strange automobile with a mulatto. In a way you have to applaud the broad-mindedness. I didn't at the time of the anecdote really even notice that she'd omitted the ethnic detail for so long, but there's something to applaud there as well, you'd have to concede, though if you —'

Q.

'The crux being that despite the terror she is somehow able to think quickly on her feet and thinks it through and determines that her only chance of surviving this encounter is to establish a quote connection with the quote soul of the sexual psychopath as he's driving them deeper into the woody secluded area looking for just the right spot to pull over and brutally have at her. That her objective is to focus very intently on the psychotic mulatto as an ensouled and beautiful albeit tormented person in his own right instead of merely as a threat to her or a force of evil or the incarnation of her personal death. Try to bracket any New Age goo in the terminology and focus on the tactical strategy itself if you can because I'm well aware that what she is about to describe is nothing but a variant of the stale old Love Will Conquer All bromide but for the moment bracket whatever contempt you might feel and try to see the more concrete ramifications of — in this situation in terms of what she has the courage and apparent conviction to actually attempt here, because she says she believes that sufficient love and focus can penetrate even psychosis and evil and establish a quote soul-connection, unquote, and that if the mulatto can be brought to feel even a minim of this alleged soul-connection there is some chance that he'll be unable to follow through with actually killing her. Which is of course on a psychological level not all that implausible, since sexual psychopaths are well known to depersonalize their victims and liken them to objects or dolls, *Its* and not *Thous* so to speak, which is often their explanation for how they are able to inflict such unimaginable brutality on a human being, namely that they do not see them as human beings at all but merely as objects of the psychopath's own needs and intentions. And yet love and empathy of this kind of connective magnitude demand quote unquote total focus, she said, and her terror and totally understandable concern for herself were at this point to say the least distracting in the extreme, so she realized that she was in for the most difficult and important battle of her life, she said, a battle that was to be engaged completely within herself and her own soul's capacities, which idea by this time I found extremely interesting and captivating, particularly because she is so unaffected and seemingly sincere when *battle of one's life* is usually such a neon indication of melodrama or manipulation of the listener, trying to bring him to the edge of his seat and so forth.'

Q.

'I observe with interest that you are now interrupting me to ask the same questions I was interrupting her to ask, which is precisely the sort of convergence of —'

Q.

'She said the best way to describe focus to a person who hadn't undertaken what were apparently her denomination's involved and time-consuming series of lessons and exercises was to envision focus as intense concentration further sharpened and intensified to a single sharp point, to envision a kind of needle of concentrated attention whose extreme thinness and fragility were also, of course, its capacity to penetrate, and but that the demands of excluding all extraneous concerns and keeping the needle thinly focused and sharply directed were extreme even under the best of circumstances, which these profoundly terrifying circumstances were of course not.'

Q.

'Thus, in the car, under let's keep in mind now enormous duress and pressure, she marshals her concentration. She stares directly into the sexual psychopath's right eye — the eye that is accessible to her in his aquiline profile as he drives the Cutlass — and wills herself to keep her gaze directly on him at all times. She wills herself not to weep or plead but merely to use her penetrating focus to attempt to feel and empathize with the sex offender's psychosis and rage and terror and psychic torment, and says she visualizes her focus piercing through the mulatto's veil of psychosis and penetrating various strata of rage and terror and delusion to touch the beauty and nobility of the generic human soul beneath all the psychosis, forcing a nascent, compassion-based connection between their souls, and she focuses on the mulatto's profile very intently and quietly tells him what she saw in his soul, which she insisted was the truth. It was the climactic struggle of her spiritual life, she said, what with all the under the circumstances perfectly understandable terror and loathing of the sex criminal that kept threatening to dilute her focus and break the connection. Yet at the same time the effects of her focus on the psychotic's face were becoming obvious — when she was able to hold the focus and penetrate him and hold the soul-connection the mulatto at the wheel would gradually stop ranting and fall tensely silent, as if preoccupied, and his right profile would tense and tighten hypertonically and his dead right eye filling with anxiety and conflict at feeling the delicate beginnings of the sort of connection with another soul he had always both desired and always also feared in the very depths of his psyche, of course.'

Q.

'Just that it's widely acknowledged that a primary reason your prototypical sex killer rapes and kills is that he regards rape and murder as his only viable means of establishing some kind of meaningful connection with his victim. That this is a basic human need. I mean some sort of connection of course. But also frightening and easily susceptible to delusion and psychosis. It is his twisted way of having a, quote, relationship. Conventional relationships terrify him. But with a victim, raping and torturing and killing, the sexual psychotic is able to forge a sort of quote unquote connection via his ability to make her feel intense fear and pain, while his exultant sensation of total Godlike control over her — what she feels, whether she feels, breathes, lives — this allows him some margin of safety in the relationship.'

Q.

'Simply that this is what first seemed somehow ingenious in her tactics, however daffy the terms — that it addressed the psychotic's core weakness, his grotesque *shyness* as it were, the terror that any conventional, soul-exposing connection with another human being will threaten him with engulfment and/or obliteration, in other words that *he* will become the victim. That in his cosmology it is either feed or be food — God how lonely, do you feel it? — but that the brute control he and his sharp implement hold over her very life and death allow the mulatto to feel that here he is in a hundred percent total control of the relationship and thus that the connection he so desperately craves will not expose or engulf or obliterate him. Nor is this of course all that substantively different from a man sizing up an attractive girl and approaching her and artfully deploying just the right rhetoric and pushing the right buttons to induce her to come home with him, never once saying anything or touching her in any way that isn't completely gentle and pleasurable and

seemingly respectful, leading her gently and respectfully to his
satin-sheeted bed and in the light of the moon making exquisitely
attentive love to her and making her come over and over until she's
quote begging for mercy and is totally under his emotional control
and feels that she and he must be deeply and unseverably connected
for the evening to have been this perfect and mutually respectful
and fulfilling and then lighting her cigarettes and engaging in an
hour or two of pseudo-intimate postcoital chitchat in his wrecked
bed and seeming very close and content when what he really wants
is to be in some absolutely antipodal spot from wherever she is from
now on and is thinking about how to give her a special discon-
nected telephone number and never contacting her again. And that
an all too obvious part of the reason for his cold and mercenary and
maybe somewhat victimizing behavior is that the potential profundity of the very connection he has worked so hard to make her feel
terrifies him. I know I'm not telling you anything you haven't already decided you know. With your slim chilly smile. You're not
the only one who can read people, you know. He's a fool because he
thinks he's made a fool of her, you're thinking. Like he got away
with something. The satyrosaurian sybaritic heterosapien male, the
type you short-haired catamenial bra-burners can see coming a mile
away. And pathetic. He's a predator, you believe, and he too thinks
he's a predator, but *he's* the really frightened one, *he's* the one running.'

Q.

'I am inviting you to consider that it isn't the *motivation* that's the
psychotic part. The permutation is simply the psychotic one of sub-
stituting rape, murder, and mind-shattering terror for exquisite
lovemaking and giving a false number whose falseness isn't so immediately evident that it will unnecessarily hurt someone's feelings
and cause you discomfort.'

Q.

'And please be aware that I'm quite familiar with the typology behind these bland little expressions of yours, the affectless little questions. I know what an excursus is and I know what a dry wit is. Do not think you are getting out of me things or admissions I'm unaware of. Just consider the possibility that I understand more than you think. Though if you'd like another I'll buy you another no problem.'

Q.

'All right. Once more, slowly. That literally killing instead of merely running is the killer's psychotically literal way of resolving the conflict between his need for connection and his terror of being in any way connected. Especially, yes, to a woman, connecting with a woman, whom the vast majority of sexual psychotics do hate and fear, often due to twisted relations with the mother as a child. The psychotic sex killer is thus often quote symbolically killing the mother, whom he hates and fears but of course cannot literally kill because he is still enmeshed in the infantile belief that without her love he will somehow die. The psychotic's relation to her is one of both terrified hatred and terror and desperate pining need. He finds this conflict unendurable and must thus symbolically resolve it through psychotic sex crimes.'

Q.

'Her delivery had little or no — she seemed simply to relate what had happened without commenting one way or the other, or reacting. Although nor was she dissociated or monotonous. There was a disingen— an equanimity about her, a sense of residence in herself or a type of artlessness that did, does, that resembled a type of intent concentration. This I had noticed at the park when I first saw her and came and crouched down beside her, since a high degree of unself-conscious attention and concentration is not exactly standard issue for a gorgeous Granola Cruncher on a wool blanket sitting contra—'

Q.

'Well still, though, it's not exactly what one would call esoteric is it since it's so much in the air, common knowledge about childhood's connection to adult sex crimes in popular culture these days. Turn on the news for Christ's sake. It doesn't exactly take a von Braun to connect problems with connecting with women to problems in the childhood relation to the mother. It's all in the air.'

Q.

'That it was a titanic struggle, she said, in the Cutlass, heading deeper into the secluded area, because whenever for a moment her terror bested her or she for any reason lost her intense focus on the mulatto, even for a moment, the effect on the connection was obvious — his profile relaxing into its grin and his right eye again going empty and dead as he recrudesced and began once again to singsong psychotically about the implements in his trunk and what he had in store for her once he found the ideal secluded spot, and she could tell that in the wavering of the soul-connection he was automatically reverting to resolving his connectionary conflicts in the only way he knew. And I clearly remember her saying that by this time, whenever she succumbed and lost focus for a moment and his eye and face reverted to creepy psychotic unconflicted glee, she was surprised to find herself feeling no longer paralyzing terror for herself but a nearly heartbreaking sadness for him, the psychotic mulatto. And I'll say that it was at roughly this point in listening to the story, still nude in bed, that I began to admit to myself that not only was it a remarkable postcoital anecdote but that this was, in certain ways, rather a remarkable woman, and that I felt a bit sad or wistful that I had not noticed this type of remarkability in her when I had first been attracted to her in the park. This was while the mu-

latto has meanwhile spotted a site that meets his criteria and has
pulled crunchingly over in the gravel by the side of the secluded
area's road and asks her, somewhat apologetically or ambivalently it
seems, to get out of the Cutlass and to lie prone on the ground and
to lace her hands behind her head in the position of both police
arrests and gangland executions, a well-known position obviously
and no doubt chosen for its associations and intended to emphasize
both the ideas of punitive custody and of violent death. She does not
hesitate or beg. She had long since decided that she must not give
in to the temptation to beg or plead or protest or in any way appear
to resist him. She was rolling all her dice on these daffy-sounding
beliefs in connection and nobility and compassion as more fundamental and primary components of soul than psychosis or evil. I
note that these beliefs seem far less canned or flaccid when someone
appears willing to stake their life on them. This was as he orders her
to lie prone in the roadside gravel while he goes back to the trunk
to browse through his collection of torture implements. She says by
this time she could feel very clearly that her acerose focus's connective powers were being aided by spiritual resources far greater than
her own, because even though she was in a prone position and her
face and eyes were in the clover or phlox in the gravel by the car and
her eyes tightly shut she could feel the soul-connection holding and
even strengthening between herself and the mulatto, she could hear
the conflict and disorientation in the sex offender's footsteps as he
went to the Cutlass's trunk. She was experiencing a whole new
depth of focus. I was listening to her very intently. It wasn't sus-
pense. Lying there helpless and connected, she says her senses had
taken on the nearly unbearable acuity we associate with drugs or extreme meditative states. She could distinguish lilac and shatter-
cane's scents from phlox and lambs'-quarter, the watery mint of
first-growth clover. Wearing a corbeau leotard beneath a kind of
loose-waisted cotton dirndl and on one wrist a great many bracelets

of pinchbeck copper. She could decoct from the smell of the gravel
in her face the dank verdure of the spring soil beneath the gravel
and distinguish the press and shape of each piece of gravel against
her face and large breasts through the leotard's top, the angle of the
sun on the top of her spine and the slight swirl in the intermittent
breeze that blew from left to right across the light film of sweat on
her neck. In other words what one might call an almost hallucina-
tory accentuation of detail, the way in some nightmares you remember the precise shape of every blade of grass in your father's
lawn on the day your mother left him and took you to live at her sister's. Many of the cheap bracelets had been gifts apparently. She
could hear the largo tick of the cooling auto and bees and bluebottle
flies and stridulating crickets at the distant treeline, the same
volute breeze in those trees she could feel at her back, and birds —
imagine the temptation to despair in the sound of carefree birds and
insects only yards from where you lay trussed for the gambrel — of
tentative steps and breathing amid the clank of implements whose
very shapes could be envisioned from the sounds they made against
one another when stirred by a conflicted hand. The cotton of her
dirndl skirt that light sheer unrefined cotton that's almost gauze.'

Q.

'It's a frame for butchers. Hang by the hind feet to bleed. It's
from the Hindu for leg. It never occurred to her to get up and try to
run for it. A certain percentage of psychotics slice their victims'
Achilles tendons to hobble them and preclude running for it, perhaps he knew that was unnecessary with her, could feel her not resisting, not even considering resisting, using all her energy and
focus to sustain the feeling of connection with his conflicted despair. She says now she felt terror but not her own. She could hear
the sound of the mulatto finally extracting some kind of machete or
bolo from the trunk, then a brief half-stagger as he tried to come
back up along the length of the Cutlass to where she lay prone, and

heard then the groan and sideways skid as he went to his knees in the gravel beside the car and was sick. Puked. Can you imagine. That *he* is now the one puking from terror. She says by this time something was aiding her and she was completely focused. That by this time she was focus itself, she had merged with connection itself. Her voice in the dark is uninflected without being flat — it's matter-of-fact the way a bell is matter-of-fact. It feels as if she's back there by the road. A type of scotopia. How in her altered state of heightened attention to everything around she says the clover smells like weak mint and the phlox like mown hay and she feels the way she and the clover and phlox and the dank verdure beneath the phlox and the mulatto retching into the gravel and even the contents of his stomach were all made of precisely the same thing and were connected by something far deeper and more elemental than what we limitedly call quote unquote love, what from her background's perspective she calls connection, and that she could feel the psychotic fellow feeling the truth of this at the same time she did and she could feel the plummeting terror and infantile conflict this feeling of connection aroused in his soul and stated again without drama or self-consciousness that she too could feel this terror, not her own but his. That when he came to her with the bolo or machete and a hunting knife in his belt and now with some kind of ritualistic design or glyph like a samekh or palsied omicron drawn on his tenebrous brow in the blood or lipstick of a previous victim and turned her over into a rape-ready supine position in the gravel he was crying and chewing his lower lip like a frightened child, making small lost noises. And that she kept her eyes steadily on his as he raised her poncho and gauzy skirt and cut away her leotard and underthings and raped her, which given the kind of surreal sensuous clarity she was experiencing in her state of total focus imagine what this must have felt like for her, being raped in the gravel by a weeping psychotic whose knife's butt jabs you on every thrust, and the sound of bees and meadow birds and the distant whisper of the interstate and his machete clanking dully on the stones on every thrust, she claiming it took no effort of will to hold him as he wept and gibbered as he raped her and stroking the back of his head and whispering small little consolatory syllables in a soothing maternal singsong. By this time I found that even though I was focused very intently on her story and the rape by the road my own mind and emotions were also whirling and making connections and associations, for instance it struck me that this behavior of hers during the rape was an unintentional but tactically ingenious way to in a way prevent it, or transfigure it, the rape, to transcend its being a vicious attack or violation, since if a woman as a rapist comes at her and savagely mounts her can somehow choose to *give* herself, sincerely and compassionately, she cannot be truly violated or raped, no? That through some sleight of hand of the psyche she was now giving herself instead of being quote taken by force, and that in this ingenious way, without resisting in any way, she had denied the rapist the ability to dominate and take. And, from gauging your expression, no I am not suggesting that this was the same as her asking for it or deciding she wanted it unquote, and no this does not keep the rape itself from being a crime. Nor had she in any way intended acquiescence or compassion as a tactic to empty the rape of its violating force, nor the focus and soul-connection themselves as tactics to cause in him conflict and pain and gibbering terror, so that at whatever point during the transfigured and sensuously acute rape she realized all this, saw the effects her focus and incredible feats of compassion and connection were having on his psychosis and soul and the pain they were in fact causing him, it became complex — her motive had been only to make it difficult for him to kill her and break the soul-connection, not to cause him agony, so that the moment her compassionate focus comprehended not just his soul but the effect of the compassionate focus itself on that soul it all became divided and doubly complex, an element of self-consciousness had been introduced and now was itself an object of focus, like some sort of diffraction or regress of self-consciousness and consciousness of self-consciousness. She didn't talk about this division or regress in any but emotional terms. But it was going on — the division. And I was experiencing the same thing listening. On one level my attention was intently focused on her voice and story. On another level I — it was as if my mind was having a garage sale. I kept flashing back to a weak joke during a freshman religion survey we all had to take as an undergrad: the mystic approaches the hot-dog stand and tells the vendor Make me one with everything. It wasn't the sort of distracted division where I was both listening and not. I was listening both intellectually and emotionally. I — this religion survey was popular because the professor was so colorful and such a perfect stereotype example of the Sixties mentality, several times during the semester he returned to the point that distinctions between psychotic delusions and certain kinds of religious illuminations were very slight and esoteric and had used the analogy of the edge of a sharpened blade to convey the thinness of the line between the two, psychosis and revelation, and at the same time I was also remembering in near-hallucinatory detail that evening's outdoor concert and festival and the configurations of people on the grass and blankets and the parade of lesbian folk singers on the poorly amplified stage, the very configuration of the clouds overhead and the foam in Tad's cup and the smell of various conventional and nonaerosol insect repellents and Silverglade's cologne and barbecued food and sunburned children and how when I'd first seen her seated foreshortened behind and between the legs of a vegetarian-kabob vendor she was eating a supermarket apple with a small supermarket price sticker still affixed to it and that I'd watched her with a sort of detached amusement to see whether she would eat the price sticker without taking it off. It took him a long time to achieve release and she held him and gazed at him lovingly the entire time. If I had asked a you-type question such as did she really *feel* loving as the mulatto was raping her or was she merely *conducting herself in a loving manner* she would have gazed blankly at me and had no idea what I was talking about. I remembered weeping at movies about animals as a child, even though some of these animals were predators and hardly what you would consider sympathetic characters. On a different level this seemed connected to the way I had first noticed her indifference to basic hygiene at the community festival and had formed judgments and conclusions based solely on that. Just as I am watching you forming judgments based on the openings of things I'm describing that then prevent you from hearing the rest of what I try to describe. It's due to her influence that this makes me sad for you instead of pissed off. And all this was going on simultaneously. I felt more and more sad. I smoked my first cigarette in two years. The moonlight had moved from her to me but I could still see her profile. A saucer-sized circle of fluid on the sheet had dried and vanished. You are the sort of auditor for whom rhetoricians designed the Exordium. From below in the gravel she subjects the psychotic mulatto to the well-known Female Gaze. And she describes his facial expression during the rape as the most heartbreaking thing of all. That it had been less an expression than a kind of anti-expression, empty of everything as she unpremeditatedly robbed him of the only way he'd ever found to connect. His eyes were holes in the world. She felt almost heartbroken, she said, as she realized that her focus and connection were inflicting far more pain on the psychotic than he could ever have inflicted upon her. This was how she described the division — a hole in the world. I began in the dark of our room to feel terrible sadness and fear. I felt as though there had been far more genuine emotion and connection in that anti-rape she suffered than in any of the so-called lovemaking I spent my time pursuing. Now I'm sure you know what I'm talking about now. Now we're on your terra firma. The whole prototypical male syndrome. Eric Drag Sarah To Teepee By Hair. The well-known Privileging of the Subject. Don't think I can't speak your language. She finished in the dark and it was only in memory that I saw her clearly. The well-known Male Gaze. Her seated pose a protofeminine contraposto with one hip on a Nicaraguan blanket with a strong smell of unrefined wool to it with her trust me on this breathtaking legs sort of curled out to the side so her weight was on one arm stiff-armed out behind her and the other hand held the apple — am I describing this right? can you — the toile skirt, hair that nearly reached the blanket, the blanket dark green with yellow filigree and a kind of nauseous purple fringe, a linen singlet and vest of false buckskin, sandals in her rattan bag, bare feet with phenomenally dirty soles, dirty beyond belief, their nails like the nails of a laborer's hands. Imagine being able to console someone as he weeps over what he's doing to you as you console him. Is that wonderful, or sick? Have you ever heard of *the couvade*? No perfume, the slight scent of some unrefined soap like those old cakes of deep-yellow laundry soap one's aunt tried to — I realized I had never loved anyone. Isn't that trite? Like a canned line? Do you see how open I'm being with you here? And who would go to the trouble of kabobing only vegetables? I had to respect her blanket's boundary, on the approach. You do not just stroll up out of the blue and ask to share someone's wool blanket. Boundaries are an important issue with this type. I assumed a sort of respectful squat just off its fringe with my weight on my knuckles so that my tie hung down straight between us like a counterweight. As we casually rapped and chatted and I deployed the pained-confession-of-true-motive tactic I watched her face and felt as though she knew just what I was doing and why and was both amused and responsive, I could tell she felt an immediate affinity between us, an aura of connection, and it's sad to recall the way I viewed her acquiescence, the

fact of her response, a little disappointed that she was so easy, her
easiness was both disappointing and refreshing, that she was not
one of these breathtaking girls who believe themselves to be too
beautiful to approach and automatically see any man as a supplicant
or libidinous goon, the chilly ones, and who require tactics of attri-
tion rather than feigned affinity, an affinity that is heartbreakingly
easy to feign, I have to say, if you know your female typologies. I can
repeat that if you like, if you want to get it exact. Her description
of the rape, certain logistics I'm omitting, was lengthy and detailed
and rhetorically innocent. I felt more and more sad, hearing it, trying to imagine what she'd been able to pull off, and felt more and
more sad that on our way out of the park I'd felt that tiny stab of
disappointment, maybe even anger, wishing she'd been more of a
challenge. That her will and wishes had opposed my own just a little more. This by the way is known as Werther's Axiom, whereby
quote the intensity of a desire D is inversely proportional to the ease
of D's gratification. Known also as Romance. And sadder and sadder that it had not once, it seemed — you'll like this — not once
occurred to me before what an empty way this was to come at
women, then. Not evil or predatory or sexist — empty. To gaze and
not see, to eat and not be full. Not just to feel but *be* empty. While
meanwhile, within the narrative itself, she, still deep inside the psychotic whose penis is still inside her, glimpsing his palm's thumb's
web as he tentatively attempted to stroke her own head in return,
seeing the fresh cut and realizing it was his own blood the fellow
had used for his forehead's mark. Which was not a rune or glyph at
all, I knew, but a simple circle, the Ur-void, the zero, that axiom of
Romance we call also mathematics, pure logic, whereby one does
not equal two and cannot. And that the quote rapist's mocha color
and aquiline features could well be brahminic instead of negroid.
Aryan in other words. These and other details she withheld — she
had no reason to trust me. And nor can I — I can't for the life of me

recall whether she ate the price sticker, nor what became of the apple at all, whether she discarded it or what. Terms like *love* and *soul* and *redeem* that I believed could be used only with quotation marks, exhausted clichés. Believe that I felt the mulatto's fathomless sadness, then. I —'

Q.

'It's not a good word, I know. It's not just quote sadness the way one feels sad at a funeral or film. More a plummeting quality. A timelessness to it. The way the light gets in winter just before dusk. Or that — all right — how, say, at the height of lovemaking, the very height, when she's starting to come, when she's truly responding to you now and you can see in her face that she's starting to come, her eyes widening in that way that is both surprise and recognition, which not a woman alive can fake or feign if you really look intently at her eyes and really *see* her, you know what I'm talking about, that apical moment of maximum human sexual connection when you feel closest to her, *with* her, so much closer and realer and more ecstatic than your own coming, which always feels more like losing your grip on the person who's grabbed you to keep you from falling, a mere neural sneeze that's not even in the same ballpark's area code as *her* coming, and — and I know what you will make of this but I'll tell you anyhow — but how even this moment of maximum connection and joint triumph and joy at making them start to come has this void of piercing sadness to it, of the loss of them in their eyes as their eyes widen to their very widest point and then as they begin to come begin to shut, close, the eyes do, and you feel that familiar little needle of sadness inside your exultation as they arch and their eyes close and you can feel that they've closed their eyes to shut you out, you've become an intruder, their union is now with the feeling itself, the climax, that behind those drawn lids the eyes are now rolled all the way around and staring intently inward, into some void where you who sent them cannot follow. That's shit.

I'm not putting it right. I can't make you feel what I felt. You'll turn this into Narcissistic Male Wants Woman's Gaze On Him At Climax, I know. Well I don't mind telling you I'd begun to cry, at the anecdote's climax. Not loudly, but I did. Neither of us were smoking by now. We were both up against the headboard, facing the same way, though addorsed is how I remember it for the story's last part, when I wept. Memory is strange. I do remember listening for some acknowledgment from her that I was crying. I felt embarrassed — not for crying, but for wanting so badly to know how she took it, whether it made me seem sympathetic or selfish. She stayed where he left her all day, supine in the gravel, weeping, she said, and giving thanks to her particular religious principles and forces. When of course as I'm sure you could have predicted I was weeping for myself. He left the knife and drove off in the unmuffled Cutlass, leaving her there. He may have told her not to move or do anything for some specified interval. If he did, I know she obeyed. She said she could still feel him inside her soul, the mulatto — it was hard to break the focus. I felt certain that the psychotic had driven off somewhere to kill himself. It seemed clear from the anecdote's outset that someone was going to have to die. The story's emotional impact on me was profound and unprecedented and I will not even try to explain it to you. She said she wept because she had realized that as she stood hitchhiking her religion's spiritual forces had guided the psychotic to her, that he had served as an instrument of growth in her faith and capacity to focus and alter energy fields by the action of her compassion. She wept out of gratitude, she says. He left the knife up to the handle in the ground next to her where he had thrust it, apparently stabbing the ground dozens of times with desperate savagery. She said not one word about my weeping or what it signified to her. I displayed far more emotion than she did. She learned more about love that day with the sex offender than at any other stage in her spiritual journey, she said. Let's both have one last one and then that will be it. That her whole life had indeed led inexorably to that moment when the car stopped and she got in, that it was indeed a kind of death, but not at all in the way she had feared as they entered the secluded area. That was the only real commentary she indulged in, just at the anecdote's end. I did not care whether it was quote true. It would depend what you meant by true. I simply didn't care. I was moved, changed — believe what you will. My mind seemed to be moving at the quote speed of light. I was so sad. And that whether or not what she believed happened happened — it seemed true even if it wasn't. That even if the whole focused-soul-connection theology, that even if it was just catachrestic New Age goo, her belief in it had saved her life, so whether or not it's goo becomes irrelevant, no? Can you see why this, realizing this, would make you feel conflicted in — of realizing your entire sexuality and sexual history had less genuine connection or feeling than I felt simply lying there listening to her talk about lying there realizing how lucky she'd been that some angel had visited her in psychotic guise and shown her what she'd spent her whole life praying was true? You believe I'm contradicting myself. But can you imagine how any of it felt? Seeing her sandals across the room on the floor and remembering what I'd thought of them only hours before? I kept saying her name and she would ask What? and I'd say her name again. I'm not afraid of how this sounds to you. I'm not embarrassed now. But if you could understand, had I — can you see why there's no way I could let her just go away after this? Why I felt this apical sadness and fear at the thought of her getting her bag and sandals and New Age blanket and leaving and laughing when I clutched her hem and begged her not to leave and said I loved her and closing the door gently and going off barefoot down the hall and never seeing her again? Why it didn't matter if she was fluffy or not terribly bright? Nothing else mattered. She had all my attention. I'd fallen in love with her. I believed she could save me. I know how this sounds, trust me. I know your type and I know what you're bound to ask. Ask it now. This is your chance. I felt she could save me I said. Ask me now. Say it. I stand here naked before you. Judge me, you chilly cunt. You dyke, you bitch, cooze, cunt, slut, gash. Happy now? All borne out? Be happy. I don't care. I knew she could. I knew I loved. End of story.'

YET ANOTHER EXAMPLE OF
THE POROUSNESS OF CERTAIN BORDERS (XXIV)

Between a cold kitchen window gone opaque with the stove's wet heat and the breath of us, an open drawer, and the gilt ferrotype of identical boys flanking a blind vested father which hung in a square recession above the wireless's stand, my Mum stood and cut off my long hair in the uneven heat. There was breath and the mugginess of bodies and the force of the hot stove on the back of my emergent neck; there was the lunatic crackle of the wireless's movement among city stations, Da scanning for better reception. I could not move: about and around me the towels trapped hair at my shoulders' skin and Mum circled the chair, cutting against the bowl's rim with blunt shears. At one edge of my vision's strain a utensil drawer hung open, at the other the beginning of Da, head cocked past the finger at the glowing dial. And straight ahead, before me and centered direct across the shine of the table's oilcloth, like a tongue between the teeth of the pantry's opening doors, hung my brother's face. I could not move my head: the weight of the bowl and towels, Mum's shears and steadying hand — she, eyes lowered, intent on her crude task, could not see the face of my brother emerge against the pantry's black. I had to sit still and straight as a tin grenadier and watch as his face assumed, instantly and with the earnestness reserved for pure cruelty, whichever expression my own emerging face betrayed.

The face in the well-oiled doors' crack hung, I inert, the face neckless and floating unsupported in the cleavage of the angled doors, the concentration of its affect somewhere between sport and assault, Da's shaggy head cocked and sightless at the tuner, two bars of strings distorted by the storm and snatches of voices found and lost again; and Mum intent on my skull and unable to see the white hair-framed face reproducing my own visage, copying me — for we called it that, 'copying,' and he knew how I hated it — and for me alone. And with such intensity and so little lag in following that his face less mimed than lampooned my own, made instantly distended and obscene whatever position my own face's pieces assumed.

And how it became worse, then, in that kitchen of copper and tile and pine and burnt peat's steam and static and sleet on the window in undulant waves, the air cold before me and scorching behind: as I became more agitated at the copying and the agitation registered — I felt it — on my face, the face of my brother would mimic and lampoon that agitation; I feeling then the increased agitation at the twinned imitation of my face's distress, his registering and distorting that new distress, all as I became more and more agitated behind the cloth Mum had fastened over my mouth to protest my disturbing her shears' assertion of my face's true shape. It ascended by levels: Da's cameo recessed against the glow of the tuner's parade, the drawer of utensils withdrawn past its fulcrum, the disembodied face of my brother miming and distorting my desperate attempts by expression alone to make Mum look up from me and see him, I no longer feeling my features' movements so much as seeing them on that writhing white face against the pantry's black, the throttle-popped eyes and cheeks ballooning against the gag's restraint, Mum squatting chairside to even my ears, my face before us both farther and farther from my own control as I saw in his twin face what all lolly-smeared hand-held brats must see in the funhouse mirror — the gross and pitiless *sameness,* the distortion in which there is, tiny, at the center, something cruelly true about the we who leer and woggle at stick necks and concave skulls, goggling eyes that swell to the edges — as the mimicry ascended reflected levels to become finally the burlesque of a wet hysteria that plastered cut strands to a wet white brow, the strangled man's sobs blocked by cloth, storm's thrum and electric hiss and Da's mutter against the lalation of shears meant for lambs, an unseen fit that sent my eyes upward again and again into their own shocked white, knowing past sight that my twin's face would show the same, to mock it — until the last refuge was slackness, giving up the ghost completely for a blank slack gagged mask's mindless stare — unseen and -seeing — into a mirror I could not know or feel myself without. No not ever again.

Gary Hannabarger

David Foster Wallace (1962–2008) wrote the acclaimed novels *Infinite Jest* and *The Broom of the System* and the story collections *Oblivion*, *Brief Interviews with Hideous Men*, and *Girl with Curious Hair*. His non-fiction works include *This Is Water, Consider the Lobster, Everything and More*, and *A Supposedly Fun Thing I'll Never Do Again*. He was the recipient of a MacArthur Fellowship and numerous other awards.

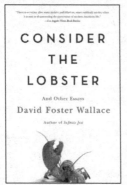